Revealing Me

TETHERED TO YOU, BOOK 3

KRYSTAL KAE

DARK ORCHID PRESS

Cover Design: Martin Endeavors, LLC
Editor: Rebecca Joy Editing

Paperback ISBN: 979-8-9895730-5-9

BEFORE YOU READ

This book contains mature sexual themes, including but not limited to public displays (not main characters) and dubious consent. It includes strong language, discussion of weight/body image issues, and familial loss. There is some crude humor regarding a temporary gender swap. The book also contains brief mention of rape (not a main character), and many violent scenes, including on-page depictions of death, murder, and gore.

CHAPTER 1

Violet

I remembered being told that when I lost weight, my boobs would be the first to go.

It had been a lie in high school, and it was a lie now.

Well, in my case it was anyway. My pants were getting a bit loose in the waist, I had extra material around the midsection of my shirts, and even my calves didn't feel as confined anymore. While I wanted to appreciate the muscle tone I'd gained and the inches I'd lost over the past several weeks, I couldn't help but scrutinize the naked image before me. My chest remained unchanged, and my bottom lip formed into a pout.

"You're unhappy."

The interruption from Kade made me cross my arms uncomfortably. My eyes flashed in his direction to find him leaning against the bathroom doorframe in nothing more than his workout shorts, body slick with sweat. Some mornings he woke with me, while others he slipped from our bed to squeeze in some cardio and catch up on the people he was watching.

I had once been one of them.

Almost three months before, I'd been among the group of humans Kade watched on a regular basis, but in a class of my own. While most were scum of the earth—people who were on the path to committing crimes against humanity—I was put on the list because of my experiences with death.

Little did I know, meeting Kade and ending things with my ex would lead me to my death and rebirth. I was now a combination of demon, banshee, and fury—a concoction that was unheard of in Kade's world. It was something that shouldn't have been possible, yet I was living proof that it was.

Oh, how my world had drastically changed into something I never could have imagined. And I had no idea where I fit into it.

"It's nothing." I shook my head, willing away my remnants of self-loathing even though I knew better. Our tethering bond saw to it that we were able to pick up on each other's feelings. It didn't help that Kade had a knack for sneaking up on me unannounced. I wished I could pick up on his presence and inner turmoil as easily as he did with me. Maybe in time I might be able to, but for now, it was a bit irritating.

"Violet…"

"Don't." I clenched my eyes shut, attempting to push my desire to change my body out of my mind.

Kade neared and I stiffened, knowing he was going to try and pry my worries and troubled thoughts out of me. His hands wrapped around my waist, sliding across my skin and creating goosebumps inch by inch. A soothing calm began to creep over me as his chin rested on my shoulder. My heart and breaths slowed, allowing him to put my mind at ease.

"Talk to me, Violet." He pressed a kiss to my neck and my head tilted away.

I didn't want to talk, not about my insecurities. Not about the mess inside my head regarding my own body that never seemed to change in the ways I wanted it to. Demons could change their entire appearance in a matter of seconds, yet I still couldn't do anything but change eye and hair colors. And even maintaining those was a strain on my mental capacity.

"Whatever's bothering you, I can help." He planted another kiss and I squeezed my eyes shut as his hair tickled my skin.

"I don't want to talk about it. Not about this." My voice trembled, betraying the emotions I tried to hide.

"Then allow me to tell you how fucking beautiful you are."

I scoffed, but sensing his love for me was beginning to open up my chest crack by crack, pulling me out of my pity party. It didn't matter if I was fully dressed or stark naked as I was now, he always had something to say to boost my spirits. And his stronger emotions overpowered my own.

His body pressed against me, his skin a slick contrast that had me trying to pull away. I had to meet with Aleena in half an hour and I didn't have time to get tangled up in whatever Kade had planned. His hold on me only strengthened.

"I have training soon." I tugged on his arms in protest, but his grasp didn't falter.

"So be late," he whispered in my ear. A hum of want began to run through me, and my eyes wanted to flutter closed, but I resisted. Damn, was it hard to resist.

"Kade," I warned, but his lips began to traipse down my neck toward its curve.

"Aleena can wait." He released me but took my hands in his, leading me out of the bathroom. "This can't."

I eyed him suspiciously.

Kade led me down the hall, taking a right to proceed to his watching quarters—the room he had once told me I wouldn't be a stranger to. But ever since my freak disappearance and revenge on my murderer, I'd been on a short leash in here. I was never more than a few steps away from his side, and kept more than an arm's length away from his wall of mirrors. Every time I entered this part of his home, his nerves became crystal clear. Sometimes he hid them well, others not so much. The unease and trepidation he felt was like a gut punch every time.

But today was different. Kade did nothing to hide his arousal and excitement as he brought me to the wall that mirrored the room's belongings. It was much the same as any other time I'd come in here, everything neat and in its place, minus his music center in the far back corner. He must have frequented that corner more than I was privy to.

We came to a stop and he turned me to face our reflections, his hands resting on my wide hips. My eyes narrowed on him and I tried to bring my arms up to cover my chest, but he pried them back down and to my sides.

"What are you doing?" I struggled against him, but it was futile. My heart was an erratic mess, not knowing his intentions.

"I still can't believe you're mine." He peered over my shoulder as he pressed his groin into my behind. My breath caught in my throat as I locked eyes with my demon equivalent of a husband. His heated gaze stilled me.

Hearing him speak of me in that manner always made me blush.

If any of the men from my previous relationships had

spoken about me like that, I would have put them out on their asses. But with Kade, it hit differently. Probably because I felt the same way in return, even if I didn't speak it out loud. He was mine in every sense of the word. Wasn't our tethering bond proof of that?

Kade let one hand float up and tilted my head back until I met his lips. He planted slow, languid kisses as he ground his erection against me. The material of his shorts was thin enough that it was evident his weakly confined member wanted to be granted release.

His hands began roaming my body, skimming the surface one moment and cupping my breasts the next, teasing their peaks. My head lulled back to rest on his shoulder.

"You drive me wild without even trying," he purred into my ear, and my core began to ache. Knowing he was so close to penetrating me but still partially clothed was driving me mad with want. "I wish you could see yourself through my eyes."

"And what is it you see?" Breathless, my hands rose and tangled into his hair.

"The most beautiful woman I have ever laid eyes on."

"Right," I answered, unbelieving. I'd seen numerous women around Darthou, and I didn't hold a candle to the ones who had control of their appearance. Granted, I didn't know what was fake and what was real with their shifting abilities, but I still felt inadequate among the lot of them. Growing up in a society that put too much pressure on appearances had definitely taken a toll on my mentality.

"Watch me, Violet," he coaxed, and I did as I was told. He'd uttered those words once before, in the Maze of Mirrors, teasing me before vanishing. My thighs clenched as I remembered that night, our first and only date that had been eventful in more ways than one.

"As long as you don't disappear on me again," I said lowly, staring at him dead-on.

A warm laugh vibrated his chest, shaking my back. "Promise."

Kade kissed my shoulder before switching places with me, only to urge me down onto the couch. The cool fabric beneath me was a startling difference to the heat my body was producing. When Kade pulled my legs apart to expose me, I swallowed hard. I was on full display in his watching quarters with no darkness to hide in and no blankets to reach for to cover me.

Kade's eyes raked over me and I wanted to curl up into a ball; his hunger for me was overwhelming.

It was a damn good thing I was sitting down.

His hands held me at the knees before tracing up my thighs and toward my center that throbbed in anticipation. Kade wasted no time thrusting two fingers inside of me, and my head fell back. His fingers twisted and turned as they gently explored, and his thumb found its way toward my clit.

"There aren't enough hours in the day for me to show you how irresistible you are."

I writhed beneath his touch, grasping the back of the sofa in delight. "Good thing you have me all to yourself every night then."

Our entanglements in the evenings were almost a routine now, ever since I'd finally admitted my love for him. Once we were away from prying eyes, we devoured one another. It was like a honeymoon each night, wrapped up in heated exchanges. Sometimes soft and gentle, other times a little rougher. The events of the day usually impacted how much energy we had for sex, but the way we craved one another never ceased. Each time the door to our home closed, we lost ourselves in one another as if we'd been apart for weeks. We always made sure to come together at night and make time for us when the days didn't allow it.

Kade withdrew his hand and yanked me to stand, smashing his lips against mine only to let his tongue explore my mouth. It was wild, unforgiving, and desperate. I gripped his neck and held him there, trying to meet him with equal enthusiasm as he managed to remove his clothing.

He swiveled me around to face the mirrors again, and the sudden move made my balance struggle to keep up with what was transpiring.

Kade set me right on my feet before sitting on the couch behind us. Before I could turn to meet him, he gripped my hips, stopping me.

"You're going to watch yourself fuck me." My heart skipped at his command. "Give me your leg."

I swallowed hard as I lifted my foot from the ground and he brought it to rest beside his hips. He steadied me as I brought the other up as well, until I was hovering above him.

I'd ridden this man several times, but never with my back to him and a wall full of mirrors before us. His erection was already poking at my core, eager to make its way inside.

Watching myself lower onto him, closing the small gap between us, was one hell of an erotic sight.

Kade tugged at my sides, groaning as I reached his base and eliciting a moan from me in return. I rocked against him as I adjusted to his fullness.

I never tired of this—of *feeling* him. Of our connection when we joined together and became one. His hands kneaded and pulled and grasped as I moved. My body rose up, then lowered back down again, and I had little choice but to study every curve of myself in my reflection and the pink marks his touch left behind.

Irresistible. Goddess. Mouthwatering.

His descriptions of me played on repeat in my head. If he could see those things in me, then why couldn't I?

I didn't know what to do with my hands when I couldn't wrap them around him; there was nothing in front of me to hold on to. I settled on my breasts, cupping them as he often did, pinching the peaks between my fingers, knowing that they couldn't get any harder than they already were. The weight of each breast as I lowered onto him again and again was a reminder of how much he loved them, when just minutes before I'd been sulking about their apparent inability to shrink and perk up.

I almost didn't recognize the black-eyed woman staring back at me—touching myself, fucking in front of a mirror in a new place I was still learning to call home, with a man who had never let me believe for one second that he didn't love me.

And yet I kept trying to tear myself up and beat myself down.

Kade bucked into me and I cried out. My body careened forward but he caught me, drawing me back to my place and binding my wrists together from behind.

"Again," I begged as I reopened my eyes. I could barely make out the top of his head in the higher mirrors, but I knew his focus was solely on me even without witnessing it firsthand.

This body before me was still curvy, but had grown stronger and leaner in my short time since coming here. I was far from a warrior, but I was capable of so much more now. More than I even knew. I had to appreciate how far I'd come, the progress I'd made.

Kade slammed his hips against me again, and I was nearly

there, unbelievably close to exploding around him as my insides throbbed, eager to go over the edge. I whimpered another plea and with a third thrust, I lost it. I screamed as Kade chased after his release after I'd found mine so quickly.

One. Two. Three. Four. Five relentless pounds and his grip on me tightened as he came with a guttural sound. I pulsated around him as I fell back against his chest, staring at the ceiling.

We sat in silence until our breaths leveled out and we rode out our high. His teeth grazed my ear playfully and I attempted to shoo him away as I giggled.

"Do you think we could add a mirror on the ceiling?" I questioned, turning my head toward him.

"I take it you like watching?" He nipped at my earlobe and I tried to pull away but his grasp on me didn't falter.

I was a bit embarrassed to admit that it had been insanely hot to watch ourselves. Though I'd been extremely relieved and grateful to find that we couldn't be viewed by others in our home. There were enchantments in place for that, just like how no one could enter our home unless a door was open or we granted them access.

"Maybe I want to watch you next time," I disclosed, grinning.

"Mmmm… Guess I have some work to do." He captured my mouth but I drew back a few inches.

"But first, bathroom door. I've been asking for weeks. Don't you dare put a mirror up before that gets done."

Kade laughed, shaking me and making my chest bounce. "Who would have thought? I have a honey-do list already."

"Damn right, you do."

"These things take some time, Violet." He tightened his hold on me. "But, I promise it will get done."

At the mention of time, my eyes bulged.

Shit.

I glanced up at the bronze clock on the wall. I was definitely going to be late. I tried to move but Kade didn't let go.

"Kade, I need to get cleaned up." I struggled against him.

"Do you, though?" he teased while thwarting my escape attempt.

"Yes, I do. You know how important these training sessions are to me, be it with your sister or Elias."

"Fine, fine." He released me and I wobbled as I stood, my legs quivering. "At least let me help."

I held up my hands like I was trying to hold off a bear from attacking. "Nope, no. Showering with you right now is not an option. I won't get out of here for at least another hour."

"Come on," he said, feigning innocence. Showers with Kade always involved more than just cleaning up. I didn't know if they had an endless hot water supply in Darthou or what, but we had definitely used substantial amounts, and the pressure and temperature never failed us.

Eyeing a shelf by his treadmill, I retrieved a towel and launched it at Kade. He caught it without pause, all while watching me in the mirrors.

"Sorry, but you'll have to clean yourself up today." As much as I wouldn't mind getting lathered up together, I couldn't afford the distraction. Just because he didn't have anywhere to be this morning, that didn't mean he could mess with the schedule I was trying to keep.

The slickness between my legs had me making a break for the door, but Kade beat me to it, blocking my escape. I cocked my head to the side, eyes wide.

"In all seriousness, are we still on for tonight?" His humor was wiped away, replaced by something that genuinely put all joking and playfulness aside.

Once a week, we visited Xandor, scrounging up food, clothing, and essentials for those still living there. On the day of my death, they had lost many of their own in a massacre that had destroyed many of Xandor's inhabitants. It was the drive behind me learning everything I could about the creatures there, training in combat as well as trying to acquire the basics of being a demon.

Those that remained there kept us at a distance, and rightfully so. The last time they'd trusted a demon, it had led to the slaughter of countless lives. It didn't matter their age— young, old, and those in between had all been killed. We still had no idea why so many, and within such a short time frame. To our knowledge, I was the only one born again with abilities from creatures who had died.

It had never been a question that I wanted to help them, and this was the only way I knew how for the time being.

Kade had never fought me on the matter, knowing that his father and mother had once been visitors to Xandor. Tarnon, Kade's father, had promised to free the ones exiled and abandoned there, only to never return again. Little did Xandor's occupants know, he had met his end, unable to carry out his word.

Kade and I hadn't exactly discussed it, but I knew he wanted to make it right. The people there were suffering with no end in sight. Their hope had been lost, then destroyed with the massacre, and they didn't know how long they had until someone else tried to come for them or until their world came crumbling down, taking their existence with it. We didn't know how much longer Xandor had. How much longer the witch could keep up with her attempts to buy them some time.

"Of course." I nodded. "Do you think your uncle or Elias

will join us this time?"

Uncle Zan had been the one with the most resistance to our plan, but we made it a point to keep them both in the loop just in case anything should happen. Elias had come once to help us with the food. Sometimes he was outspoken about how we shouldn't be involved in such matters, while other times he was indifferent.

Kade had confided in me that he and Elias were now at odds with how they'd been brought up, being told to fear the beings that were exiled in Xandor. They'd been told that it was impossible to control or reason with the assortment of banshees, witches, furies, werewolves, and various shifters. Taught that these beings were almost as evil as their enemies, the saints, who still inhabited the world I came from.

But I didn't belong there anymore. I didn't exactly know where I fit between worlds and realms. There was no one like me around. At least, not that we knew of.

"I'll check with him, but I wouldn't count on it. He and Aleena have been going through some stuff."

"Oh?"

"Yeah, I try not to dive into that topic too much."

Kade's best friend and sister were hot and heavy one minute, total strangers the next. I couldn't make heads or tails of their relationship.

I didn't think Aleena and I knew each other well enough for me to start inquiring about her relationships. Maybe we were on a path toward that; someday she might consider me close enough to share. She loved to talk, just not so much about her personal life.

"Kade?" I looked into his eyes as he met mine with a turn of his head. "Could I please go get cleaned up now?"

A wicked grin crossed his face, and I knew if I stood here

any longer, he would attempt to take me again. And while a part of me wanted to surrender to that, I really didn't want to be any later than I already was.

"Sure I can't persuade you otherwise?" He drove his hips forward and I shook my head and ducked around him.

"Maybe some other time," I commented as I darted off toward the bathroom without a door.

CHAPTER 2

Violet

I needed a spray bottle or something to keep Kade off of me. He respected my request enough to let me shower alone, but that didn't keep him at bay for long. I even whacked him with my hairbrush when he got too close, but he playfully rebounded, scooping me up in his arms just to capture my lips once more.

"What's gotten into you?" I broke us apart as he set me down in our closet.

My wardrobe had grown exponentially since arriving, considering I'd barely had time to throw a few outfits into my bag before departing my human life. Being on a first-name basis with Rebecca didn't hurt either. The seamstress/stylist loved dressing me almost as much as I enjoyed trying things on. Rebecca was like my own personal shopper, and one of the few humans I'd had the pleasure of meeting upon my arrival in Darthou. Well, she wasn't exactly for me only, but she definitely had a knack for making me feel welcome and comfortable in her shop.

"What? I can't be in a good mood?" Kade nabbed a shirt from his right as I began running my fingers across my more loose-fitting clothes that would allow me to move easily for training, plucking out undergarments and leggings from the drawers below.

"Good mood? Yes, but it's almost suspicious." My gaze narrowed on him as I backed out of the closet. I set my things out on the foot of the bed and he met me at the other side, helping me draw up the covers. "Are you nervous at all about the council meeting today?"

He shook his head. "No, actually. I'm ready to go in there, tell them like it is, and I'm not taking no for an answer."

"And what if Staffan pushes back?" I countered, knowing that his loss of power was coming to an end with Kade's upcoming reign.

"Oh, I fully expect him to. But the rules are the rules, and as much as he loves to follow them when it benefits him, he's not able to spin the tables to his liking on this one."

Staffan had been in charge since the death of Kade's parents. When Aleena had come of age, she had no interest in tethering to secure her place on the throne, so that responsibility had fallen to Kade. And from what I gathered, the council had been less than enthused with his decision to request a tether to a human, but it had set him on the path to hold his place of power until I came into the picture.

Now that Kade had successfully tethered, when the next Blood Moon rose here in Darthou, demons from all over this world would gather to see Kade and me take our place as rulers.

The thrones had been empty and in storage ever since his parents had passed, and we would be the first to sit in them after all this time.

It would also be the only time a moon of any kind could break through the constant cloud cover of their world. Like the Blood Moon somehow had the power to cut through the film and truly shine. I was looking forward to seeing it. The lack of a visible moon, sun, or stars above us made the ache of homesickness surge in my chest.

"Well, since you have deprived me of showering with you"—Kade sauntered around the bed—"I suppose I'll go get cleaned up." Then he added with emphasis, "By myself."

"However will you manage?" I teased as I poked the center of his chest. Until Kade, I had never known that I could enjoy showers so much. Or sex, for that matter.

"Good luck today." I gave him a quick peck on the lips but he drew me in, deepening the kiss. This time I let him, without fighting. There was a very good chance I wouldn't see him again until tonight when we would get ready to depart for Xandor.

"I love you." His lips brushed against mine as he broke away.

My heart was full as I beamed up at him. "I love you too."

Reluctantly, I separated from him, our entwined fingers lingering until we were out of reach.

"Give Aleena hell for me?" Kade voiced from behind my back.

I rolled my eyes as I headed for the door. "Not a chance, I like her too much."

"Worth a shot."

The hallway was quiet and vacant as I shut the door behind me. The dimly lit corridor never changed, since it didn't have any windows, and the surrounding halls provided an endless maze that was super easy to get lost in.

I should know. I'd been lost more times than I could count. There were no signs directing where to go or indicating who lived where. Some doors were identical, and others had markings either from wear and tear or who knew what else. Lucky for me, taking a left from our place led me straight to Aleena's.

I'd been mortified when I found out she literally lived next door, since Kade and I were less than discreet when it came to our sexual acts. She'd gotten me all riled up, leading me to believe that she heard anything and everything that went on to the point that I thought I would die of embarrassment. Kade had only been able to stow his amusement for so long and was the first to break, admitting that our homes were soundproof and that his sister was known to blast her music at all times of day and night and we hadn't heard a single note.

Another thing that bothered me was that everyone traveled by pocket mirror to get around. Even more after the realization that Aleena was so close by. Was it really that troublesome to stroll down the hall when she was so near?

Then again, the amount of times I'd gotten lost made me wonder if that was why they did it. I still had no idea how to get to Zan and Sarah's place. Maybe once I was finally granted my own pocket mirror for travel, I might think differently.

Knocking on Aleena's door four times, I began stretching my arms as I waited, moving on to my quads. I was bracing myself against the doorframe when she finally answered. I was over twenty minutes late thanks to my other half.

Her eyes narrowed at the sight of me, her bright red hair ablaze in color but confined in two French braids that looked so tight I couldn't imagine how they weren't hurting her scalp.

Her formfitting tank and shorts were fit to perfection, tailored for her size.

"Sorry I'm late." I twisted my fingers together behind my back, snapping out of my stretch so I could appear as apologetic as I was.

She examined me from head to toe, then back again. "Next time he wants to fuck you on my time, tell him to take it up with me."

Stunned into silence, I raised my shirt to take a sniff. Kade had informed me of Aleena's superior and unmatched sense of smell, but I had just showered. Was that not sufficient?

Aleena shot me an annoyed look and pivoted, leading me into her apartment. She spoke over her shoulder as I came in and closed the door. "It's not your clothes, by the way."

I moved uncomfortably, crossing my arms in confusion. I had scrubbed myself thoroughly and I knew I'd put on deodorant. "What…"

"Tell him to wrap it up next time."

I followed after her before the realization hit. It made my stomach churn to think that she might smell remnants of Kade's and my…relations. It was enough to make me wonder about swearing off sex for a while. And if she could smell *that* of all things…

I shuddered, thinking about all the people and scents she might come across. Things she might be able to name and others that she might not want to know.

Aleena beckoned me to follow, and I jogged through her room and down the hallway to catch up. Her home had the exact same layout as ours, but I had no idea if she had the outdoor garden area like we did.

"Better yet, hold off until I'm done with you."

"I'm…sorry. I tried to tell him—"

She held up a hand to silence me as we came to a stop. "Let's start small today since you've spent your morning exerting your energy elsewhere."

My gaze dropped to the floor. It was almost like being scolded for being late to class, but without the audience.

While Aleena's equivalent of Kade's watching quarters was somewhat smaller, it was loaded. Her wall of mirrors paled in comparison to his and was about half the size. There were two chairs, a lounge, and a couch placed in a semicircle as a viewing area in front of them. One corner was overtaken by fabrics and a couple of sewing machines and mannequins, as well as a few trunks on wheels that I assumed housed more colorful necessities for her crafty mind. It was evident that she spent a lot of time there, as Kade did in his music section, although it saddened me that I never seemed to catch him enjoying it.

"Blinks…go." She whipped around to face me.

Startled, I tried to recover. Shaking out my hands to release the built-up tension, I turned to face the mirrors. I concentrated on the green that my eyes used to be as I shut them. I'd found that it was the easiest way to bring on the change. I'd had those eyes for twenty-three years of my life, after all.

When I reopened them, Aleena's face remained unchanged. Stoicism seemed to run in the family.

When I turned my attention back to my reflection, that pit in my stomach opened up again. This was as close to human as I felt anymore. The whites of my eyes had returned, and the black abyss was now center, small, and contained.

"Blue," she ordered, and I stuffed away the longing for my past life.

Blinking again, I thought of the eyes Kade had worn out and about with me back home. My old home. No sooner had

I achieved victory, than Aleena was powering through with more orders.

"Brown."

These were trickier. Harnessing the brown to a color that wasn't too dark to blend in with the black proved problematic, and it frequently tripped me up. Sometimes I would overthink it and make the brown so light it was almost translucent. If that wasn't a freaky sight to see.

What had helped me last time was a roll of fabric in the corner, and I set my sights on it once again. The lush, rich color reminded me of milk chocolate.

This time, the movement of my eyelids was more exaggerated, and when I reopened them, a small smirk turned up the corner of Aleena's mouth.

"Good. A bit slow, but good." She clasped her hands together. "Now keep that, and let's try hair."

Removing my tresses from their tight bun, I let my hair tumble free. Trying to save time in the shower, I hadn't washed it since I'd been pressed for time and knew I was more than likely going to get sweaty and gross if Aleena's session involved any physical activity.

She never clued me in to what her plans were for me; I just showed up and went with the flow of whatever she decided to teach that day. It was best not to know what she had in store, since I would just stress about it anyway, and she knew that.

While I enjoyed spending time with Kade's sister, it was also cause for concern. Aleena had to report weekly to the council on how I was adjusting to this new world and my demon status, just the same as my weekly follow-ups with Rafina. She, too, had to report to the council. The fact that nobody seemed to know how or why I'd been brought back to life was troublesome, and they didn't like what they couldn't explain. So while I wanted to use these sessions with Aleena to my advantage, there was an unfair spotlight on everything I did, all of my successes and failures.

Aleena and I met almost every day. I met with Elias occasionally for combat training, and with Rafina once a week on Thursdays. I always dreaded those days the most.

Tucked away in my sports bra were the two coins that the witch from Xandor had gifted me to help suppress my banshee and fury sides. While they didn't bother me, they had a negative effect on Kade, who heard a high-pitched sound that grew in annoyance the longer I had them on me. The witch had said there wasn't much she could do about it since we were tethered. The depths of the ties between us were no match even for her magic.

Even though the coins bothered Kade, they were a necessary part of keeping my sanity intact. The screams I heard when in the presence of Rafina and her tethered, Staffan, had yet to be explained, and it wasn't worth it to risk them finding out that this newly resurrected and turned demon had a lot more beneath the surface than what met the eye.

While the witch and the others stuck with her in Xandor entertained our visits, they weren't very forthcoming with information. It was expected, after the betrayal that had fallen upon them. But I was still hopeful that in time, I could earn their trust and find some answers that no one else had been able to provide.

I raised my arms to the hairline on my forehead, and Aleena cleared her throat, shaking her head in disapproval. Last time she had informed me that I needed to start bringing on color changes without the use of my hands. It helped to be able to concentrate on changing the color inch by inch with the movement of my hands, but she wanted me to move away from that and to stop relying on it.

"Focus. Keep your eyes brown and change your hair."

I bit my tongue, wanting to argue with her. She made it sound so simple.

I had crazy respect for the long periods of time that Kade had kept his blue-eyed appearance at the carnival and at my grandma's house. One minor distraction and I could lose the hold I had on the blinks or hair changes. It was a talent that required continued attention and focus. With how often my thoughts jumped from one subject to another, the struggle was real.

Picking a spot on the ground before me, dark wooden floors that had streaks of black throughout, I mustered up enough courage to give it a shot, something that I was never brave enough to do back in high school.

Visualizing my scalp, strand by strand, I urged black to seep in and take over my strawberry-blond hair. I imagined it spreading until I could see it in my periphery. I grinned as I continued down to the tips.

"Damn, good job. That's really dark, Violet." Aleena's smile now spread to both corners of her mouth, but then faltered. "Careful, you're bleeding."

"What?" Panicked, my gaze snapped to the mirrors. Sure enough, the pupil-like centers of my eyes were bleeding out and into the brown irises, slowly taking over.

Shit.

"Just stay calm, focus. Reel it back in," she soothed with a gentle voice. She did have a softer side, but it was a rare thing to come across.

I knew that these lessons were more than likely a reflection of Aleena and her abilities for the council, and I also didn't want to disappoint her. I wanted to be worthy of her time and efforts.

As I stared ahead, I mentally pushed the tiny streams of black toward the center of my eyes. But just when I almost had it confined, I lost my hold on my hair. The black faded away in less time than it had taken me to change it in the first place, and my temperature rose in frustration.

"Fuck," I muttered as I braced myself on the mirrors.

"Forget the hair, just focus on your eyes."

"Why can't I get this?" I pushed off the glass surface as soon as my irises had returned to the brown hue I'd chosen. It was beyond aggravating that I couldn't hold on to the changes as easily as Aleena could. I had no idea what her hair color actually was, as she changed it so often. How did she make it look so effortless?

"Give yourself a break, Violet. You *are* making progress."

Hands on my hips, I began pacing. Sure, compared to day one, I was making progress. But it was disappointing because demons my age had these abilities well under control. "It doesn't feel like it."

"Blinks aren't something you just learn overnight."

"Yeah, well, you demons have had your whole lives to conquer these things. You make it look like child's play."

"What's with the rush?"

My feet came to a stop as I faced away from her. I did my best to school my emotions.

Aleena had been kept in the dark about me, about Xandor, about almost everything since I'd come to Darthou. Her intimate history with Rafina had put me in a strange position, one where I had to lie to one of the few people I wanted to trust around here. And yet, I didn't feel as if we could really, truly be friends while these secrets remained hidden.

The room fell silent as I wound my hair back up and into

a bun. It was a bit off-center, but I couldn't care less after my failure.

Well, *failures*. I knew my eyes had slipped back into their black pits and I pushed to shift them back to brown.

Aleena was standing still in a contemplative state when I turned, probably planning what action to take next. Since we didn't seem to be on the verge of a combative lesson, I had the suspicion that traveling by mirror might be next.

Great, another task that I hadn't conquered yet. Well, not with the coins on me anyhow.

For whatever reason, when it came to passing through mirrors, the coins had a negative impact on me. Whenever Kade and I had some alone time to spare, he was teaching me the skill, and those secret sessions had proved more fruitful than these with his sister.

Kade was worried about the countless deaths I might see upon looking into Aleena's eyes if I wasn't wearing the coins. She was a seeker, actively carrying out justice on humans who didn't deserve to live, so he was afraid of what all I might witness.

If that happened, we would have to come clean about everything before we were ready.

But it seemed as if we were never ready. Our questions continued to outweigh our answers.

"I have an idea." Aleena clasped her hands together rather excitedly, and I rose a brow. "Field trip."

CHAPTER 3

Violet

Aleena all but bolted from the room in rather large steps. She was taller than me by almost a foot, her lengthy legs carrying her faster than I could possibly follow at my walking pace. I stopped at the entrance to her closet as she flipped on the light. It was neat and orderly to the point of obsession. Her wardrobe was color coded from brights to darks, from whites and yellows all the way over to dark navy then black. This woman loved color, and it showed in everything she wore and how she decorated.

"Where are we going?" I watched as she plucked a smokey top that shimmered a pale pink and put it on. It fell off of her shoulder, and I was a bit jealous of her defined clavicle. She then grabbed a pair of leggings that cut off just above the ankle and slipped on a pair of tennis shoes. Judging by what she was picking out, I assumed that my workout attire was still an appropriate choice for today.

"Have you been to the school yet?" she questioned as she passed me. She smelled of a sweet fragrance that I couldn't place, but it was divine.

"Sarah showed me around a bit when I first got here. It was closed when I saw it, though."

"Perfect. We're going to pay them a visit." She ushered me out into the hallway. "Do you remember how to get there?"

My mouth twisted to the side. I knew I would probably head off in the wrong direction if she asked me to lead the way. "Do we have time to get lost?"

A lighthearted laugh escaped her as she closed her door. "Follow me, and try to keep up."

Aleena took off at a slight jog and my eyes bulged. There was no way I was going to be able to do that. Keep up with her?

I barreled down the hall after her as she made a right, then cut left. My arms pumped at my sides as I moved, willing myself to stay in the zone but channeling my inner strength to keep running. I loved to walk, but even with all my training since coming to Darthou, I still *hated* running.

She moved in silence while I, on the other hand, felt like an elephant bounding through hallway after hallway. My breath quickened and I pushed off of each foot with force; my calves and shins soon started to feel the effects of being used like this.

Aleena took another right.

By the time I made it to the turn, she was already halfway down another hall and gaining more distance. Did Aleena run 10k's or something? I was going as fast as my body could carry me, and it wasn't enough compared to her.

My chest struggled with the exertion as she took another

left.

Right, left, right, left, I thought. The second left had been a sharp one, the first hallway we had come across.

Rounding the corner, I came to a stop, heart beating rapidly, and I let my hands come to rest on my thighs.

Where the heck did she go?

I glanced around to my right, left, and straight forward in the direction I could have sworn I saw her go. It was too quiet, and I couldn't make anything out over the sound of my panting. I tried to slow my breathing and level it out.

The fragrance that I had smelled when Aleena passed me earlier returned, and I spun around to find her behind me, hair and skin in pristine condition as if she hadn't been leading me through a maze in the castle-like structure of Darthou's main hub.

"Where did you stash your pocket mirror?" I swallowed hard, trying to coat my throat. I hadn't witnessed her retrieve it before leaving her place, and I couldn't see any outline of it in her leggings. There was only a small line from her shorts.

"In my bra." She laughed and rolled her eyes, as if that should be common knowledge. I couldn't argue with that, since it was the exact same place I was hiding my coins.

"Remind me again why there are no signs around here?" I was perturbed at the complexity of navigating around these halls. Would it kill these demons to put up a few markers for directions? I was sure the humans around here would be in agreement with me on this.

Aleena passed me and continued down the hall at a slower pace, thankfully allowing me to walk by her side.

"In case of intruders," she responded. "While we hope for that never to happen, we can't be too careful. There are multiple routes for some destinations, but you'll get the hang of it eventually. Just as you will learn all there is to know about being a demon."

I scoffed at that as I folded my arms across my chest. "Everybody seems to have more faith in me than I do."

I hadn't exactly been an A-plus student in school, but for whatever reason, the fact that I couldn't get these skills down any quicker was a constant nagging reminder that I wasn't good enough. I wanted to succeed in this new life I'd been granted, even if there were sides of me that Aleena had no idea about yet. I hoped that one day I would get to share the truth with her, as I knew how important she was to Kade. I hated that we had to lie to her.

"Look, I know this isn't how anyone pictured you coming to Darthou, and it isn't the life you thought you would have, but I have every belief that once you get the hang of things, you're going to kick ass."

While her statement was a bit touching, I couldn't keep all of the attention on me. "Probably not as well as you." I nudged her with my elbow and smiled.

"Maybe not *that* well." Her voice had an undertone of amusement. "But between Kade, Elias, and myself, you'll get pretty damn close."

I wanted to believe that, to be that optimistic, but it wasn't exactly in my nature.

Coming to a stop at a door at the end of the hall, she tapped a glass handle three times then turned the knob to the right two times, then back once to the left.

"Three for the school?" I remembered Sarah doing the same when she brought me here. Aleena and Kade's aunt might be human and unable to travel by mirror unless a demon accompanied her, but she could still access spaces like the school, kitchen, and various other public spaces by a series of taps to the handles, another enchantment much like those on the doors to homes. If a door remained open, anyone could come and go.

Within my first few weeks here, I had to prick my finger and dot the doors in Kade's home so I would be able to come and go as I pleased. He then had to repeat the action with his own blood, sealing his approval of my entry—but only his main entrance and the one leading to his backdoor oasis. After my revenge on Brett, Kade had chosen to leave the door to his watching quarters out of the question. Perhaps the enchantments were the holdup on getting a door to the bathroom; I hadn't thought to ask about that until now.

Aleena nodded as she opened the thick wooden door. Noise began filtering into the hallway that made me think of children at recess, and when I followed Aleena inside, I found exactly that.

A substantial play area was illuminated by numerous skylights. Even though the cloudy skies here in Darthou never changed, they still let in more than enough light.

I made sure to close the door behind us as I took in the scene of young kids at play. Some were running wild, others playing with jump ropes, and others hanging upside down from a monkey bar–type dome. There were slides, swings, and everything you might see in an outdoor playground, only indoors. The squeals of glee and children at play made my heart soar. There had to be about three or four dozen kids having the time of their lives.

A familiar face emerged from the group, making a beeline toward us and launching into Aleena's arms. The action reminded me of my younger cousin Lottie, and my heart's fullness became tainted and heavier.

"Causing any trouble today, Ajax?" Aleena asked as we

skirted around the perimeter of the room in the direction of what I assumed to be the teachers on duty. They were conversing amongst themselves but were quick to wrap up as we closed in. Their postures straightened as we neared, and then there was the bothersome bowing that I'd asked people to stop, but they never seemed to listen.

Then again, I really didn't get out much.

"Not today!" Ajax's excitement and maniacal laugh had me stifling my amusement. Sarah was the first to admit that while her eldest was smart, he also had a knack for causing a bit of trouble. And he was getting better at hiding it.

"Hi, Violet!" He beamed at me as he waved over Aleena's shoulder.

I returned his greeting and scanned the kids' area again before we came to a stop at the group of four adults—three females and one male who were all oddly similar in height.

Several children began leaving the play area, some bolting and others walking as fast as their little legs could carry them over to Aleena. Their faces were alight with joy as they crowded in around her. I took a step back to allow them more room. It was like gravity was pulling all of them toward her.

Setting Ajax down, she granted hugs and smiles to each child who approached, naming them all as if she knew each one individually. For all I knew, she really did.

"What brings you here today, Aleena? Violet?" One of the women spoke up, her locks pulled back and secured. "I apologize, we weren't expecting you."

Aleena stood, telling the kids to go have some fun. Even though they tried to protest, they eventually listened and begin to disburse and resume their activities.

"Nonsense. I apologize for not giving you a heads-up." She waved to a little girl who seemed too shy to approach, but once she received Aleena's attention, she giggled and took off to join her peers. "I was just hoping to show Violet around and drop by the Modifications class. As long as that's not too much trouble."

The woman flashed a pearly white smile. "Of course. You know you're always welcome. As long as you promise to stop by and read for the children sometime."

"I would *love* to do that again, yes." Aleena grinned from ear to ear, a genuine one that diminished her hardened exterior. "You let me know what time works best. I already have a few books in mind. Oh!" She stopped abruptly. "Where are my manners? Violet, this is Tani, and this is Sharsten but she goes by Shar. This is Varnon and Kim." She gestured to each one as she went down the line.

There was something off about the last woman, the way she held herself and diverted her attention when I tried to make eye contact.

"Nice to meet you all." I tipped my head in their direction, but most of their names were already lost to me as we all nodded our greetings to one another.

"If you need anything else while you're visiting, please don't hesitate to ask." Tani had a kind voice that was neither too loud nor too soft.

"Will do." Aleena tugged on my arm for me to follow, but not before the teachers offered small bows again.

Not knowing if any of them had any superb skills like Aleena's sense of smell, I waited until a door closed behind us before asking her about one of the demons we just met. We were now in a wide gray corridor with speckled and shiny flooring that felt too clean to be a part of a school.

"Kim…" I started, not sure how to skirt around what I really wanted to ask. She had demon eyes, for sure. But the name didn't fit around here, and she had appeared nervous.

"She was human before, yes." Aleena led the way, passing by multiple doors until we came to the end. Again, there were no markings or signs, the same as the countless hallways on our way to the school. "She was the last successful transition. She's been a demon for…well…you know, I'm not exactly sure how long. Probably since Kadriel and I were kids."

I mulled that information over, estimating that it would have been well over twenty years ago. I knew one major consequence of attempting to transition to a demon was literal death. It was a fifty-fifty chance that you would be born again as a demon. I didn't like those odds, but it wasn't like I'd ever had a choice in the matter.

It was that fact that set me apart from the rest of the humans who had attempted the transition. It was still a mystery as to why I'd come back, when my heart had stopped beating before entering the waters of Obsidian Falls—a place that was apparently very sacred to demons.

"I'm not even going to ask how to tell which room is what here. Darthou doesn't make any sense."

Aleena grinned as she tapped the glass knob four times instead of three. "There is a method here, believe it or not. From the door we came in, from left to right you go from youngest to oldest. This door and the one we passed there would be the equivalent of high schoolers for you. Evenings it holds adults who are furthering their studies but not quite to the extent of what you might consider college."

I stole a glance down the way we had come, all doors evenly spaced, before following Aleena in. As I shut the door behind me, my back went straight as a rod.

Three stories of pristine mahogany filled my sight, with gold accents of light fixtures and decorative pieces. The first floor housed thick black desks with two chairs each and a massive whiteboard at the front. It was a classroom setting that I wouldn't mind being a part of, but how on earth could you concentrate with the magnitude of it all?

My brain went haywire for a moment, trying to figure out how this giant space fit, when out in the hallway, the doors were much closer together. This shouldn't be possible, and yet I was standing here and gawking like an idiot.

The second floor had rows and rows of books, a library of sorts filling it from left to right, all the way to a seating area with couches and chairs that I had to crane my neck to see.

The third floor was where I caught signs of movement. From what I could tell from their size and age, these were teenagers. There was a quiet chatter among them, but I couldn't make out what anyone was saying. Their voices were too light and too far away to discern anything.

Before I could take another step, Aleena swiveled and her eyes focused on something behind me. I followed her gaze to find Jacobi coming out of a doorway through which I could just narrowly make out a glimpse of a tiled wall before the door closed behind him. My heart sank when I saw his puffy eyes. I hated how my mind flitted back to memories of me crying in countless school bathrooms over the years growing up.

He cleared his throat as he bowed his head, and I took a step forward. "You really don't have to do that." I examined him as I crossed my arms. "What's wrong?"

Jacobi didn't bring his gaze up to mine. "Nothing, I'm fine."

Sadly, it wasn't the first time I'd witnessed him in this manner. Something was bothering him, and I could only assume that the restroom was his only option to be alone. Bathrooms and the catwalk of my high school theater were the spots I had frequented when I needed to get away.

"Modifications?" Aleena questioned him, and Jacobi shoved his hands into his pockets uncomfortably. "Is it Mave?"

He stiffened at the mention of her, and I knew that Aleena was spot-on with that assumption. He didn't need to answer verbally; his silence and the fact that he was unable to look her in the eye was telling enough.

Aleena's lips thinned as she glanced up at the third floor with its growing chatter. Returning her attention to Jacobi, she spoke quietly. "Two minutes and you come up. Got it?"

Jacobi nodded and went back into the bathroom. I shot Aleena a quizzical look. But there was a gleam in her eyes and a devious smirk on her face that I didn't know how to decipher. Or perhaps worse, didn't know what could result from it.

Aleena grinned. "This is going to be fun."

CHAPTER 4

Violet

When Aleena and I finally reached the top of the spiral iron staircase, I was a bit winded and my quads ached. It hadn't seemed that intensive looking up from the first floor, but now that we were here, I attempted to recover quickly as we had now become the center of attention.

The attention of an older man with styled but graying hair and several—and I mean a lot—of teenagers. Their voices became hushed as their eyes raked over us, before they collectively started to bow.

Seriously. Stupidly annoying. I was never going to get used to all of the bowing.

"Aleena! What a pleasant surprise!" The high tenor of a voice came from the man as he parted the swarm of teens and clapped his hands together. He wore a long-sleeved, white button-up with the collar fastened all the way to the top and a sweater vest over that. "And Violet, welcome."

"I'm kind of a big deal," Aleena said in a tone meant for my ears only, winking at me. The man placed a closed fist over his heart and bowed at the hips instead of the usual tip of the head. The two embraced and he squeezed her for a few seconds before taking a step back.

"You look great, love the red." He was very animated with his hands as he examined her. "To what do we owe the honor of this visit?"

"It was kind of a spur-of-the-moment thing so I'm sorry to show up unannounced. I was wanting to show Violet the school, and I knew it was around time for Modifications."

"Yes, yes. Well, you know you are *always* welcome." He turned toward me and I offered a polite smile.

"Hi, nice to meet you Mr.—"

"Oh please, none of those formalities here. We're all on a first-name basis. I'm Bexly." I repeated his name over and over in my head as he flashed a warm smile and added, "It is so nice to finally meet you."

"Likewise, but I think I might have seen you at my tethering celebration." His posture was so proper; I remembered him dancing with another man with the same straightened back. Very ballroom-esque from what little I could recall.

"You very well could have, yes. I wouldn't have missed it, and congratulations. Welcome to Darthou."

"Thank you," I acknowledged his greeting, but whispers from behind him were trying to steal my attention away.

"And might I say, good job on the eyes. How long are you up to now?"

"Um…" I didn't really have a sense of how much time had

passed since we'd left Aleena's place. I looked to her for an answer but she left me hanging on my own. "Maybe twenty minutes, give or take?"

"Splendid. Just wonderful." Bexly came across as a very laid-back yet involved sort of authority figure. I didn't detect any arrogance or better-than-you attitude, and it put me at ease a bit, much the same as I felt around Rebecca. "You've got a wonderful teacher, but if you ever need a break from her, I would be more than happy to assist you."

His teasing earned a playful yet mocking scoff from Aleena.

"That's really thoughtful, thank you," I acknowledged.

Movement behind Bexly vied for my attention, and I wasn't the only one, judging by how Aleena stilled. The conversation came to a halt as a familiar-looking teen began whispering louder than the rest. The girl she was speaking to covered her mouth as if something was funny. She looked eerily similar to someone else I'd met, someone I didn't like.

I had an inkling that the teenagers here could probably be just as cruel as the ones I'd grown up with.

Some footsteps came from behind, and Jacobi rejoined his classmates but at the edge, crossing his arms as he focused on something perhaps invisible on the floor. He didn't make eye contact with anyone, and I couldn't blame him.

"What do you say to a demonstration, Aleena?" Bexly placed his hands behind his back as he rocked on his heels. "Give the kids a glimpse at the possibilities of their abilities? Hm?"

She didn't skip a beat in her response. "Absolutely."

"Teacher's pet," that same, dark-skinned teen mumbled in the background, and Aleena's attention snapped to her.

It had to be Mave. The sister of Dimitra who, as I recall,

had been described as a throne chaser in her efforts to get to both Aleena and Kade. Mave locked eyes with my demon trainer, not an ounce of fear or regret in her frame. She didn't cower and kept her head held high.

"Mave, dear. How generous of you to offer to join in the fun." Aleena's voice turned sickly sweet.

Jacobi stirred on my right, readjusting his stance.

"Please, join me on the podium." Aleena strode through the sea of students that parted for her.

Mave sneered something inaudible at her friends and made her way up too. Her tight copper tank top and fitted jeans showed off her petite figure as she followed after Aleena without arguing otherwise.

The wooden podium was about two feet off of the ground, several feet wide on all sides. Its height granted everyone a view of both seeker and student as they stepped onto it. Next to each other, it showed just how tall Aleena was. Her defined muscles stood out just as much as the sleek lines of Mave's body.

With the crowd of students turning their attention toward the girls up ahead, I took a step closer to Jacobi. They crowded the podium in clusters, but he remained in the back with me. I had only seen him a time or two since the tethering celebration when he had been working. He frequently watched Zan and Sarah's kids, but he was never much of a talker. The kids loved him, though, and were always saddened when it was time for him to leave.

Those feelings of wanting to protect him resurfaced, and I reminded myself not to come across as overbearing.

"Have you conquered all of your blinks and minor shifts?" Aleena questioned Mave, loud enough for her voice to be heard by everyone present.

Changes made in the blink of an eye, Aleena had told me at our first session. It wasn't just the change of eye color, but hair as well. We hadn't even made it to body alterations yet. That was something I was equal parts nervous and excited to try. Shifts, she had called them. They required a lot more concentration, stamina, and effort, morphing your body into something it wasn't.

Mave crossed her arms, as if bored of this encounter already. "Top of my class, even though Bexly won't admit it." Her heavy annoyance was not at all what I had anticipated to spill from her. The way she called out her teacher on something like that made my nose scrunch.

"Now let's behave." Bexly made his way to the front and parked himself between the two of them on the floor, the hard part in his hair now evident from this angle. The kids crowded around and almost swallowed him to the point that all I could see now was his head. I guessed they were as invested in this as I was, and I took a tentative step forward.

"Eyes blue," he ordered, speaking clearly.

Seconds apart, they blinked, the blacks of their eyes now barely seen as they shrank to the size of pupils.

"Green."

Another blink, almost in unison this time, and both Aleena and Mave nailed it.

"Brown." With the mention of that color, I could sense my loosening grip on my own, and I took a moment for myself, breathing in deep, willing the color to stay.

"Red."

The order drew my attention away from my own plight, and I witnessed Aleena's eyes as red as her hair. Mave's weren't as bright, and more dull in appearance. Her right eye noticeably twitched twice before Bexly spoke up again.

"Steady now, hold it." Then he ordered, "Hair. Brown."

Aleena's change barely took a second, washing over her from her roots to the tips of her French braids. It earned a few gasps from the onlookers. Her opponent, who already had dark hair to begin with, opted for a lighter color that took a few heartbeats.

"Platinum."

Again, Aleena gained on Mave, and with such speed that it warranted a few raised murmurs as Mave tried to catch up. The red eyes and platinum blond hair was a sight that belonged in a horror film. The unnatural combination made my skin crawl.

"Streaks of your choosing."

Aleena's hair turned to lime green, black streaks unfurling along with it, twining through her hair until both colors reached the bottom, and somehow she simultaneously lengthened her braids about three inches. I blinked in disbelief.

After all the times I'd regrettably given myself bangs, I might be able to grow out my hair like that someday?

The volume among the viewers picked up with their excitement, and Mave struggled to catch up. She kept her long, wavy hair platinum, and chose to weave what looked to be brown through it, but her eyes were starting to grow darker.

"It's okay to tap out." Aleena didn't even spare a glance at her side to see what the rest of us were witnessing.

"Play nice, Aleena," Bexly chided, but I could barely hear it from back here.

"Keep going," Maze said through gritted teeth. She was getting angry, and that was only going to hurt her. Emotions as strong as that could be to your detriment, like when I lost my grip on my hair earlier. I couldn't concentrate through my frustrations and hold both my eyes and hair in their changed states. It was too many things to juggle.

"I really don't think—"

"Just keep going," Maze cut off her teacher, and her classmates started growing restless.

Bexly shook his head in disapproval.

A hand shot up from a kid who was swallowed up by the group, and Aleena pointed to him, not giving Maze any of her attention.

The young man's hand wavered before lowering. He cleared his throat before piping up, "Is it true you conquered blinks and shifts your first year here?"

She placed her hands on her hips, studying him for a moment. "Is that really what you want to ask?"

Another kid tentatively raised their hand. I could tell by the nail polish and size that it was a young girl, but that was all I could make out. "I think we all want to know if you really completed a whole body shift while in school."

As if struck by lightning, Mave lost her grip on her changes. Her eyes zapped back to black and her hair washed away the fake color in one swoop. She heaved forward and grasped her stomach, taking in deep breaths.

"We already know you're the youngest seeker there's ever been." I couldn't pinpoint which one spoke up. They seemed to be done raising hands now.

Aleena grinned. "My brother and I conquered blinks at a younger age than most. Before starting school in this very room." She scanned the room carefully, but there wasn't any superiority or ego speaking, just…Aleena. She seemed at ease up there. "But bodily shifts in my first year here, yes."

"How?" another near the back asked.

"I'm assuming Bexly still instructs you to practice single blinks at home but not multiple blinks and shifts, correct?"

There were several nods all around and I wondered where

this was going. Why could they practice one and not the other together? Sure, she had informed me of the warning signs if I was doing too much, but that was it. And we hadn't tackled bodily alterations yet.

"I won't apologize for it, but I'm the reason for that."

Heads were turning and the kids started conversing in hushed murmurs.

"As you can see"—Aleena gestured to Mave who was being helped down from the podium by her friends—"blinks alone can be draining, especially if you're forcing it before you're ready. But when you factor in shifts, you can push yourself too far. I did so on numerous occasions and found myself blacking out to the point that I would be in the infirmary for days."

Damn. Talk about commitment.

"There were a few months that you were in the infirmary more than in my class." Bexly spoke up as if in warning. "I still stand by that rule."

"Could Rafina not heal you?" Another voice, another question. Just hearing her name made my stomach cramp.

"There was only so much she could do. I was relentless and deprived my body of the rest that it needed. The only way to get me to stop was to keep me in a coma-type state to let my body fully heal.

"I'm sure Bexly has told you to be aware of headaches and chills. Nosebleeds and uncontrollable body shakes means you're on the verge of blacking out. If you get to that point, back off. You can still achieve your goals in a timely manner, but you have to listen to your body. And most importantly, do not compare your successes and failures to anyone else's. Everybody has their own timeline and you need to respect that."

The way Aleena commanded the room made me realize

that she was some sort of oddity or legend around here. Maybe both. It probably depended on who you asked. I'd had no idea that she was the youngest seeker they'd ever had in Darthou. That was as inspiring as it was worrying. Imagining a younger version of her, in a coma due to her rigorous efforts, shed new light on her.

"But to answer an earlier question…" She cracked her neck left and right before widening her stance. Popping her knuckles out in front of her, she paused before letting her hands come to rest at her sides as if waiting for dramatic effect. "How about a little glimpse?"

Aleena's hair began shortening and turning gray, shrinking up as stubble began to form around her growing jawline. The once slender face filled out and sharpened in tandem with the rest of her frame. An Adam's apple protruded from her neck. Eyes blackened. Shoulders broadened slightly, her chest appearing to flatten and her eyebrows thickening. Before I knew it, a carbon copy of Bexly was standing at the front of the room wearing Aleena's clothing.

But what was even more fascinating than all of the changes taking place was the noticeable bulge between her legs.

A collective gasp erupted from the room, and I was soon clasping my hand over my mouth to stifle my own shock. The group before me began to cheer in admiration and praise.

I couldn't help but join in. Bexly was right—I really did have a good teacher. I'd had no idea what she was really capable of until now.

Aleena held her hands up to quiet everyone and when the room fell silent, she grinned. The bob of her throat caught my eye, tearing my gaze away from her groin area.

"If anyone can help me out with the voice, though, I am *all* ears." Aleena's voice had remained unchanged, and we all burst into laughter. Hearing such a feminine voice spill from the muscular figure before us seemed like a magic trick. I tried to think of a time when I had laughed this hard since coming to live in Darthou, but came up short.

Bexly didn't look surprised or amused by Aleena's chosen appearance for her demonstration, just shook his head as if he should have known better.

Aleena hopped off the podium and the class erupted into their own bits of chatter. The teens were experimenting with blinks here and there, and seeing them all talk excitedly when a change occurred was uplifting. The entire atmosphere was better in here now, a playful one, and Aleena had brought that to the room.

Not only did she have a positive effect on the younger children at school, but the older ones as well. Perhaps if she wasn't a seeker, teaching could have been another option for her. Mave aside, she had apparently won everyone over.

"Is this the first time Aleena has visited your class?" I scooted closer to Jacobi and asked.

He nodded and a long pause fell between us. And just when I thought I wouldn't get an answer in words, he proved me wrong.

"Honestly, everyone is kind of afraid of her—Bexly's most prized student who defied odds. He talks about her a lot." He leaned against the railing, appearing more casual and less guarded. "She caused some trouble, but still became the youngest seeker in our history."

I nodded, but pushed to keep him talking. "Doesn't seem like they're so scared now."

"Probably because she sounds ridiculous with that voice in that body." Jacobi cracked a smile and I giggled.

"It is kind of outrageous, I mean…really? Nothing on the

voice? It's like a lion with the voice of a mouse."

This time, a laugh sounded from his chest. I loved witnessing this breakthrough with him. He was always so quiet and reserved on his own, never one to break the silence or offer small talk. It was like I'd only ever seen him comfortable around Ajax and Brighton.

"Jacobi, you're going to lunch with Violet and me. Bexly already approved it, I just have to bring you back before one."

Our heads snapped in Aleena's direction and I searched her eyes, trying to find the woman I had arrived with. Sure, she wore the same clothes, but the physical appearance was so drastically different that I couldn't keep myself from giving her the once-over twice before speaking.

"Should I call you Alex? Alec?" I joked as she closed the distance between us.

"Ha. Ha," she teased as we followed her down the spiral staircase, the noise from the scene behind us growing.

"Is it really lunchtime already?" I guided myself down with the handrail. I had thought going down the steps would be easier, but the height was surprisingly making me a bit dizzy.

"It is now, I'm starving."

"What, did becoming a man bring an appetite with it?" I joked as we neared the halfway mark.

"You have no idea."

CHAPTER 5

Violet

Aleena changed her appearance back shortly after leaving class, as she led us to a kitchen. It was decent in size, as I expected a school kitchen to be, but almost too clean. The staging looked like it could be in a magazine. There were three stainless steel fridges and multitudes of sage-green cupboards with butcher-block countertops. Rows of recessed lighting filled the room to the point that there were no shadows.

Aleena made herself comfortable, nabbing a package of assorted meats and cheeses from the first fridge she stopped at, then settled on top of a counter. She popped a piece in her mouth and leaned her head back in appreciation, eyes closed.

"That was amazing, Aleena. I had no idea you could do that." I blinked rapidly, still stunned by her little show and ability to change her entire form. She had the ability to literally change herself into anyone.

Jacobi had remained silent at our sides since leaving, but leaned up against one of the two islands that were almost the size of a double bed.

"It's exhausting, is what it is," Aleena quipped as she took another chunk of food in her mouth.

"How long can you do that for?"

She chewed for a bit and reached for another piece. "Sadly, not long. It's not a change that I can sustain for extended periods of time. It wears me down, mentally and physically. It's extremely draining."

"Is that why Bexly put that rule in place? No multiple shifts or whatever at home?"

Aleena slowed, her mouth twisting to the side, before she nodded.

"Then why risk it?" Jacobi pushed, and I was just grateful that he was speaking up at all. Even if it was just out of curiosity.

"Because if I ever wanted to be taken seriously as a seeker, I had to do something that got attention. Yes, it was risky, but I became a force to be reckoned with. Grown men couldn't do what I did at that age."

"Grow a dick?" The words were out of my mouth before I could stop them. Then all three of us lost it in droves of unflattering cackles. Jacobi was even clutching his side before we trailed off and a quiet settled over us.

"Want to know a secret?" Aleena's amusement was evident on her face as her top half leaned forward. I angled toward her. "It's only an illusion."

My eyes widened as I processed. "Shut. Up."

"No way," Jacobi called out, disbelieving.

"I shit you not." She sat back. "I can manipulate my nether regions to make it look that way, but if I weren't wearing any clothes…" Aleena let our minds wander, and the image that decided to settle had my face pinching.

"Still, it's insanely believable. I never would have guessed otherwise." I spared a glance at Jacobi who appeared just as taken aback as I was.

"You have everybody fooled. It's brilliant, really." Jacobi's voice was light as he tried to recover. "Your secret's safe with me."

"Me as well," I stated. "Although, I'm not sure who I would tell anyway."

Aleena shrugged as if it was no big deal, but I found that hard to believe. Letting us in on something like this felt almost monumental in some ways. She didn't have to share this information, and yet, she chose to. With Jacobi and myself.

"Kadriel, Elias, and Rafina are the only ones who truly know. And now you two." She eyed us both, a warning evident.

"Circle small, got it." I nodded in understanding. It totally made sense that her brother and Elias were in on it. I could understand that with her reputation, she would choose to keep that tidbit on the low. I still couldn't believe that it was nothing more than a show, a contortion of sorts that looked so real, just as much as the other shifts she had made.

I tried my best to skim over Rafina's involvement in the matter. That woman kept popping up, and it gave me a bitter taste in my mouth.

"Of course," Jacobi agreed, pulling me back to the conversation.

"Now—" Aleena clasped her hands together. "This isn't cutting it for me. I need more sustenance." She hopped off the counter and sealed the container of meat and cheese before placing it back in the fridge. "How about we go to the mess hall?"

Before we could respond, she reached out and grabbed both of our hands, transporting us by pocket to the kitchen that I had only been in once before—at my tethering celebration. There were a few at work, some food prepping and others doing dishes. A voice sliced through the noise that made Jacobi jump, and his hand slipped from Aleena's.

"What are you doing out of school?" Jacobi's mother, Jaxana—I was reminded again how alike they were in features—approached us and tipped her head.

"My doing, and I do apologize for not coming to you first," Aleena butted in cooly. "I had a little demonstration at the school and asked Bexly if Jacobi could join Violet and me for lunch. I hope that's alright."

Worried lines were forming on Jaxana's forehead as she looked between the three of us. She hesitated to speak, and I took it as nerves. "I don't mind. I just thought something might be wrong and I wasn't expecting the lot of you."

Aleena was quick to try and put Jaxana at ease. "I apologize, but might I trouble you for some protein of some kind? If you have something in the fridge, that'll do. It doesn't have to be anything special."

"I have some leftover braised beef and veggies from yesterday."

"Perfect, that will work. Thank you."

"As for you two?" Jaxana looked between her son and myself. I hadn't been expecting her to wait on us like this.

"Um…that's fine for me too. Thank you."

Jacobi agreed and she left us as we made our way out to the main hall. I had been here occasionally to eat, but most of my meals were spent at home or Zan's place. I still found it funny how none of the living quarters I'd been in had their own kitchens except for Zan and Sarah's. They were the only ones that had a formal dining area and kitchen. Sarah had been more than willing to share the information that it was one of her requests after her tethering. She wanted their quarters to feel like a home, complete with those areas. Zan had been more than happy to oblige in making that happen for her.

And here I was, still waiting for a damn bathroom door. She got a freaking kitchen *and* dining room. Was I really asking for that much here?

The mess hall was the center of all things food related. Kade usually ordered food for the two of us and would let me pick what we dined on. Fried foods, however, were something I had yet to come across in Darthou. Their meals centered around fruits, veggies, and meats. While it was rare, from time to time they would have rice or potatoes as a side. And those little pastries that I had obsessed over at our tethering celebration were apparently a delicacy that was reserved for special occasions such as that. What I was really craving as of late were pancakes, but I hadn't seen those offered at all.

There wasn't even a menu that I knew of. Kade would just spout off some usual offerings, or if I said something in particular sounded good, he would point me in the direction of something similar if that couldn't be done. But you couldn't tell me that in their vast kitchen they didn't have the ingredients to make pancakes. Something as simple as that had to be an option. Perhaps I just needed to ask. Or hell, if they let me into the kitchen to cook, I would gladly try to whip up a batch myself.

We sat at the first table we came upon. A few others were scattered about the great hall, some studying with books open, others chatting, and some grazing on food. I could make out a cluster of grapes on one plate, but the others were so distant that I was unable to decipher what they were eating. The large round tables could easily seat over twelve people each, but I could tell they had removed some in the wake of our celebration, granting more space in between them all.

My sights landed on the front of the hall where Kade's family and I had sat, knowing that this coming weekend, the thrones of his parents would be placed back in their spots for the coronation. My heart began pounding at the mere thought of it.

Once again, I would be thrust into a giant social gathering, and would be the center of attention. Up until today, I'd been more or less sequestered away as I began training. When you threw in the weekly check-ups with Rafina, and my secret getaways with Kade to the exiled in Xandor, it left little time for much else. Knowing that this go-around with the masses would be different—now that I had the coins to suppress the screams that had became too much at our celebration—helped my anxieties regarding the matter.

Then again, there was the fact that there hadn't been a coronation since Kade's parents. Meaning that countless demons from both Darthou and other kingdoms would be in attendance. No one would be turned away, as all were welcomed to attend. The thought was almost gut-wrenching, and I was soon drowning in my worry.

"Nervous for the coronation?" Aleena asked as she propped her feet up on the chair next to her. She began rubbing her temples in a circular motion as if she was fighting off a headache or something.

"That obvious?" I crossed my arms and leaned forward on the table for support. I'd been informed that Aleena and Kade's family would be at the front with us just as they had been before, and that the order of events would be pretty similar to what had already taken place at the celebration.

"You'll be fine. You won't be alone."

"No, I'll just be the one singled out as queen." I sighed heavily. Kade had told me that there might be some other creatures in attendance too, but he wasn't exactly going through RSVPs to find out who. This was a word-of-mouth type of affair.

I wasn't supposed to have met any other creatures yet, not to anyone's knowledge besides Kade, Zan, Elias, and Sarah. It was just one of the many secrets being kept under lock and key. No one knew that I had already met a witch and the two remaining eerie furies, among the select few that still lived in that other world.

"Will you be working again?" I asked Jacobi, and he froze at the sudden eye contact. He'd had to pitch in and help as a server at the last occasion.

"Probably. Mom needs all the help she can get." He quickly broke the connection and fixed his focus on the table. His hands were clasped below, and he returned to his muted state.

"Care to share what happened before we got to your classroom today?" Aleena interjected, and I sat back to let her take the reins. I knew Jacobi wasn't much for sharing, but I wanted to know too.

He became a statue, still and unblinking. I couldn't tell if he was trying to ignore her or just suppressing an urge to react.

"Mave seems like a piece of work. Just like her sister," I expressed, going off of what little I knew. If I remembered correctly, I thought Mave might have been the reason Jacobi had been so upset during our celebration.

I'd only been graced by her older sister Dimitra's presence a few times, but it was enough to know that I couldn't stand her superior attitude and rudeness regarding humans. And judging by what little I'd seen at the school, it must run in the family.

Jacobi's hands tightened into fists as he took a deep breath. When he spoke, it came out through gritted teeth. "Mave has the whole class believing that I'm weak."

"Why on earth would she think that?" I looked between the two for answers, not following. He was a freaking demon. Born as one and probably ahead of me in my studies as I tried to live up to the title.

"Because of your dad." Aleena didn't pose it as a question. Just a soft voice of understanding.

Jacobi's jaw trembled ever so slightly before he turned away from us, keeping his face from our view.

His dad had been the last human to try and transition, but it had proved unsuccessful, leaving behind a wife and young son. I didn't know how old Jacobi had been, but still. He'd lost his father too soon.

"I'm sorry, but I don't understand. Why would that make *you* weak?" I failed to see the connection.

"Because Jacobi has human blood. Kids can be cruel. Hell, full grown-ass adults can be too." Aleena's expression turned sour, appalled. "It's a load of crap. You're just as capable as the kids surrounding you."

"They don't see it that way," he argued.

A familiar presence approached from behind and before I could whip around to greet him, he pecked my cheek with a kiss. Surprised at his arrival, I tipped my head up to look at him. "What are you doing here?"

Kade flashed his charming smile as I stood. "Grabbing a

quick bite before the council meeting. What are you guys up to?"

"Trouble," Aleena spouted. "Always."

"No doubt." He was dressed a little more formal than usual. A dark button-up with black dress pants and sleek shoes. The top two buttons remained undone, which suited him. Every time he came home with one of those on, I couldn't stop myself from unbuttoning it the rest of the way. What I really wanted to do was rip it off of him, sending the buttons flying everywhere. But the thought that I would look like a fool if I failed to do so stopped me every time. Not so sexy or romantic if I didn't succeed.

Jaxana came from the kitchen hallway with a balancing act of three plates. "Oh, Kadriel. I have your order ready and it's on the pass. I'll get that for you in just a moment."

She began setting our food down on the table, retrieving sets of silverware from her apron.

"No worries, I'll grab it real quick. Thank you, Jaxana."

"Of course." She bowed before leaving, now that she was free of the food she had delivered. Then she scurried off, only to pop back in with three glasses of water in hand.

"I'll see you tonight?" Kade brushed my ear with his lips as his arms wrapped around me in a hug. I shot him a wary look. I picked up on some excitement, which didn't exactly match the heaviness of our plans to visit Xandor later.

I only nodded as he backed away. I was limited as to what I could say, what I could ask. But it didn't stop Kade from offering a small wink before leaving us for the kitchen.

He winked. Had he ever winked at me? Was there something I was missing?

Who better to ask than his sister.

"Okay, he's been in a weird mood. Like, oddly playful

and…happy." I turned back to the rest of the group, Jaxana included as she hadn't left yet. "Does anybody else see it or is it just because of our tethering that I can feel it?"

"Do you guys have any plans tonight?" Aleena asked as she grabbed a fork and stuffed a chunk of meat into her mouth.

Alarmed that we did but I couldn't speak of it, I blurted, "Um…not really?"

She paused before taking a second bite, exchanging glances with Jacobi and his mother.

"What?" I stuck my hands on my hips, apparently in the dark about whatever was known to everyone else here but me.

Aleena chewed faster, then cleared her throat as she set her fork down. "Of course he didn't tell you. That's probably why he canceled it, just like he does every other year."

"Cancel what? *Tell* me what?" I pressed on, urging her to continue.

"It's his birthday eve."

I blinked at her a few times in soundless confusion. It took a few seconds before a newfound panic set in.

And when I was finally able to find my words, they came out a bit louder than I intended and it caused everyone in the mess hall to turn their heads in my direction.

"His birthday what?!"

CHAPTER 6

Kade

I strolled into the council chambers just as I finished off the last of my meal, wiping my fingers on a napkin Jaxana had placed around the package. The other men had already assembled before me—as per usual—but now that my coronation was just around the corner, their conversations came to an abrupt halt. Normally, I would waltz in here and plant my ass on my chair, waiting for Staffan to call the meeting to order. Now, it would seem that they were preparing for the shift of power.

Good.

Each head bowed, my uncle's included, as I came to my seat. It was like my blood was buzzing, eager to get this show on the road and piss off some councilmen. If this meeting ran too long or if I received too much pushback, I knew it would drive me over the edge with the growing ringing in my ears. I just had to remember that wearing those damn coins was for Violet's own good. For her safety and for those around her.

Many, or really *countless*, demons had taken lives. Some for lifetimes. Violet hadn't witnessed any visions since that first time in Xandor, and thankfully so. She could see those murdered as if viewing their deaths from the killer's perspective, just by gazing into a person's eyes. It had been enough to give her the bloodlust to kill the unnamed witch, but it had been merely a shock when she saw mine. It was something I'd feared would scare her off, cause her to run from me, but Violet was proving to be one surprise after another.

I—*we*—couldn't risk Violet's sight happening around Darthou with anyone she might come in contact with. Especially Aleena. Her kill score when it came to seeking was one to be reckoned with, and now she was tasked with training Violet in our demon ways. I loathed the position I'd been put in, keeping my own flesh and blood in the dark regarding my tethered mate, but it was safer this way.

For the time being.

"Good morning, gentlemen." I glanced at the men who sat at my sides. The curvature of our placings allowed us all a good view of one another. "I hope you don't mind that I begin today's proceedings. If anyone objects, please speak now."

I eyed Staffan, fully expecting him to insert himself at once, but when he remained stiff jawed and tight-lipped, I moved on.

"First order of business, Abeck. How are we with the coronation? Everything on track?"

Abeck was the eldest of all the council members and had served long before my father's time even. There were no such things as term limits in Darthou. You sat on the council until you died, stepped down, or were voted to be replaced. Although Abeck was a hard one to read, and often quiet, he had a distinctive and gravelly voice.

"Yes, Kadriel. The Blood Moon and your coronation are causing quite the stir amongst all creatures. We expect this to be the biggest turnout yet."

The mention of the moon caught my attention, perhaps more than it should have. I was momentarily transported back to the dinner at my aunt and uncle's when Violet had first learned about the Blood Moon. In Darthou, you couldn't see the sun, moon, or stars, just a constant cloudiness that hid whatever hung in the sky. Rays could escape from time to time, but when the coming moon emerged in its entirety, it was a magical sight that many gathered for. Some even threw parties just to honor it and its presence. It only happened once every year.

"What's so special about this Blood Moon?" Violet had asked.

"We demons are at our most powerful then. Such a special night is the only time for a king and queen to rise to power," Uncle Zan had offered as a small explanation.

"Why can't it be a Blooming Moon? A Rising Moon, or a Super Moon?" Violet had let out a snort of a laugh that she was quickly embarrassed by. Her cheeks had reddened as she tangled her fingers in her lap beside me.

"She has a thing about blood," I'd interjected, trying to keep the conversation light as I teased her. "I promise you, Violet. We may be demons, but not everything we do involves *actual* blood."

I was snapped back into the present when another member confirmed Abeck's words on this upcoming event.

"And are we prepared to entertain them all? Will we have

enough space?" I asked. My own tethering celebration had felt like we were at capacity. I could only imagine how crowded it would become if all available demons and some non-exiled creatures were able to be in attendance.

"That has been cause for concern, yes." Abeck was a bit slow to continue, placing his hands on his armrests. "If needed, we can overflow into the gardens. I have been coordinating to make sure that particular food needs are met so we will be able to accommodate all who wish to attend."

I nodded in understanding, pretending that the ringing wasn't bothering me. "Thank you, Abeck. I know our kitchen was overwhelmed with the response at my celebration, I just want to make sure we're better prepared for this."

Shifting in my seat, I readied myself for the topic that was sure to ruffle some feathers. I needed to get this out of the way now.

"Next order of business before I let you gentlemen take the floor." I sat up straighter, mentally preparing my statement. "I am ready to go to the next Summit."

"Absolutely not," Staffan interrupted right after the last word left my mouth.

And there it is.

"I am missing this Summit by one day, Staffan. I have missed years of them because I hadn't tethered yet. That ends now."

These meetings were for the leaders of each of the five kingdoms—including Darthou—who met two times a year to discuss any happenings or problems that might need attention. It was exactly the place I needed to be to discuss the growing number of saints working together. A fact that should have been concerning and handled by now, but no. We were still waiting…still gathering "intel."

"You tethering to a human was of your own choosing," Staffan spit back, and I suppressed the urge to raise my voice to meet his level.

"Yes it was, Staffan, and I would do it all over again if I had to, but I see no reason why I should miss this one. It would also be a great introduction for Violet to meet some of them before the coronation."

"You want to take *her* with you?" He acted as if it was the most ludicrous thing he'd ever heard.

"Don't pretend like you've never taken Rafina with you," I countered.

"Perhaps we should ask to reschedule," Qantan, on my far left, offered. While I appreciated his attempt to help, he was met with a unified response from Staffan and myself.

"No."

"How about we take a minute to think this through," Zan pleaded, and I realized I'd been leaning forward in my seat, almost ready to pounce. I settled back into my chair as he continued once he had our attention. "I understand why you want to go, Kadriel. Narrowly missing this Summit doesn't—"

Staffan cut in, "But I—"

"I'm not finished." Zan raised his voice and the room went quiet. The anger on Staffan's face was clear as day for all to see. I was stunned to see him heel like that. It wasn't like him to back down and bite his tongue.

"A lot has happened since the last Summit, especially your successful tethering, Kadriel. While I understand Staffan's...hesitancy to give up his place and your eagerness to get started, how about a compromise?"

Staffan and I exchanged hard looks, unclear of Zan's aim in this. I didn't know what my uncle had up his sleeve, and the thought was a bit unsettling. I feared that this was nothing we had discussed on our own behind closed doors.

"What if the two of you attended together?"

"Absolutely not," Staffan puffed in agitation.

While I was less than thrilled with that idea, I was trying to seek Zan's reason. I gestured for him to continue.

"What if Kadriel accompanies Staffan to the Summit? This could provide a sense of closure for Staffan as acting lead."

"This is ridiculous." Staffan stood from his chair, his temper getting the best of him.

"Would you sit down and shut up?" Abeck's voice echoed through the room until it went silent once more. Collectively, we all turned in his direction, more than surprised at his outburst. "You're acting like a child."

I wanted to bark out a belly laugh at the last comment, but I refrained. I was loving Staffan being in the hot seat right now, as things were obviously not going according to his plan. Which then begged the question, why was this Summit so important to him that he had to go? Why couldn't he just let me step up and into my place? It was inevitable. His time was up.

As much as I didn't want to play into it, I had to be the bigger man and do it, pretending to see reason and go along with it, no matter how much I didn't love the idea. "It would be a good opportunity for him to introduce me. I have met a few of the other leaders over time, but this might not be the worst idea. I can take Violet another time."

I then directed my attention to Staffan, who remained the center of attention with his defiance. What was stopping him from fighting back?

"What do you say, Staffan? I'm willing if you are." I pretended to offer an olive branch, even though I would rather ram it straight through his back.

The next time we butted heads, I wouldn't be settling, as my word would be final, no matter the vote amongst the rest of them. Once I was crowned king, I could take their words and opinions into consideration, but it was my orders they would have to obey.

I would have the final say.

"Fine," he seethed, unable to look at me as he backed into his chair. I swore I could feel the heat rolling off of him, like opening the door to a sauna.

"Very well then, that matter is settled." Zan settled back into his place, crossing one leg over the other. Ever the perfect poker face. The fine pressed lines of his pants showed off Sarah's impeccable ironing. It was something that Rebecca had done for him prior to his tethering, but now his mate had taken that on as a job of her own.

"Next order of business." I cleared my throat coolly. "How are we with recruits for our guard, Hyett?" He was the leader of security measures and in charge of those sworn to protect. He bore the responsibility of the guards and their actions, no matter what Staffan believed. Hyett was the one who recruited, trained, and evaluated them.

"Here we go again." Staffan rubbed his temple in annoyance. "You're beating a dead horse, Kadriel."

"And I fail to see how you don't think that the growing number of saints working together isn't a problem. That, and the fact that the one known as Damian has a shard of glass from Violet's mirror. The one that released me."

"Speaking of that, and pardon my interruption." Everyone's focus turned to Clefus. His pin-striped, black-and-gray suit complemented the chosen wisps of silver in his hair. His face was more youthful than the coloring he'd chosen above it.

Clefus was a bit of a wild card, and I never knew which way he was going to sway. One day he would be hell-bent on making my life miserable and siding with Staffan. The next he would have my back as if he had been there all along. Each situation or problem was different.

"We do have cause to be concerned."

My body went rigid as I eagerly waited for him to continue. Of all of us, he looked the oldest, even though age-wise, Abeck had him beat. Maybe his hair made him look wiser, I really couldn't be sure. He was the least muscular amongst us, choosing to bury his head in studies but never one to teach. Watching and observing, but never fully taking on the job. He had his hands in many things here in Darthou, but he himself was a library of knowledge. If I could pick anyone's brain about all they knew about banshees and furies, he would be the one to ask. But not knowing where his alliances truly stood was troublesome enough for me not to open that door.

"I know you have all been harping on me to narrow down the pool of saints that this Damian could be, and I have done so. But I wasn't ready to say something until I was absolutely certain."

We all exchanged looks of curiosity. I was anxious about both the news he was about to bring and the ringing in my ears that seemed to be loudening with each passing second. It had only been a few hours since Violet had grabbed her coins, but it was long enough that the annoyance was growing worse. I only hoped that she returned home soon so I could get a break from their annoyance. The witch hadn't anticipated the side effect, but it was one that I would endure to keep Violet safe.

"By all means, you have our undivided attention." Zan nodded for him to continue.

Clefus adjusted himself in his seat as his face grew grim.

The sinister silence that fell upon the room while he let us simmer in dramatic effect was almost maddening.

Just speak, dammit.

"I have narrowed this Damian saint down to two individuals and Kadriel, you were certainly right in the knowledge of his age. Both are well over two hundred and fifty years old," he began, and I hung on his every word. "But one of the possibilities is too much of a coincidence to be ignored." He shifted, uncrossing his legs and putting his feet flat on the floor. "In my opinion, and I'm sure many of you will agree, there is no way it is merely that."

"Is this going anywhere?" Staffan inserted himself, and I shot daggers at him with my eyes.

Clefus scowled at the interruption, although he didn't turn to face the one responsible. Instead, his gaze pivoted to mine. "Noliathan."

If the blood could have drained from my body and left me for dead, it would have.

"No," Zan uttered in disbelief as he pushed himself up from his chair and began to move away, putting distance between himself and the rest of the council.

It felt as if I was witnessing things from a bird's-eye view. Watching myself in my own out-of-body experience. I couldn't breathe, couldn't speak. The ringing in my ears increased to cut out the chatter of the men commenting around me. They could have been yelling at each other, slaughtering one another, and I wouldn't have had a clue. I couldn't make out what anyone was saying.

That name. *That fucking name.*

I had been so close to ending him. So fucking close!

I wasn't sure how loud my voice was, but all I could manage to say before zapping myself out of here was, "Recess."

CHAPTER 7

Kade

Once in the confines of my living quarters, I pried my shirt apart at my chest. Even with the first couple of buttons undone, I was still suffocating. The news that Noliathan had returned, and even worse, had kept Violet under his thumb and eye for so long, was debilitating. That he could have ripped her away and I wouldn't have known his true identity—disastrous.

Clefus had been tasked with this project weeks ago, and I didn't know what I'd expected him to come up with, but it certainly wasn't this. I never could have imagined this revelation. I didn't want to believe it, but if he had whittled it down to two, then it was a no-brainer that this…

My heart was beating so fast, threatening to break from its cage. My head was pounding as if it was about to split in two.

Like a sword's blade had found its way into my skull.

The ringing, the fucking ringing! It was all I could hear and at this point, I could almost *see* it.

I sank to the floor, covering my ears as if that could provide the littlest comfort, and let out a strained cry that I couldn't even hear. It tore through my throat, making it raw as my eyes began to well with tears. My vocal cords strained again and again, vibrating to an extent I'd never experienced before. I waited for them to snap from the pressure they were under.

"Kade," Violet's voice rang through, slashing through the unbearable torment but only at a surface level. Worry washed over me in a wave that swept through my body, lightening my load of pain and agony. Hunching over on all fours to the floor, I tried to combat the exhaustion that wanted to show. But a hollowness began to settle in my belly and I heaved.

"Kade," she repeated as a hand came to lie on my back. "What's wrong?"

"Does someone want to tell me what the fuck is happening here?" Aleena's raised voice was a stark contrast from the soothing of Violet's and I groaned. Of course she was here too.

"Aleena, how about you retrieve Elias and bring him here. There's something that needs to be discussed. It's urgent."

Uncle Zan was here as well. For fuck's sake. Why couldn't I just be alone? Better yet, Violet was all that I needed.

Violet pressed softly on my back, creating calming circles. It was working to an extent, but there was still one thing.

"The coins," I croaked in a voice I didn't recognize. Placing a hand to my throat, I healed it. It took longer than expected, but I swallowed in relief as Violet removed her coins, jogging to the bathroom to place them on the counter in their usual spot.

When she returned, there was the smallest wrinkle

between her brows and I could sense her warring panic even though she was trying to suppress it. Violet was getting quicker with her attempts to squash her emotions before they became too big. Keeping emotions from her face, though, was still a work in progress.

"Are you okay?" She searched my eyes, my face, as she lowered down in front of me. "What happened? I've never felt that from you before. Like...ever."

She took my hand in both of hers, offering a gentle squeeze. I glanced up at my uncle, who had his hands shoved into his pockets with a heavy look that told me he was struggling with this news as well. I was sure the blow that had been delivered in the council room was a hard hit to the both of us. Although, I wasn't sure how he was hiding it so well.

Zan met my stare briefly, then shook his head to look away.

I didn't want to believe it either.

Aleena returned with Elias, the two of them separating like oil and water as she positioned herself on the opposite side of Zan.

"Okay, will somebody tell me *now* what the fuck is going on?" My sister crossed her arms, and it looked as if she was resisting the urge to tap her foot as she waited.

"We received some rather...distressing news at the council meeting just minutes ago. We have a brief recess, but we need to figure out our course of action." Zan then returned his attention to me. "Kadriel—"

I held up a hand before he could continue. "I'm fine."

But I really wasn't. I couldn't be further from it. My grip tightened on Violet's hand as we stood together, then I gestured for him to go on. How could he remain so...calm?

"Aleena, I hate to deliver this news with an audience but

this…" Zan's gaze dropped again while wheels turned in his head. "We believe Clefus has figured out who Damian is. Narrowed it down to two, to be precise. But one of them…"

I couldn't even bring myself to utter that name. Couldn't fathom my mouth making the movement to say it. Violet wrapped her other arm around mine, leaning in close as if to steady me.

"Noliathan."

The name held so much grief, so much power over me, and I witnessed Aleena's face shift into one of denial. In a matter of seconds, the red hair atop her head began to fade to a dark brown to match my own. Her natural color was rare to see anymore, and I was left speechless by her slip.

Even if she was taking the news better than me.

"Fuck," Elias muttered as he ran a hand over his face.

"It's no wonder he attached himself to Violet." I finally spoke up, feeling all eyes on me now. "But we need to know who introduced them. There's no way he found her on his own." I swallowed hard, loathing myself for not finding any kind of link before now.

"I'm sorry, but…I'm lost," Violet piped up gently. "Who exactly is this Nol-i-athan?" She drew out his name as if testing it.

Zan stepped forward, wearing a somber expression that aged him within the shadows of the bedroom where the light of the windows didn't reach. "He's the saint that claimed the lives of Tarnon and Audra, then vanished without a trace."

Just hearing my uncle speak my parents' names sent a lance of pain through me, and I struggled for air. That sword to my head had moved to stab me in the chest.

"No." Aleena shook her head as she took a step back from the group. She stifled a choke of a sob and Elias moved to try to comfort her, but she stopped him.

Noliathan had taken our parents—our *world* from us. His little army of saints had almost taken out Aleena too the last time we'd been face-to-face.

That smug face that he'd worn—he knew who we fucking were and we had been none the wiser. Now that we knew the truth, there would be no stopping us in our pursuit of finding and ending him.

In the weeks that had followed Violet's disappearance, he'd resigned from her old workplace and told his coworkers he'd secured another job several states away. He hadn't even waited for a replacement to come, but had tried to leave on good terms, especially since there was still an investigation underway since one of his employees was missing and presumed dead. Since then, he had retired to the apartment building that he called "home," but he hadn't been seen in well over a week now.

Elias, his dad Eleandor, Zan and I were all tasking ourselves to keep a watchful eye. We were hell-bent on figuring out his next move while trying to come up with a plan of our own to capture and end him.

The apartment he was hiding in was a fortress in itself, with no mirrors or reflective surfaces inside, like it was sealed off from the world. It was too much of a risk to enter it ourselves without knowing what we were walking into. There were people coming and going occasionally, resuming what looked from the outside to be normal lives and routines, but Damian—or Noliathan—must have taken it upon himself to arm his home just as he had his workplace. We were unable to see anything once he stepped inside. It was understandable that he would have taken great measures to make sure the place was secure, but the fact that no others could be seen in there was unnerving beyond belief.

Perhaps now the council would take me more seriously, knowing that the one responsible for killing their last king and queen had come back into the picture. Hell, *had* been back in the picture for some time now, and right under our noses.

Watching. Waiting. Planning whatever fucked-up scheme was at play.

"He…what?" Violet's confusion and heartbreak as she sorted through the news was staggering.

As much as I wanted to be comforted by her mere presence, I couldn't bring myself to look at her. She was gazing up at me, but I was still rocked by the blow I'd been struck with. It shook me to my core, and its grip on me had thrown me off. Way off-balance.

"What happens now?" she asked when I remained unmoving and silent. It was the exact opposite of what I needed to do, what I needed to be. That I was letting this information bother me to this point was not a good sign for my upcoming leadership. I had to prove that I was worthy and ready to lead and dammit, if this was a test, it was my biggest one yet.

I had failed to rid the world of him the last time we'd met, but we had been ill prepared. We hadn't been ready for the unknown army he had at his command, and it couldn't happen again.

We had almost lost Aleena.

Violet had died.

The next time we met, there would be no escaping.

I locked eyes with Aleena, who seemed to have come to terms with the news quicker and quieter than I had. Her ability to lock down her emotions and get to business was a quality that I admired, but it was also a hard wall to break down if you needed to. And I had flown out of the council chambers moments after Clefus had spoken his name, unable to be among others for fear of showing weakness. Aleena was currently handling it all way better than I had, but now I was coming up on the other side of it.

And I wanted blood.

CHAPTER 8

Kade

"Council will resume in an hour. I think a recess was much needed," Zan expressed upon his return to my watching quarters where we had all congregated. He rejoined us as we gathered around my wall of mirrors.

I began swiping at them, bringing up images of Damian's apartment building through the various car mirrors that would grant us a look at his so-called residence. The two-story building felt tiny compared to the size of Violet's past building. Judging from the outside, it housed about twelve apartments; Elias had come to the same conclusion after digging up some blueprints. The white vinyl siding and black shingled roof were still in pristine condition even though the building was nearing ten years old. Each window was framed in black, with inside coverings that didn't allow anything to be seen in its interior. They were never opened. In the evenings, if you were lucky, you would see silhouettes of occupants, but that was all. An occasional passerby, a glow from a possible television, but nothing that helped our efforts to decipher what was happening indoors. Sending someone in would be a suicide mission, not knowing what lay ahead.

We had vetted everyone who claimed residency there, tracked them back to when they first moved in and where they had lived before that. It was all useless information that did nothing to tell us why Noliathan had decided to set up shop here.

They carried on their day-to-day routines, and there was never anything to make us think they were in danger. Saints only had a problem with you if you cheated death. Hiding amongst innocent lives kept them safe for the time being.

I held my breath as I took a step back to join Violet at her side. She took my hand again as she searched the images I'd laid out before everyone. It was the middle of the day and several cars were still parked in the lot, one of them being the truck that belonged to her old boss.

"We need to figure out how to get eyes on the inside," Elias began.

"We can't afford any collateral damage if things take a turn," I added, while not disagreeing with him.

"Who…what is this place?" Violet questioned. "I see…" She paused, and I felt her nerves taking root as her heartbeat quickened. "That's Damian's truck. Does he live here now or something?"

I turned my focus to her. "This is the only place I've known him to live, Violet."

"No, he lives up north. Or…so I thought." She returned her attention to the mirrors and I loosened a breath.

"He has lived here since before you went to work for him."

"Oh," she said quietly, a bit deflated. I knew she had beaten herself up on more than one occasion for not knowing something was off about Damian. But how could she have known? She'd had no idea of the world of demons, saints, and creatures until I came into her life.

Damian had kept her in the dark, just how he wanted to. Until I came into the picture and everything had fallen apart.

One of Violet's previous coworkers turned into the parking lot, taking her place in her usual spot near the far right side. Her silver sedan came to a stop and she exited the vehicle with purse in hand, home for her lunch break.

"Wait, Theresa?" Violet took a step forward and without realizing it, I reflexively tried to pull her back and away from the glass surfaces.

She whipped her head around, emotionally hurt by my action while her face showed a warning. The memory of how she had crossed through without so much as blinking an eye when she killed Brett had caused me to react without thinking it through.

This morning, these mirrors had been nothing more than reflective surfaces for our personal enjoyment, but now? They could be a one-way ticket to mayhem if something sparked in her. Violet's fury side was lying in wait to come alive and take over.

I also knew that she didn't have her coins with her right now, so the possibility of her crossing through was greater, should she feel the need to do it.

But Aleena was with us, and we couldn't speak freely of it at present. Was it time to finally bring her into the fold? The longer we waited to include her, the more she would take offense to it. I wasn't exactly looking forward to her wrath.

Violet jerked her arm away, eyes lingering on mine for a moment before turning, and it stalled the air in my lungs. She studied the mirrors and different perspectives of Theresa, a coworker she used to favor, as she proceeded down the sidewalk. Her gray hair was long and the top half was pulled up and away from her face by a large clip. Dress shoes clicked against the pavement as she moved at her usual speed.

"Wait a second." Something was stirring inside of Violet that I couldn't quite place. Her emotions were going a bit haywire. "That's not Theresa."

My pulse quickened as I blinked at the back of her head, unsure of the conflicting emotions flowing between us, and her observation.

Theresa opened the door to the main entrance, offering a small window of opportunity to glance inside, but it was nothing we hadn't seen before. Tiled floors and a well-lit hallway was all we were granted a view of before she closed the door promptly.

"What do you mean, Violet?" Zan approached us as he swiped at the mirror to rewind what we had just watched. He tapped the surface to pause it on Theresa's face as she exited her car.

"She's not wearing her glasses." Violet looked up at him and in return, he cast a loaded glance at me.

"Perhaps she forgot them?" he responded, but she only shook her head.

"Unless she's had a major eye surgery or something, there's no way."

"Please, clarify for us, Violet." Zan gently ushered her to speak again.

She turned to face the rest of us, hands on her hips. "Theresa *has* to wear her glasses and her prescription lenses. She is, and I quote, 'as blind as a bat without them.' Her words, not mine, I swear. Something about how when she was born, she was way overdue and it really messed with her eyesight. She will not do contact lenses, she *hates* them. Glasses or it's a no-go."

Elias inserted himself into the conversation. "When was the last time we saw her with glasses?"

He, Zan, and I all shrugged at one another.

"I don't recall her having any type of procedure, but let me go back in the footage to see if I missed anything." Elias reached in the pocket of his jeans for his mirror, and I assumed he was reaching out to his dad.

"I highly doubt you did, Elias. But it doesn't hurt to double-check." Zan lifted a finger to his chin, thinking. Elias and I had begun chaperoned watching duties in our teen years, well over ten years ago now. Elias took watching just as seriously as I did.

The three of us should have been able to catch a detail like that, no matter how small. "Could Damian be shifting as her?" Violet spoke up, trying to make sense of it all.

I paused briefly, staving off the anger at the mention of the saint, then offered my opinion. "With his age, it seems like a rookie mistake. It doesn't make sense for him to risk going out as her. Especially if he knows Theresa as well as you do."

With Damian acting like a civilian and working with Violet and her coworkers for a few years, how could he not know?

"Which means it's probably another saint." Aleena found her voice again, stepping forward. Her hair was blazing red again and her face was set in a scowl. "For all we know, they have a whole network of them inside."

"With the army you three were met with on your last

encounter, I don't think that idea is that far-fetched. We've expected as much." Zan returned his attention to the mirror before directing his focus to me. "What say you, Kadriel? How would you like to move forward?"

Biggest goddamn test of my life.

I took a beat as a plan began to unfold in my head. I knew I couldn't exactly call the shots as of yet, but we needed a course of action before we went back to the council. No matter the path I chose to take, it had to be reasonable, solid, and without hesitancy.

"I want a watcher on each tenant, around the clock. Guards at the ready at a moment's notice. We need them on high alert and they can take shifts."

"Good, how many on each shift?" Zan pressed.

I met him with an answer straightaway. "Thirty, at least."

"That's a lot to ask for." His eyes widened. "The council won't like it."

"Well, if there's a chance the saint army has grown since we last met, I would rather not be blindsided again. Numbers on our side would be a bonus. Besides, is this not what we have them training for?"

"Good. Now, are you wanting to interrogate Noliathan? Others involved?"

As much as I would love nothing more than to kill Damian on sight, I knew he was getting information from a traitor on our side—but the question was who? Damian had slipped through my fingers once, but he wouldn't again. Someone had led him to Violet, informed him of my tethering courtship schedule, and provided him a way into our realm that he had chosen not to use yet. I only hoped we would beat him to the punch and he wouldn't have the opportunity for that before we made our move.

If the council didn't approve my course of action today, then they would be met with it as my first order of business as king when they had no other choice.

"We need answers, yes. But any other saint involved has signed off on their own deaths."

"A swift death is too easy on him." Aleena glared through clamped teeth. "I want him to suffer."

The feeling was mutual as I met her stare. "Limb by limb."

"Eye by eye," she joined in.

Zan and Elias united with our voices. "Scream by scream 'til death comes by."

Everything went quietly still, only to be broken up by my other half, a small, bright light that burned through the heaviness of our words.

"That is one freaky nursery rhyme." Violet looked at each one of us before settling back on the images of the apartment building in the mirrors over her shoulder. "What can I do?"

"I just feel like I should be doing more." Violet held my hands in hers and quieted her voice. "I *can* do more, I know it."

I cupped the side of her face, and she leaned into it without delay, deepening her gaze. I knew she meant well, and she wanted to put her banshee and fury sides to use to help if she could, but it wasn't worth the risk. We couldn't, *I* couldn't, put that responsibility on her. What we could do was use her knowledge and insight of her world and the people she'd once known. She had been of help within seconds of seeing Theresa, or who we thought was Theresa, possibly identifying another saint. She wanted to help, and maybe she could, but from afar.

Damian's army had severely wounded Aleena in our last encounter. I couldn't entertain the possibility of Violet so much as getting close enough for something like that to happen to her.

"For right now, just stay here, please. I need my head on straight for this meeting and then I will return first thing, I promise."

Violet pursed her lips, unhappy about my request. "I don't like house arrest."

My heart sank at the mere mention of that. "I'm sorry, I didn't think of it like that."

"I was actually enjoying my time with your sister. And Jacobi. We went to the school today." A small smile crossed her lips, lightening the ache in my chest. "It was more normal than I had expected. It was…its own kind of beautiful. Like a wizarding school but with demons.

"And they adore Aleena," she added, and I couldn't suppress my amusement at those words.

"They might now, but she was certainly a problem child growing up. Good grades, but they had their hands full with everything else."

"So I'm beginning to hear." She closed the gap between us, entwining her fingers with mine. "Were you a model student?"

"He liked to skip school. Cut class with Elias," Aleena butted in as if she'd been a part of the conversation this whole time.

I rolled my eyes as Violet took a step back from me. I hated the distance, no matter how little.

"I thought you had left." I let my head cock to the side in annoyance. Elias and Zan were still conversing in my watching quarters while I'd ushered Violet to the bedroom for a moment alone.

"You thought wrong, little brother."

I flinched unwillingly at that remark. I hated it when she called me that, and she was well aware of it. I tried not to give her any more satisfaction than the betrayal of my reaction to her words.

Aleena proceeded to cop a bit of attitude. "I guess I'll be on my way."

Ignoring that my sister was in such close proximity, I pulled Violet in close, crushing my lips onto hers.

"Oh gag, didn't you mark her enough this morning?" Aleena began to retreat and Violet blushed from embarrassment as she broke the kiss.

"Don't make her late again!" Aleena called out, but I wasn't going to honor her with the time for a response.

"Ah, but she didn't say that I couldn't make you come again," I whispered into Violet's ear, earning a playful smack to my chest. I wanted to grab her wrist, throw her onto the bed, and make good on that. Losing myself in her would be a much more pleasant afternoon delight than meeting with the dreaded council again. I had seen enough of them for one day. The news about Noliathan? It did more than create havoc on my mental state.

While I had tried to be feasible and accommodating to the joint Summit idea, this matter with Damian was one in which I was planning on being bullheaded.

"Damn right, you will. But not right now."

Her truthfulness had me grinning like a fool. I wouldn't be able to be back with her soon enough.

Violet had done well in front of the mirrors this morning during our intercourse, and just now with the images she had seen. Perhaps I could try, in short sessions, to allow her into my watching quarters. She wanted to help, and maybe I could begin to let her observe my duties. I hated keeping her from the room, but all I could see was Violet crossing into that cabin where she'd taken Brett's life. She knew I was nervous to let her back in, but I had to trust that now that she'd taken the life of her murderer, her fury side that sought vengeance might be sated.

For now.

With Aleena gone, Violet and I began down the hall again to join Zan and Elias, but she brought us to an abrupt halt. It was astonishing that she hadn't noticed it when we first came to the bedroom, her excitement hitting a high.

"The door!" she exclaimed as she flipped on the bathroom light to examine it. Just earlier she had been reminding me of it, her one request since coming to Darthou. Little did she know, that was how my time had been spent this morning after she'd left and before the council meeting.

"Kade, thank you." She swung it open and closed again, smoothing her hand over the dark wood. It fit like it had always been a part of my home, even though it was the newest addition.

"You're welcome. I was serious when I said I wanted this to feel like home to you. If there's anything else I can do, please just say so."

She beamed, appreciative of my efforts and follow-through. I hadn't been lying when I told her it would take some time to procure it.

Violet left to retrieve a pocketknife from one of the drawers in the closet and returned, looking up at me while blinking her dark lashes.

"I still plan on fucking you in the shower," I admitted lowly, my voice growing rough. "And often."

"And I will leave the door open a crack if you are

welcome," she teased right back. She drew the blade against the tip of her finger and ran it along the door before handing the blade to me. She hadn't even made a face with the action. My cock stirred at the thought of her trying to keep me out while she was naked and bare in the shower. Did she really think she was going to get that much alone time now?

Taking the blade from her, I did the same to myself and marked the door over the top of her swipe of blood. "In case you're forgetting, leaving it open might invite others."

She blanched, realizing the error she had made. She was becoming more and more demon every day, but it was a lot to take in, our world. There was still so much to learn.

"Come, let's get back." She shook her head as her shock faded away and we met up with the others who ceased their conversation as we drew nearer. I then addressed the room. "I think we need to revisit the topic of bringing Aleena in."

I didn't like the silence I was met with.

Violet stirred beside me. "If my vote matters, I'd like that. I've been spending so much time with her, it would be nice to have another woman I could speak to. Freely. And it would be more time I could spend without the coins which we know aren't doing Kade any favors."

When she looked up at me, a warmth spread through my chest, one that only she had ever provided. Regardless of our tethering, she made me feel so much. She'd softened me and yet somehow made me stronger at the same time.

"I think it's doing us more harm than good by keeping her out any longer," I added, urging them to speak.

"She's going to be pissed." Elias finally spoke up.

"She will, but once we explain it all surely she'll see why."

"Still going to be pissed," he reiterated, eyes wide.

My uncle began to pace, forefinger and thumb beneath his

chin. "Could we wait until after the coronation?"

"Why then?" I stepped toward him, pulling Violet along with me. She leaned into my side and I wrapped an arm around her, enjoying her closeness while I still had it before I had to leave again.

Collectively, we all waited for him to answer.

"We all know she's going to have a reaction. We can't do anything to jeopardize our united front with your coronation and impending reign."

I hated that he was right. Aleena wasn't going to be happy, but we'd kept her in the dark this long, so what was a few more days at this point?

Elias cleared his throat. "Maybe after the coronation and getting Aleena on board, you can call off the weekly meetings with Rafina? Violet can choose to keep training with Aleena if they both see fit, but then their choice can be entirely theirs. You can also get rid of those check-ins with the council too."

I nodded. That very action had crossed my mind more than once, but Zan had told me to keep that under wraps for now. Not to bring it up with the council just yet. I had to keep my cards hidden and not demand too much before coming to power. We didn't want to cause suspicion or gather any more unnecessary attention than we'd already received.

"Maybe I won't be so incompetent in my training with Aleena." Violet's mood plummeted. "If I don't have to wear the coins, that is."

"From what I hear, you're doing just fine. You're picking up on things a lot faster than born demons," Elias stated, and he only spoke of what was true. Violet was so hard on herself for not latching onto things any faster than she was. How she could fail to see the wonder and miracle that she was, was beyond me.

"Doesn't feel like it," she mumbled, and I gave her a slight squeeze.

"It's settled then—after the coronation, we bring her into the fold." Everyone nodded in agreement, and what should have been a small weight lifted from my shoulders. Aleena really was going to be pissed. It had been months since Violet arrived, and we had kept her out of the loop. My own flesh and blood. But I would place all of the blame on me if I had to. I was willing to.

"We should get going, Kadriel. The council is probably gathering as we speak." Zan made his way toward the door to exit.

I nodded reluctantly in agreement. "Let's get this over with." I placed a kiss on Violet's head, unsure of how to part while she was still in my watching quarters.

As if sensing my hang-up, Violet sighed. "I know, close the door behind me. I just wanted to reach out to Sarah real quick, if it's not too much trouble." She pleaded with her eyes. "Hopefully Elias can supervise real quick before he leaves too?"

"No problem." Elias strolled up to her side. "Let's see how fast you can establish the connection."

Violet might not have conquered passing through mirrors on a regular basis yet, but when it came to contacting someone, her odds were better. She had even successfully opened the portal to Xandor four times now, and that alone was impressive.

CHAPTER 9

Violet

I escaped out to the garden while I waited for Kade to return. The moment Elias had left and saw to it that the watching quarters were closed and off-limits to me, I'd moped around and eventually sought comfort out here. The aromas of the flowers welcomed me as I shut the door, sealing me out of my home.

Doors.

Careful what you wish for.

I'd wanted a door to the bathroom so badly that I hadn't even considered that if it remained opened, someone else could pop in. Kade had to seal my blood into the door with his to grant me access, so I could open and close it as I pleased. He'd done so now with the front, garden, and bathroom doors, but not the door to his watching quarters. I started to wonder if he could ever truly trust me.

Honestly, I didn't even know if I could be trusted. What happened with Brett had all transpired so fast, and while I'd wanted nothing more than to end him, I didn't know if I could have stopped if I'd wanted to.

I hated to think that Kade was right. I'd felt so hurt as his arm snapped out to stop me when I'd set my sights on the woman they thought was Theresa. It wasn't the first time he'd acted like that, but it gutted me every time. I didn't want this rift between us. I wanted him to have faith in me just as I had a blinding faith in him.

But perhaps I really couldn't be trusted alone with his wall of mirrors. The bathroom mirror was totally separate from other reflective surfaces meant for travel and communication. It was enchanted with something that didn't allow for those kinds of connections, which helped put my mind at ease when I was stark naked or getting fucked by Kade.

Sitting upon the iron bench that was parked amongst the mass of flowers, I gazed fondly at the yellow ones to my right—the very kind that Kade had brought me before our carnival date. My fingers delicately skimmed a few petals as I relaxed before sitting back and tilting my sight to the sky above. The clouds never changed, nor did they move with the wind. I couldn't make out any animal shapes either, to my disappointment. Just giant, gray, boring clouds.

While I didn't love the heat the sun had brought back home, I did miss the feel of a toasty day on my skin. How it warmed you after being inside an air-conditioned room all day or how it illuminated the skies at dusk in a beautiful show of color.

The first time Kade had taken me outside in Darthou was a memory that was hard to forget. The grass had crunched beneath my feet as if frozen by frost, the trees glazed over in an icy coating that glistened even though the sun's rays couldn't touch them. It was a foresty terrain all around as far as the eye could see and yet, here in the little garden Kade's parents had made, flowers blossomed in abundance, full of life as if in the height of spring.

Since I was a demon—well, partially demon—I wasn't affected by the temperatures as much as humans were around here. They wore longer sleeves and pants, whereas I could strut about in shorts and a tank top, never the wiser to how cold it was for them. Kade said the weather stayed the same, between forty and fifty degrees Fahrenheit, and it was never changing. It was the perfect weather for snuggling up with a hoodie or a blanket, something I used to love to do. Before my rebirth.

I lay back against the iron slats of the bench, getting as comfortable as I could while staring up at the sky. But my mind could never go blank or cease in its worries.

Damian. Noliathan. The one responsible for the death of Kade and Aleena's parents. Zan's brother. The last king and queen to rule over Darthou. And for whatever reason, this saint had meddled and made his way into my life. I hated the uncertainty that came along with his actions. We still had no idea what he truly wanted. Even though he'd admitted to me at one point that it was me he was after, I highly doubted he felt the same way now that I was a demon. What the hell would he want with me now anyway?

I was now residing in Darthou and tethered to Kade, and we were both supposed to be stronger because of it. Kade couldn't rise to his status as king before tethering because of that fact, so how could Damian have anything to gain now? What was his angle?

My eyes flitted until they closed as I recalled the gut-wrenching agony that had overtaken me in the great hall during lunch. I'd thought I was going to lose my food as it came on. It was an anger and despair so great, I'd thought I might come apart. My connection with Kade was a strong one, but I hadn't felt feelings like that in… Well, since the truckload of warring emotions I'd felt the day I killed Brett. There had been so much unraveling so fast—it was too much.

After trying to get my words out to tell Aleena that something had to be wrong with Kade, she'd whisked me away, leaving a rather concerned and confused Jacobi behind with plates of uneaten food. Seeing him—no, *feeling* Kade so distraught and enraged at the same time was nothing short of heartbreaking.

I couldn't imagine what Kade, Aleena, and their uncle were going through with the knowledge that the saint responsible for ending Tarnon and Audra all those years ago had inserted himself into our lives. And that saint was growing an army that was apparently a big cause for concern, as that was abnormal amongst their kind.

If I were to come face-to-face with the man responsible for taking my family away, I didn't know how I would cope with it. Luckily, his life had also been claimed in that terrible accident, so I would never have to know. But it was saddening, angering, and frustrating beyond belief that Damian had been right under their noses without them knowing.

He had been hiding in plain sight. Plotting and planning something that remained to be seen.

I wasn't sure how much time had passed, as my mind continued jumping through time hoops. Reflecting on my life in my human form, and the hybrid that I was now. I began to think about tonight and our return to Xandor. Its inhabitants were always so guarded and aloof, and they honestly had every right to be. We could bring supplies for months or years even, but I didn't know how to win them over. I had to find a way to get them talking.

Sure, the coins had proved useful thanks to the witch, but I didn't think of them as a long-term solution. I couldn't just suppress my fury and banshee sides indefinitely. That felt like I was begging for trouble.

My breathing slowed as I hugged myself, relaxing into the bench as well as I could with its hard slats. I tried to focus on Kade and our connection. I knew he was still with the council as I honed in, imagining him in the center chair that he belonged in. Sitting upright, proper in posture and engaged in a heated conversation that began to stir worry within me. My eyes darted back and forth beneath their lids as I tried to recall the line of faces to his left and right, but I could only remember where Zan and Staffan had been seated. The others were blank faces, men in black that I couldn't place.

This council wanted to know everything about me and all that transpired during my trainings and meetings with Aleena and Rafina. I really should get a proper introduction to the lot of them. My first encounter in their chambers had definitely been less than ideal. I'd met a few at our tethering celebration, but there hadn't been enough time to try and commit their faces to memory.

"Trying to spy on me?"

My eyes shot open to see Kade crossing the short distance to meet me. I swung my legs down to sit up, rubbing my eyes.

"Not exactly."

Sitting beside me, he raised an arm to rest it around my shoulders. As much as I wanted to nuzzle into him, I was eager for information. "How did it go?"

Kade hesitated as he picked something off of his dress

slacks. "Could have been better."

"Why? What happened?" I pressed when his answer was too vague. He was back to the cool, calm, and collected facade. There was a hurt brimming at the surface, but he squandered it away swiftly.

"They're split right now. And since I don't get to vote until this weekend, I can do nothing against it."

"What? How?" I stiffened, repulsed by this news. "So what? They're going to wait?"

"They want to see the evidence that Clefus has to corroborate his theory. They still think there's a chance that it could be another saint and that he's jumping to conclusions."

"You're joking." I stood and moved away, careful about my foot placement so I didn't trample any flowers.

"In the meantime, we've been allowed to task three watchers to keep tabs on every person—be it saint, human, or whatever they are—in that apartment building. I've granted Zan access to my files so he can give them what I have so far on its tenants. But as far as the guards go, they didn't see the need to go that far and cause such a stir."

I gaped at him, annoyed at how ridiculous this council sounded. Kade rose from his seat to meet me on the little path.

"There's nothing more that can be done right now. They've made their decision and I'm not going to waste time trying to sway their opinions when some are so pressed to see me fail."

"Like Staffan," I practically spit. Any time I saw that man, I wanted to punch his nose so hard it caved into his face. And I would rather listen to nails on a chalkboard than hear his arrogant voice again.

"I just have to get through this Summit, and then we get through this coronation together. Once those are behind us, things are going to change. Right now? I think I'm more of an annoyance. But once I'm king? They'll either have to get on board or I will surround myself with those who will."

The way he spoke sent an unsolicited shiver through me. His determination and the fire in his expression alerted me of how after the coronation, things were most likely going to get messy. And perhaps worse? Maybe even ugly before it got better.

All I could manage was a nod before stepping into his space and wrapping my arms around his waist. We held each other for a few moments, minutes possibly.

As much as I was dreading the coronation and what came after, I feared what his new title might have in store for us. We were already treated differently, which didn't help matters when I wanted to fade into the background and go unnoticed. But what did it mean for our day-to-day routines? How would it affect what little time together we seemed to have now? With my training sessions with Aleena and Elias, traveling to Xandor, failing research with Sarah, weekly checkups with Rafina, and the saint problem? Even now, we were lucky enough to have a night together without interruptions.

"Do you have any plans this afternoon?" Kade's chest vibrated with his words.

I stirred, wiggling my way out of his hold so I could look up at him.

"Do *I* have plans?" I offered a light laugh. The goal had been to spend the day with Aleena, but after the day's events I had been confined to our home so Kade could concentrate on his council meeting without the ringing from my coins.

Kade separated from me and took a few steps back toward the bench. He bent down and examined one of the yellow flowers, skimming its petals before gliding down the stem to a notch that was just about an inch from the ground. With both hands, he snapped at the lump quickly, separating the flower from it and returning to me, holding it out.

"Thank you?" I eyed him curiously as I accepted it. With a magnificent garden such as this out here, I didn't see the need for him to do that.

"Come, I think it's time I finally show you something." While it didn't read in his expression, there was a nervousness lurking beneath. Taking his hand, I let him lead me back inside and straight down the hall to his watching quarters. "Forgive me, as I'm not ready to grant you full access yet, but…baby steps."

Kade guided me to the mirrors that we had just screwed in front of this morning. The very same ones that his family and best friend had just gathered in front of a while ago.

I warmed at the imagery that sprang to mind, but cleared my throat to try and shake it away.

A small chuckle erupted from his throat, and I knew that my naughty thoughts had been caught, but he left it unsaid. He began swiping at mirrors, bringing up image after image. Homes, supermarkets, parks, even a hotel. There were so many people and places popping up that I lost count. The cacophony of it all loudened with each video-type surveillance he pulled. I couldn't focus on just one for too long before jumping to the next, fascinated by the world laid out before me.

My old world. The one I was first born into.

"Is this…" I couldn't even finish because I knew. I'd wanted to see this for so long, and he was finally letting me in. Even if it was as he said, baby steps.

"Everyone I watch, yes." He came to a stop at the end, leaving a few mirrors blank that only cast back his own reflection.

"This is…amazing, Kade." Some images were distorted slightly. Others were as clear as if I were standing before them. A woman working a register at a grocery store. Another driving in a car—judging by the view of her I was granted, it must be from the rearview mirror.

"And overwhelming," I added.

I made my way down the line, careful to keep my hands to myself, crossing my arms. I knew he was on guard, waiting to see what could happen. But when I finally met up with him at his end, I couldn't help but stare at him in wonder.

Kade might have watched me for six years, but he definitely had a whole hell of a lot going on here. He'd admitted that there were over twenty who were under his "care," but there had to be more now.

My smile faltered as something churned in the pit of my stomach. It registered with Kade almost instantly, and I studied him as I tried to make sense of it.

"I *feel*…something."

Kade passed me and began swiping at mirrors to close the connections, but I pried at his arm to get him to stop.

"Wait," I commanded with a steady voice. And that was when I saw it in his eyes.

Fear.

I sensed it in him. His concern that I was going to revert back to how I'd been that day when I killed Brett.

But this was different. That day I'd been blinded by my rage and quest for vengeance. This was something else. Maybe even familiar.

I turned, eyeing each mirror as I followed my gut in search of something. The further I moved, the stronger it stirred. Kade remained almost attached behind me, no doubt ready to pull me back if things went south, but I had no intention of letting that happen. If I could help it.

A hushed scream formed in my mind and I came to a halt, causing Kade to bump into me. I searched the images frantically, trying to locate where it was coming from, and when the voice rose, I locked in on the man in the image. He was young, perhaps a few years behind me even. No facial hair, and there was a youthful glow to him that was diminished by his deep-set eyes. He was scraggly, in clothes that didn't fit and surrounded by a clutter of a mess. Papers, trash, and dirty clothes were littered about the table next to him. His greasy hair shone under the luminescents.

"I hear it." I spoke aloud so Kade would know that I was still very much aware and present. I reminded myself that I was in control. That I could and *would* control this side of me. "A scream. It's faint but it's there."

"Him?" Kade pointed to the man I was fixated on, and I nodded. I clutched my arms tighter in my hold, careful not to make any sudden movements that might make Kade abandon this venture.

"Who is he?" I asked, unmoving as I stared at him, hatred swirling around in my stomach with brute force.

This was the first time I'd heard a scream with anyone else besides Rafina and Staffan. Perhaps it was quieter because I wasn't standing before him in close proximity? I honestly had no idea, but I was grateful for it.

"His name is Stanley."

My mood took a turn now that I could put a name to the face. Something didn't sit right with him. It was in his eyes; something was off.

Another scream erupted and my head snapped to the left. I begin searching once more to find who it belonged to, but not before Kade began swiping at mirrors behind me. His nerves were at an all-time high as he closed connections.

"Stop it," I ordered, but he wasn't listening. I pointed to the mirror when I located a woman in what appeared to be a restaurant kitchen, hard at work. Kade snatched my outstretched hand, yanking it away.

I was fuming at this point. "Who is she?"

"I think you've seen enough." His words had a bite to them, but I ignored it and repeated myself.

"*Who* is she?" I seethed, knowing that something was wrong with her in the same manner as Stanley.

"Maria." Kade swiped the image away, removing her from view, and I couldn't help but give him a shove in my agitated frustration.

"Why did you do that?" My voice rose as the scream emitting from her ceased. The one from Stanley was now gone as well as I looked down the line of vanished surveillance feeds. But another was quick to come alive.

My eyes darted to find it, but before I could zero in, Kade removed the rest of them from view.

"Kade!" I screamed, then started to demand, "Bring them back!"

"No," Kade stated, as if his word was final.

"No?" I repeated, appalled that he would deny me. My breaths became short and the pounding of my chest made its way to my ears. "Why show me and then rip it away?"

"Because I can feel you slipping!"

I took a step back as his panic rose before he replaced it with the tranquil calm he was willing me to feel. My chest ached like I'd been climbing a cliff, and I turned my back on him to put some space between us. Energy pulsed through me as adrenaline rushed through my veins.

I had no idea who these people were, but I certainly

despised Stanley and Maria. Considering I had never met them, the rapid reaction to each of them was shocking.

But a part of me knew why I hated them, even if I was afraid to admit it.

"Who are those two?" I shook my hands out to release the built-up tension, but it did nothing. Knotting them together didn't help either, so I just began fidgeting uncomfortably. "There was another, but you stopped me."

I was perturbed that he'd done so. I wanted to put another face to the scream. That was just the thing, though—the screams didn't belong to those I saw on the mirrors. Each one was different. A different rasp. A different pitch. A different tone. All three were distinguishable in their own ways.

"Violet." Kade placed a hand on my shoulder but I violently shrugged it off.

"Who are they?" I spoke again through gritted teeth, my temper unrelenting. I shoved his chest with my palms, frustration boiling over. It barely knocked him off-balance, but he regained his composure just as fast. I pushed again, hating how weak I must be in his eyes, but he caught my wrists. "Who?!"

His lips smashed onto mine as he forced me down onto the couch. I struggled against him, turning my head to break away from the harsh kiss.

"Calm down, Violet," he urged as he stared into my eyes. There was a moment of nothingness, and at the slightest loosening of his grip, I escaped his hold and scrambled to stand.

Calm down?

My eyes slanted as I repeated those two words over and over. Each time, the voice in my head grew louder and louder. "Don't tell me to calm down. There is something seriously wrong with those people, Kade!"

I wanted answers. He was holding back information. He *knew* something about those individuals. Why show me a glimpse into his life, the very job he'd been tasked with, only to turn me away the moment I...

The moment I wanted to kill.

That realization hit hard as I recognized it for what it was and the person I'd become. But I couldn't decide where to start. Each scream was practically begging me to help, to avenge the lives taken from them. Voices of the helpless and lost souls that had been snuffed out in tragic ends.

Never since that first scream had erupted in Rafina's presence had they been so…identifiable. It was like they were calling to me. Perhaps seeking my attention in the only way they could communicate.

Through their deaths.

I turned away from Kade, barely holding myself together both mentally and physically. I'd gone from one extreme to another, from thirsting to end lives by my own hands one second to mourning for those killed the next.

My eyes didn't even have a chance to burn before tears started to fall down my cheeks. Every time I thought I had a small grasp on this new me, it exploded, leaving me stranded out on some desolate island with no help in sight.

"Are you cold?" Kade gently spoke up from behind me, so close I could almost feel his body heat. A shiver wracked through me and I snapped my mouth shut in an attempt to quell the sudden chill that buried itself bone-deep.

I couldn't be cold. I shouldn't *feel* like this. Like I'd stepped outside to a blustery winter back home without a coat on.

Kade was careful to round me, his slow movements showing his hesitancy. But that didn't stop him from brushing his thumbs across my wet face, the black substance of my tears evident on his long fingers. He was strangely warm against my skin.

Kade popped out of view momentarily and returned with a sweater of mine. He gently tugged at my arms until I caved and accepted the sweater, slipping it on. The woven fabric was comforting as I crossed my arms again and muttered a faint thanks.

Turning, I approached the mirrors once more, ignoring the worry that bubbled up in my other half. He was never more than an arm's reach away, and I didn't know if there would ever be a time when he wasn't so on edge with me around mirrors. It didn't seem promising at the present moment.

"Who are they, Kade?" This time, I was exactly what he wanted me to be. Calm. Collected. Nonthreatening.

I had been slipping indeed, into the madness that consumed first, leaving the destruction and aftermath to deal with later.

Kade joined me at the wall, folding his arms around me in a snug hold as he rested his chin on my shoulder. All expressions were wiped clean from his face.

"You said you would never lie to me, please don't start now," I said, urging him to say something. I needed more than the names he had given. I *needed* facts. To have someone else confirm what I already believed to be true. "This was the first time I've heard screams since Rafina and Staffan all those weeks ago. I have to know."

Keeping me encased, he let out a slow and controlled breath. "I'm guessing that your fury and banshee sides might be at work."

"Isn't that obvious?" I pressed, unamused. My coins weren't a part of the equation, so I was more susceptible to those sides of me now. I wanted him to quit beating around the bush and just answer me already.

"They both have taken lives recently."

"They've killed," I stated plainly. They were murderers. Killers. Still walking, talking, breathing air when they had stripped their victims of those very functions.

"They have. And they more than likely will again."

CHAPTER 10

Violet

"Can we talk this through? Just the two of us? Please," I begged Kade, after he'd initially wanted to bring Zan and Elias in to discuss this new revelation. While I understood wanting to keep them informed, I hated that everything had to be discussed out in the open with them at all times. I was constantly sharing Kade, though at this point I should expect nothing less. He was soon going to be king of Darthou for crying out loud. Maybe it was possessive of me to want more of him to myself, but at the same time, I didn't care.

"If that's what you want."

"It is," I clarified immediately so there wouldn't be a single doubt. "I just don't understand," I blurted as I knelt on the couch beside him. "You've killed people. I've seen it. Witnessed it, even through your eyes, and I didn't have this kind of reaction. So why is this happening with complete strangers?"

Xandor was where I had first discovered "the sight" as the furies called it. Kade ascertained that it was because of my connection and proximity to them that it had been so strong at that time. The furies usually remained together as a united front.

But I hadn't seen anything when I laid eyes upon Stanley and Maria, just experienced an unsettling bodily response, paired with those screams that had my stomach churning, heart racing, and the will to make them pay.

"I have a theory that might fit."

Bringing my gaze back to Kade, I gestured for him to take the floor with this one. "I'm all ears."

"Like I said, Stanley and Maria have killed recently. Maybe your reaction is stronger because of that. Furies seek vengeance, and swiftly. To my understanding, that's why they were exiled."

I nodded in understanding. The furies had been banished because they didn't wait and ask questions. They carried out their justice fast. And according to what demons had been led to believe, there was no swaying their minds otherwise when they made up their minds to kill.

"I think that the key here for you is innocents. Someway...*somehow*, you're able to discern who is deserving of punishment by death and who isn't. Without using the sight even."

It was a struggle to swallow as I reflected on his words, but it made perfect sense. Witnessing through Kade the lives he had taken hadn't given me the visceral reaction I'd just had. It had been shocking, sure. But it was entirely different to how I felt when I set my sights on Maria and Stanley. Those screams had alerted me. It was all I could listen to. All I could seem to focus on.

Kade picked up my hands, loosening the knotting of my fingers. "I should probably apologize for going overboard. I shouldn't have brought up all of my charges at once. I should have been more cautious."

Shaking my head, I lifted my chin to meet the gaze of the man who had enraptured me since the first time we met. "Don't be. It means a lot to me that you let me in like that. Even if I kind of went off the rails."

But there was still a large part of me that was hung up on the power couple of Darthou. "What does this mean for Rafina and Staffan then? That they killed someone? Multiple someones, before my rebirth?"

Kade sighed through his nose, and my gut twisted at the thoughts that must be pummeling through his head. But there was one idea I could never fully let go of. "Are we absolutely sure that they didn't cause the deaths of all of those in Xandor? The timing is—"

"I know," Kade cut in. "But their whereabouts for the day are for the most part accounted for. All except the time Rafina must have spent with you before bringing you to the infirmary. With the amount of lives taken in Xandor, there's no way she could have done all of that, cleaned herself up, and retrieved you."

The witch had said it was a woman who had caused the destruction, but one who was younger in years. According to Kade, Rafina didn't meet that qualification. I still wasn't used to the age thing around here.

"If they didn't do it, then who did they kill? Those screams were the worst, Kade. The ones today were minimal in comparison. Whatever they did, it's not good."

The severity and reality of my words threatened to put me in a chokehold. Rafina and Staffan were two highly prominent demons who just so happened to be tethered together. The fact that Staffan was losing what power he'd held over the council for the past several years had been brought up on multiple occasions. Was this all just an elaborate play to get his hands on the throne?

And what of Rafina—the almighty healer that Kade had held in such high regard before I came here? Was she involved without a choice in the matter or was she a willing accomplice in all of this?

"I'm sorry I blew it." Pulling my hands away, I buried my face in them. This time, the tears threatening to spill were from a place of sorrow. I had failed him and wasted this one, small act of inviting me into his watching space. I'd only further nailed the door shut on the opportunity to gain Kade's trust.

"You didn't blow it." He drew my hands away as my eyes welled up. "Please don't cry. We learn and we adapt. One mirror at a time from now on, not dozens."

"But you work in here. You spend a lot of time in this room. And I don't mean to sound needy, but I want more time with you. Even if it's just in silence while you watch. I'll find a hobby or something."

A stray tear fell and Kade brushed it away with his thumb before it could mark my cheek. "Then we will figure out a way to make this work…together. We'll go slow."

Standing up, he held out his hand to me and I accepted it without delay. I followed him to the mirrored wall. Without breaking eye contact, he swiped his hand over a mirror and produced an image of a young boy who couldn't be older than ten, sitting on a bed. It was a narrow and horizontal view, but I could still see him in his entirety.

One of his legs was propped up on a pillow in a cast, and upon further inspection, there were little scribbles and names on it. My eyes traveled over him, finding a healing bruise on one of his arms and a rather large one on his jawline. He was thoroughly engrossed in a comic book, and for some reason that felt so much more adventurous of him than zoning out watching television.

"Do you feel anything?" Kade asked.

Alarmed at the idea that I should, I spoke up. "Please don't tell me he's a killer or going to be. He's just a kid."

"Hate to tell you, but there are some that have signs way younger than him."

My eyes widened at the mere thought. I didn't want to believe in a future like that for this boy. He seemed normal to me.

"Do you feel anything like you did before? With Stanley and Maria?"

I studied the boy for a few more seconds, making sure a scream didn't erupt from god knows where. But no ailments came to plague my body.

When all remained silent and undisturbed, I finally answered, "No."

"Good." Kade placed his hand on the small of my back. "You shouldn't."

I cast a curious look his way, unsure of his meaning, but then a light bulb went off.

"Is he like me? I mean, has he cheated death?"

Kade tipped his head in acknowledgment. "Climbed up a tree and hit the concrete when he came down. He was in a medically induced coma for days after flatlining. He's one of my latest charges."

The boy flipped the page, moving on in whatever world he

was submersed in. His straight dark hair swooped to the side of his forehead, and I could barely detect the moment of his eyes as he followed the words on the pages before him.

Not long ago, Kade had been watching me in this same manner. Just a woman in a mirror before him, but one he was pining after.

"I think your gift could prove useful. We just have to figure out how you can control it to your advantage. If you want, that is." He backpedaled a little on that last bit.

My head bobbed in a newfound excitement. "Yes, yes I do. Baby steps, though."

"Baby steps," he confirmed.

"Can I try closing the connection?" I was reaching the point where I felt odd to be peeking in on this boy, watching him when he was in an environment that should hopefully not lead him to any harm.

Kade's breath caught at my question, but he recovered. I couldn't help but wonder if he had panicked this much before our tethering.

"Sure."

Slow to act, I raised my hand. I thought of a blank, reflective surface, empty of any images except that of our own. But in the split second it took to close it, my thoughts darted off to a memory of my grandma and before I knew it, I swiped.

Before me now was the woman who raised me, in her rocking chair where she currently sat with embroidery materials on her lap, an image left unfinished. She had a far-off look as she rested her chin upon her hand. Her lips were pulled down at the corners in a sadness that took hold of my heart like a wrench tightening.

"Step back, Violet." Kade's voice was soft but stern, as if he knew how hard it was for me to see her. I hadn't since the day before I had died. His hand pressed into my stomach, guiding me to do as instructed, and while I wanted to resist, I did as he asked. My heart ached for her. I wanted to talk to her and tell her that I was alright and not dead, even if she didn't need to know the particulars and how loaded of a statement that would be.

"H-how is she?" My words were quiet, shaky even with the image before me. But I already knew the answer.

Heartbroken. Sad. Absolutely beside herself that the entire family of one of her daughters had been wiped from existence.

"Managing as best as she can."

I'd wanted to ask Kade to see her multiple times, but I'd always skirted around it. Was she safe? Was Aunt Cindy helping out? Was Damian bothering her?

Kade began rubbing small circles on my back, much like I'd done for him earlier after the news about Damian. Noliathan. Whoever the hell he was. Two-faced fucker.

"Just remember, she's not alone. Your Uncle Steven has even been visiting more frequently."

Funny how he could finally make time to get away from his farm to come see her. Just took me dying for it to happen. But Steven was her only son, so I was sure she appreciated his visits nonetheless.

"Margaret is still holding out hope that you're alive. She's even paying for your apartment in case you come back."

"What?" I was flabbergasted at that news. "How can she afford that?"

I wasn't going to pretend that I knew all of my grandma's finances, but she was on a fixed income now that she was retired. There couldn't be much left after all of the month's necessities were paid for.

"Cindy and David are pitching in for now, but it's for a

limited time. They keep trying to persuade her otherwise, but she won't listen."

They had three kids of their own and all those costs to worry about, so that didn't make me feel any better.

Before I could protest, Kade swiped and my grandma vanished. Now I was met with a view of my apartment. The last place I'd called home before Darthou. The curtains and blinds were open, letting daylight pour in. Everything was in its place and just as I remembered leaving it.

Except for my mirror.

Memories flooded back of my frantic packing, my worry for Kade as he went off to find Damian, the knocks on the door that had almost made me jump out of my skin.

Instinctively, I reached out and touched the glass. The next thing I knew, I was standing at the foot of my bed. Kade arrived at my side in a flash.

The bed was made, almost too neatly. Tucked in just like my grandma would do after wash day. Pillows propped up and blankets smoothed out to the point that I was afraid to touch it. It was how she made her bed every day. A mark that she had been here.

To my left, I witnessed the remnants of my mirror. The one that had been passed down to my mother and then to me. The frame had been propped up against the wall, broken off of its hinges, and one of its legs had been snapped off entirely. There was no glass in sight as I skirted around the bed. When I had been shot and fell, I'd taken it down with me. There had to have been glass everywhere, but was any of this even salvageable at this point?

"The glass had to be destroyed after Damian retrieved a piece. That's the only thing we've touched, everything else was cleaned up by your grandma and aunt."

I thought I nodded in understanding, but I was having trouble controlling my body. Being here after what happened, after what had transpired, was messing with my head, sending me through a roller coaster of emotions and countless what-ifs about the day that had forever changed the trajectory of the rest of my life.

Turning to take in the rest of the apartment, I examined it all in its pristine condition. I never would have defined myself as a slob by any means, but it had certainly never been this clean and tidy. Even the vase that had held the flowers from Kade was now gone; no doubt they had died shortly after my departure.

Emotion clogged my throat, and I tried to focus. I wasn't sure if I'd ever get this chance again, and I had to remind myself to get my head on straight and think clearly.

"Would it be alright if I took a few things? There are some...items I would rather them not find. That is, if they haven't already."

Kade was wary of my ask, but instead of denying it, he approved after mulling it over. "As long as it does nothing to alert them someone has been here."

I made quick work, grabbing a grocery bag from beneath the kitchen sink, careful to leave things close to how they were before. Lucky for me, clothes had been taken care of thanks to Rebecca, but there was one sweater that I nabbed from my dresser as a comfort item.

Kade busied himself, browsing around the apartment, allowing me some time to gather the things I wanted and not hovering. There wasn't far to go in here, but I was appreciative of him for giving me this. Letting me have more time when I had been robbed of it due to my own neglect in listening to him. But what would have happened to my neighbor had I not answered the door? Would Brett have killed her instead?

I blinked out of my spiraling thoughts, trying to remember what else I had come here for.

My eyes bulged as I dived into my nightstand, removing sex toys and lube that honestly, I didn't need anymore. But I wanted to be the one to get them out of here. Nobody else needed to discover or dispose of these kinds of things.

Wadding the items up in my sweater, I shoved them in the bag and gave the place another once-over.

Kade, as if sensing I was trying to wrap things up, stopped his slow perusal and approached with his hands stuffed in his pockets.

"It wasn't supposed to be like this," I whispered, my throat beginning to constrict again. Today had already been trying in more ways than one, for the both of us.

And the day still wasn't over.

Silence grew between us, but Kade did nothing to rush me out of here. I closed my eyes and listened to the traffic outside. The hum of the fridge running. The air kicking on and blowing through the vents. The urge to shut the curtains was strong, but I know I shouldn't touch them. I knew I couldn't give anyone reason to suspect that someone had been in here. Someone who was missing and presumed dead.

Probably by everyone but my grandma.

"I'm ready to go home now."

CHAPTER 11

Violet

Xandor hadn't changed at all since our last visit. The gloomy skies and sparse and dying land made Darthou look normal in comparison. Every time I stepped foot in this desolate land I was met with the urge to bring these people back with me. These creatures might have been banished ages ago, but they were still *people*. People with lives and feelings, living in this world that was only surviving by the witch siphoning off the magic within so she could support those who remained. Those who hadn't been slaughtered in the massacre.

Elias had chosen to join us tonight, and all three of us had our hands full with food, clothes, and I even tossed in some books that I'd collected since last time.

Kade had apparently worked something out with Rebecca,

taking old garments and creations off her hands. I'd been with him the first time he'd inquired about helping those in need, and while I could see the skepticism in her facial expression, she hadn't questioned him about it. She'd only asked about the climate for their clothing needs and possible sizes. She even included little sewing packs in case there were things that needed altered.

As for the food, Sarah had been making dishes and baked goods for us to take. With the privacy of her kitchen, and Elias's quick trips to the human world for supplies, she was busting things out of there like she was a one-woman factory. I helped her as much as I could, taking her direction without hesitation. Her kindness in the matter only made me appreciate the woman that she was all the more.

And her two boys were quite the kicker. Rotten little guys who loved butting into the kitchen to try and swipe whatever sweets were being made.

It was still strange to me how Darthou was run. I'd come from a world where money was key to practically everything, but here it was favors, asks, and trades. Nobody was greedy when it came to food, and besides my first initial shopping trip to stock up on clothes, my wants were pretty minimal. There was no cost for education. No rent or bills to be paid. It was all so…simple.

Dressed in our protections—still adorned with weapons even though I argued that they weren't needed—our feet crunched with each step across the dry plain. We never had to venture far; they always found us within minutes of our arrival.

Kade and Elias were always quick to remind me that these creatures had been banished for a reason, even if it had been decades ago and before our time. Also, that the inhabitants here had just been betrayed by a demon who had claimed the lives of many, so we needed to always be at the ready should things take a turn. Prepared for the worst but hoping for the best.

My steps faltered under the weight I was carrying when I found the witch in the tree line. Only this time, she was not alone. Heart rate kicking up a notch, I readjusted my grasp on the bags and moved on, not giving much attention to the side glance from the men at my sides at my fumble.

It was a bit of an understatement to say that I was excited to see the furies again. The last few visits, they'd been nowhere to be found, and when I'd asked about their whereabouts I was met with silence from the witch. I couldn't place an ounce of blame on them for being protective, especially with everything they'd been through. But after today's events, I was more determined than ever to try and get through to them.

"Hi," I chimed rather excitedly, instantly regretting how chipper my voice sounded. I set my supplies on the ground as the two furies and witch examined us and the items we'd brought. They were cautious, still, and quiet as they looked us over. But I wasn't going to let this opportunity pass me by. "I was really hoping I could talk to you two today, if that's alright. Something happened today and…I was really wanting to see if you could make sense of it."

Thing 1 and Thing 2 wore sweaters and slacks from our last visit, items that hid their skeleton-like figures beneath. Perhaps the food we'd been bringing still wasn't enough. We had no idea just how many creatures were left in Xandor and if our efforts so far were even reaching all who lived here. But it did provide a small comfort knowing that some were at least getting use out of our help. Perhaps the hairbrushes I'd brought too, deducing by their tamed hair.

Still, it didn't seem like enough in the grand scheme of

things.

The furies exchanged looks, but their slim faces remained unchanged. In unison, they nodded their heads once and turned to leave. I chose to take that as my sign to follow.

Kade's hand latched onto my wrist lightning fast, his apprehension doing nothing for the nerves that were already taking root.

"Kade, I have to do this. Maybe they'll be more comfortable if it's just me," I pleaded with every fiber of my being, peeling his fingers from their hold one by one. Without another word between us, I left him, Elias, and the witch behind to follow the only two who might have answers.

About me. About furies. About *us*.

I kept a small distance between them and myself as I followed. We veered off into the dying and empty trees on a winding path worn down by being traveled. It was almost unnatural how the two in front of me remained practically soundless as they moved, making me all the more aware of how loud my movements were. Each step, each rub of my thighs together, the sway of my arms, and the air leaving my nose all made too much noise compared to them.

There was very little known about furies, and upon perusing the libraries of Darthou, Sarah and I had found even less than what the demons had heard by word of mouth over the years. We didn't know fact from fiction at this point.

Zan was starting to think that any materials, books, or scripts that contained data on those banished must have been moved and kept under lock and key, much like the instructions that Kade's father had uncovered on how to cross over to Xandor. Everything had been zapped from existence as if someone, or multiple someones, didn't want it found.

They had unfortunately done a good job hiding it all.

We came to a small clearing, a circular formation of rocks that looked to be here for a reason. Boulders was probably more like it—large round surfaces with a smoother spot on top for someone's rear end to go.

I followed their lead and sat on the nearest one. It was the perfect height for me to take a seat, and my fingers twisted together in my lap, waiting.

I didn't want to come on too strong, but I wanted nothing more than to pick their brains about today and the past. Both theirs and mine. Their recently deceased sister too, if they'd let me. There was so much to ask and I didn't want to unload on them with a slew of questions at once, like I did with Kade.

"We heard you've been inquiring about us," one began.

"What do you wish to know?" the other picked up.

Blowing out a slow breath, I suppressed the need to spill it all out at once. I needed to tread lightly. They could hate my guts, for all I knew. After all, I'd been born on the death of their sister, as I'd been told upon our first visit.

"While I appreciate what the witch has done for me with the coins, the side effects are affecting Kade, and I would like to get to the point that I don't need them anymore. But I don't know enough about furies and banshees to even begin."

Thing 1's expression turned almost sorrowful. "The last banshee here died."

"She kept to herself," Thing 2 said in almost a sneer.

For once, they didn't act like they were on the same page, and it had me raising my arms up in defense for some reason. "I know. I don't expect you to know everything. I just want your help, in whatever might be fury-related. You have no reason to believe or trust me, and I sincerely hope that in time, you might. I can't stress enough that I didn't ask for this. All that matters is that I don't hurt the people that I've come to love, and this chance at a new life that I have."

The two exchanged an identical glance, as if speaking with one mind, their freaky connection weighing in on just how out of place I felt.

"What has happened?"

"What transpired?" the other added, barely a beat behind.

I didn't wait, starting from the beginning with my rage and Brett's death, leading up until today when Kade had shown me numerous images of the humans he watched. How different today had been, and the gut reaction I'd felt at the sight of certain individuals compared to my feelings when I'd killed my ex-boyfriend. It was a whole other side of me that only made me ask more questions.

When I finally drew to a close, the two joined their hands that were closest to one another.

"It's blinding, the rage." Thing 2 on the right spoke first this time, as if recalling something.

"Especially when met with the one who murdered you," the other responded, and they shared another look, one that spoke louder than words ever could. Because they knew. They knew *exactly* what I was talking about.

"But I didn't feel that today," I reiterated, so there was no confusion there.

"Because you don't have a personal connection with them."

"Because you do not *know* them."

My breath caught at how our thought processes were aligning.

"He was a boyfriend, correct? The one you killed."

"A lover?"

My eyes were darting between the two of them to keep up.

I wanted to scowl at the use of that term. I wouldn't have

considered Brett to be a lover, but instead of correcting them, I skirted around that minor detail. "We had been together for some time, yes."

"You might not feel that level of revenge again unless there is an emotional connection."

"He wronged you, he *murdered* you." The voice from the left one turned almost threatening.

"I wish I could have seen it." The other turned to face her sister, as if in glee. "His murder."

"How did it make you feel?" they questioned in unison, turning their attention back to me. Both sets of eyes met mine and I froze as I was put on the spot.

"I…" As much as I had tried to repress the memory of murdering Brett, I couldn't deny that it was now ingrained in me. Each touch, each feeling and emotion were now a core piece of me that could never be forgotten. And as much as I had been taught growing up that violence wasn't the answer, that murder was breaking one of the Ten Commandments in my grandma's church, I couldn't deny these furies the truth. Especially when I desired their trust and honesty more than anything right now. I couldn't lie to myself about it any more than I already had, even if it scared me.

"I felt…"

"Yes," one hissed in intrigue.

"Go on," the other pushed as they leaned forward.

"Taking his life when he had taken mine was…powerful. Like I was righting a wrong and balancing scales."

"And you liked it."

"I did." I didn't hesitate in my response, and the valor with which I spoke of it was almost freeing.

"You have tasted vengeance."

"You have done what many others cannot."

"You've done it once."

"And you'll do it again."

I shook my head as if I could bring myself up and out of the downward spiral into familiar territory. The darkness that came with it shouldn't feel so…comforting. "But I'm not some sort of assassin. I don't *want* to kill anyone. Anyone else, that is."

"That is a lie." Thing 1 stood.

"Do not take us for fools." The other followed suit.

I stood to meet them, not wanting to be looked down upon. "I—"

"Do you know *why* we were banished here?"

"*Why* the demons didn't want to work with us anymore?"

"What?" I shook my head. What did they mean by "*work*" with them?

"Because we didn't want to serve them anymore."

"To follow *their* rules."

They stepped forward and together, creating a wall in front of me. My stance widened in response.

"They couldn't control you," I spouted off, suddenly angered by the very thought. I mean, there'd been no controlling me when I killed Brett. But today, Kade had said that he'd felt me slipping and he had pulled me out of it, had torn my mind away from what it was after.

"They can't do that…can they?"

Their eyes blazed with a heat that resonated with my body, a kinship that started a small kindling within my strengthening frame and ignited something in my soul. The thought of the furies being used as weapons reminded me of the speculation of what I had been created for—to kill Kade. To stop the tethering and his rise to king.

"Find your sight." The one on the right grabbed my hand,

sending a jolt of energy through me.

"Make it right." The other mirrored her action and another zap of electricity spread at her touch.

My body temperature rose as my body began to pulse in a rhythm that matched theirs. Static filled my ears as I looked between the two of them, unsure of where this was headed and what would become of it.

Whatever it was…it was too much. I was burning from the inside out by flames I could not see but could feel.

With a crack of lightning, the sky above us lit up, and my vision turned white before I could blink from the pain of it. It was harsher than the sun I had once known.

CHAPTER 12

Kade

It was blinding. The brightness that came from the lightning. The skies had been overcast like always, and while dark, they had been calm up until this point. Elias and I exchanged glances once we recovered from it, on high alert. The strike had come from the direction where Violet and the furies had disappeared. At the speed of their walk, they couldn't have gotten far.

They'd been gone for maybe ten minutes, leaving me to ten minutes of failed conversation with the witch in the meantime. She would nod occasionally, offer vague responses when I tried to ask open-ended questions. She was more than happy to take the supplies we brought, but I couldn't get a damn straight answer out of her for anything.

But my impatience was diminished with the worry of

Violet being out of view, away from the protection I could provide. I'd tried to give her the space she needed, the time to get some answers without Elias and myself hovering. Now I was regretting that.

The lack of emotion coming from our tethered connection was causing me to grow more concerned.

"What was that?" I questioned the witch vehemently. I was ready to bolt to find Violet, but I was having a tough time getting a read on her. She was here and in this realm, that I knew for sure, but something was off. "What's happening?" I stepped closer to the witch as an amused grin crossed her features. Her red eyes crinkled at the corners, sending an unwelcome chill through me.

She knew something.

"We should get going." Elias stepped forward to meet me at my side and I nodded in agreement while I maintained eye contact with the woman before me.

"Calm down, boys, they're already on their way back."

That was the most words she'd used in a single sentence since we'd arrived.

While Violet had made up her mind in her hopes to rescue everyone here in Xandor, I couldn't bring myself to get on board with this witch. She had sorted through Violet's, my uncle's, and my mind and yet she still chose to keep her cards hidden close to her chest. She knew all that she possibly could about the three of us, but besides supplying Violet with those coins, had done absolutely nothing to win me over.

I shook my head, unbelieving. "I would rather find out for myself."

Elias followed after, keeping a pace about three steps behind. I would have transported myself to find her except for the fact that I didn't want to spook the furies if I didn't need to.

Switching into a jog, I was careful not to use too much energy. Not knowing what lay ahead was gnawing at me.

I knew the creatures here had no reason to trust us, but the same could be said about them from our positions. No one in Darthou seemed to be able to locate any documentation as to why these creatures had been exiled to this realm. Everything we knew had been spread by word of mouth. We hadn't been able to find anything concrete regarding Xandor or its inhabitants.

Which gave me the idea of checking in with the other kingdoms. I was mentally sorting through, compiling a list of possible and discreet accomplices, when the witch materialized in front of me, bringing me to a skidding halt. I steadied myself and readied my stance—to fight, to run, to stand my ground, whichever was necessary to get Violet and go.

"Do you still feel connected?"

My fear knew no bounds as I mentally pulled at my bond with Violet. I sought her out, eyes fixated on the witch.

She was still here in Xandor, distant in our connection, but not in distress.

Why would the witch ask such a thing? Was there a reason that I shouldn't feel her?

I glared as if I could burn a hole right through her, churning with a lividity not to be trifled with. "Why do you ask?"

"No reason." She shrugged, the fabric on her shoulder inching off the edge of her figure before she pulled it back into place.

I stepped forward, ready to blink to Violet's location. I didn't care what I could be interrupting between the three of them. "Tell me, *witch*."

"Back off, *demon*," she retorted.

A rustling behind her signaled their return, but I was not overcome with the relief I expected to feel. My initial reaction was to rush to Violet's side, but the unfolding scene sobered me.

Violet was leading the furies out of empty trees as they flanked her on each side. Step by step, they walked in perfect harmony as their images became clearer. A heaviness settled in my chest.

Not only was I sensing a rising anger in her, but there was more—a collective anger that was staggering, suffocating to the point where I struggled to take in air.

Violet looked like a warrior, lethal in her demeanor alone, as her face was set just like the others. There was a bond now between them that hadn't been there before. I could almost see it, although I would swear that my eyes were playing tricks on me. A stream of energy connected them, almost like a triangle.

"What...what happened?" I rubbed at my chest as I tried to expand my lungs, but the air was too heavy. "Violet," I let out in a pant. "Are you alright?"

There was so much hate, so much emotion coursing through the three of them, that I thought I might black out.

"They mean no harm," Violet said, but it was not directed to me. It was to the unnamed furies behind her, as if she was their leader. "They are not to be touched, as well as Zan and his family."

The furies nodded in understanding, together. I blinked hard, unbelieving.

"To harm Kade is to harm me."

With Violet's words, the weight on my chest lifted and I rolled my shoulders back as air came rushing in. I couldn't explain the hold, the heaviness that had taken over, but I didn't like it one bit. It would have rendered me useless if any kind of battle had ensued.

This was the second time Violet had overpowered me. Whether she even realized it or not, I had no idea. We were supposed to be stronger together, and yet she kept rising and I seemed to be faltering. First when she killed Brett, and now with whatever in the hell was going on between her and the furies.

"Ah, so it is still intact." The witch spoke and my head swiveled to meet her. "I can't wait to see how this turns out."

Instead of giving her the satisfaction of my puzzlement, I ignored her. "Violet…"

I wasn't sure how to tell her that it was time to go without it sounding like a command. I wasn't going to pretend I knew what was going on, but I hated how the witch seemed to have an understanding that I didn't currently have on the situation before us.

"Same time next week?" the witch called out to Violet.

"Or sooner," she answered, pinning the witch with a loaded stare that should make my hair stand on end. As she began to leave the furies behind her, Elias and I met her halfway.

I studied her with every step and once she was within reach, I got us the hell out of there.

Violet's eyes fluttered rapidly as I grabbed her shoulders, looking her over for any signs or marks of injury. I'd whisked her back into the privacy of my watching quarters.

"What the fuck was that?" Elias appeared at my side.

"Don't tell me she's one of the creepy furies now."

"Shut up, Elias." My voice rose more than it should. I wanted to know the answer to that question too, but our tethered connection still felt...offbeat. Like it had been tampered with. My arm tingled for a few seconds before it subsided, leaving me with nothing but the memory of it. "Violet, are you alright?"

She swayed a bit before her hands latched onto my elbows for balance. "I think I need to lie down."

Just seconds ago she had been leading the furies back from who knew where, as if she was the center of their trio and possibly in charge, and now she'd done a complete one-eighty. I was half-tempted to return to Xandor, but I couldn't leave her now. And to go it alone and without any kind of backup was a rookie's mistake. I couldn't let my emotions and worry get in the way, not now.

As if snapping out of it, she held my gaze for a moment before she placed a hand to my chest. "Kade."

"Yes, yes, I'm here," I assured her, cupping her face, but her bare skin felt warm. Too warm.

"I'm tired," she muttered softly.

"I'm going to get Zan." Elias vanished without my approval. I wasn't sure how my uncle was going to make any sense of this either.

Exhaustion pulled Violet over the edge and sleep attempted to claim her. "Violet, please. Don't fall asleep. Just tell me what happened."

"I'm fine." She was weak as she pushed me away, eyes closing before she repeated herself. "I'm fine."

"I'm sorry, but I'm having a hard time believing you right now."

Violet's body went limp and I just barely caught her,

scooping her up into my arms. More than shocked by the turn of events, I stood there, dumbfounded. In my arms, Violet drifted off without another word.

I carried her out and down the hall, headed straight for our bed as Elias returned with my uncle. Their voices were anything but quiet as I laid Violet down, propping her head up on her pillow. I sat beside her, moving a stray piece of her hair out of her face, tucking it behind her ear. Again, I noted just how warm she was. She felt almost feverish as I skimmed her exposed skin with the back of my fingers.

Vanishing to the bathroom, I retrieved her coins, and when I returned to her side, I placed them inside a small pocket on the underside of her arm. I scanned her thoroughly with attentive and scrutinizing care—searching for some kind of ailment or injury unseen. When I couldn't make anything out, I took her hand in mine and tried to heal her, hoping that she might awaken. When she didn't, I set it back down in defeat.

I stared at her softened features and let my mind wander, although my train of thought wasn't exactly pleasant.

Was Violet any better off now that she had met me? I didn't understand how she could be so understanding and empathetic to everything she'd come across in my world so far, and yet she tackled each new day with valor. She had a newfound determination and drive to take action, no matter the price. Was that the fury side of her that wanted to eliminate threats immediately and ask questions later? Or had this always been a part of her that had lain dormant, that she could never act on until now?

Sleep seemed to be the only time she got a full reprieve from everything that occurred in our daily routines, but it killed me to not know what had transpired with that lightning strike. Before, during, and after.

Now that we were back home, I could tell without a doubt that our tethering was still intact. Why did the witch have reason to suspect that it wouldn't be?

I made quick work removing what few weapons she had hidden on herself. It was only a few hand blades that were small and easily concealed. She hadn't had much practice with weaponry in her trainings so far, but at least she had something to defend herself if she ever needed it.

"Kadriel." My uncle beckoned me, and I held up a hand to signal for him to give me a minute. I took off for the closet, retrieving Violet's blanket she had brought from home, and returned, draping it across her. My fingers lingered as I touched her cheek, willing her to wake up and talk to me. When she didn't budge, only then did I finally leave.

Leaving the door open a crack in case Violet decided to wake and search for me, I turned to face my uncle and best friend. Zan had changed out of his clothes from the council meeting and was now in his usual shirt and jeans attire that he normally wore while at home.

Today had been nothing short of a shit show, and it was wearing me down. Barely anything had gone according to plan, and it was a reminder of how I was practically being handed the keys to the kingdom—so to speak—this coming weekend.

"I filled him in but…what the fuck, Kadriel?" Elias was anything but subtle in his frustrations. Hell, I didn't even know what I was feeling right now.

"She won't wake. I can't identify any problems, tried healing her, but nothing. She's completely knocked out."

"Her body must need it, but it's definitely poor timing."

I raised a brow at Zan, a bit irritated by his comment. "Sorry, I didn't think to run this nap by you for approval." I pinched the bridge of my nose, almost ready to kick them out.

"I didn't mean that, Kadriel, it's just…"

When I reopened my eyes, I witnessed the two of them exchanging glances.

"Spill," I ordered, and rather heatedly. "I'm really not in the mood."

I moved to the little stand beside my couch and poured two fingers of the strongest stuff I had. They remained quiet, watching and waiting as I polished off the drink, but it did nothing to stifle my agitation at their failure to speak.

"Either tell me or get out." I pointed to the door while still handling my glass.

"It's your birthday eve, Kadriel," Zan gently acknowledged, not the least bit bothered by my aggression.

I scoffed. "I really couldn't care less about that right now. Nor do I any other year."

"That may be so." He rubbed at the back of his neck, stealing another glance with Elias before stepping forward. "But now Violet knows."

My eyes darted between the two of them. "And why is that?" I certainly hadn't spilled that knowledge to her; I hadn't celebrated it in years.

In Darthou, we didn't really do birthdays like Violet did in her world, but we celebrated the eve before the birth. It was normally a private affair for the parents and the child that came forth from their union, to commemorate the life before the new addition. There were no elaborate parties or soirees or such, no fuss. After all, when you had immortality before you, the years didn't really seem to matter.

The thought stirred that Violet might have had something up her sleeve if she'd known about this. And now she was currently passed out on our bed.

"Was she planning something?" I questioned them, and their silence was confirmation of my assumption.

"Fuck," I grumbled as I ran my hands through my hair. The length of it curled around my fingers.

"She meant well," Zan piped up. "We can reschedule it, she'll understand. Your sister, on the other hand..."

"Aleena told her, didn't she?" I presumed. Violet had spent time with her this morning and I highly doubted anyone at the school would have divulged the information. It concerned none of them. "I'll deal with her later."

"Can we please get back to the freaky furies? Am I the only one bothered by this?" Elias crossed his arms, eager to dive back into our latest visit. "She left one minute, came back as if she were one of them," he pushed.

"So what if she is?" My voice rose at his remark, as if he were insinuating that it was a terrible thing. The two men before me blinked in surprise. "As you stated yourself, *uncle*, she has the vengeance of a fury. Are we really surprised that she has found some sort of camaraderie with them? For fuck's sake, one of the furies was slaughtered the day Violet was reborn."

I was defensive now, trying to protect Violet even though I had no idea what had happened in that short amount of time she was away and in their company. If Zan and Elias began to doubt her, there would be no hope that anyone else would accept her.

"We are well aware, Kadriel," Zan rebuked.

"But why would the witch ask you if your tether was still intact?"

I shot a disgusted look at Elias, who seemed to be on any side but my own.

"We could test it. That brought her out of it the last time we were unable to get through to her."

"No!" I scolded my uncle for even suggesting it. "She's there, I can *feel* her. She has some sort of link with the other furies, yes. But our tether is still there."

"What kind of connection?" Zan prodded.

"I don't know, exactly. It's like they're connected by some sort of bond. I could almost see an energy of some sort flowing between the three of them." I hated to speak this out loud, but I didn't see the use of hiding it. I had no idea what Violet had witnessed or her part in it all. "Did you see it, Elias?"

He shook his head in denial.

"First thing," my uncle began. "I don't believe I should have to say this, but I'm going to. No one, and I mean *no one*, is to travel to Xandor until Violet wakes up and we get some answers."

"Fine," Elias and I echoed each other.

"Second, furies have always been, as far as my knowledge and memory goes, depicted in groups of three. Those two lost their third, so Violet can fill that void. She can complete the set."

"But why? Why would they want to replace their third with the one who was born from her blood?"

Elias brought up a good point. Would they ever truly see Violet as one of their own? She wasn't even all fury.

"They're stronger together," I started, realizing that now. Violet was becoming strong on her own, but with them? Who knew what she would be capable of. "I felt it when they returned."

I toyed with the idea of spilling what had happened with Violet earlier, and then blasted straight ahead. I had no idea how long she would be out for; I should get it out of the way now.

"There's also something else you need to know." I cleared

my throat as I stood. "Earlier, I let Violet see all of my charges. Brought up all thirty-two of them."

"You did what? After Brett?" Elias's eyes bulged. "How could you be so reckless?"

"Will you shut up for a minute?" This side of Elias was getting on my last nerve. "She was coherent, present, and even though I felt her slipping, our connection faltering, she did something I didn't know she was capable of."

"Go on." My uncle's curiosity knew no bounds.

"She said she heard a single scream, and when she located where it was coming from, she landed on one of my charges. One that had just recently committed a murder."

Stepping toward the mirrors, I brought up the images Violet had seen earlier. I paused on Stanley and Maria before turning to face them again.

"She did it not once, but twice. She identified killers by the sound of the screams she heard. There was another, but I ended the rest of the feeds before she could spiral."

I had to make them see the possibilities here, to show them what she could be capable of if we could figure out a way to harness her abilities.

"Then when I showed her Tyler"—I motioned toward the boy who was now stumbling into his kitchen to rummage through the snack cupboard—"she knew he hadn't committed anything of the sort. No screams, no gut feelings or hunches that he was bad. Nothing."

"Hm…" Zan didn't honor me with any words as he studied the images.

"Are they on track to kill again soon?" Elias began, his voice more level now. I'd given him information to chew on, and he wasn't arguing with me so that was a plus.

"Maria, possibly." She had taken too much glee in

poisoning her victim. Her background in food and its flavors put her in the perfect position to do so. Now that she'd tasted the power she had, I had little doubt she would move again before Stanley did. Maria had a list of people who had wronged her stashed at the bottom of an antique cookie jar.

"It doesn't make any sense, though," Zan finally said. "Banshees are normally predictors of death. But nothing has happened to either Staffan or Rafina since Violet's first encounters with them and those screams. Why are these different?"

"And that's just it," I interrupted. "Violet heard multiple screams with both of them. With these charges, it was a single scream that practically drew her to them."

Zan crossed his arms and tapped a finger to his chin, thinking. "Makes me wonder what will happen now that the furies have accepted her."

His words held a massive weight. This was all uncharted territory, and we were fumbling through the dark trying to find answers. We weren't much better off now regarding Violet and her abilities than we had been when she first received her coins from the witch.

But that woman had to know something. I knew it in my core.

CHAPTER 13

Kade

I couldn't concentrate. Couldn't focus on anything. I had changed out of my protections into some sweatpants and had been sitting on the bed next to Violet for hours. At the foot of the bed sat a cake, and I studied it as if I could memorize every curve and swipe of its whipped frosting.

Violet had asked Sarah to help her procure a cake for my birthday eve, because she hadn't been able to do so herself. Sarah had been so eager to help since I hadn't celebrated it in so long; of course she would have dropped everything to help. I wasn't sure how she'd found the time to make it, but I had little doubt that this very treat had been made at home in her own kitchen.

The fact that Violet could have so much going on in her own head, in her own life, and still be concerned about celebrating something like this, only hardened my love for her. She was always thinking of others. Wanting to rescue those in Xandor. Worrying about Jacobi at our tethering celebration and how Elias had been missing from the party. Fretting about Aleena and her injury when they hadn't even met yet. Asking me what I wanted to do on her last day in her world, in her hometown, not knowing when she would get the chance to return.

She was selfless.

As much as I wanted her to wake, and for her demon eyes to meet mine, I still felt like it was my fault that she no longer had her green ones. That she was a trio of different creatures combined, and we had no idea just how she was functioning.

And to think there'd been a time that I would have trusted Rafina with my life. I would have run to her with Violet's first symptom, knowing that something wasn't right, ready for her to examine and explain.

Even though I hadn't approved of her relations with my sister, I had looked up to her. I couldn't deny the powerful healer that she was. Even now, I was still struggling with the idea of going to her and trying to seek answers.

But there was a reason Violet didn't trust her. A reason Violet wanted nothing to do with her.

It made me wonder, after the events of today with the furies, what would happen now if Violet were to meet Rafina without the coins? Would she still hear the screams? And if she did, would they still be as debilitating?

When she'd first awoken in Darthou and was met with Rafina, the screams were the worst they had ever been. We still had no idea why.

We kept running into wall after wall after wall.

Taps alerted me to my pocket mirror and I pulled it out,

tossing my tablet onto the bed a few feet away. When I answered, I was met with a fiery and artificial redhead.

"What the fuck is going on, Kadriel?" Aleena was cross with me, definitely more than her normal sibling self.

I stole a glance at Violet by my side, still fast asleep and unmoving since I had laid her down. Only the soft rise and fall of her chest was any indication that she was still slumbering peacefully. Even though I highly doubted a conversation was going to stir her, out of respect, I left the bed and headed for my watching quarters. But not before nabbing the cake from the bed and taking it with me.

"Hello? Are you ignoring me now?" Aleena continued to pester me.

Flipping on a light, I set the dessert on my desk and moved toward the couch and my liquor stash. Again.

"If I answer yes, will you leave me alone?"

Appearing at my side, Aleena was busting at the seams to unload on me. "Not in the slightest."

"What is it, Aleena?" I poured myself a double from the closest bottle, not caring enough to peruse them and choose something particular at present.

"Where's Violet?"

I paused briefly as I brought my drink up to my lips. I took a beat before responding. Perhaps being honest would get her out of here faster. "Resting, so pipe down."

"Bullshit!" she spat as I downed my drink. The burn made my throat constrict, but its fire quickly receded as it settled in my belly.

"Check for yourself." I poured myself another. It was a daily guilty pleasure of mine to toss a few back, but this felt oddly comforting right now. It wasn't exactly an ideal time to flirt with alcohol, but I wasn't sure how else to cope with my sister's attitude, my mate knocked out, and the news about Noliathan.

Out of my periphery, Aleena went to check on my statement. She must have seen enough of Violet's covered frame, but when she returned, her walk was slower. Her face was morphing from one of confusion to skepticism.

I raised a brow, waiting for her to unleash something on me.

"Since when do we hide things from each other, Kadriel?"

And there it was.

She was soft-spoken, almost hurt, and it angered the liquid in my stomach. Keeping my composure, I set my glass down. "I'm not sure I know what you mean."

"Cut the crap." Her voice rose. "I know something is going on."

"What makes you say that?" I met her gaze straight on, unwavering, turning my entire body in her direction.

"You really want me to dive in?"

I gestured for her to continue. I was curious as to just how much she had bottled up.

"I am happy that you have secured your tethered mate, Kadriel, but you've been hiding her away."

"And that's a problem because…"

"Because she's going to be queen. She needs to get out there and be seen. These little meetings with Rafina, Elias, and me are not enough. Nobody really knows who she is."

"Noted. Thank you for your concern." The grip on my glass tightened ever so slightly, but I made sure to keep my face void of any expression.

"I'm not done," she overruled me with defiance, silencing me. "What I don't understand is how someone can be reborn and minutes later, pass through a mirror flawlessly only to fail in doing so again and again for weeks after. She's holding back in her sessions, I know it.

"And don't think I don't know about your little meetings with Zan and Elias. With Sarah and Violet. I'm not sure what you guys are up to, but I don't appreciate being left out of what little family I have."

That stung a bit.

I had been worried about this exact thing. Aleena was anything but a fool. It made me wonder how long it had been since she'd caught on to the secrets being kept. The truth was on the tip of my tongue. But she was losing the grasp she had on her anger, her attitude. Her hardened exterior was fading away into nothing more than a sister, concerned and exhausted and beside herself.

I could probably count the amount of times I'd seen this side of her on one hand. The vulnerability had me turning my head away to look at something else. Anything else.

"It's your birthday eve, Kadriel. Violet was so excited to share that with you. You know how important birthdays can be to humans. I hope you're not going to brush off hers like this."

"I will not," I stated, gathering courage to speak. "And you had no right telling her about it, however it came up."

"Well, you made her late this morning and she said you were in an incredibly good mood. Which is the exact opposite of what you normally are at this time of the year."

It was hard to believe there'd been a time when I was actually excited for my birthday eve. It really had been a long time at that—before our parents had died, even. It was difficult to find joy in an occasion when the two who had brought me into this world were no longer a part of the equation.

"I'm not exactly sure what I did to piss you off, but please, don't shut me out. I like Violet. I want to get to know my sister. But I would also like to spend more time with her outside of training. I don't want her to think of me as the sister-in-law that's all work and no play. That has never been my choice. That was you and the council."

I bit my tongue, trying to reel back the thickness getting caught in my throat. The truth of her words was a hard pill to swallow. While I'd been trying to protect Violet, I'd been shutting out Aleena like she was the damn enemy. And she was anything but.

There had been a time when a younger Aleena begged Mom and Dad for a sister. The fights we would have over having a brother or a sister, like our parents could have a say in the matter, earned nothing but lighthearted laughter and answers of "maybe someday" from them. Who knew if we would have had another sibling if they'd only had more time, if they were still with us to this day.

"I can assure you, you have done nothing to piss me off and…" I searched for the right way to put this. Zan had agreed to tell her after my coronation; we only had to make it through a few more days. "There is something, Aleena."

Her head perked up in my periphery, intrigued. Looking into her eyes, I couldn't help but wonder about the lives she had taken. Her death toll would put mine to shame, no comparison. What would Violet see if she were with my sister without her coins? Violet had had a glimpse at mine during our first visit to Xandor, but Aleena? How would she handle that?

Breaking this news would require more thought. Not only did we need to fill Aleena in on what all Violet was, but the trouble with Xandor. And to top things off, a certain healer that Aleena had messed around with on occasion.

"It's not my news alone to share, but I promise you—after

the coronation, we will tell you everything."

CHAPTER 14

Violet

Stiff. It was as if my body hadn't moved in days. I stretched my limbs as far as they let me and rubbed the sleep from my eyes. My sleeves were too constricting, and I glanced down, observing that I was still dressed in my protections. I tried to remember how I got here and in my bed, covered in the blanket my grandma had made me. I took hold of it as I sat up and surveyed the darkened and vacant room. A small sliver of light was coming from Kade's watching quarters, and that was where I would start—after I used the bathroom.

Closing the new door gently, I contorted my arms to pull down the mini zipper. Usually, Kade helped me with this task, but dammit I had to pee and I wasn't going to wait. I pried my protections from my body and laid the suit on the bench next to Kade's.

After relieving myself, I grabbed Kade's shirt from earlier and buttoned it up, stopping just above my breasts. Raising the sleeve to my nose, I inhaled deeply. The citrus on him smelled ten times better than in the garden. It only furthered my desire to find him.

When I opened the bathroom door, a bare-chested Kade was leaning against the wall with his arms crossed. His mood wiped the grin from my face instantly.

"What's wrong?" I blinked, worried.

"What's *wrong*?" he repeated, unmoving except for the words that left his lips.

The shadows at his sides from the unlit hallway almost made him look angry, but sexy as hell at the same time. A few unruly curls made their way onto his forehead, practically begging to be pulled on.

I swallowed hard, unsure why I was being met with such an odd greeting just after waking. "Did I do something wrong?"

His eyes narrowed, brows pitting against one another.

"What?" I asked again, uncomfortable. What was I missing?

Kade pushed himself off his perch but didn't cross to close the gap between us. "Violet, what's the last thing you remember?"

I helplessly searched his dark eyes as if there was a chance I could see the intent behind his quizzing me.

Returning to the start of our day, I recounted everything I could remember.

Waking. Sex. Aleena and the school. Lunch. The news about Damian or whatever the hell we were calling him now. The mirrors and those I had identified. Our trip to…

Xandor.

Deep in thought, concentrating on my last known whereabouts, I focused on every single action. From loading up on supplies, to crossing over with Kade and Elias. The furies were there and—

"Fuck," I muttered as my memories unraveled. We hadn't even spoken much, but it was enough to bring it all back and into focus. Those final moments sent a chill through my spine.

Find your sight. Make it right.

The jolt when I had joined hands with each one of them. The shock wave that had swept through my entire being, and the lightning that filled the sky after doing so. It had been powerful and overwhelming, but welcoming at the same time.

It was as if they had accepted me without even knowing me. They felt like friends who I'd known all along, a kinship like no other I had experienced since coming to Darthou, since being reborn. But as much as I enjoyed that sense of bond, there was a collective anger that was brimming beneath the surface. A hatred that wanted a release, but it was being suppressed.

"Do you remember?" Kade inquired, but I had a feeling he already knew the answer.

I nodded. I was still calling these furies Thing 1 and Thing 2, but the urge to protect and save them was now at new heights of importance. Why did I have the need to have them by my side even now?

"Did they hurt you at all?"

My gaze snapped to his, appalled. "Of course not!"

"Then tell me what happened. You've been asleep for almost ten hours. Whatever happened, it knocked you out. You collapsed shortly after returning." There was an urgency to his voice and I could sense his anxiety. His unease.

So that was why I'd still been in my protections. I could

recall a brief and fleeting moment of our return, a glimpse of Kade before it was lights out for me.

"You're connected to them now, aren't you?" There was an underlying trace of understanding buried beneath his worry. Kade and I both seemed to have that in common, but he was doing nothing to hide it right now.

I was a bit afraid to admit it, but there couldn't be secrets between us. Not if we were going to continue moving forward together. And by the way he asked, he already knew.

I nodded again. I was at a loss for words. I was still trying to make sense of it myself. It had all happened so fast. Our weekly visits were normally short, and not exactly a party, but this one had to be the most eventful since we had first crossed over.

At least nobody had tried to kill one another this time.

"Talk to me, Violet. Please." He took a hesitant step forward. "I need to know that you're alright."

Kade scooped up one of my hands and held it in his. After all our time spent together thus far, his touch still brought about a comfort that couldn't compare to anything else. I tilted my head up to witness the concern etched in his face, to the point that he had turned to stone.

When I met his eyes, I saw a flash of a moving image, and I jumped, heart in my throat. My hand jerked away from his hold as I witnessed a man slain by Kade's hands. A man I had seen only once before, a saint that Kade had killed in the ambush at the factory.

There was no stopping the gasp that ripped from my chest, a sound that left me before I could get a chance to squash it.

"The sight." My breathless statement stumbled out before Kade could get a word in. "Find your sight. Make it right."

"Sight?" Kade pushed for more, stepping into my space

again.

"Find your sight. Make it right. That's what the furies told me." I searched the darkness around him, almost afraid to meet his gaze again. I didn't want to see death every time I looked at him; I didn't know if I could deal with that. He was my comfort and my safe place. He was my home now. I didn't want to be reminded of the lives he had taken each time I peered at the man I loved, the man I was tethered to and planned on spending the rest of my life with.

"Then don't hide from it."

I turned my back on him, confused and alarmed by his statement. "I don't want to see you killing people every time I look at you."

"Violet, look at me."

"No." My voice shook. The thought occurred that I needed my coins, and I left to retrieve them. But they weren't on the counter in their usual spot.

"Look at me." Kade spun me around and grasped my shoulders. I squeezed my eyes shut, unwilling to follow his order.

"I have killed, yes. You know that I'm a demon, and why I have done the things that I have. You didn't have the urge to kill me when you first experienced the sight, so don't fight it now. Let it run its course."

"I don't want to," I pleaded as I tried and failed to push him away.

"Look at me!" he demanded, his voice escalating to a higher pitch, and when my eyes reopened, the focus was instant. My pulse went haywire as the man I saw once before appeared again. I fought the urge to look away, knowing that Kade would continue to push until I did it. As if sensing my turmoil, his hands moved from my shoulders to the sides of my head, holding me in place.

I didn't want to see it, not with him. It was one thing to imagine Kade killing murderers and ending lives. It was another to witness it for myself.

The image morphed into another, what I assumed was another saint, judging by the same vast, dusty room. Kade ended him too, though not as fast as the first.

Person by person, they came to the surface as I stared into his eyes. Life by life, snuffed out by his hands. Some swift, quick, and clean. Others, it was obvious that their deaths were drawn out, their bruised and battered bodies showing that I was only getting a small taste of their drawn-out encounters and ends. I began to lose track of how many I was bearing witness to. Body after body, I watched the light fade from their eyes, but there was one thing they all had in common.

They had it coming.

Cue the chorus of ladies from "Cell Block Tango."

Each one was guilty of crimes that made my gut roll in disgust. I didn't place an ounce of blame on Kade, who was playing executioner, as each one moved into frame, practically begging to be killed. I couldn't explain the satisfaction that started to ooze over me with the unfolding of each scene.

Maybe demons and furies weren't all that different to begin with.

When the last image faded, I gasped for air. My frame tried to fall forward, but Kade caught me and my buckling knees. While I might have been holding my breath, my body was almost on a high after seeing the scales being balanced by this one man, this demon before me.

He had every right to kill them. Each one was justified. They deserved it. Every. Single. One.

"Could you see any of that?" I didn't know what effect it

would have had on him, if any. Did all of those deaths rise to the surface in his mind as I discovered them? I didn't know why I worried; there was nothing for him to be ashamed of. I, on the other hand, felt like I was intruding. Watching something involving him without his permission.

I couldn't bring myself to look at him, for fear of it unraveling all over again. Kade only shook his head, and I attempted to put some distance between us. This time, he let me go.

"What did you see?"

My fingers itched to tangle together, but I crossed my arms instead. Ever since he'd pointed out the habit, I was overly cautious about it now. "Pretty sure I saw every life you've ever taken."

I should have been startled by it, *rattled* by the images I had seen, but I was growing more concerned about how I wasn't. It felt like ages ago when he first told me that he carried out justice himself, and that had felt like a heavy burden then. So why wasn't I bothered by this now? Was it because I was no longer human?

"I stand by those actions. I've never hid any of this from you. Never lied to you about it."

"I know." I studied the sink that I'd claimed as my own, centering my attention there. I didn't blame him, and I would stand beside him just as I had up until this point, but I didn't understand how I could be with him, truly be with him, if all I was going to see was his past every time I looked at him. That alone was horrifying and cruel.

"I'm sorry I pushed you." His hurt was more than evident. In his tone, in his stance. "I didn't know it would upset you so much."

"It's not that." I hung my head down low. "I'm just afraid

that I'm going to see the same thing every time I look at you. *That*, I don't want."

There was a long pause, the silence filling my ears to the point that I wanted to turn around, but I was too scared to look at him. I loved staring into his eyes. It was the first feature of his that I'd grown fond of, no matter how bizarre they were. And even though I now had a set of those black demon eyes myself, it didn't mean I appreciated them any less.

"You won't know unless you look at me again, Violet." The way he used my name was coaxing for me to do it. "Start with the mirror."

Kade pressed against my back, snaking his arms around my waist as his chin sat upon my shoulder. I held my breath, mustering up the courage to talk myself through it. I hated how this small act of looking at him brought a fear that I never thought I could have.

"Look at me," he whispered into my ear, bringing goosebumps to the curve of my neck. I bit my bottom lip, trying to push myself to follow through.

When my lids opened, I froze. I met his gaze straight on in our reflection, and I waited.

And waited.

When nothing happened, I released a heavy exhale. Relieved that nothing had spurred those images, those occurrences to begin playing again. But it was only half the battle.

"Focus on us," he said as he planted a kiss on my neck. "Focus on what we have. The connection that we share."

Kade dragged his lips up my neck, and one of his hands tilted my head to the side so he could capture my lips. He was gentle at first, carefully testing before leisurely prying my lips apart so he could explore my mouth. When his tongue met mine, the tense edge I'd set myself on began to fade away.

Time passed, and I couldn't begin to think how much of it, but it was enough to warm my entire body within our embrace. When Kade finally broke away, we were both trying to catch our breaths. The small laugh we shared wasn't forced. It was more relieving than anything.

That was when I realized that I was looking at him, straight on. Not a slashed throat, plunging knife, or body cracking in sight. Zero deaths.

"Oh thank fuck!" I threw my arms around his neck, overcome with joy that I hadn't been met with the same replay of events that I'd just seen minutes ago. He returned the embrace, securing us together, and just when I thought all was well—even if only briefly—it all came to a screeching halt.

I'd been passed out for ten hours?

"Oh no!" I released him, a hand snapping to my mouth. "Have you heard anything from Sarah?"

A knowing smile formed on his lips, and it was evident that he was already aware of my plans for tonight. Well, last night.

Dammit. Well, that plan had totally backfired.

Without a word, Kade escorted me back to his watching quarters, and my eyes landed on it right away. On his desk that he rarely used sat the cake that Sarah had been willing to bake for the occasion. One that she swore was his favorite flavor.

Being human herself, Sarah knew all about the importance of birthdays and had even brought that tradition with her to raise her own children by celebrating them each year. Zan had been happy to oblige, as long as they could also commemorate their birthday eve as well.

When I had contacted her earlier, I didn't even have an idea of where to start with Kade. If he liked cake or not, what flavor, and if he would prefer anything else. Cheesecake, cupcakes, brownies, or cookies. Maybe he didn't even like cake. Maybe he was an ice cream, gelato, or frozen yogurt kind of guy.

Come to find out, of all the things I would have guessed, it certainly wasn't lemon blueberry cake with a whipped lemon frosting. Sarah didn't hesitate, knowing exactly what he would devour, and she had prattled on about having all the ingredients at the ready and how she could have it done in time.

I'd only been planning on a small get-together, between myself and those closest to him. Aleena, Elias, and Zan's family would have been enough, as I knew what they all meant to him. I had inadvertently messed it all up with our visit to Xandor.

"I hope you're not upset with me." My heart sank along with my eyes, but he promptly lifted my chin up with a single finger. My breath caught for a brief second, fearing what I might see again, but when nothing came to pass, my shoulders sagged with ease.

"I'm not sure why you think I would be."

"Well…" I scrambled for words, but decided to just come out with it. "It didn't seem like you wanted me to know about it at all. Were you ever going to tell me about this birthday eve business? It's my first one I get to celebrate here. To celebrate you."

His jaw clenched and unclenched, as if ready to respond but steering away. It was obvious that he hadn't planned on me finding out, at least not yet.

"I care, Kade. Though I wish I would've heard it from you first." A shiver raked through me and I hugged myself tight. It didn't go unnoticed, and he raised a brow.

"And for that, I'm sorry. Perhaps we'll save this for later." He gestured to the cake before running his hands up and down my arms in a warming manner. "I'm sure my cousins are more than willing to help us annihilate it."

As I grinned at the image of Ajax and Brighton shoveling cake into their mouths, Kade disappeared within a blink, then returned with my blanket in hand, draping it around my shoulders. "Are you really that cold?"

My head bobbed as my bare legs pressed together to try and find some more warmth. "Did it get colder in here or something?"

He shook his head in denial. "Come here."

I sat with him on his couch, and he swung my legs over the top of his, drawing my blanket as far as it reached to try and comfort me. "Did you talk about anything else with the furies? Anything at all."

I sighed, shrugging at the lack of conversation the three of us had had. I hadn't really been gone long, and those two weren't exactly the type to talk things out.

"Not really. I told them what had transpired today, er, yesterday I mean. They mentioned the sight and then joined hands with me. There was this…" I swallowed, trying to find the right words without sounding ridiculous. "This jolt of energy that came over me with each touch. I felt stronger almost immediately. And there was this understanding between the three of us, without anything being said."

"There's some significant anger there. I felt it." His thumb rubbed my bare ankle back and forth as he concentrated on the ground before us.

"Oh, there's a lot of anger," I agreed. "They're pissed at demons in general. They lost their sister by the hands of one. Were banished by them. There's a lot they have to be angry about."

"It was suffocating." His thumb stopped, as if he was recalling it. Perhaps stuck on the memory. "That's why you told them we weren't to be harmed."

"It was," I confirmed. The witch knew from our first visit that we were not a threat, had searched through our memories and seen that none of us were responsible for the massacre that had taken place in that realm. But it did little to hush the hatred of demons that had been building for decades. I didn't know the age of anyone there in Xandor, but they had certainly had a lot of time to stew on it, that much I knew.

"I think that's what they want most right now. Revenge for their lost sister. They want it more than to be free at this point."

"And I'm willing to bet that they're hoping you'll be able to carry it out."

My eyes widened at the thought. "The sight…"

"Exactly. You can come and go, they cannot. They are bound to that realm right now and you're their only help in carrying out that mission."

I gulped, realizing that what he was saying could very well be true. I wasn't sure if I should be impressed or scared at the fact that they might be expecting me to exact revenge for someone I had never even met.

"With the sight—if it's as strong as what you just witnessed in me—it could prove very useful but also dangerous."

"What do you mean?" I pressed, even though I had an inkling as to what he was referring to.

"Violet, if your sight is as strong as what you just witnessed in me, you could probably sniff out the demon responsible for that massacre in no time. If you really did sift through the years and occasional times that I played seeker within a matter of seconds, you should have no trouble doing that to others."

"But what if I do find them?" I stammered, getting worried about the next thing to spill from my mouth. "What if I lose control again? Like with Brett?"

"And that is exactly what makes it so dangerous. We have no idea how you'll react. Or who is responsible and what else they're capable of."

"That reminds me," I started, "the furies mentioned that I had such a reaction to Brett because there was a personal connection with him. But when I saw those two that you were watching, I *did* feel more in control."

"You were slipping," he interrupted faintly.

"But you brought me back."

"You were walking a fine line. Remember all that pent-up energy you had? You were about ready to combust."

I was angry that Kade had removed the images of those wrongdoers. Cut me off before I could find another. I had needed a release for the build that was taking over. The urge to do something. But was it the urge to kill? I still had no idea.

I reflected on all of the funeral pyres I had witnessed after the massacre in Xandor; I had made a vow to find the one responsible and to make them pay. The devastation it had caused loomed over me as I recalled the grieving father who had lost a child, the furies who had lost a sister, and other mourners who I had not seen since. I'd given none of them a reason to trust me, but I'd be damned if I didn't have this odd and unpredictable gift for a reason.

Perhaps this was my purpose that I was finally beginning to accept. Claiming the life that had taken so many, and for what? You couldn't tell me that I was the sole purpose of the bloodshed that had taken place that day. There had to be more to it. If their plan had been to get me to kill Kade, that had majorly backfired.

I had been a nobody before I released Kade from my mirror. A human that a demon had requested a tethering for, and nothing else. So why were there so many slain when I only had demon, fury, and banshee now running through my veins?

"Kade?"

"Hm?"

"Do we know how many different creatures were murdered that day?"

He thought that through for a moment, perhaps trying to make a tally in his head. "I can only recall what I saw on the pyres closest, but I'm not entirely sure, why?"

"There were at least a dozen bodies, were there not?"

"Where are you going with this?" His eyes slanted.

"If I only have banshee and fury sides within me, what happened with the other creatures that were slain? Why would anyone go through so much trouble to destroy so many and to only use the blood of two for me?"

"We've discussed the possibility of others like you. Well, maybe not *exactly* like you. But out of all the kingdoms, you and I were the only tethering request granted. There's been nobody else since."

"Well..." Apparently Kade, Elias, and Zan had been talking more than I knew about. I tried not to let it bother me, at least not right now. "Any unexpected deaths to charges or..." I was grasping at straws as Kade rubbed my leg above the blanket. "Strange occurrences with born again demons?"

The sound that came from his chest was like a forced and failed attempt at a chuckle. "We have a few people around Darthou and other kingdoms keeping tabs on things. Discreetly, of course. But there haven't been any red flags as of yet."

It was on the tip of my tongue to ask who they were, what they did, and just how much we could trust them, but I refrained. I knew Kade wouldn't have told them any specifics about me, so how would they know what to look for? And just how often was he having these little get-togethers with his uncle and best friend?

"But you'll tell me, right? If you find something? If *they* find something?"

Grabbing a hold of my calf, he grinned. "Maybe don't fall asleep for ten hours and I can keep you up to speed."

I smacked his arm with the back of my hand, then crossed my arms. "Rude."

He lifted his hands up in surrender. "Low blow, I know. I'm sorry." This time when he laughed, it was genuine but cut short. "One way or another, we're going to get to the bottom of all of this."

But at what cost?

CHAPTER 15

Violet

Elias was an early riser, so Kade and I started with him this morning. I purposely left my coins behind, as we were going to try and test out my sight on him. We had gone weeks without any leads, and we were ready to hit the ground running.

"Everyone?" Elias questioned as he threw on a tank that fit tightly around shapely muscles. We had caught him in the middle of a workout and sweat was rolling off of him. His hair was pulled back tight and out of the way as he caught his breath, steadying it.

"Pretty sure, yeah," I hesitantly acknowledged. Kade had never verbally given me a number, and I had quickly lost count of the lives he had taken. I didn't know if I really, *truly*, wanted to know that figure, though.

"You're not squeamish at all about them?" Elias's eye contact was heavy, and I was the first to break it. I was suddenly nervous about what else I might find.

Kade squeezed my hand and my reply staggered out. "Honestly, it all happened so fast. They flashed by so quickly I didn't really have time to react. It was just one right after the other. Maybe a few seconds with each one."

Elias mulled that over before approaching me. I looked to Kade for guidance, but he only nodded his reassurance before taking a step away.

"Bring it on." Elias came to a stop about two feet away, motioning for me to come at him like he so often did in our combat training.

I wasn't even sure how to bring on the sight—to find what I was looking for. He was slightly smaller than Kade, but their physiques were strangely similar. It felt strange staring into his eyes, the black pools of another man and Kade's best friend. At this close proximity, it was an intimacy I reserved only for Kade.

My focus bounced from eye to eye, searching for some kind of sign. But when nothing unraveled, I began to lose hope.

"I..." Defeat hit me in an instant. "I don't know exactly how I brought it on before." I hated to admit that, and I started to think about the scenes with Kade. Was it all just dumb luck at this point?

"I've killed, you know that." Elias's face hardened. "Use that."

Taking a deep breath, and evening my stance, I honed in again. Waiting. Urging myself to find something, anything. Surely he had killed on his own and not just when in the company of Kade and Aleena. It made me wonder what his death toll was like compared to theirs. Kade had been a seeker on occasion, even though he was usually a watcher.

"Focus, Violet," Kade instructed with a gentle yet stern tone. "You can do it again."

I was a bit perturbed at my failure so far, and Kade's words did little to soothe my rising anxiety.

"I'm trying," I said through gritted teeth. This was embarrassing, staring into Elias's eyes and waiting for something that might never come.

Just when I was about ready to throw in the towel, a flash of an image rolled though. The sharp crack of a neck, of an already broken and beaten man. The room they were in was filthy, trashed even. And Kade was there, standing watch with his arms crossed.

Then it all shifted. A new location. More bodies and more faces.

The swords that Elias favored sliced through someone in a place that looked identical to the first scene I had witnessed with Kade. This death might be clean-cut and swift, but the thud from his falling body caught me off guard.

I jumped back, breaking the contact and cupping a hand over my mouth.

"You saw something." Kade was at my side with a hand on my shoulder.

I nodded once, the gruesome act of that man meeting his end frozen in my mind. "You said when you battled the saints, it was at an old factory?"

"An abandoned one, yes," Kade confirmed.

"What did you see?" Elias's intrigue was more than evident as he closed the distance I'd just tried to put between us.

"You slicing away and cutting through a man like he was nothing more than butter. Before that, you snapping a man's neck."

I didn't appreciate the smug look of satisfaction that rolled over his face. Proud of his work.

As if sensing my inner turmoil, Kade was ready to let me off. "Is this too much? We can stop."

I shook my head vehemently. "No. I want to keep going. The sooner I can control this, the sooner we can get some answers." There were two demons in particular I would *love* to use this sight on. Rafina and Staffan.

"I understand that, but we don't have to do this all in a day. If it gets to be too much, say something."

I assured Kade that I would.

"You said each one only lasts a few seconds?" he inquired, making sure he had his facts straight.

I nodded. "It seems quick, but at the same time, like it's lasting forever."

The two exchanged glances, almost as if they were speaking telepathically. It was a bit annoying, but I guessed it could be expected when they were so close and had grown up together.

"What is it?" My eyes darted between the two of them before Kade finally spoke up.

"I'm just worried about my sister's death toll. That might be quite the trip when we bring her into the fold."

My eyes bulged at the realization. Aleena had been the youngest seeker ever, and she took joy in what she did. She didn't watch full-time like the two before me, and they still had high body counts, in my opinion anyway. The thought of unraveling Aleena's past victories was a bit unsettling. But the practice I could do on her might prove useful when the time came.

As if Kade could sense my worry, he said, "Maybe we'll

work up to her."

"Sure." I bobbed my head.

"Can you talk while you're viewing my memories?" Elias asked as he stepped in close again. He searched my eyes as if he could find something there, when I for one didn't even know what in the hell I was doing to search out the memories in others.

"Maybe, why?"

"Can you say something each time you see a new one? So we can keep count?"

"That would be helpful," Kade added, "if it's not too much to ask."

"I can try, sure." Perhaps the more acquainted I became with the sight, the more I would be able to expand on it. I didn't know if I could draw out the scenes longer or if I might be able to pause on them to describe what was happening in more detail. But for now, I would just concentrate on this. Talk myself through it, and out loud.

I shook my hands out, nervous once more at what I might find. I thought of the furies and the connection we shared. How I wished they were here, and that they could help me. Hell, they were probably the reason this sight was stronger and more prevalent now.

Though, whether this sight was a blessing or a curse, that remained to be seen.

Taking my stance in front of Elias again, I took in a deep breath through my nose and slowly released it, recalling the snapped neck. The recollection stirred and once I opened my mouth to tell them, I was taken to the factory again.

The words rolled off my tongue in a rush. "Snapped neck. Now the saint."

Another man took his place at the same location. Elias's

blade went straight through his chest, sending a spray of blood at the impact.

"Another," I breathed out, trying to focus as it shifted once more to a third. It went on and on, victim after victim and death after death. It felt wrong referring to some of them as victims when I could taste the evil in their soul. Some perpetrators made me want to vomit with the hatred in their eyes, hatred that soon turned to shock in their last moments of lingering life. Some deaths were quick, others more drawn out.

It was a full-on decapitation that pulled me out of my trance, drawing me back to the present. I gasped to fill my lungs, stunned.

"Are you alright?" Kade was at my side and steadying me. I wasn't even sure when I had stopped taking in precious air.

When I finally got my bearings, I glared at Elias. "You decapitated someone?!"

The man had to have been in his twenties. He was a wicked one, but he was a bloody pulp before the action that claimed his life. Out of all of the images I had witnessed with Kade, this one with Elias had affected me the most. I wasn't completely repulsed by it, although the image might be regrettably ingrained in my memory, but I wasn't exactly in favor of it either.

"Says someone who ripped a man's heart out with her bare hands."

"Elias!" Kade scolded.

I opened my mouth to say something, but refrained. Elias was right, even though I didn't want him to be. I didn't know what was worse, and I certainly was no better than him. The cruelty of my actions didn't paint me in any better of a light.

Pressing a palm to Kade's chest, I gently pushed him away. He was more than ready to come to my defense, but there was no need for it right now.

"He's right," I acknowledged, owning up to it. "I'm not sure why that one affected me so much. More so than any of the others I've witnessed."

"I have to admit, it's pretty damn impressive." Elias's words gave me a little kick of a confidence boost. I might have my ass handed to me time and again with training, but this? If this earned his praise, I'd take it. It chipped away at the repetitive feelings of not being good enough, of being weak.

"Just within that short time frame, you've almost witnessed everyone I've ever hit."

I glanced between the two men. "Any idea how many?"

If I had to guess, it was more than Kade at this point.

"Ninety-four," Kade confirmed. "Assuming you informed us of everyone you saw."

"I think I did." I nudged Kade's shoulder playfully, trying to find humor in a grim subject matter. "Slacker. I think Elias has your score beat."

Kade broke into a small smile as Elias's laughter filled the room. There wasn't enough time for laughs anymore, especially as of late. I couldn't help but grin at the poke I'd made.

"I'm afraid that being in line for the throne doesn't permit me many chances to seek. The council doesn't like me going out there for it often."

"Well, I may not agree with the council on much of anything, but I can confirm that I don't like the idea of you seeking either," I offered, just so there was no doubt regarding it all.

"Noted." Kade pulled me in and kissed me on the top of my head. My hair was still damp from my shower and pulled back into a low bun so it didn't get my sweater wet.

"Are you feeling alright?" Kade asked, suddenly serious.

Taking a beat, I gave myself a mental overlook, making sure that everything was in check. "I think so, but I think I've seen enough for now. No offense," I stammered out, suddenly alarmed that Elias might take that remark the wrong way.

"None taken." He held his hands up. "Although, I am a bit saddened that I don't get to relive all of those encounters with you."

"Really?" I was surprised by that. Why the hell would he *want* to do that?

"Yeah, especially Marcum. That guy I decapitated. He raped and murdered teenagers who never stood a chance. I had some fun ending that fucker."

"Which brings us to the conclusion that using your sight on Aleena might have to wait a while," Kade concurred.

My stomach soured at the thought.

"We pale in comparison to the lives that she has taken. You need to be mentally and physically prepared before you tap into that. I wouldn't be surprised if she needs to give you a quick briefing before you dive in there."

I knew Kade meant well, but it felt like he was tossing stones into my tummy, weighing it down.

"The more serious the crimes committed, the more she tortures them," Elias clarified. "It's more than just a job or a game for her. Seeking is her everything."

Thinking back to the school, I remembered how the children's faces had lit up at seeing Aleena. How she was welcomed and received by both students and teachers, young and old. It was almost bizarre to think of Aleena carrying out justice, seeking and delivering death to those identified by the watchers.

The way she balanced two drastic sides of herself was

something to be admired.

But then there was her even less spoken about love life. Well, if love was even in the equation. I really couldn't be sure.

I hadn't seen Aleena and Elias together since our tethering celebration. In the great hall, they had been fighting and on the verge of causing a major scene. Then, I'd witnessed them in a back hallway, and Aleena had him pinned up against a wall. It had been a heated exchange that made me a bit hot and bothered just remembering it. I was sure I wasn't supposed to have witnessed that, but then again, they could have chosen to go somewhere else. It was their decision to display their affections in a hallway not too terribly far off from where the festivities were being held.

I hoped that one day, and maybe someday soon, I might be close enough to Aleena to ask her about their relationship. I wasn't sure why it bothered me so much, perhaps just because I knew that she and Rafina had a past.

Pushing all of those thoughts aside to sort through at another time, I continued onto another subject—the revelation that Kade and I had been discussing at length and believed we were now ready to bring to Elias. We would get to Zan and Sarah later.

"There's another thing that Kade and I think we might have a lead on, although we're a bit stumped at the moment. Perhaps another brain might help."

Elias shifted his weight to his other foot and crossed his arms. "Alright."

I glanced at Kade to see if he wanted to discuss this himself, but he gestured for me to continue.

"As we know, there were several slaughtered in Xandor. Two of which were a fury and a banshee." I signaled to myself with the point of my fingers so he would get the picture. "I would like to think that if I had anything else in me, we would have found out by now. So what happened to the blood of the other creatures?"

"There was a lot of death, and we still have no idea why," Kade offered.

"Is someone trying to make more of me?"

"But how?" Elias questioned. "Isn't it a stretch? Tethering with humans…even the requests to do so are minimal. There's a slim chance that it will happen again for some time."

"So are the requests to become a demon," Kade stated. "But what is the one thing that all of these have in common? Who would be at each transition, be it successful or not?"

"We keep circling back to them. Staffan and Rafina. But we have no proof, just suspicion." Elias shifted again, as if uncomfortable. "Even so, for the most part, the two of them have been accounted for on that day. They couldn't have been responsible for the deaths in that realm. The witch even said it was a demon, younger in years, but obviously they were old enough to have conquered their shifting abilities. They never showed who they were in Xandor, not their true selves."

"But now we have me." I tried to stand a little taller. I knew that this world, this body and its abilities were still raw and new and fresh, but I refused to let it all be for nothing.

Elias stared at me, a piercing glare that I didn't shrink away from. Images began flooding me again on repeat, starting with his most recent kill, and going back. It caught me off guard for a moment, before I continued.

"If I can…" I concentrated on the connection, pushing further and trying to form words as I let the images fill my head. "If I can control my sight enough, I should be able to start weeding out demons who are not responsible."

"And what if you do find them?" Elias challenged. "How

will you keep yourself from ripping out their heart right then and there?"

My mouth tightened as my heart rate kicked up. I didn't like how he kept dangling my past actions in front of me. There was no hiding from it; what happened couldn't be changed. But the fact that he held that situation in front of me, as if I should be ashamed of it, was upsetting. It was like he didn't trust me or something. But then again, had I ever given him a reason to?

Death by death replayed as I took in an uneasy breath. I was trying so hard to remain in the conversation while simultaneously trying to keep the connection with Elias's memories going.

"The furies said that I had that reaction because there was a personal connection there. Yesterday, it was different when I was in Kade's watching quarters. I didn't kill anyone, even though I knew there was something seriously wrong with those individuals."

"But you were watching them through mirrors, remember?" Kade reminded me, and as much as I wanted to turn toward him, I couldn't. I had to keep the connection with Elias. I was now at the decapitation death, and determined to move past it and continue.

"What happens when you come face-to-face with the demon responsible for those deaths in Xandor? Will you be able to hold back, or are you going to seek vengeance right then and there? After all, they were responsible for the death of one of the furies. How do you know you won't blindly react in the moment?"

"I don't know." My agitation grew, bringing on pain in my temples that spread quickly to my forehead and between my eyes.

"Is it worth the risk then?" he pushed, unrelenting.

"It is if we can bring them to justice! They shouldn't be able to get away with their actions. They killed a fucking child in Xandor!"

"Violet." It barely registered that Kade was pulling at my arm, perhaps trying to reel me back in, but I gave him a shove as I fought to keep eye contact.

"What are you going to do then?" Elias was mere inches away and pressing on, hitting buttons that were infuriating to no end. "Are you going to go up to every demon in Darthou and stare them dead in the eyes in the hopes that your sight will reveal the memories in each one? That's not going to look suspicious at all."

"Elias, enough!" Kade maneuvered between us, and while his best friend didn't budge, I did. I stumbled back, disoriented.

The ache in my head reached an all-time high but I tried to ignore it, knowing that I'd been victorious. I had been present and aware of everything playing out before me as I sifted through the visions that took over. I'd carried on a conversation—better yet, I had fought—and was still able to use my sight.

My lips turned up at the corner, and for once, I felt like I was gaining the upper hand.

I saw a horrified look reflected back in a man's eyes as Elias stabbed him, over and over again. Blood stained the sand around them. The man with the receding hairline begged and pleaded for him to stop, claiming his innocence, which was useless from what I could surmise. There was nothing clean nor orderly about this kill. It was downright brutal. Elias's hesitation in ending him only drew out the inevitable—his death.

Elias shook from the encounter, from taking a life. There was a remorse that I hadn't witnessed before, a trepidation as he came to terms with what he had done as a life slipped away.

"Tell me, Elias." I took a step forward but planted my feet firmly. "Were you nervous before your first kill? Quite the progression, if you ask me. From that first man by the river to the last man that you killed in a dirty room."

At that, he was stunned into silence, trying to conceal whatever emotion was begging to come make itself known.

"You made it to the beginning." Kade blocked my view of Elias, squandering the high I was feeling. My success.

"Yeah," I mumbled as I closed my eyes, pressing the heels of my palms to my temples. The ache was subsiding, but left the remembrance of it in its wake.

"You're pushing yourself too hard, too fast. You need to be careful," he cautioned.

"I've waited long enough. I may never be able to fight as well as the rest of you, but if this is how I can help, then I'm going to do it to the best of my abilities."

"But—"

"Kade, they're practically sitting ducks over there. How long before someone returns and tries to claim more lives? So far, they've gotten away with it once. I'll be damned if I'm going to let that happen again. Not when I can finally do something."

"She's right," Elias said from across the room, perhaps wanting distance from me. He must have traveled over there by pocket, because I never heard a single step.

Whatever I had uncovered, it had been unpleasant for him. He wasn't able to hide his emotions as well as Kade and Aleena, and it read on his face. While I was proud of myself for what I had accomplished, I didn't like the position it had put him in.

But if he had been trying to get a rise out of me in the first place, it had worked.

"Kadriel, are you still planning on asking the council about Xandor once you see your coronation through?"

"I am." Kade directed his attention toward his friend as he took my hand in his. "They better come forth with some answers when I do. That and…Noliathan"—he struggled to get that name out—"are top of the agenda at our first meeting."

"Good."

"I believe we have taxed you enough for this morning, Elias. Thank you for your help."

Before I could offer a word of anything, Kade took us back to our place.

CHAPTER 16

Violet

"Hey!" I slapped him on the arm for the abrupt departure. I was suddenly unsure whether I should have apologized to Elias or not. My words had come out without me even thinking them through, and I had been so caught up in the moment. In hindsight, perhaps I was a bit harsh. "I wasn't finished."

"But *he* was," Kade assured me. "Now how about some breakfast?"

I hadn't eaten anything since lunch yesterday with Aleena and Jacobi, and that was now clearly evident. But I didn't want the usual fruit and occasional meat for breakfast. My lips protruded in a small pout, not wanting to disappoint him but tired of the usual fare.

"Can we go to the kitchens for a change?"

Kade's entire posture stiffened. "Um…if you really want to."

"I do." I didn't skip a beat. That wasn't an outright *no*. "Where are my coins?"

Kade made his way to my side of the bed, which admittedly was messier than his. My nightstand held books, water, and the necklace he had gifted me, whereas his stand was empty of any contents. Retrieving the coins from the little drawer in it, he held out his hand for me. But there was an apprehension as his hand hovered above mine.

"What's wrong?"

His lips thinned, but other than that he remained still, coins still clutched in his grasp.

"Kade," I pressed, "tell me."

I didn't know if I would ever get used to our tethering connection and our ability to sense what we felt in each other, but I didn't need to use our bond to see that something was bothering him. His actions, even though minimal, were enough.

"You've changed…since yesterday."

When he didn't continue, I urged him to go on. "So…"

"Never mind." With a shake of his head, he dropped the pieces into my waiting hand and I tucked them into the front pocket of my jeans.

I knew why he was nervous. After the events of yesterday, he had good reason. Not only did I feel different—more powerful, even—but the sight that I was now experimenting with was becoming more prominent. But as long as I had the coins, I should be fine.

Flashing a smile, I gave the coins in my pocket a good pat. I was just grateful that I didn't have to stuff them in my bra again today. With the one I was wearing, there was a good chance the coins would wiggle their way out of there. That had unfortunately happened a time or two. Or more than I cared to admit.

We appeared in the kitchen, and my gaze found two others at work, one at a stove and another chopping fresh fruits. The moment they realized our presence they froze what they were doing to acknowledge us. Recognition set in—I'd seen the gentleman chopping fruit before, and he made his way over to greet us, wiping his hands on his apron.

"What can I do for you two this morning?" If I had to guess, he might be in his thirties, perhaps not that far off from Kade. But I didn't know why I still tried to figure out anyone's age around here. With their shifting abilities, he could be hundreds of years old.

"I don't believe we've formally met. I'm Violet." I held out my hand and I was surprised to see the man glance at Kade, as if he needed some sort of approval to accept my gesture.

"It's just a hand," I whispered lightheartedly, a bit annoyed that he would do that.

"Sorry, I—" He wiped his hands again before accepting it, bowing this go-around. "I'm Lorenz." He was incredibly tan and his shapely hair was molded to perfection.

"Nice to meet you, Lorenz." Placing my hands on my hips, I glanced around the kitchen that was way quieter than I had ever experienced before. But then again, I thought I could count the times I'd been here on one hand. "I was hoping you could point me to a stove that would be out of anyone's way. And perhaps I could bug you for some flour, eggs, milk, and butter. Oh, and a pan and some vanilla extract."

"If you would like some pancakes, I would be more than happy to make some for you."

The smile that flitted across my face came naturally.

"That's alright. I won't pretend I'm a master chef in the kitchen, but I wouldn't mind whipping some up on my own. As long as that's not too much trouble."

"Of course not, let's get you to a station." He beamed before turning, beckoning me to follow him to an unused and empty corner of the kitchen.

Kade disappeared for a moment while Lorenz set me up to cook. He diligently showed me to the cabinets that housed the ingredients I required, and the nearest fridge for the rest of them. Once we'd collected everything, we met Kade back at the stove, only now he had a few strawberries in his hands.

"It's really no trouble. I can make you breakfast if you would like to wait out in the hall." Lorenz tried once more to persuade me, but I waved it off.

"You all do so much already. I appreciate it all, truly. But I've got this, thank you."

"Of course. Please let me know if there's any other way I can be of service." With a pivot of his heel, he left us.

Two more demons had joined us in the vast kitchen. When I made contact with each, they tipped their heads. I flashed my usual and awkward hello, and we all busied ourselves.

"So far, so good?" Kade asked, and I rolled my eyes as I began scooping ingredients into the bowl that Lorenz had nabbed for me.

"So far, so good," I repeated to hopefully put his mind at ease. I hadn't been provided any measuring cups, so I went off of memory, hoping for the best.

"Lorenz was a seeker before he found his love of cooking."

I stole a glance at Kade, my hand shaking as I poured the flour. The white substance spilled onto the counter. "No way."

"Yes way," he teased back.

"But he's so..." I wanted to say friendly, and not

intimidating in the slightest, but I was afraid to admit that out loud in case someone else might hear. He seemed so different compared to Aleena who looked like she could snap literally any person in half. Either by her stare or her sheer strength.

"Remember when I told you that even if you pick an avenue of interest—a certain job, so to speak—you are not bound to that your entire existence?" He leaned forward as he spoke, his voice lower. "He's the perfect example." Kade then proceeded to hop up on the counter and I glared at him.

"What?" His expression shifted to that of confusion.

"Get your ass off of the countertop. We're in a kitchen," I scolded him, but his face was alight with amusement.

"That you are, Kadriel. You should listen to her."

A booming voice carried through the kitchen and I jumped as if the words were spoken right behind me. A rather large man who towered over the both of us had suddenly appeared, no doubt traveling by pocket. He was sleeveless, showing off the black ink of tattoos surrounding his robust arms. His shorts were so tight, it looked as if his thighs were going to rip through them if he flexed.

Kade hopped off the counter and met the man with a shake of his hand and a pat on the back. At least by their reactions to each other, they appeared to be on good terms. I began whisking my batter together as I awaited an introduction.

"Violet, this is Tamian. He's on the guard, and quite the drill sergeant."

"It's a pleasure to formally meet you, Violet. Welcome to Darthou." I couldn't get over how deep his voice was. He would most likely bust the speakers in my old car.

"Thank you, it's nice to meet you too." I paused briefly on his eyes, suddenly grateful for the coins in my possession. Surely a member of the guard had taken lives, right? How bad would seeing it be with him, compared to Kade and Elias?

"Kadriel, haven't seen you in some time. Will you be at the party tonight?"

"Party?" I questioned. "You guys party around here?"

Tamian chuckled and I tried not to let my eyes bulge. "Well, it's the first football game of the season. Elias usually makes a big deal about it."

"As I recall, so do you. Aren't your opposing teams playing tonight?" Kade expressed his knowledge on the subject between his comrades.

I rolled my eyes as I kept whisking, scraping the sides of the metal bowl. The thought of getting out and to a party of any kind had been a promising turn of events.

"Not a fan of football, I take it?" There was no denying that Tamian's words were meant for me, and I looked up at him. He was someone I certainly didn't want to go up against at any point in my life. Now *he* was intimidating.

"Of sports in general. If I know someone playing, then I'll watch. But I just don't get the hype. Especially with football. It's all start, stop, start, stop. Tackle, kick, score. I swear those are the longest games ever created."

He laughed again, causing almost all the heads in the kitchen behind him to glance in our direction, only to hurriedly look away as if they might get in trouble. Except for Lorenz, that is. I noticed how his eyes lingered on Tamian.

"Very well then, she's out. Are you in, Kadriel?"

"You should go," I beat him to the punch, warranting an uneasy look from him. Ever since coming to Darthou, everything had been so serious, from the dramatics of my new life and everything that had spiraled off from that.

Kade needed a reprieve. A night out. *Something* to get his mind off of everything before things picked up again with our upcoming coronation. I knew firsthand that he hadn't been granted any fun such as this since my arrival.

"Maybe not this time," Kade tried to object, but Tamian cut him off, swinging an arm around his shoulders and giving him a squeeze. It was comical to witness.

"Come on, Kadriel, it's been ages since we've all been together. Listen to your tethered mate, maybe she needs a break from you."

This time I let out a small laugh, as it was probably the other way around. Kade used his pocket to pop out of Tamian's grasp, appearing at my side as he straightened himself out. That earned another booming laugh from our guest that swallowed up any sound around us.

"He'll be there." I popped my hip out to the side and bumped Kade playfully.

"Wonderful. Again, it was nice to meet you." Tamian tipped his head and left us, heading over toward Lorenz and whatever he had been working on with the vegetables at another stove.

"What did he mean by *formally* meeting me?" I poured a splash more milk into the bowl, as the batter had become too thick.

"He might have been present at Obsidian Falls the day of your rebirth. It was brief and you were…"

"Dead," I finished for him. That wasn't awkward at all. There was this empty experience that was missing from my memory on that day due to my death, and I hated it. I knew I couldn't be mad at myself for not remembering, but for goodness sake, what all had transpired between when I last laid eyes on Kade in my apartment to waking in the infirmary? It was something that kept me up at night on occasion.

That is, when Kade didn't keep me awake. Unwinding

with him every evening, no matter the time, was one of my favorite activities.

Adding a bit more flour, as my milk had been a bit heavy-handed, I began whisking again.

"How about you get some more of those strawberries? And bananas if you can."

Kade pecked me on the cheek, then let his lips linger on my ear as he whispered a line from another one of my favorite movies. A not-so-subtle reminder of my past, and the time he'd spent watching me.

"As you wish."

CHAPTER 17

Violet

I hadn't meant to feed the entire kitchen, but with the amount of batter I had mixed up, the pancakes needed to be eaten somehow. They could have tasted better, but everyone ate them whether they liked them or not. I was hoping they weren't indulging me just because I was going to be queen in a few days and they were afraid to offend me, but at the same time, it was nice breaking out of the usual routine. Making food myself for a change. Talking with new demons and watching them communicate and tease one another.

They all seemed so…normal. The more I got to know them, the more at ease I felt.

At our tethering celebration, there had been so many people in attendance, so many introductions that it was impossible to keep track of every single one of them. Sure, a few stood out among the rest, but there were many I hadn't been in contact with since.

Lorenz vanished for a couple of minutes, only to return with an assortment of syrups, and I was giddy as could be when I laid my eyes upon the strawberry one he'd collected. The kitchen fell into a hush when he disclosed he had run to a grocery store real quick. It had never dawned on me that demons would visit the human world for such things as syrup. A majority of their fresh produce was taken care of here, but it didn't stop them from retrieving a few other items from my world.

I joked about them having a Costco membership and was met with a roar of laughter, but nobody confirmed or denied my remark.

There were some demons—Lorenz, for example—who had been granted permission to come and go as they pleased due to their occupation here. As long as Lorenz was bringing back supplies or goods for the community here, it was an approved task.

But I still had trouble believing that this lighthearted and dashing man before me used to take lives for a living. I guessed he was a "looks can be deceiving" type of guy.

"Can you come and go whenever you want?" I asked Kade as I popped a stray banana piece into my mouth.

"I can, but it is heavily frowned upon. I guess you could say that I'm kept on a short leash. You know...the crown and all." His voice was quiet as we spoke to each other amongst the chatter in the kitchen.

I was amazed at how the kitchen worked, and at the demons who arrived to get their fixings of food before vanishing. Some lingered a bit or offered a word, while others popped in and out as if they were on a mission and couldn't be bothered with pleasantries. Being here was a nice change of pace. I thought I could get used to mornings like this.

"Is it safe to say that I will be met with the same rules? Even after I…acclimate?"

"Violet," he said, as if in warning, eyes sliding to mine.

"Not to visit my family, I know." I tried to brush off the hurt that threatened to bubble up. "I know I can never visit as myself, but once I conquer my shifts and sustain them for longer periods of time, is it possible for me to go back?"

I moved to the kitchen sink so I could rinse off my plate. Kade had finished his food long before me, practically inhaling it, but I took his dish along too.

He wrestled with himself as he thought of an answer. His stoic face was unwavering while I fought to control my own emotions.

"Perhaps. But now is not the time for that discussion."

All I could manage was a slight nod. It wasn't a rejection, so I would accept that answer for the time being.

"Shall I see if Zan and Sarah are ready for company?"

"Sure." I smiled, even if it didn't reach my eyes.

Lorenz began to approach us, wiping his hands on a towel before throwing it over his shoulder with such precision it was like he knew where it was going to land on the counter behind him.

"Was there any other way I can be of assistance to you this morning? Either of you?" He looked between us as he awaited a response.

But before my voice could find its way out of my throat, a familiar voice cut in.

"Is there a problem?" Jaxana approached, bowing before providing an uneasy half grin. The commotion that had taken over the kitchen was on its way out, a collective hush falling over it with her mere presence.

"Not at all," I tried to reassure her with a sweet smile. I never really knew where I stood with Jacobi's mother.

"We were just on our way out." Kade placed his hand at the small of my back, beginning to lead me out of the way.

"Um…thank you. Everyone. It was nice to meet you all." I tried to offer a polite farewell as Kade weaved me around everyone and out a hidden doorway in the cabinetry. With a push on one of the cupboards, we stepped through into a long corridor.

Once we were out of view, I removed his hand and whipped around to face him. "What the heck was that for?"

Kade only shook his head in warning, offering a raised finger to his lips to silence me before snagging my hand and leading me down the hall. It didn't take long for me to realize that this was the very same hallway I had rushed through on our day of celebration to find the tiniest bit of solace. I anticipated revisiting the throne room, but Kade brushed past it and headed for the next door. Once the door clicked shut, he swiveled to meet me. I almost shrieked at the abruptness.

"Coins, please." His focus narrowed on my pocket where I had stashed them, and I quickly removed them, placing them on a small wooden table just barely within reach.

This room didn't differ much from the one next to it. Furniture pieces were covered, draped in various cloths, but yet there wasn't a single speck of dust to be seen. Someone was keeping up with cleaning around here, even if its contents weren't actively being used. But before I could try to decipher what was hidden beneath each one, Kade stepped into my line of sight.

"What's wrong?" The words left me right as a pulsing wave of want hit me like a blow to my chest, making its way down my body.

Kade closed the gap between us, driving me up against the door. My head made an impact with the solid surface behind me, and when it bounced back off, I met his lips. Hard, pressing, and desperate lips. I took his face in my hands as he hiked one of my legs up, but my jeans weren't very forgiving to the stretch. His hips rocked into me and I moaned into his mouth, appreciative of his evident erection.

Who knew making him breakfast would make him so feral? I should have asked to make pancakes sooner.

My hands twisted into his hair and my lips met his neck. Tilting my head, I kissed down the line toward the collar of his shirt.

I wasn't sure what had brought this on, but I was going to take advantage of the lust that overcame us. Kade deserved it after everything I was putting him through.

Pushing on his chest, I directed him back. I undid the button on his pants and drew his zipper down, quick to grope him through the thin fabric of his boxer briefs. His eyes blazed through mine as a low moan escaped his throat.

"You should sit." I squeezed his erection as I guided him back to a singular chair covered in a dark fabric. The eagerness in his expression only excited me more.

As he sat, I knelt before him and freed his member from its holding. I maintained eye contact as I let my hand stroke it. Slow and steady I worked him, preparing myself to take him in my mouth.

Kade's want was radiating off of him like a furnace, and my face was reddening with its heat. My own body ached for him in return, but for now I only sought his pleasure.

As I took him in my mouth, a sharp hiss left his lips. I teased his tip, tasting him, dragging my tongue slowly across to put on a show. One of his hands fumbled to grip the armrest of the chair while the other came to lay on the side of my face. He stroked my cheek twice before guiding me to take him to the back of my throat.

The ground beneath me was unforgiving on my knees as I moved my upper half. Kade directed me gently as I worked him over, using my hand when my mouth was absent. My cheeks hollowed with each draw and his breaths quickened with excitement.

Peering up at him, I found a man, *my demon*, gearing up to come apart.

"I'm not going to last if you keep this up." There was an edge to his voice, and I continued full steam ahead. As much as I would have liked to break away and straddle him, I squandered that thought for now. I wanted the power of causing his release just from my mouth alone.

I took him as far as I could possibly stand it. My throat threatened to fight back, but his answering groan spurred me to keep going. It drove me wild in the best way, and I fought to continue my sharpening movements.

His hand applied slight pressure to my head, helping to drive me down each time. I let him use me to his liking, taking joy in the sounds emitting from his throat. It was such a turn-on, hearing him become vocal as he chased his climax. He soon found it.

I let him ride the waves of his orgasm, swallowing as I maintained contact to keep up with his slowing thrusts. When his grip loosened on me, I finally let go and wiped off my mouth.

"Fuck," he mumbled as he gazed up at the ceiling, slumping against the back of the chair. All I could hear was his ragged breaths in the empty room.

Kade ran a hand through his hair, the mess a bit longer than I could recall. I couldn't remember the last time I had looked at him—I mean, *really* looked at him—to appreciate the man that he was. The demon that he was.

He was so breathtakingly attractive. And yet mine. All mine.

Tapping.

There wasn't a rhythm to it like when he and Elias communicated to each other, just a dampened sound emitting from his pocket that made me wonder who was trying to get ahold of him. It still felt early in the day, but then I had no idea just how long we had been with Elias this morning and in the kitchen either. Time felt so different in Darthou.

Kade tucked himself away, not bothering to zip himself back up before retrieving his pocket mirror. My hands moved down his inner thighs and muscled calves as he answered.

"Kadriel, we're free if you would like to come by," his aunt's voice came through, and I froze.

"Yes, I can reach out to Aleena. As long as it's alright with you and Violet," Zan spoke up, although he didn't harbor the same chipper attitude as his other half. "That is, if Violet is up for it. Elias said he'd already seen the two of you earlier."

"I'm a bit busy at the moment." Kade's words came out quickly, as if he couldn't be bothered with it. Since my passing out yesterday, his birthday eve had been put on hold, and I felt terrible for it even though he'd had no idea about the little party I'd been planning for him on such short notice, but I wasn't about to let him escape it a second time.

Celebrating Kade was something I wanted to do, and with all the drama that surrounded us, we needed to remember that we were lucky just to be alive. While I understood why it might be painful to think about the past birthday eves he might have cherished with his parents, I thought it was important to try and create new and positive memories so it wouldn't be a night he dreaded, a night that only reminded him of what he and his sister had lost.

Aleena still celebrated her own, even if it had taken a few years after the passing of their parents before she did. But something told me she went a little more all out for herself. She did like the spotlight, which was something I couldn't relate to.

"Just give us ten minutes," I spoke up, but I was met with a look from Kade that told me he clearly wasn't on board with this. I had the feeling he had other plans for us.

"Maybe an hour." Kade's eyes narrowed on me, completely ignoring his family on the other side of the connection.

"Ten minutes, and we'll be there with the cake." Without seeing the image on the screen, I swiped at it, hoping to close it. Judging by the lack of voices after my motion, I must've been successful.

Kade clenched his jaw, studying me. Time was ticking on those ten minutes, and he tucked the mirror back into his pocket before leaning forward.

"I need more than ten minutes with you." His hand was back on my neck, making sure my attention couldn't wander elsewhere.

I was more than turned on. Painfully so. But this little party was more important than the desire that was boiling between us at present.

"You can make it up to me later," I teased, biting my bottom lip, but his thumb was quick to free it. "If you must."

"But I want to do it now." The demand in his voice almost made me crumble before him and surrender. However, there was a small part of me that couldn't let that happen, because then we might not ever get out of here. His family would be joining together without the cake that still sat at home, and a certain sibling of his would be in attendance. A certain bright-haired woman with an immaculate sense of smell.

My stomach did a little tumble.

"You can have me later. But right now, I want to brush my teeth before we see Aleena."

The moment we appeared at Zan and Sarah's place, Ajax and Brighton came barreling toward us. Kade greeted their little attack, scooping them both up with ease. I, on the other hand, moved out of the way for fear of getting knocked over and losing my hold on the cake.

I met Sarah in the kitchen, setting the celebratory dessert on the counter. There were remnants of the kids' breakfast to my left and crumbs on the floor, so I opted to hide out in the kitchen and help clean up until we were all present and ready.

"I am so sorry about last night." I met Sarah at the sink as she retrieved a dish rag.

"Oh, Violet, you don't need to apologize for anything." She beamed an appreciative smile, just as she had yesterday when I'd made the request of a cake for Kade. "I can't tell you how thrilled I am that he's even entertaining the idea at all. You bring out the best in him, you know."

Sarah loved to remind me of this. Sure, Kade had pined over me for years, unable to make a move or meddle in my life until he was released. From the day I had touched my mirror with the smallest amount of blood and set him free, he had practically been a new man. Sarah had repeatedly informed me of that. It was almost as if it was her mission to remind me time and time again of the positive effect I had on him, even though I felt as if I was proving to be more troublesome than any of us could have imagined.

Pushing her sleeves up to her elbows, she washed and I dried. I'd been over here enough that the two of us found our own rhythms in the kitchen and created small talk, covering my visit to the school yesterday and my horrible sense of direction and memory as I navigated the fortress we lived in.

The squeals from the boys in full-on laughter caused the both of us to look over our shoulders. Kade was on the ground and had them pinned down, tickling them relentlessly until Ajax began hitting the floor with the palm of his hand as if he was tapping out.

The boys' faces were reddening with the sudden turn of events, but that didn't stop them from climbing all over Kade like they were monkeys.

"Can we sing 'Happy Birthday' now?" Ajax was clinging around Kade's neck.

"Happy birthday to you…" Brighton began singing. My chest expanded with the affection radiating off of Kade, and when matched with my own, I could have sworn my heart was going to burst. Their little voices joined together in a loud and partially off-key serenade.

Kade stood as they wrapped up their song and thanked them at the end of it, prying them from his body and tossing them playfully onto the giant sectional that took over half of their living room. There were toys scattered about and he had to scoot them out of the way to continue their torment. Their high-pitched screeches and howls soon had Sarah and me both laughing.

"Starting the party without me?" Aleena popped into view

and joined us in the kitchen. She held two bottles of what I assumed to be liquor and set them on the counter next to the cake.

If we'd had the chance to celebrate last night like I had originally intended, it would have made sense. My face betrayed me and it must have been enough to catch Aleena's attention.

"Relax, Violet. One of them is sparkling grape juice." She was still wearing her fiery red hair, but she was dressed more relaxed today with a slightly oversized shirt and leggings.

"And the other?" I questioned her.

"Oh, definitely alcohol."

It was thoughtful to have both options. And I appreciated the fact that even though we were still keeping Aleena at bay with all matters related to my…complications, I was starting to get to know her. The woman that she was. Her cares and interests. She was kind of an awesome sister-in-law.

"Ah, looks like everyone has made it." Zan rounded the corner with Elias at his side. I couldn't help but wonder if they had been discussing me after recent events.

Elias's platinum hair was slicked back as if he had showered recently, but it wasn't fully dry yet. He wore a coordinated sports jersey and shorts, a color combo that reminded me of the game tonight. He was decked out all the way down to his shoes that looked brand-new.

"They playing at your party tonight?" I gestured to his choice of attire, but my query was met with a guarded expression. His eyes slid from mine, to Aleena's, then toward Kade in the other room who was trying to make his way in here. Only then did he allow himself a slight grin.

Elias was so serious in his expressions most of the time. But then again, I was having trouble remembering times when he was around that *I* wasn't the center of trouble.

Even so, I had to admit he had a really nice smile. It made me wonder why he hadn't tethered yet himself. He seemed accomplished, trusted, and loyal. Why hadn't he been snatched up yet?

I wasn't going to pretend to understand Aleena's love life, especially since she had been involved with Rafina in the past. However, I couldn't help but think that Elias might have stronger feelings for Aleena than she might have in return. The two of them made a cute couple, but the only time I had seen the two of them involved and in a "friendly" state hadn't exactly been an occurrence I was meant to see.

"They are, yes." He cleared his throat. "I'm assuming Kadriel told you about it? You're...welcome to come."

I shook my head, sensing his discomfort on the forced invitation. "Tamian might have mentioned the game. Thanks for the invite, but sports aren't really my thing."

I didn't have a single urge to go to that party. Besides, Kade could use a little break from everything we'd been battling lately.

"Kade should be there, though," I offered as I noticed he and the boys were headed to meet us all in the kitchen where we were all congregating.

Elias offered a muttered reply after dropping our eye contact. "Nice."

Aleena was making herself at home in the kitchen, grabbing glasses from cabinets with ease. Sarah was at the other end of the counter collecting some small plates and silverware. It felt odd celebrating a birthday just after breakfast. If it was weird to anybody else in attendance, they didn't say.

"Do we get to sing again?" Ajax slid down Kade's side and climbed up onto a barstool at the counter.

"Does he get a candle?" Brighton was now positioned at Kade's hip. "I can blow it out for you," he offered, and there were a few amused laughs around the room. His small voice was a lot softer than that of his older brother's. I still couldn't get over the family resemblance between Zan, Sarah, and their children.

My mood took a turn at that thought. Kade and I had spoken briefly in my human life about the possibility of children, and while we hadn't fully disclosed whether we wanted them or not, with his impending reign I had little doubt that he would want to continue his family's claim to the throne.

While we were both in agreement that we didn't want them yet, I became worried that we might someday. Before, we had been human and demon, talking about our tethering and the possibilities of a child. Now, we found ourselves in a future that neither of us had planned for. What would it mean for our children, since being a demon was only a sliver of who I was?

Obviously, in the two boys in front of me, demon genetics had been passed down. But could the same be said for the fury and banshee in me? What would happen if a child came into this world with my predisposition? I was already, in lamest terms, hiding who I was. A baby would be an uncontrollable and unpredictable bundle of terrifying joy that would only further my anxiety about, well, everything. I was unlocking a new fear.

First I was going to become queen, then I would be responsible for a possible baby from—

"Violet." Kade's voice broke through my downward spiral and when I met his gaze, I found everyone's attention on me.

"I'm sorry, what?" Embarrassed for zoning out, I tangled my fingers behind my back, completely out of the loop on what had been transpiring around me.

"What would you like to drink?" Aleena butted in without delay, shaking an empty glass back and forth in front of me.

Suddenly, drinking alcohol in the morning didn't seem like such a bad idea. "Wine, please."

Once we all had glasses in hand, Brighton the only exception with a sippy cup, the boys led us all through the birthday song once more. This time, the melody was there, and I noted Sarah's soprano tone beside me. Out of everyone here, she had the most captivating voice. I wondered if she sang lullabies to the boys with such beautiful deliverance.

Kade blew out a single candle with the help of Brighton, and everyone clapped. Ajax was ready to dive in, and took a swipe at the frosting on the side only to be scolded by his father. Even though the time of day was a bit strange for a birthday party, everything else was as normal as it could be. The cake, the song, the gathering of those closest. I hoped it made Kade realize that he was reason enough to celebrate.

"To Kadriel, our soon-to-be king!" Zan boasted loudly, a bit too much for the company we had.

"To Kadriel," we echoed him and toasted each other, then took a drink.

It was obvious that Kade had his sights set on me; no doubt my little episode of concern and stress were on full display for him. It was times like this that our connection was annoying. I couldn't just play it off as being lost in thought. He knew better, and would be inquiring about it later. It was something I wasn't ready to openly discuss yet. Hell, I didn't even like entertaining it in the confines of my own head.

Sarah began cutting the cake, using the blade of the knife to scoop it onto plates, and slices were passed around. I noted how Ajax was all about the frosting, while his brother was scooping the cake into his mouth so fast it was a miracle he was able to chew at all.

Kade made his way around and I stilled, trying to focus on the piece of lemony goodness I had stuck my fork in. It was an airy mixture that smelled divine now that it was before me. I shoveled it into my mouth as his hand came around my waist. He held his plate out and away so he could lean in. Lips brushed past my ear as my chewing slowed. "Everything okay?"

I couldn't lie to him, but this wasn't exactly the time or place for the truth.

"Later," I mumbled, after I worked to swallow. The cake was nothing but divine, and I almost wanted to devour it like the little ones in front of me. "We had a less than ideal start to our morning, and I never formally wished you a happy birthday."

I mustered up the best smile I could, hoping it would help curb his curiosity. He wouldn't be one to forget, that I knew. "So happy birthday."

Kade's fingers dug into my side with slight pressure, and I paused, stealing glances at the other party guests who were all involved in their own conversations.

"You know you didn't have to do this."

"I did." My voice quieted in response to his. "I wanted to."

"And what if my birthday wish was to simply be inside you tonight?"

"You can still do that." My mouth was going dry, and I reached for my wine, not that it would help. "*After* you go to the party."

There was an annoyance that didn't go unnoticed, and he removed his hand. "And what are you going to do while I'm away?"

"How about she hangs out with me? I'm not going to the

football party." Aleena downed the rest of her drink and snatched up the bottle on the counter, polishing it off. There was a bouncy pep in her step as she joined us.

"No training?" I questioned her, intrigued.

"None, unless you really want to."

I couldn't suppress my excitement. I had no idea what she might have in store, but it would be nice to be with Kade's sister without the whole training bit looming over us.

"Count me in, yes. I would love to." The words came out in a gush.

"As long as you don't get into any trouble," Kade butted in, possibly even more perturbed now.

There was an upturn in the corner of his sister's mouth, one that held a hint of wickedness. "Oh, Kadriel, don't be a buzzkill."

CHAPTER 18

Violet

After Kade's party, Zan and Sarah were off to take Ajax to school, and Brighton tagged along. Elias and Aleena remained at opposite sides of the group at all times and never uttered a word to each other, but they each took their own turns conversing with us. I was hoping that if I got close enough to Aleena, maybe someday I could ask her what was going on between them.

Kade wasn't exactly forthcoming with any information pertaining to them, just the usual "it's complicated" and "I try not to get in the middle of it." I could understand his stance, seeing as he was literally in the middle of it between his sister and best friend. I wasn't exactly the meddling type, but for whatever reason, having those two on the outs felt odd, considering how Kade had mentioned that they all were so close. That he trusted his life with the two of them. How could that still hold true if they weren't even on speaking terms?

After snagging some lunch from the kitchens, Kade returned me home just to go off and tend to more business. I snacked on my food between reading a book, rummaging through my closet for something to wear tonight, and pacing around our main bedroom area.

At one point, I considered what it might be like to gut our home and add a kitchen, but I had difficulty visualizing how we could turn this giant bedroom into more. Zan had done so with Sarah, and from what I gathered, without hesitation. It would be nice to have our own kitchen and not have to depend on their version of room service, or having to go to the kitchens to retrieve food. Maybe I might think differently one day, once I could travel by myself, but for now, I missed the small touch of something I had never gone without until I came to Darthou.

It wouldn't even have to be anything extravagant. It wasn't like I was planning on hosting parties and feeding dozens of people, but if I could just have a small little setup like my old apartment, that would be enough.

Sitting on the edge of the bed, I glanced about the space I had come to call home. The main focal point, and the piece that always drew my focus regardless of what was on my mind, was the stained glass windows. Even though I couldn't see out of them, the light that filtered through was a beauty that I loved to get lost in. That was something I was adamant wouldn't be touched in here. The garden outside, too, was perfect. Perhaps when things settled down—or better yet, *if* things ever settled down—Kade and I could talk through some possible changes around here.

As much as I wanted it to, it still didn't fully feel like home.

He'd told me over and over again that if there was anything I wanted or needed changed, all I had to do was say the word. But I didn't want to take over and make things over in my image. I wanted to find a balance between the two of us. After all, we had come from two entirely separate worlds.

There was a knock at the door, and I stilled as my head twisted in its direction. I hadn't been expecting any company, but then the only ones who normally came by were family, with the exception of Rebecca who would bring our clothes once they'd been washed, fixed, altered or repaired in any way. Occasionally she would toss in a few more items if she thought I might approve. It was always a sweet gesture to be thought of in that way.

The knocking sounded again, and I made a beeline for the bathroom to retrieve my coins. I didn't bother hollering that I was on my way with the place being soundproof. I opened the door, but didn't find the seamstress. It was someone who made my stomach fall to my feet.

"Hello, Violet." Rafina barely tilted her head as she stood before me. The white dress she wore was modest but still breathtakingly stunning on her figure. Her hair was swept up into a high ponytail, but it still showed its great length. "I heard you have been unwell, is everything alright?"

"Um…I'm fine. I'm not sure I know what you mean."

Rafina had never shown up at our home before. And now a house call out of the blue? That, and the fact that she thought something might be wrong with me, made me wonder who in the hell might have led her to believe that in the first place.

I had an urge to avoid eye contact with her, but thankfully with my coins on me I could meet her stare anyway. She gave nothing away, acting like she cared for my well-being like she always did in our weekly encounters. The sweet smile that others might have thought was genuine wasn't fooling me.

"I'm available now if you would like to get this week's session over with. I'm sure you and Kadriel have packed schedules with the upcoming coronation."

I bit the tip of my tongue, weighing my options. It wasn't like I was doing anything of importance right this minute, and the thought of getting this over with now and out of the way was somewhat promising, though unexpected. The only thing stopping me was that Kade had no idea about this, and I'd told him I wouldn't leave until he returned. If it was anybody who'd been present at his party earlier, I wouldn't have a second thought about it and I would go. The problem was, it was fucking Rafina.

"Kade and I weren't expecting it today—perhaps we should keep it for tomorrow as planned."

But then again, Kade was supposed to go to the Summit thing tomorrow and he would need his head clear of all things coin related so he could focus. While I hated to admit it, getting it done today would be more beneficial to him in the long run.

Rafina was about to take her leave, until I stammered out my changed decision.

"Actually—" She ceased mid-turn and waited for me to continue with my inward dilemma. "Better yet, maybe you're right. Let's get it done today."

Kade would be able to find me, but hearing the ringing sound from the coins might be worrying enough when he hadn't expected me to leave at all. I would beg for forgiveness later if I had to, but I was doing this so he could have his head on straight tomorrow.

As I closed the door behind me, Rafina grinned. I could have sworn the temperature around me dropped about ten degrees. She had this fake, too-nice persona that she used at our weekly meetings, but I didn't really have any other option than to go along with it.

With her hand on my shoulder, we appeared in the infirmary. I hopped up onto my usual slab and placed my hands in my lap as I awaited for her to begin the usual line of questioning that she did each week.

How are you feeling? Any changes you're concerned about? How are your trainings with Aleena? Any lingering side effects?

"Are you nervous for the coronation?"

My reflection on past visits skidded to a halt. I blinked at her a few times, trying to focus on the question I hadn't anticipated. She had caught me off guard with that one.

"The coronation?" I repeated back to her, suddenly unsure about this unscheduled visit.

"Yes, it's a very big day. Bigger than your tethering celebration." She slowly clasped her hands together in front of her.

"So I hear." I swallowed. "I'm nervous, of course. I haven't even met all of the demons in Darthou, and now there's creatures coming from all over for this."

She studied me for a moment, remaining still. I couldn't even see the rise and fall of her chest. "Understandable."

A long pause fell between us, and my fingers began to tangle. I internally scolded myself before flattening them out on my lap. I looked around the room, practically at anything but her. Nothing was ever out of place here; it was neat and orderly, never a mess in sight.

"Are you cold?" Another query threw me off.

"W…why do you ask?" I tried not to let my stutter and frustration read on my face.

"You're dressed rather warmly." She pointed to my sweater as she crossed her arms. I was normally in workout gear when

I came to these meetings, so I ran with that.

"Well, I hadn't planned on going anywhere today. This was just a comfy, lounge-around option."

Rafina's dress showed off most of her arms and her collarbones, and its length stopped just above the knee. Her dainty white flats showed no scuffs or wear and tear on them. Everything about her was polished to perfection.

And here I was in a sweater and jeans, laid-back and casual because…well, come to think of it, I was kind of cold.

Perhaps when I made it back home I could take a dip in the hot tub in the garden. That would be super comforting right about now. Anywhere else would be better than this at present.

Rafina took a step forward and held out her hand, and I placed one of mine in hers. She pressed her two fingers to my pulse, and we sat in silence until she was finished. I noted how icy her fingers felt, much the same as when Kade first arrived in my world. If I could feel the difference between our temperatures, I knew it was blatantly obvious to her as well.

That was when it dawned on me.

Something had changed within me now that the furies had accepted me. Not only was my sight stronger and more frequent, but it had messed with my body temperature too. I only hoped that Rafina wouldn't bring this change up before the council. I didn't want to jeopardize anything when it came to Kade's reign that we were drawing so close to. Something that had been years in the making and predated me.

I was antsy as I waited for her to bring it up. This week's visit was entirely different, and unfortunately so. I should have stayed home. I should have said no and see you tomorrow and informed Kade about her unexpected arrival.

"Violet," she said, pulling me out of my spiral.

"Yes?" I raised my brows, a bit too quick in my response as I almost cut her off.

"You know you can talk to me about anything. I'm not the enemy."

My eyes narrowed at her choice of words. From the start, I had never called her an enemy, but when I wasn't around her, I sure treated her like one. The chorus of screams I'd been greeted with upon our first meeting in this very infirmary had solidified that. I couldn't tell if it was that very recollection that made my stomach start to turn, or if it was something else unfurling deep within me.

One might think I had stomach issues with everything it put me through.

"I never said that you were." The air between us grew uncomfortable.

"Well, something is the matter, your raised body temperature tells me that."

Dammit.

If she was trying to back me into a corner, it was working. I had no idea how to get myself out of this one. I knew the chances of me leaving on my own accord were slim with the coins in my possession, and stress began to creep across every inch of me.

"It's highly unusual, and a bit troubling. I would like to draw some blood—"

"No." I was firm in my interruption. I hadn't even given her the chance to turn away from me. "I don't like needles."

Her demeanor shifted, her friendly face now gone from view. "It's harmless, I assure you. I can heal you as I do it."

"And I said no." I hopped off of the counter and crossed my arms. "You've never asked to draw blood before. Perhaps I just have a chill."

Her head tilted to the side, studying me. I hated it. Like I was some sort of specimen trapped in a cage. And maybe I was. The infirmary certainly presented itself as a cage.

"It's not *normal*, Violet."

"I'm fine." I crossed my arms as if it could create a barrier between us. "We all know that I didn't have a *normal* transition in the first place. So why are you just now wanting a blood draw?"

"New symptoms showing up this late after your transition are cause for concern." Her lips thinned as she took a step forward. I straightened my back, but I still couldn't meet her height. "You wouldn't want to do anything to risk the coronation, now would you?"

My face cracked, even if for only a fraction of a second. But it was enough to know that she witnessed it in its entirety. I had no idea what my blood would tell her, if anything. Would there be some sort of markers of other creatures in my blood? If Rafina really had nothing to do with my transition and rebirth, would this be the thing that outed me to everyone?

I didn't know much about demons, but while some were more than accepting of human-to-demon tetherings, there were those who were still opposed. What the hell would they do if they found out that their soon-to-be queen was a compilation of different beings?

"In your expert opinion, what could my change in body temperature mean?"

She shook her head as if amused. "Demons rarely get sick, Violet."

"Then what do you need healers for? Just battle wounds?"

"Again, let me remind you that I am not the enemy."

"And yet you keep using that word," I spat back at her. "While we're at it, how about you tell me about the 'change' you referred to several weeks ago."

"When you learn to trust me." Her voice rose, only infuriating me more, and mine rose higher.

"When have you ever given me reason to?" I was only a foot away from her at this point, and as close to her face as I dared to get. She didn't even flinch at my surfacing anger. Instead, she kept her facial expression cold and empty and turned away, putting some distance between us, a whole slab to be exact.

My heart was pounding wildly and out of control, the pit in my stomach opening, and I wanted nothing more than to remove my coins and meet Rafina head-on. I didn't know what I might see when I looked into her eyes, but I was growing impatient waiting to find out.

"If you are not the enemy, then who is?" I spoke through gritted teeth, my words laced with frustration. The only enemies in my mind were the one who had slaughtered all of those creatures in Darthou, and Damian. If Rafina had nothing to do with either of them, then she was no one I would concern myself with right now. But her actions and words in my short time since knowing her did nothing to help change my view of her.

"I think we're done for today." Rafina's voice carried an authoritative tone.

Panicked by the news she might bring to the council if we parted on these terms, I began to backpedal slightly.

"Not if you're going to throw a wrench into Kade's coronation."

"It's your coronation too, remember." She whipped around, her hair a blond flash that swayed with the movement.

As if I could forget. Queen. The very word was terrifying, but I couldn't let it show.

"There has never been a king or queen of mixed descent. You will be the first." Her voice was gentle now, as if she was treading lightly.

"But I am a demon. I was reborn."

"And your body temperature is reason enough to believe that you are not *all* demon."

I held my breath, unsure of how to follow that. How was I to know that something so minimal to me such as a difference in my temperature was enough of a giveaway that something had gone awry with my transition?

"What else would I be?" I tested her, waiting to see if she would bite.

But there wasn't a flicker of emotion. No glimmer or glimpse that she might know. "The sooner you learn to trust me, the sooner we can figure that out."

Her answer was not what I wanted to hear, nor was it what I expected out of her. It was like there were two sides to her, and I never knew which one was going to come out to play. She could be intimidating and forceful one minute, kind, caring, and relaxed the next. These mixed signals told me that I still shouldn't trust her. Especially when she was ambitious enough to try and get me to do exactly that.

"Trust is earned. I will not give it blindly."

Rafina took a few moments to ponder that, as if mulling something over in her head. "Then let me take the first step."

She tilted her chin ever so slightly. "I will not speak of this to the council, so the coronation can move forward as planned. But—" She held up a finger to draw attention to whatever she was going to deliver. "Should this temperature of yours worsen or get out of hand, I expect you to come to me."

Eyeing her warily, I wasn't easily convinced that this olive branch of hers was worth it. Or that my body temperature was as big of a deal as she was making it seem.

"I wouldn't want anything to tamper with your tethering with Kadriel."

I hated to admit it, but she was good. She cut through to me with that last statement, and it was almost enough to crack my exterior. Little did she know the trials our tethering had already put him through, from the moment he experienced phantom symptoms of the bullets that had caused my death, to Zan trying to dig up our tethering cord to see if we still had our connection. Add in the constant pain of the ringing Kade had to go through each and every time I wore the coins, and I was definitely putting him through the wringer.

Was I really worth all of it? Was he really any stronger since we had joined together? It felt as if I was doing more harm than good, even if he might never admit it.

"I think I'm ready to go home now." I let my head hang a bit in defeat, uncomfortable with the thoughts rolling through my head. "You've…given me a lot to think about."

It was my intention to give her a fragment of hope that I might be leaning toward trusting her in the future, even if I didn't right now. If I could get her to believe that, maybe she really would follow through with the action she spoke of.

"Of course. Until we meet again." Rafina rounded the slab and placed a hand on my shoulder, transporting me back to the hallway before my door. She had whisked me off and away alone, and I was exponentially grateful and relieved to be out of her presence.

I made my way in, kicking my shoes off as I continued to the bathroom to rid myself of my coins. I reached into my pocket to retrieve the pieces, and the light clink of them hitting together made me look down.

On the edge of one of them, a small crack was beginning

to form on the surface. As I glided my nail across it, it caught, and my heart leapt up into my throat. I wanted to believe that it was nothing more than a minor imperfection from wearing them so often, a blemish from wear and tear.

But something inside of me stirred, recalling my reaction in the infirmary with Rafina. The turn of my mood that caused me to lose my temper, that gut feeling I had experienced from time to time.

Deep down I knew it wasn't a coincidence, and I feared what this small crack could mean.

CHAPTER 19

Violet

The second Kade entered his watching quarters, I could tell. The familiar feeling of his closeness sent me dashing down the hall and I began knocking rapidly until he opened the door.

He swung it open, eyes wide and a look of frustration on his face. What I hadn't expected was the half a dozen demons behind him, including Elias, who all turned in my direction at my intrusion.

"I'm sorry, I didn't realize you weren't alone." I kept my voice quiet, shying away from the doorway. Kade stepped through, leaving the door open just a crack.

"Is everything alright?" There was an edge to his voice that I didn't like, an urgency that put me on edge.

"I guess I should be asking you that." I glanced around him

once more, not recognizing the rest of them. "Is it Damian?"

No wait, scratch that. Lorenz and Tamian were a part of the group.

Kade's eyes closed briefly, as if pained by the name. Noliathan and Damian might be one and the same, but I was sure it didn't make Kade hurt any less knowing that he was responsible for the death of his parents.

"We're coming up with a plan for Damian and the saints. Elias and I have rounded up some watchers and seekers to get a head start on things since the council has been less than helpful. We want to hit the ground running after the coronation."

I nodded. "Is there anything I can do to help?"

He cupped the side of my face and I leaned into it, comforted. Unfortunately, I knew by his demeanor that the answer was no.

"We're short on time, the football game starts soon." Tamian's distinct voice had no trouble reaching my ears.

"Yeah, we don't want anyone getting suspicious if we're late," another chimed in, but I couldn't see who that voice belonged to.

"Then that's my cue to get ready to meet with your sister."

"Is everything alright? Earlier—"

I pressed my lips to his to silence him, hoping to stifle his worry so he could try not to focus on what he undoubtedly had sensed of my encounter with Rafina. When I backed away, he was puzzled.

I brushed a stray curl of his dark hair away from his forehead, but it only fell back into its place. I wondered how close he was to needing to tie it back, or if he would even let it get to that point.

"I'll talk to you later about it. Go take care of things and try to have some fun at the party. You deserve a chance to unwind."

"I can think of other ways," he mused rather wickedly. The mere thoughts racing through my head made every muscle in my body clench.

"You can come find me when you're done." I kissed him once more before pulling away.

"You can bet on that." It didn't take much for him to spark desire in my blood, and I knew he fully intended to follow up with how we had left things after breakfast.

"Now go, they're waiting on you." Turning on my heel, I returned to our closet and began rummaging through it again.

I had no idea what Aleena would have in store for tonight, if we would just stay in or if we might venture out once more. I'd loved visiting the school, but then we had been on the clock, so to speak, as it was technically a time for instruction.

Opting to keep my jeans, I found a gray, long-sleeve shirt with a low V-neck that revealed some cleavage. If there was a chance we were going anywhere, it was appropriate without being too much, and if we stayed in, it would be comfortable enough to unwind and relax.

I placed the black obsidian necklace around my neck and clasped it, letting the bar rest on my chest. Its cool temperature was a stark reminder of Rafina's discovery of my change.

Did she really have no idea that there was fury and banshee within me? Before today, I would have sworn up one side and down another that she was responsible for it all somehow. But now I was questioning that. Was that her purpose? Did she intend for me to start second-guessing everything? I had been so sure, and now doubt was seeping in at a rapid pace.

I shook my head, as if I could do the same with my train of thought. I wanted to have fun with Aleena tonight, no matter what we did. I didn't want to dwell on what-ifs and endless possibilities.

Seizing the coins from the bathroom counter, I examined them again. I flipped them over in my hand, my attention centered on the jagged crack that I hadn't noticed prior to today. I drew in a deep breath as I sent up a silent prayer to who knows what, that they would continue to do their work as they were supposed to. I couldn't afford any slip-ups, not when Rafina was already suspicious.

I had chosen to keep my hair down in the hopes that it would provide a little warmth, and I fluffed it out and over my shoulders. I stowed lipstick in my pocket should I need it and left, turning off the lights and firmly closing each door that I passed through. I made my way down the short distance to Aleena's door, knocking three times.

Aleena greeted me within about two seconds, wearing nothing more than a robe. Her hair was dark, like I'd seen when Kade had delivered the news about Damian. It was odd seeing her hair in what I imagined to be her natural color, but it suited her. Honestly, I didn't know if there was a color that she couldn't pull off.

Her face was alight with excitement as she greeted me and pulled me into her home. There was music playing as she dragged me in, the atmosphere as inviting as she was right now. I came to a stop as she spun around, releasing me. She was in high spirits, I'd give her that. It was uplifting and refreshing.

Her bed remained unmade, pillows and blankets all thrown about in a shape that I could only assume she would sleep in the middle of. She rarely, if ever, picked up before I visited. I didn't know if that was because she was comfortable around me or if she just didn't care. Either way, it didn't matter.

"I was thinking," she began, and I eagerly awaited to hear what plans she had for us. "If you want to stay in that's fine, but I had another idea. If you're uncomfortable with it, just say so."

Well, color me intrigued.

"Go on," I pressed.

"Well, I know Kade was wanting you to meet other creatures at the Summit tomorrow and that plan fell through. But what if you could meet some tonight?"

I was overly cautious as to how I reacted, trying to pull out my inner actress with curiosity and confusion. "I'm not sure I follow. What did you have in mind?"

I was a bit uneasy at the thought of not having Kade by my side as he had been any other time I was in the presence of other creatures. Creatures that Aleena had no idea I'd met, or that I was more familiar with them than she knew.

"Well..." She clasped her hands together. "There's this place in Torenca—think of it as a type of club—where all creatures can gather without fear of ridicule."

"Is it legal?" I asked, suddenly unsure of her plans. Torenca sounded familiar, though. I thought it was another demon kingdom, if memory served me right.

A lighthearted laugh erupted from her throat, but it didn't do much to put me at ease. "It is in your terms, yes. It's sort of a...how do I put it? A place where you can be free to act like you want, say what you feel, and carry out your darkest desires all in one place."

"Didn't Kade say not to get into any trouble?" I pushed back lightly. While I was heavily intrigued, especially about visiting another kingdom, doing it without Kade didn't feel right. Even if it was with his sister.

Aleena rolled her eyes. "If it helps, he's been there before.

And I go pretty frequently by myself." She opened a rather large black chest that had wheels on the end of one side. "It might also be where I tend to unload some of my creations."

The chest was chock-full of garments in different materials and fabrics. Some had tassels, some were made of lace, others of leather from what I could tell. The assortment of colors had me reaching into it and I pulled out a yellow lacey piece that was oddly shaped. I wasn't even sure how one was supposed to wear it.

"What is this even supposed to cover?" I asked as I held it out.

"Not much, that's the point," she offered with another giggle. That, I could clearly see.

I picked up another number, a turquoise one that shimmered as it caught the light. Its fabric was more stiff, a bit more structure to it but not quite strong enough to be considered a corset.

"So this is what you meant by helping me with any undergarments." I knew by her own admission that she had worked alongside Rebecca and learned all that she had to offer when it came to sewing and designing. But Aleena had gone out on her own path, choosing a bit more risqué avenue when it came to dressing. "Do you sell these there?"

"Oh no, I just give them away."

"You what?" I shot her an incredulous look. "You're joking. There's got to be dozens of items in here and you just *give* them away?"

She nodded. "I'm not driven by the need or want for money. I love doing this. I don't expect anything in return."

I was dumbfounded, but in the best way. To go through all of the trouble to make these just to give them away?

"That's kind of amazing, Aleena."

"Oh, stop." She waved her hand as if it were nothing. "So how about it? Want to live life a little on the edge tonight? Get out of Darthou?"

When she put it that way, I perked up a bit. I mean, it wasn't like I was going alone. I was sure if anything were to go south, she would protect me. And I had trouble seeing how she would ever think about voluntarily putting the future queen of Darthou in any kind of dangerous or unnecessary situation.

"Ah, that got your attention, didn't it?" That wicked smile of hers spread across her lips and I tried not to seem too overzealous. I wasn't sure Kade would approve, and if I had transitioned to a demon and nothing more, perhaps I wouldn't be faced with the hard decision before me now.

I knew with Aleena by my side, no harm would come to me. And even though I was a bit concerned about the crack in one of my coins, I didn't want to miss out on this chance to hang out with her. To get to know her outside the concrete confines of Darthou.

"Let's do it."

CHAPTER 20

Violet

Who knew that my hair was capable of such volume? The wavelike wand and product combo Aleena had used on me was quite the duo, I'd give her that. But while my head was covered with lustrous tresses, Aleena was sleek and refined with her hair smoothed back. We were total opposites.

She was more heavy-handed with the makeup tonight, compared to the last time she'd had complete control of the brushes and my face. She was incredibly quick with contouring and winged eyeliner, which I'd never mastered. While I had my doubts about the bold, darker color she opted for on my lips, I had to admit it managed to pull the whole look together.

What she had selected for me to wear, however, was an entirely different matter.

"You can't be serious." I looked at her in shock when she

retrieved the pieces from her creative design corner.

"Do I look like I'm kidding?" She popped a hip out to the side as she waited for me to take the garments.

"Maybe all your shifting yesterday has gone to your head. Where did I agree to go tonight? A strip club?"

"Well…" Aleena pursed her lips as her gaze left me.

"Aleena," I all but scolded, but she apparently only found humor in the situation.

"Relax, you don't have to go anywhere you're not comfortable with."

That wasn't exactly a no on the strip club. What had I signed myself up for?

While it was great seeing this side of Aleena, I was beginning to have my doubts. I had no idea just where we were headed, or how far away from Darthou it was. When you could travel by mirror and pocket, the space between seemed so insignificant.

"If you're curious, we'll venture out a bit. We won't do anything or go anywhere that makes you uncomfortable."

I wasn't quite sure how to respond, seeing as I literally had no idea just what I had agreed to. While Aleena's heart might have been in a good place, wanting to introduce me to some different creatures prior to the coronation, I didn't know what she expected or what her intentions were for the evening. Sure, she was apparently planning on doling out scandalous outfits for free, but you couldn't tell me that was the only item on her agenda. Especially if we were both going to be dressed in her creations too.

"Or we can stay in, if this is too much."

I must have blanched, as I was getting lost in my own head again, drowning with uncertainty and self-preservation. Doing my best to push all the negative thoughts aside, I took charge and snatched the garments from her hand, hustling off for the bathroom.

Aleena whistled as I hightailed it out of sight. I made quick work ridding myself of my clothes and slipping into a number that I wouldn't normally leave home in.

The black leather skirt was fitted but zipped up the side with ease, settling low on my hips. The corset was mostly see-through at the sides, with patches of lace across the breasts and upward to my shoulders. The vibrant green straps of the garment were barely an inch wide, but I assumed once the back was fastened, it would help lift my breasts and secure them.

"I guess I need a little help," I called out as I held the fabric to my front. There was no way I was getting in or out of this without an extra set of hands. My bra was definitely a no-go and I slipped it off.

"Yes, you do." Aleena bounced around the corner and into view. "Stand up straight."

I did as instructed and watched as she intently began hooking strands of emerald ribbon through the back and began to cinch me in. I always imagined that being corseted would be painful, but it wasn't as bad as I'd expected it to be. Pull by pull, she fastened me in until the swell of my breasts filled the top of the material.

Now that she was nearly finished, I could really see the lines of the garment. It was slimming, drawing your attention toward my bosom and then directing your attention down in a V-shape. There was a sheen of gold amongst the nude parts that I'd thought held no hue, but it was mesmerizing as she gazed over my shoulder.

"You have no idea how long I've been waiting to dress a figure like yours." Aleena beamed as she stepped to my side, crossing her arms as she looked me over and examined her work in her bathroom mirror. "You look fucking delectable."

I could have been dressed for the Moulin Rouge in this creation of hers. But I had to admit, even I might fuck me at this point.

"I don't think I would have ever given this the time of day if it weren't for you. It's absolutely stunning."

"Correction, *you* are stunning. The garments only flaunt your assets." She mimicked a chef's kiss and left a few words as she departed. "Let me change and we'll get going."

I turned from side to side, admiring myself in the mirror. Not only were my breasts lifted and on display, but my ass looked amazing as well. I fixed my hair, drawing some of it over my shoulders so it hid the straps, making my outfit—if I could call it an outfit—appear even more scandalous than it already was.

I argued with myself about whether or not to change my hair color, and decided what better time to try it out than right now? After all, I didn't really feel or look like myself, so why not?

Focusing on my roots, I let a jet-black shade take over, sweeping over me and filling out all the way to the ends. Turning my head this way and that, I made sure that every inch of my strawberry-blond hair was covered. It added an edge that I'd never been brave enough to try out in high school, and I decided to just go for it.

Once I was satisfied with my shift, I began to fold my clothes, and my coins slipped from my pocket. They dropped to the floor before I could catch them, the metallic sound as they bounced off the floor and scattered sending me into a panic. My movement was restricted as I attempted to bend over, so I had to kneel to collect them. I had just barely shoved them into my bust as Aleena rounded the corner and we came face-to-face.

That was a close one.

"Love the hair, we'll both be dark beauties tonight."

She wore a lace halter that bared her toned midsection; it was a mixture of baby pink and black that displayed ample cleavage. I was a tad jealous of her long black pants. Even though they were skintight, I would have preferred that to a skirt. Aleena fastened a choker around her neck that seemed too stiff to be fabric, and flashed a smile as she looked me up and down again. She reached around the corner and pulled out a pair of boots.

"I know you're not a fan of heels, so hopefully these will do." She knelt down and I stepped into them one at a time, and she fastened them up for me. Thank goodness they weren't high, and the wedges on them ensured more balance.

"What exactly did I agree to?"

She did nothing to hide her amusement. "How do you feel about public displays of affection?"

I was taken aback for a moment. "Like, hugging, kissing—"

"Fucking." She crossed her arms under her chest, pushing her breasts up even more as she waited for an answer.

"People do that? In public?"

"Some do, yeah. We'll try to stay in the center of the hub and you don't have to venture out anywhere you don't want to."

I stared at her blankly, stunned at the unknown world I was about to walk into. I'd thought I was just going to be meeting some different creatures and standing alongside Aleena as she doled out her creations, but now I was starting to wonder if I should be doing this at all.

"Come on, it's really not that bad." She took my hand and

led me out of her bathroom. "Unless you want it to be."

With a wink, she used her free hand to shut her trunk and latch it, then picked it up by a handle on the side so it was brought up to its wheels.

"Ready?"

"Jury's out on that one," I said nervously. I only hoped Kade wasn't picking up on it; I didn't need him rushing over here. I wasn't sure what he would think about seeing me dressed like this and going out in public. And without him to boot.

In a blink, we were in a dimly lit room with music filtering in through a large metal door. The walls were covered in dark drapery, and I couldn't make out any windows. Just a room with a single door, and nothing more than a chandelier that hung in the center. If I had to guess, it sounded like this club might lie on the other side.

"Just relax, you're here to explore. Enjoy it!" Aleena's heels clicked as she made her way to the door, and she banged on it four times in a row, evenly spaced. A metal slide moved over and a set of glowing red eyes came into view. Eyes that reminded me of the witch in Xandor.

Without a word from either of them, the metal seal slammed shut, and I could hear gears clunking as mechanisms were being used. When the door swung open, a tall and slender woman dressed in some kind of wrap stood with arms wide open as the music loudened and filled our space.

"Bonsoir, Aleena!" When she spoke, her accent was thick on her tongue.

The two bumped cheeks on each side before they embraced as if they were good friends, squeezing each other instead of the awkward pat on the back that I sometimes witnessed between others. Then the red eyes landed on me and my breath stalled.

"And who do we have here?" She studied me with careful precision.

I crossed my arms uncomfortably in front of my midsection. It was one thing to be dressed like this in front of Kade's sister, another to be showing it off to who knows who. I should have asked for a cover-up or something. Although, surprisingly, I wasn't cold anymore, which was a nice change since I'd been bundled up most of the day.

"This—" Aleena scooted me forward so I came to stand before the woman who towered over me. "Is Violet. Kadriel's tethered. I'm hoping to introduce her to life outside of Darthou before the coronation. He's been keeping her all to himself."

"Ah…well, any friend of Aleena is most welcome here." She moved with such grace, skimming across the floor as she made her way over and offered me the same greeting, minus the hug. She smelled of something woodsy, but there was a floral undertone I couldn't quite place. "I am Brigitte."

"Nice to meet you." I offered a shy smile as she looked between the two of us.

"I can sense your nerves." Her head cocked to the side, the hair that framed her face never swaying from its place. "Please know we welcome all. You can merely observe if you wish. Your involvement is your choice. This is a place where we can gather together and be our truest selves without holding back."

I nodded in understanding. So far, not so bad, but we hadn't even stepped through the door yet. The door that held no light, just a black abyss.

"Are you headed to the hub? I see you have some gifts with you this evening." She gestured toward the chest that was sitting upright, and it was then that I noticed how crazy long her fingernails were.

"We are," Aleena spoke up. "Figure that would be a good spot to make some introductions and kind of dip her toes in."

"Of course, follow me."

Aleena directed me to follow as Brigitte exited through the door. Though hesitant, I followed blindly into the darkness. Once through the threshold, I could start to make out the stone walls that formed around us. We were in some sort of tunnel, with a blue light filtering in from up ahead, almost calling us toward the music that filled my ears. The sounds of our steps and the trailing of the chest behind me was soon drowned out by what sounded like a live performer, a woman singing a slow tune that was hauntingly beautiful.

I began to notice carvings on the walls, some symbols, some words. From what I could tell, they were in different languages, and I moved closer to try and inspect them.

"What are all of these markings?" I asked as I slowed, tracing my fingers over one of them.

"Some are enchantments to protect us, others are messages from those who found what they were looking for here," Brigitte said as she came to a stop, and we all stood still as she began to point to a few. "Freedom. Acceptance. Thank you." Then her gaze fell upon me as she gestured to another. "I don't have to hide anymore."

I froze, staring at the phrase on the wall. I couldn't help but wonder if that was really what it translated to at all. Did Brigitte know about me? Or worse, could she tell from my mere presence that I wasn't just a demon? What if she had some sort of power like the witch from Xandor that allowed her to see more than anything surface level?

I couldn't shake the feeling that she might be onto me. It didn't help that I had another witch's coins hidden in my clothing. I had no idea if she could sense that or not.

The rest of our walk was quiet, except for the music that constantly grew louder. The blue light grew thicker, illuminating the mouth of the hallway as it opened up to a giant room filled with people—or better yet, creatures—of all shapes and sizes. Some were hanging in the air, others listening to a woman on a small stage. The different heights, features, and skin colors were fascinating, and though I didn't mean to, I came to a complete halt, causing Aleena to bump into me.

"Come on." Aleena grinned as she took my hand and we began following the path Brigitte made through the crowd. She didn't seem so tall now that we were in here among countless others.

It was almost like an auditorium with the high ceilings and the acoustics that were perfect for the silver-haired woman on stage. Splotches on her skin shimmered in the lights as she sang into the mic, and some in attendance hung on every word, as if they were in some sort of trance.

Aleena offered a few greetings as we passed, and as we were exiting through a doorway in the back, I noticed that we had a line of followers behind us. Mostly women, from what I could tell. They were a giggling bunch that didn't seem to be speaking English, but it would appear that they were having a good time. One of them had demon eyes, but the rest were mostly human, from my quick observation. Honestly, I didn't know who was what at this point. If other creatures could shift as demons could, I had no idea who or what I was looking at.

This time, our path was lit well with torches on the walls, and the small hallway soon opened up into a circular room with mingling guests whose attention turned toward us as we approached. One came barreling forward and attacked Aleena, causing her to drop her chest with a thud. She was extremely petite, couldn't have been anything over four feet tall. She leaped onto Aleena and wrapped her arms around her neck. But it was the wings at her back that I couldn't help but stare at.

They glistened as they fluttered excitedly, a stunning iridescence that was captivating. The two began conversing as Aleena set her on the ground, but I couldn't make out a word they were saying. It didn't sound like a language I'd ever heard before.

"Violet—" I dragged my gaze away to look up at Brigitte, who was standing patiently with her hands folded in front of her. "I do hope you enjoy yourself. I hope we meet again."

"Thank you, Brigitte."

Another squeal from behind made me swivel around to see another conversing with Aleena as if they hadn't seen each other in forever.

I examined our surroundings—what I assumed to be the "hub" that was referred to earlier. It had the same dark drapery on the walls of the dome-like room, with a much larger golden chandelier. It was about triple the size of the one in the room we'd first appeared in.

We had become quite the spectacle as others gathered around us. Some were curious, while others acted more annoyed and made their way out in different directions. Including the way we'd come from, there were six different doorways leading out. Music filtered in, but it wasn't loud or overbearing, and neither was the chatter amongst all of the guests in here.

I noted a couple in the far back making out, and rather heatedly without a care of who saw them. It reminded me of Aleena's words about the possibility of seeing people screwing around. I couldn't help but wonder if one of these doorways led to even more risqué destinations where one might witness such things.

So far, this club didn't seem so bad.

"Come here." Aleena pulled me out of my thoughts and I joined her at her side. "Everyone, this is Violet," she introduced as they all turned their attention to me. I froze momentarily before offering an awkward wave of my hand.

I wanted nothing more than to shrink up and become a wallflower at this point.

Aleena began stating names and what type of creature they were. I had no idea how some of the names rolled off of her tongue, as they didn't even make sense in my head. Some offered their own nods, or waves, while others wrapped me in a hug in a more friendly manner.

There were fairies of different sizes, a vampire, a goblin, a siren, and ghouls. There was another witch who didn't have the same glowing red eyes as Brigitte and the one from Darthou, which I found curious, but I couldn't exactly let on how much I already knew.

The way Aleena would make an introduction and then smoothly shift from English to another language was a talent I was witnessing for the first time. She soon opened her trunk and began pulling out her arsenal of designs, and the women around us were quickly swooning over them.

One with a dark complexion ripped off her top, baring it all, only to replace it with a silky red number that was so short it showed off the underside of her breasts.

"Nzuri!" Aleena clapped her hands together as she praised the top. Her face was alight with a joy that was infectious, and I was happy for her.

I was thankful that Aleena hadn't tried to put me in something like that with absolutely no support. Although I had to admit, Nzuri's perky breasts could certainly get away with it. She could practically walk the catwalk in a fashion show. I was pretty sure she'd been introduced as a ghoul, but she looked so human. I had no idea what a ghoul really was in this world.

Or goblins. The only thing I noted about the woman who was supposed to be a goblin was her ears, how they protruded out and away from her face while the fairies had ears that were similar in shape to mine but came to a point at the top.

"You are the new demon, no?" A thick-accented man met me at my side.

"Is it that obvious?" I fidgeted with my fingers as I met the gaze of the alluring stranger. His hair was short and his shirt unbuttoned about halfway down with dark hair showing, but I lingered on the points of two of his teeth.

His smile broadened as he held out a hand as if taking notice of my perusal. "I am Nicolae."

I offered my hand for a shake but he brought it up to his lips and kissed it. While I wanted to think this was just his way of being polite, it felt oddly intimate. And awkward.

I cleared my throat before I could find my voice. "Violet, nice to meet you."

"You as well." His teeth shone and I had to remind my swirling thoughts not to get hung up on them.

Was any of this real? Was I hallucinating? There were so many creatures and so much going on that I thought my head was going to explode.

"Nicolae, love." A brunette came up from behind him, settling her head on his shoulder as he released my hand. "Who have you found here? Someone to join us?"

Her eyes landed on my breasts, a gleam in her brown eyes. Why was she looking at me like I was something to eat? She was missing the fangs that Nicolae had, but I could recognize the hunger in her.

"She's unavailable, you guys, sorry." Aleena swooped in to save the day. "You'll have to find someone else for your orgy."

My eyes widened in shock at the realization. "Yeah, sorry. Happily tethered."

Nicolae let out a few tsks with his tongue, as if that wasn't a good enough reason. "Doesn't mean you can't have a little fun."

"He could join us, if you like." The brunette was beginning to run her hand through Nicolae's chest hair.

"Nope, nope. I'm good." My face was overheating. "Thanks for the offer, though."

"Suit yourself." Nicolae wrapped an arm around the woman and led her out of the hub, disappearing through one of the doorways at the far left.

When I turned back to Aleena, I was gawking. "An orgy?!"

She laughed. "You're hot stuff. I would be surprised if that's the only invitation you get tonight."

I shook my head, unbelieving. "Wherever they're headed, I am *not* going in there."

"No problem. How about we get ourselves some drinks?"

"Sure, I guess. You lead the way?"

She nodded and took me by the hand. "Help yourselves, everyone. I'm going to show Violet around a bit."

There were a few parting words before Aleena led us out of the hub and through the second doorway from the right. Techno music began taking over, a beat that I could feel in my chest before the music consumed my ears.

"Just remember—" Aleena's voice was raised. "Don't be afraid to tell someone you're not interested. They'll move on and forget about it."

I tipped my head in understanding, and that small movement made me think to inquire about something before we were drowning in beats. "I'm not complaining, but nobody has bowed to us here."

Aleena turned her face to mine, exaggerating a sigh of relief. "Great, isn't it?" I had no idea if it bothered her as much as it did me, but her comment made me think that it might. "It's more of a status thing for us, especially in Darthou. Here, we're all equals, just seeking what makes us happy."

And getting invited to orgies as if it's no big deal. Totally normal, sure.

We entered a cave-like room that was a chaotic mess of various colored strobe lights. Some were gyrating and dancing with drinks in hand, others devouring each other's mouths as if they were drinking their life from them. I laid eyes upon the woman with the short red top. Her breasts were being revealed each time she raised her arms on the dance floor, but a man at her side scooped them up into his hold as she moved.

The party in here was definitely at a different level compared to the singer in the auditorium. Things were getting a bit spicier in here, and I pried my eyes away as if I might get in trouble for looking.

We came to a stop at a bar that had a neon orange backlight on the shelves of liquor bottles. We weaseled our way in and Aleena pounded her fist on the countertop to get the attention of one of the shirtless men behind it. Each one was ripped beyond belief, but what was startling was their eyes. They were snakelike, small slivers that I blinked at, making sure I was seeing correctly.

Aleena made a gesture of the number two and then signed something with her hands. He nodded in understanding, swinging a cloth over his shoulder as he retrieved two glasses and began mixing.

I wasn't even going to ask what he was, but I could say with one-hundred-percent certainty that I preferred demon eyes to whatever he was wearing. It gave me the creeps.

The music in here should have been loud enough to hurt my eardrums, but instead, it made me want to move. I wasn't exactly the dancing type, but my foot began tapping to the beat as I took in the sights. I was in sensory overload, yet I didn't want to leave.

Nobody was bothered by the fact that other patrons were practically fornicating around them. Some were half-naked, but there didn't seem to be a single soul that cared. If there was ever a place to fade into the background, this was it.

The words *freedom* and *acceptance* came to mind. Words the witch spoke of upon entering this club. I wanted to believe that I could achieve that here, a sense of normalcy. Would the creatures here accept me if they truly knew who I was? *What* I was?

With a tap on my shoulder, I turned back toward Aleena who had two shot glasses in her hands. I accepted one that held a pink ombre liquid that sparkled. I didn't think she would be able to hear me if I asked what it was I was about to partake in, but we cheered and I brought the glass to my lips.

The smooth liquid hit my tongue and it instantly began to tingle. It trailed down the back of my throat, settling low in my belly. It was sweet, with a tart aftertaste that lingered.

I signaled to Aleena and tried to shout for another, but she shook her head no and mouthed, "Just one."

She took my glass and set the both of them on the counter, dragging me out into the throng of creatures as we weaved our way in. I was lost in a sea of them, and for once, I didn't feel like I had a spotlight on me.

The music had shifted into another beat, but it was still captivating and in sync with the light show around us. Aleena raised her hands and began to move, and I surrendered to the pounding rhythm as I followed her lead.

A joyful warmth spread over me, and a slight fuzziness swept through my brain as if I had downed a few drinks when in reality I'd only had one shot. Perhaps whatever it was, was so strong that Aleena had limited me to one.

There was an occasional bump from the bodies around me, but it never bothered me or them. My hands floated up just to come down again as I cherished the anonymity I had here. I was just one of many, surrendering to the atmosphere and letting my body move how it wanted.

My hair began to stick to my neck, and I longed for a hair tie of some sort, anything to cool me down just a little.

Whatever alcohol was in my stomach had me buzzing, and a bit turned on. My skirt was rising, working its way up my upper thigh, but I wanted to rid myself of my clothes altogether. I was starting to get hot, my temperature rising from the masses and my movement. When I opened my eyes to look at Aleena, she was grinding against a man I didn't recognize, capturing his mouth with hers. His hand trailed its way down her front and into her pants, although how he managed to fit in there, I had no idea.

A caress along the back of my leg startled me, but awareness of my soon-to-be demon king of a lover took over. I grinned at the realization that he had joined us.

I had no idea how much time had passed or if his football party was really over, but nevertheless, I was happy to have him near, especially now that Aleena was enjoying herself with another.

My hands floated up and around his neck as I pressed my

ass against a hardened cock. Bare arms wrapped around me and I grinned, closing my eyes. I couldn't even talk to him in here if I wanted to, but just his presence alone revved my body up even more.

I turned in his embrace, his face now illuminated by flashes of red light. Only, it wasn't Kade's face.

CHAPTER 21

Violet

My heart leapt up into my throat as I jumped back, but his firm grip on me kept me close. The man before me had sandy blond waves, facial hair to match, and demon eyes. Dressed in fitted leather and a man's corset, every muscular curve was shown off. But it was the emerald-green details on his clothes that matched mine that had me searching his face.

"Kade?" I attempted to shout, but I couldn't hear myself over the noise.

I knew he could shift, but I hadn't experienced it firsthand other than the changing of his eyes some time ago. It was strange, feeling our connection when the man before me held hardly any facial resemblance to the demon I had come to love. When he grinned, I thought I might lose my mind.

Throwing my arms around him, I attacked his mouth. The action caused us to bump into a few strangers, but it felt so right to have him here. Every touch had a fire igniting beneath my skin. He gripped me tight, holding me so close that I might lose the air in my lungs. When he pulled away, I felt even more dazed than before he had shown up.

Taking my hand, he proceeded through the crowd. I ducked, narrowly missing a stray arm that came my way, and it threw off my equilibrium momentarily. It was like my brain was sloshing around in my head, and I centered my attention on the emerald-green fastenings on Kade's back.

What kind of dress code had there been for this football party? Had I been missing out?

I tugged at my skirt that was now riding up my behind, as I wasn't too keen on exposing any more skin than I needed to while we made our way forward and out of the crowd. Cheers and hollers erupted from the scene behind us, but I resisted the urge to look away from Kade for fear that I might stumble.

What the hell had been in that drink?

Kade made a stop at the bar, pressing me up against the counter and trapping me against it. I wanted to protest as he signaled for a drink, but I couldn't turn. The same bartender with the weird eyes returned with a clear liquid and left just as quickly as he had surfaced.

I shook my head, not wanting anything else at this point. I didn't want to be shit-faced after two drinks. How pathetic would that be?

I attempted to push his hand away, but Kade confiscated my wrists, binding them together as he pressed the glass to my lips. He used its edge to tug at my lower lip and I caved, almost unable to keep my head up.

It tasted horrible, bitter even. I squeezed my eyes shut as I forced my throat to swallow it. Kade and his sister definitely had different palates when it came to alcohol; this was undeniably awful.

When I opened my eyes, I centered myself. The fogginess that had invaded my head was lifting ever so slightly, my tummy buzzing with a weird fluttering. I noticed how Kade hadn't ordered a drink for himself, and given the effects of this clear drink, I could see why. It must have been some sort of cure for my alcohol-based state of being.

Setting the empty glass down on the counter, Kade led me out of the booming atmosphere and through another hall. He ducked into a small alcove, pushing me up against the wall. My chest heaved with excitement as he closed in, nestling into me.

"Someone's been having fun." His voice was unchanged, unlike his appearance.

I brought his head to mine, exploring his mouth without hesitation, pushing my tongue inside to taste him. My hand skated across his facial hair, creating another layer of sensations that made my head spin in all different directions. I arched into him as best as my confines would allow, savoring the remnants of whatever liquor he had consumed. It was a messy, frenzied meeting of our mouths as I gripped his biceps tighter. I could see why Aleena had said there might be fucking, as that was the only thing on my mind right now.

"Take me," I ordered between kisses, my need pounding between my legs to the point that I might go mad if he didn't touch me there soon. I wouldn't stop clawing at him until he made me come, maybe even thereafter. I could be leaving marks on his skin for all I knew, but it would only be a sign to let others know that he was mine.

He broke away, the face of a stranger coming into view again. "Not here."

Was my corset tightening? I couldn't seem to catch my breath.

I followed him as he led the way out of the hall, passing through the main hub where I caught a glimpse of Aleena's chest still being rummaged through. When I realized Kade was headed for the entry that the vampire Nicolae and that girl had gone through, I tensed.

A sultry tune began to waft into the hall as a low-lit room came into view, but nothing could have prepared me for what awaited us in here. Everything was in shades of red, outfitted with golden fixtures that hung from the ceiling. Countless faces and bodies were engaged in sexual acts, performing for any and all who dared to watch. There were moans and groans of pleasure and screams of ecstasy as we skirted around the perimeter, and there were numerous pieces of leather furniture that some were carrying out their revelry above, below, and on top of.

Then there were those who merely stood by and watched as the scenes unfolded before them. I hadn't exactly had this in mind when I asked Kade to fuck me, and I began to grow nervous.

I couldn't help but notice the lingerie on a few of the occupants that were dressed, if you could call it that. One number, on a man, only covered a small section of his top half. As I looked closer, I could see that he wasn't just kissing the neck of the woman before him, but he was feasting on her. A trail of blood fell down her back, the thick crimson an unmistakable sign of the truth of what was playing out. I noted how her ears were pointed, possibly another fairy if I had to guess.

My eyes lingered on a man who appeared to be half wolf and half human; the amount of hair on him made it hard to believe he was anything else. He was pounding away into a girl who was hunched over a chair, quivering as we passed into another darkened corridor.

I was beginning to think that the maze of wherever the hell we were was no easier to navigate than Darthou.

We didn't stop walking until we came to a wooden podium with a woman behind it, leaning on her elbows as if she might be bored. What was curious, though, was that she was blindfolded by a black strap that disappeared into her golden bob hairstyle.

She began to speak and Kade slowed to a halt, bringing my hip up to his side. I tilted my head slightly, wondering what language this was. My head whipped in Kade's direction when he responded to her, awed by the ability I'd just witnessed with Aleena earlier.

Without any introductions, Kade led me away and we passed on her right. The same metal doors, like the one Aleena and I had entered through when we first arrived, lined a hall, with markings at the top of each one that I didn't understand. There was a soft flow of music as we continued door after door, but I couldn't make out where it was coming from. All that was visible were the stone walls and occasional mounted torch that was higher than my head. It was almost like some sort of underground hotel from an earlier century.

Kade came to a stop and placed his hand on a door. A metal clank sounded, and he opened it, pushing it in to reveal a small navy-colored padded room. I stepped in, observing the small table that was raised and tilted toward me. I pressed into it, noticing how soft yet firm the material was.

To my left was a wall with several metal bars, both vertical and horizontal. There were indentations on some of them, and I had the distinct feeling that on more than one occasion, people or creatures had been restrained using them. I swallowed hard as I pivoted back to Kade, noticing a floor-to-ceiling mirrored wall, all one magnificent piece. It was clean, crystal clear, and showed no imperfections. I couldn't help but think about how impossible it must have been to get that thing through the door in the first place.

Kade sealed us inside, the metal clank sounding again, but there was no lock that was visible to my eyes. I crossed my arms below my breasts, eager to see where he was planning to take this now that we were finally alone.

"So..." I began as I took a step closer. "You speak a different language."

Even though this man before me didn't look like Kade, I couldn't mistake the need that was emitting from him. It was almost enough to make me weak in the knees now that I could focus on it and nothing else.

"I speak many, in fact." He advanced another step, and we were now within reach once more.

"Mhmm...that's kind of sexy." I poked him at the top of his chest that was exposed, admiring the similarities between our outfits. "And this, have you been holding out on me?"

He wrapped his fingers around my hand, drawing me closer. "Aleena might have left Elias and me something to open after the party."

"Oh?"

"We bolted here as soon as we did." His hands moved down to my waist, the tips of his fingers curling under the tight fabric.

"Well, I'm glad you did," I mused, appreciative that I would now get to spend the rest of my evening with him. I dug into my breast, pulling out the coins and tossing them onto the floor. I should have been more careful with them, considering their state, but that would be a problem to deal with later.

They scattered about and before the last one rolled to a stop, Kade's mouth was on the swell of my chest, his head buried. He bumped into my necklace but moved it out of the way as his hands roamed my backside. I drew the zipper down the side of my hip, and he was quick to slide it down, leaving my panties. But even those were of no interest to him. He tore through the fabric like it was nothing, leaving me bare as the scraps fell to the floor.

Kade turned me by my waist, tearing his mouth away as he began pulling on the ribbon that strapped me in. I used the small table to brace myself, pressing my ass into him to feel his erection. He groaned at the friction, and I turned my head to watch him in the mirror, my black and poofy hair threatening to block my view. He gripped my right cheek with his hand, squeezing as he returned the thrust, sending me forward onto the table, but he pried me back up again by the closure at my back.

This table was the perfect height if he decided to take me here, as long as I kept my boots on.

I stayed there, watching him as he pried ribbon after ribbon to rid me of the rest of my attire. The intensity with which he carried out the task as his gaze remained fixed to my backside was a heady display for my eyes only. The fastenings on my back loosened, and when the sides of the corset fell away, he pulled me up to standing, taking hold of my chin as his lips met my neck. His tongue lashed out, grazing my skin as a hand worked over a breast, kneading it with such pressure it was on the verge of pain as he pinched the peak. I inhaled sharply at the motion.

Then he vanished, my skin void of all contact with him. I searched the small room, confused and dazed by the fact that I was the only occupant. The solid glass wall and my solo reflection was startling. My cheeks were flushed and my body was warm. I crossed my arms to cover myself.

When he appeared before me again, I grabbed at my throat in a yelp. "What the fuck, Kade?"

My heart was pounding with his little disappearing act, unsure of why he would leave me, even if only momentarily. The corner of his mouth turned up before he grabbed me by the waist, lifting me onto the table. I stifled my surprise at the quick movement.

"Hands out," he ordered, and I raised an unsure brow, holding out my fists in front of me, my breasts pressed together at the movement.

Kade reached behind me and produced a set of black fabric handcuffs.

"Oh," I mouthed as he began to pry the thick Velcro apart. He wrapped them around each wrist, and they were secured together by a link of four chain-like circles.

"Gee, do I need a safeword?" I joked, suddenly nervous. I had only been bound by Kade's hands prior to this. Handcuffs were an introduction to something different, but I was ready to submit, however he wanted me.

"I'll know how you're feeling through the bond, and I promise to stop if you're too uncomfortable." Then he added with a wink, "I also promise to not do anything to you that I wouldn't be able to heal."

I gazed up at him, shocked by his honesty but outrageously turned on by his reasoning. My mouth went dry as I was suddenly overtaken by a desire that was so close to consuming me.

"If you did need one, what would it be?" He took my chin in his hand, keeping my focus fixed on him as I searched for a word in my head, which had gone blank. It had to be something I wouldn't accidentally say out loud.

Settling on one of my fondest memories of our time together, I let the word leave my lips. Hopefully, for the only time tonight.

"Carnival."

His jaw tightened, visible even with facial hair in the way. Our lips crashed for a few seconds but before I could deepen the kiss, he drew my hands up and arms high, ushering me to lie back against the table. I stretched out for him as he secured my hands to something beneath the raised back, but due to my angled view in the mirror, I couldn't make out what it was.

Kade returned to the other side and lifted each foot, removing my boots and socks, letting them each drop to the floor with a clomp. I gazed down at him, waiting for him to undress as he was wearing far too many clothes for my liking, even if he was drool worthy with that men's corset on.

Wrapping his hands around my ankles, he lifted them, settling them on the edge of the table. My necklace settled at the base of my throat, its weight almost too much with my jagged breaths. My knees wanted to fold in, but he drew them apart once more, shaking his head.

A roll of black tape came into view, and with a drawn-out drag, he peeled it out and began to wrap it around my bent leg. He circled it several times, locking me into place before he broke the tape off, then repeated the same maneuver on my other leg. Not only were my hands literally tied up for the first time in my life, but I couldn't say that I'd ever been taped before either. When he was done, he tossed the roll of tape to the side and it rolled across the floor until it stopped.

He pulled apart my folds, exposing me fully, and bent down, his blond head now hovering above me as his breath mixed with my heated center. The smooth softness of his tongue lashed out and began to explore. He nuzzled in there, taking me in as he drew circles with his tongue, teasing me.

The urge to run my hands through his hair was strong. I wanted to hold him there, greedy for him to make me come with nothing more than his mouth. He was relentless, showing no signs of slowing as his arms came around my legs, holding me to him. The climb was a steady one, building and raising my body temperature higher.

His lips closed in on my clit, sucking. My hips fought to leave the table but he forced me down with ease. I was securely fitted against him and bound. Completely at his mercy.

Tipping my head to the side, I could only make out the top of his head as he moved, bringing me closer and closer until I came. I knew I wouldn't last very long, not when I'd been so worked up to begin with.

"Fuck!" I shouted as if I were in pain, but I was far from it. The sensitive nub was released from his mouth and he came into view, lips glistening. He swiped at his lips with his thumb, then took his thumb into his mouth. And I'd thought he couldn't look anymore fuckable.

"I've been wondering…" Kade spoke as he kept one hand on the outside of my thigh and his other hand fished something out of his pocket. When he pulled out the purple vibe I'd taken from my old apartment, I was stunned into silence. I had thrown all of that into my new nightstand when we returned and had never given it another thought.

The realization of what he held and his possible intentions did little to help me cool down from my high.

"Why is this so special?" He pressed the button for a few seconds and it reared to life, the vibration evident in his hold.

I swallowed hard as I squirmed on the table. That vibe and

I had a relationship that rivaled all of my ex-boyfriends. I really didn't have a need for it anymore, not with Kade in the picture. He never left me unsatisfied. Hell, I didn't think he could even if he tried.

His hand lowered, and my gaze fell with it. I lost sight of it beneath the curls between my thighs. Dipping it into my core, he drew it up from there, and it easily glided along to my clit. I pulled on my restraints as the vibrations and the moisture from my arousal deepened the sensations from its pulses. I closed my eyes, back arching, savoring the long-lost feeling of an old friend. Hands fisting, I writhed against it as he held it steady.

Okay, so maybe I did still need it.

I knew he was watching, no doubt appreciating the show before him. Opening my eyes again, I verified that he was fixated on me. The hunger in his face told me that he wanted me, but he was letting my vibe get in the way of that. His vision bounced between my center and my face, like he couldn't decide which he wanted to watch more.

"I'd rather have you inside of me," I moaned as I rocked against the vibe. While I relished the attack with his tongue, and the different sensations the vibe provided, I still wanted *him*.

Kade grinned, pressing a finger into me, the click of a small button kicking the vibrations up a notch. "You'll get me…eventually."

I failed to swallow at his admission, lost as another finger joined in. He moved the vibe up and down the length of me and when he applied more pressure, I whimpered.

My insides began to quake as another climax began to build. He curled his fingers as he reached inside and stilled, letting the vibe take me to an orgasm that tore through my lips and warranted an unfiltered cry. His fingers remained as he cut the sound of the toy and removed it as I rode out the waves of the aftermath. Each clench around his fingers was a stark reminder that he wasn't done.

"Well, you held on to your blink for a little while." An amused laugh left him, settling in his chest. I turned my head toward the mirrored wall once more. My once-voluminous black hair had faded back to its strawberry-blond strands. The waves were more evident now that they weren't in a sea of darkness.

There was a click, as if something was being opened and squeezed, but when I looked down, I couldn't make anything out. I searched the mirror, hoping I could get a sense of what was going on, but my limbs were beginning to feel heavy. Two orgasms ripping through me with little time between was proving taxing, but I would stay the course until he could bury himself in me. That would be my undoing.

What I hadn't expected was something foreign pressing into my ass, and I tried to buck off of the table.

"Easy, easy, Violet. Just relax," he coaxed as he remained fixated on what he was trying to accomplish.

"That is *not* one of my toys." I gasped at the fullness of something down there. There was one guy before Kade who had wanted to try anal, but I hadn't allowed it. He hadn't even known what he was doing when it came to the basics of sex half the time, so why would I let him anywhere near my rear end?

"I thought I might add to your collection." Kade lowered his head, kissing my inner thigh as I tried to adjust to the object he had penetrated me with. "Do you want to safeword?"

My lips pressed together, and I was on the verge of doing so but I fought it off as I began to settle down. My cheeks were aflame, knowing that my plight was on full display, just as my body before him. Sweat began to form along my hairline, as well as along my back on the table, and between my legs that were secured together by the tape.

"No," I assured him. Kade had already claimed every other part of me prior to today. I could give him this. We could try something new, even if we hadn't discussed it before now.

I was confused about how my body could still ache for him. No. *Throb* for him, when I had already come two times. Despite having something shoved up in an unfamiliar place, I still wanted his member inside of me. I wouldn't feel complete until I had it.

"If you honestly don't like it when we're done, I'll never use it again."

I nodded in understanding, unable to form any words as I focused on the complex and warring thoughts over whether I favored it or not. Its entrance had been slick, swift and quick, an invasion that I hadn't been expecting. But I had to admit, it wasn't all that terrible now that the shock was wearing off.

The rustle of his movements as he left his post caused me to open my eyes once more. My lids were becoming heavy, just like the rest of my body, exhaustion threatening to take over and ruin our time together.

Lips brushed against mine in a teasing manner. I raised my head to chase him, but I could only graze his lips in return. My head hit the table in defeat. A positively sinful smirk played across his face, and I rolled my eyes.

"You're having way too much fun with this," I muttered as I failed to roll my wrists. I hadn't realized how hard I'd been pulling on my restraints until now. While they were made out of a soft material, the edges of them had some bite.

His hand began to caress my swollen clit, and I moaned.

Between his oral and my vibe, it had already been put through the wringer. I wasn't even sure how much longer my body could hold out, even as a steady throb began to fill my ears.

Kade's yearning for me was strong and unwavering. It oozed over me in droves that left me panting for more. He took his place at the center of my satisfaction, and I heard the zip of his pants. I smiled, more to myself than anything, as this was what I craved, this was what I wanted.

The head of his cock hovered at my opening, waiting. I tried to rock forward to feel it, but within a nanosecond he pulled it away. Not knowing if he was going to take it slow or slam into me had my head spinning, but I fought through it as I opened my eyes to meet the stranger before me.

"Wait," I expressed with a broken voice. While I hadn't used the safeword, he still froze, studying me.

"Ch—change yourself back." I squirmed, eager to see the man I knew, the one I had accepted what seemed like ages ago, and I begged, "Please."

Immediately, the blond hair began to disappear. His dark hair returned and he ran his hands through it, making it the messy head of hair I longed for. I hadn't realized how much I enjoyed the facial hair until it began to fade away, leaving his sharp jawline in its wake. Perhaps later I could tell him I didn't mind the scruff; it had certainly added to the experience when he was down below.

With a jolt of his hips, he entered me, and I cried out. My legs strived to break free of the confines of the tape, but it wouldn't budge or break. Kade placed a hand on my side, keeping me in place as he produced the vibe once more.

Oh. Fuck.

Turning it on again to its lowest setting, he placed it on me and I wanted to leap from the table. His hips began to move, picking up the pace, and my brain was scrambled, sending mixed messages of pain and pleasure, fighting against one another. I was overstimulated on my clit, but it was becoming overpowered by the way his balls pressed the anal toy deeper with each thrust—it all had me screaming uncontrollably. I didn't even recognize the shrieks bursting from my throat.

My arms were sore, my throat turning raw as I took everything Kade was giving me. He pumped into me harder, faster, grunting with each press, and my eyes began to seep tears through the outside corners. I couldn't form any words, and even if I could, they wouldn't make sense.

My body shook as he increased his speed, and I thought I might split in half. The pressure was too great, building toward an explosion that would have no mercy. His grip on my side was firm as the vibe drove me higher and higher until a violent orgasm seized me. My heart was in my head, hammering away relentlessly as he pressed on.

Kade held me down, making me continue to take him as he grunted with each strike until he broke. The vibe disappeared and he pulled the toy from my ass, eliciting another cry from my lips at its removal. He curved over me, resting his head between my breasts as he rocked the last of his load inside. I pulsed around him, throbbing around his member. If he so much as looked at my clit, I would probably have to use my safeword. Either that or I would pass out. There was no possible way my body could take another touch, toy, or anything of the sort down there. I was spent beyond belief.

A silence stretched on, mingled only with our jagged breaths as we came down from our peaks of exertion. Kade kissed my stomach before leaning up and removing himself. I winced, trying to shrink away, but I was still being held, locked in place. He began to unwrap my legs and then he gently closed them, guiding them down to one side. I could sense him rounding the table next, coming to free me from the hold on my wrists, and when he brought them down I hugged myself across my chest.

"Take me home," I whispered, although I wasn't entirely sure if he could hear me. My voice sounded distant as my head fell in his direction and I drifted off.

CHAPTER 22

Kade

Violet was a tangled mess in the sheets, cuddled up against me. Her head was tucked beneath my chin, her fluffy hair a minimal annoyance that I had to keep pushing out of the way. She'd passed out before I even brought her to bed, but that hadn't stopped me from cleaning her up a bit first.

Surprisingly, I'd been able to heal her wrists while she slept without having to use her coins to do so. The cuffs had marked her fair skin, and I didn't want her to wake to find the blotches. She had been slightly pink from the tape that was wrapped around her legs, but it quickly faded without my help. It was gone by the time I'd cleaned up the playroom and settled into our bed with her.

Getting out of my corset, however, had been quite the

performance. I'd almost ripped it to shreds in an attempt to get out of it, but resorted to shrinking my frame to remove it. The way her eyes had devoured me, I knew it was only a matter of time before Violet would ask me about it, perhaps requesting I wear it again.

If Aleena hadn't told her yet, Violet would soon find out that Elias and I had been Aleena's models when she started dabbling with menswear. Or her version of it, anyway. It certainly wasn't a habit to parade around in Aleena's designs. I usually told her to keep quiet or I wouldn't be of any help to her. Elias, though, would parade around stark naked if Aleena asked him to. He would jump through hoops and walk through fire at her request without a second thought. He would give everything for her. I couldn't fathom why she could never do the same for him.

And yet, she had welcomed him with open arms last night on the dance floor. She had to have known when she provided us with outfits, that we would drop everything and meet them there. I wasn't exactly thrilled at my sister for introducing Violet to Torenca without me, especially given the stakes. But since the night had ended on such a high note, I really shouldn't complain.

Violet whimpered beside me, her body going rigid. Fists clenched as her breathing kicked up and heart-gripping fear flooded through our connection.

My grip on her tightened as I attempted to push the fear away and take deep breaths, willing her to ward off whatever plagued her dreams. I'd never witnessed her having nightmares like this before her death, but now that she was here and our coronation was drawing closer, they had increased. I'd tried asking her about them twice now, but I was always met with a nonchalant shrug. These night stirrings seemed to bother me more than her, and I would just leave it at that.

Perhaps it was her unease with my world and the slew of things that came with it. Finding out I was going to be king and she a queen. The stress of being the center of attention when she was never one for the spotlight to begin with.

With a jerk of her body, she stilled and I ensured my hold on her, willing everything I had in me to chase off her malicious dreams and calm her. It must have worked, as I felt her body soften against me, the air leaving her more slowly now through her parted lips.

I let out a long exhale of my own in relief.

I was too wired to sleep. Too high on the memories of her bound before me as I coaxed her to come again and again and again. She had held out until the very end, even though I'd sensed she was at war with herself, doubting everything one minute to desperately begging the next. It was even better than I could have hoped for.

Violet's head nuzzled into my chest and I carefully readjusted my position. I brushed a stray hair away from her face, noticing how warm she was to the touch.

Ever since returning from Xandor, her body temperature had been affected. She should have no problem running around in a tank top and shorts without ever feeling a chill, but now she was snuggled close as if she were searching for heat in the dead of winter. Even while wearing the thicker clothes that the humans wore on the regular here in Darthou. I didn't know how long we had until someone took notice, and I only hoped that others might think it was nothing more than a wardrobe choice.

It might work, considering we'd been hiding Violet ever since her arrival. My sister, even though I hated to admit it, was right. The people needed to see her. They needed to get to know her. Tomorrow she would be crowned at the coronation, and nobody knew who she was. The mystery that surrounded her rebirth had given everyone enough to talk about already.

And now that the fucking furies had blessed her with the sight that was working in full force, we had an even bigger problem on our hands.

She was a vengeance-seeking fury, let loose amongst loads of demons who had tortured, maimed, and killed. Aleena, Elias, and myself were just three out of countless others.

I held my breath, trying to pull myself off the ledge that I was pushing toward.

They weren't the enemy.

I shouldn't be trying to place any blame on them. Seeking vengeance was the core of who they were, and it wasn't fair to displace my hate onto them for this. Violet was just a pawn in someone else's game, and the thought that her different sides put her in that much more danger was almost suffocating. Even now when I finally had her by my side, I feared for her very existence.

If anything else were to ever happen to her…

"Did you have a good birthday?" Violet's voice broke through my mental drownings of unease, and I pulled my head back to meet her gaze.

"The best." I kissed the top of her forehead. Very little light was filtering through the upper half of the stained glass windows, casting her hair in a golden hue. It was only brighter when she stepped into the sun on a bright summer day. Only, that was something she would never get here in Darthou.

"How long do we have before you have to go to the Summit?"

"I have a little bit of time, what did you have in mind?" I poked as I rolled my hips against her. She groaned and attempted to push away from me, but I wouldn't allow it.

"Back off, you fiend." She was tousled and heavy from sleep. "Haven't you had your fill of me?"

"Never." I cradled the back of her head and took her mouth. My cock was spurred to life, ready to take her once more, if she wasn't too sore. It might be a bit devilish of me, but I wanted her to plead for healing so I could fuck her again. It would be a glorious start to the day.

"Do you think we could discuss some changes around here? If it's not too much trouble? I know we've got a lot—"

I silenced her with my mouth, my chest expanding with the immense intensity of my feelings for her. When I pulled away, I let my lips playfully bite down on her lower lip. Her cheeks filled with a blush of color, lips full and begging to be taken again, but I resisted the urge to do so. I would hear her out.

"What's on your mind?"

Fully expecting Staffan to put on a suit, I reluctantly did the same. I had no idea how the other leads dressed, but I didn't want to be upstaged by him. I would have gladly chosen dress slacks and a button-down shirt, but until I knew what everyone else's dress code was, this would have to do.

Violet had chosen a navy blue suit for me at Rebecca's shop, and as soon as I was ready, I whisked her away to Elias for some training. I banged on the door multiple times and even tried communicating by my pocket mirror, only to be met by a grumbling mess of him answering the door in nothing more than a towel around his waist. I didn't wait around long enough to see if my sister was there with him, and I escorted Violet back to our home where Elias would retrieve her later when he was more…decent.

At least when Violet was with him, she wouldn't have to wear her coins. A thankful reprieve, since I would be at an important meeting today that only took place a few times a year.

Prior to our conversations this morning, I'd thought she would only have them on for a short while when she met with Rafina for her weekly checkup today. I had seen nothing but red when Violet informed me of Rafina's unplanned visit yesterday, ahead of schedule. A schedule that Rafina never tampered with. The matter of this supposed blood draw she had requested was almost enough to make me come undone.

Rafina had become more reclusive since Violet came to Darthou. You used to see her wandering around the great hall or occasionally accompanying Staffan to meetings, but not as of late. It was almost as if she was hiding as much as we were hiding Violet. That, in itself, I considered practically an admission of guilt. Violet had seen more of her than I had in their weekly meetings, and she had made herself scarce.

I had expected the council chambers to be vacant when I arrived, and I was less than enthused that Staffan had beat me here. His appearance never changed. The same hair, same skin tone, same body mass, only now he was—as I had guessed correctly—sporting a dark gray suit. What caught me off guard was Rafina, who poked her head over his shoulder, her eye contact sending a jolt of frustration through me as their hushed whispers came to a halt.

"Care to tell me why you saw fit to see Violet yesterday instead of your scheduled meeting today?" I shoved my hands in my pockets as my mouth closed, jaw tense.

Staffan moved himself out of her way, allowing us to look at each other head-on.

"She came with me willingly, maybe you should take that up with her." Rafina's face was void of any emotion as she spoke. There was no apology or skirting around to diffuse the situation. Her usual bedside manner, gone.

"She was just as surprised as I was." I took a step forward, making my shoulders square. "And for the record, these bullshit weekly meetings will cease immediately following the coronation. She can train when, where, and with who she wants without the unnecessary microscope of the council."

For the most part, Rafina remained unmoved. There was only a slight narrowing of her gaze as she raised her chin. "Understood."

She clasped her hands in front of her long dress as she took a few steps away from Staffan and me. The dress had uncharacteristically lengthy sleeves that stretched toward her knuckles.

"Safe Summit, everyone." She bowed her head and vanished without so much as a glance at Staffan.

I could never understand the lack of intimacy between the two of them. They had been together for decades and yet, besides the occasional dance or linking of arms, that was as comfortable as they got together. Had love ever been a part of their relationship, or had they merely sought positions of power that they'd agreed to on their own terms in their union?

Suppressing my agitation, and questions I might never have answered, I focused on the soon-to-be ex-member of the council. Maybe that should be my second order of business tomorrow, after calling the hounds off Violet.

Get rid of Staffan and finally get Elias in the game.

But for now, I plastered my best fake smile on my face,

attempting to play nice. "Where are we headed today?"

The Summit was held at a different location with each meeting, and never the same place two times in a row. The decision was held off until the last minute because those in attendance were all royalty of some sort. Some were leaders by blood such as myself, others by democracy. There was always a fear that there would be an attack, so the secrecy of the location was something everyone abided by. I was curious whose home would be used for our meeting today. For all I knew, Darthou could be playing host.

"Islands of Isatar."

I could feel the strain of my left brow striving to rise. I hadn't heard anyone speak of them in ages. Land sirens—much like those of Greek mythology—had wanted to claim the islands as their home on land, but there were also water nymphs that sought to claim it as their own. There had been a battle between the two groups, one that was barely covered in textbooks but enough to raise awareness of the lengths they would go to for battle. It had been a bloody one, and both sides had recruited other creatures in their fight to claim the islands. In the end, no one was victorious. The losses on both sides were too great.

"I thought the islands had been abandoned?"

It was curious. The decision of the meeting place. Usually the meetings were in a realm or home of one of the attendees. This was out of the ordinary. This alone gave me pause.

"The trolls have inhabited the territory for quite some time, using it as their own safe haven." There was a disdain in Staffan's voice for those creatures. He was never one to support the underdog, just those who had power and status—alliances and numbers that he could count on should we ever be faced with battle.

Trolls, in particular, shied away from the spotlight due to their appearances. They didn't possess the ability to shift. However, as far as I could recall, they weren't exactly fans of the sun. The Islands of Isatar didn't seem like a suitable home for them. But then again, I didn't normally find myself in the company of any trolls who were interested in chatting, to truly find out for myself.

"Outcasts." I put the word out there, fully aware that I had heard him use that term before in reference to trolls.

Staffan's chest rose slowly with a rather noisy and exaggerated inhale, then out once more. He didn't bother with a response. Actually, he didn't quite seem like himself. Other than being dressed to impress and a singular snide remark, he was unusually quiet.

Speaking of quiet, I glanced about the room. We were still the only occupants in the darkened council chambers.

"Is Tamian accompanying us today?" Every attendee brought at least one form of security to these meetings, or at least, that was what I had been led to believe. It was my understanding that these events were civil, but as a precaution, you were to never attend alone.

Staffan was one for punctuality, but there wasn't a guard in sight and I knew for a fact that Tamian was frequently his plus one. I knew this was a task he would be loyal to, even given the man he was escorting.

"I'm not waiting around for him, he'll reap the consequences when we return." Staffan turned on his heel and began to make his way toward a wall mirror, swiping at the surface and bringing up a view of a white sandy beach. The fading sun glistened off of the clear waters, showing the time difference between here and there. Before I could object to leaving our home without a member of the guard, he passed through, feet sinking into the ground before him.

Retrieving my pocket mirror, I tapped on it in the hopes of getting ahold of Elias. Someone had to be aware of what was transpiring, as this was against protocol. When he answered, the words flooded out of my mouth before he even had the chance to speak. "Find Tamian, something's not right. Islands of Isatar."

Stowing the mirror in my pocket, I followed after Staffan on high alert, eyes adjusting to the sun's rays in the distant horizon. I hadn't seen it in person since I had been in Violet's world. Although it stung my eyes, it was a beautiful sight to behold, but I couldn't linger on it for long.

My head was on a swivel, taking everything in. I could barely make out a string of islands, and we were on the end. You could easily swim to each one, should you dare to enter the water. The one we had arrived on was probably the length of five football fields, if I had to guess, the beach littered with delicate and petite shells.

To my right was a building that looked to be ruins of something very old. It was a mixture of stones, some broken and others whole, weathered and covered in mosslike growth. What furthered my doubts was the singular arched doorway up ahead.

One way in and one way out—that wasn't exactly promising. From an escape standpoint, that was a major red flag. I only hoped that once inside, I could locate other means of access.

To be honest, I couldn't remember the last time Staffan had informed the council of where the Summit had taken place. It was something I should have noticed, something I had regrettably missed.

"Whose turn was it to decide the meeting place?" I

questioned as I followed after him. He made his way to the entrance that had obviously been built with the height of trolls in mind. Now that we drew nearer to it, the building appeared larger than what I had initially believed. A weird optical illusion made it appear smaller than it actually was.

"It was mutual," he muttered as he made his way in first. I was more than glad to let him take the lead. My only regret was not bringing more weapons with me. I had a small switchblade tucked in my pocket, but nothing more. It wasn't like I expected to be patted down upon my arrival or anything, but I didn't like going in empty-handed. Maybe old habits of moonlighting as a seeker were still buried within me.

I entered the crooked doorway and rounded the corner, following after Staffan.

Now that the background noise of the ocean was fading away, voices began to echo through the hall. We were soon swallowed up by a thick fog that lasted a few steps, only to evaporate into a wide room with many already present. Trolls were the first ones I spotted, towering over most of the guests. They were busying themselves with drinks and seating everyone, but no one really paid them much attention. It was as if they were servants.

That very observation was disheartening. The trolls had supposedly found refuge here, and yet they were having to work for us? Why? Had they agreed to play host for this occasion?

"A drink, sir?" One troll approached Staffan, barefoot and wearing a light ensemble of a flowy white shirt and khakis that were too short, cutting off well above the knees. His face was almost rectangular in shape, nose about the size of my fist, and brows thick and close to one another.

"Off with you." Staffan acted like he was appalled at the

mere interaction, and I stalled. I knew he looked down on other creatures, but seeing him react like this when face-to-face with one was appalling.

The troll shuddered as he attempted to shrink away, obviously hurt by Staffan's response. He tried to recover, shoulders caving in and unable to make eye contact with me as he approached. There was a stutter to his voice now, one that hadn't been there before.

"A-and you, sir?"

I blinked, trying to regain my wits as I looked at the creature. "What is your name, sir?"

He froze before me, a giant who had been reduced by one man's rude manners, but somehow found his balance again after Staffan left us behind.

"I apologize for his actions, as he never will himself. I am Kadriel." I stuck my hand out in the hopes of a pleasant greeting. I purposely left off the soon-to-be king, for fear of his reaction. I wanted him to view me as an equal and without titles.

"I-I…" He was searching the ground as if he had lost all train of thought.

"I assure you I mean no ill will. Just a name so we might get better acquainted," I tried to assure him, hoping it would pull him out of his quandary.

"I am afraid my name may not be pronounced by your tongue."

"Try me," I said, perhaps a bit more forward than I meant to be.

A grumble came from his chest as his mouth moved and contorted into a name that I didn't think I could repeat even if I tried. Instead of diving into the embarrassment of not being able to replicate it, I let a broad smile break out on my face.

"I hate to admit it, but I think you're right, my friend. If I try, I might ruin your good name. What would be acceptable for me to call you?"

He shook his head, still wearing a look of defeat. "You need not call me anything. I am only here to serve."

"Nonsense. I am only a guest here and I would rather us be on good terms." I stepped closer, causing his gaze to meet mine. His eyes were large, just as every other piece of him, but they drooped down on the outside corners. "If it helps, today is his last Summit. If he gives you any more trouble, please let me know. You have no reason to trust me, I get that, but he has no right to treat you that way."

He took in a breath as if he was ready to speak, but we were interrupted by a vampire who I hadn't expected to make the journey yet, as the sun was still present outside. That very thought gave me the idea that there was another entrance, but it did little to ease my uncertainty around here.

"Kadriel, how nice of you to join us!" Nicolae approached with a woman hooked on his arm, two holes evident in her neck that he must not have had the urge to cover up. The smooth-talking Romanian wasn't exactly my favorite creature in charge, but he definitely wasn't the worst either. He was more about pleasure and living in the moment, rather than actively planning ahead.

Not only would there be representatives from each of the demon kingdoms, but some from other circles that had evolved much like our own.

"Nicolae, it's been too long." I shoved my hands in my pockets casually. The man was eerily similar to my stature, but I couldn't focus on that for long before noticing an amusement behind his gaze. There was something on his tongue, just begging to come out.

"I had the honor of meeting your tethered mate last night."

And there it was. I hadn't been aware of this encounter, but it was more than likely since Nicolae's sexual tastes knew no bounds. Torenca was a second home for him.

"Violet." The articulation of the last letter of her name when it left his lips was an odd sound that lingered in my head. "No wonder you're so smitten with her. Her blood…" He pretended to search for the words he wanted to say. "It sings. She is absolutely mouthwatering."

My eyes narrowed on him for a moment. I had no idea how to respond to something like that. Was he simply interested in Violet, or was he catching on to something? Could he tell that she was more than a demon, even while she had her coins in her possession?

The jealousy that unfurled in me at his words was an unexpected turn of events. I knew full well that Violet would never give him the time of day—or night—but the thought that he might try to seduce her left a foul taste in my mouth.

I had to divert the conversation before I paused any longer. Glancing at his silent companion, who was oblivious to what we were speaking about, I leaned forward as I spoke to snag her attention. She had been innocently surveying the room without so much as a word so far.

"And who is this exceptional young vampiress you've brought along with you today?" I had seen her a time or two, but we'd never been formally introduced. Her bob and short dress reminded me of the flapper era.

"This is my darling Petra." Nicolae squeezed her side harder and she offered a hooded smile. "He's tethered to that deliciously tempting demon we met last night. Shame we couldn't have had more time to get to know her."

Yep, that was enough of that.

Trying to bypass any conversation deriving from last night, I moved on. "Will we see you at the coronation tomorrow?"

"Of course," he all but bellowed, as if it were brainless of me to ask.

A chorus of boisterous laughs sounded, tearing our attention away from our small and growingly uncomfortable chitchat. Staffan was standing with the king of the goblins and one of his henchmen who served as a bodyguard, along with the leader of the river serpents and two other demons of royal lineage. It was an interesting lot that he was aligning himself with, but I noted the stares from others around the room before they returned to their own conversations.

"I take it that Staffan is not well-liked?" I muttered lowly, and that remark earned a loaded expression from Nicolae's arm candy. Her face turned sour.

"Tell me, Kadriel." Nicolae patted her arm. "Are you planning on running these meetings as if you are in charge?"

I studied him for a moment, unsure of his implication. I was hesitant to speak, hoping he would continue, but he only awaited my response.

"The soon-to-be king of Darthou has no higher power in these meetings than any other leader present. The Summits are used to swap knowledge, protect each other, and retain order throughout the realms. Why would a single one be in charge?"

Nicolae shook his head in annoyance. "Either you are naive or being lied to."

My mood turned turbulent, anger beginning to bubble beneath the surface. I widened my stance and stole another look at Staffan, who was thoroughly engrossed in some kind of discussion. The river serpent at his side began talking, his tongue slithering out so quick it would have been easy to miss in the blink of an eye.

"Nicolae," Petra finally spoke, her voice sensual as she stroked his arm affectionately. "Perhaps you should go easy on Kadriel. This *is* his first Summit."

I held my tongue. Perhaps today would be better spent just observing. It looked like Staffan had already racked up a list with those less than enthused with his involvement in these proceedings so far.

"Tell me, whose idea was it to have the meeting here at the Islands of Isatar? Just a few minutes ago, I had thought they were still abandoned."

The two exchanged glances, almost as if they were sharing a thought before returning to me.

"Staffan." Nicolae spit out his name as if he was trying to expel it from his mouth like tainted blood. It was entirely mutual. "He was rather adamant on the matter."

CHAPTER 23

Kade

"Shall we get started?" Staffan's voice carried over the room, bringing everyone to a collective hush. He took a seat in a wooden chair not far off from where he and his party were gathered, and they shortly followed after.

There were about a dozen trolls in attendance, all wearing the same type of clothing and all men. They had taken it upon themselves to arrange all of the chairs into one giant circle, but had allowed enough space between the walls and the chairs so they could easily maneuver behind. No one bothered the tables scattered about, and most guests left their food and drinks behind, choosing to not take things with them when they moved. The lighting in here was bright enough to see clearly but still low enough that it cast shadows in the corners. There were numerous torches lit, yet it was still cool. You would figure that being on the beach, it would be warm, but it wasn't.

I had been pleased to witness Nicolae and Petra and their encounter with another troll. It had been the polar opposite of what I had experienced with Staffan upon our arrival, and while I admittedly wasn't the biggest fan of Nicolae himself, that gesture had gone a long way. I could have gone without the knowledge of a past orgy with a troll and the details he wanted to disclose, but even so, it helped broaden my narrow-minded perspective of him.

A siren, who I'd seen in a rather compromising position at Torenca last night, made her way over and didn't pay Nicolae any mind when she raised her hand for me to greet her. I had heard very little about Sakira. Her unnatural eyes were a sharp blue, and piercing at that. She sat at my right side, one knee placed on top of the other, her beaded dress pooling on the floor and showing off her slender legs.

The sirens were a tricky lot, I had to admit. Their voices could be used to sway others to do their bidding, especially humans. When in their natural form, they had a better chance of controlling any type of situation with their song. They could fuck you and kill you while making you think it was all your own idea. Luckily, the black obsidian that rimmed my pocket mirror would shield me should she try something. That stone wasn't limited to just protecting against saints and their mind games; the gifts it harbored were many.

Petra snagged a fellow demon king who I'd only had the pleasure to meet twice in my life prior to today. I remembered Edvin and his mate being present for Zan and Sarah's tethering, and come to think of it, a private meeting between my father and him. I had been quickly ushered out of the room after some small talk, and I had completely forgotten about that occurrence until now.

What business had my father had with him, for Edvin to travel to Darthou?

I stowed that recollection away as I shook his hand before taking a seat. His grip was firm, gold cuffs catching my eye, and a golden watch to match peaked out from beneath his sleeve. His kingdom was the only one that rivaled our own in the amount of demon-and-human tetherings.

Even though my attire had been fueled by the desire not to be upstaged by Staffan, I was certainly glad that I'd gone to Rebecca's to be fitted. Everyone here was in formal wear of some sort, or the best clothing of their respective cultures.

Violet had teased me this morning about needing a haircut, and while I probably could use one, I hadn't shied away from informing her of the satisfaction that came from her twisting her fingers through my hair and pulling on my scalp as she called out my name on the verge of an orgasm. It was an occurrence that had never held any importance or enjoyment until she came along.

My cock stirred at the remembrance of those entanglements, and I shifted in my seat. Now was not the time to get thrown off my game. I had to be attentive, fully immersed in my first out of many Summit meetings. What happened today would set the stage for my future encounters with these other leaders.

Violet was turning me into a goddamn animal.

"First order of business…" I rolled my eyes as Staffan began again. As if I didn't get enough of him barking orders in the council chambers. "Tomorrow, Darthou will open its doors for the coronation of our new king and queen. If you haven't already, please confirm your attendance through the appropriate channels."

I could sense the shift of focus to me from the attendees,

and I was already over this entire Summit. I didn't want to be associated with Staffan in any way, shape, or form. From what I had gathered so far from Nicolae, he wasn't exactly favored. I wasn't sure why they all put up with him in the first place. Why was he being allowed to run things at all?

"I'm sure most of you have noticed that Kadriel has accompanied me today, be sure to introduce yourselves if you haven't already."

Last I knew, we were all fucking adults here. Why was he treating us like school children?

Staffan's eyes flicked to the side, and the sliver of the river serpents' eyes did the same but seconds after. To my recollection, there hadn't been any sudden movement in that direction to cause them to do that. My back straightened as I tried to ascertain what had pulled their focus. I surveyed the room discreetly, trying to see if anyone else had caught wind of it, but for the most part, the focus was on the one speaking. Was it the vintage clock on the far wall?

"And haven't the trolls done a fine job of rehabilitating the fine Islands of Isatar?" A few of the room's occupants offered praise, but it quickly died down. Staffan didn't join in, or smile at the compliment. What good were his words when he treated the trolls like shit to begin with?

Sakira scowled beside me. It was obvious that our location today was still a heavy wound that she carried. I would have to make an effort to speak with her when I had the chance. She undoubtedly felt blindsided by today's chosen location for the Summit, and if Staffan was the one who had chosen it, surely she would have a few things to say on the matter.

A tap on my chest informed me that Elias was trying to reach out. Careful not to draw too much attention, I reached into the inside of my suit jacket and pulled out my pocket mirror. On it, there was nothing more than a single word, which didn't bode well.

Misper.

As of right now, Tamian was considered a missing person. The term was so rarely used amongst us demons, but that one word sent a swell of discomfort through my bloodstream. Elias had been unable to locate an important member of our guard who was supposed to be accessible at all times. It was his job, *his duty*, to be on call no matter what. The fact that Elias couldn't reach, contact, or find him, was highly suspicious.

The river serpent leaned toward Staffan and whispered something in his ear as the room fell eerily quiet once more. The serpent then got up and made his way out of the room, through a doorway that the trolls kept going in and out of. What could have been so important that he would have to leave at the start of a meeting? It seemed rather disrespectful. There had been time to converse and take care of needs before everything began.

"Now, let us discuss—" Staffan was interrupted before he could finish.

"How about we revisit an issue that you so blindly turned an eye to at the last Summit? That *many* of you did," Edvin interrupted vehemently as he stood and took a step forward to drive his point in. "I have reports of four more werewolves who were hunted down and killed by saints since the last time we gathered."

I froze, and the room suddenly grew heavy with negativity as some began to whisper amongst themselves. This was news to me, and it certainly hadn't been mentioned to those of us at council after the last Summit. Why would Staffan have left out crucial information such as this? Saints hunting down creatures of any kind was a threat to all of us.

"What proof do you have?" Staffan raised his voice as if to silence Edvin, but it didn't work.

"Are their deaths not enough proof?!"

"We, too, have had increased encounters with the saints." Another demon stood, Alba, a queen from the farthest kingdom away from Darthou. Her voice was a pure sound that matched her appearance, dressed in whites and creams. "We thought we had the situation taken care of, until three more saints took his place."

This news was beyond unsettling. Until now, I had been led to believe that this war with the saints was limited to us, but now I knew it was bigger. So much bigger that they were actively going after werewolves and demons?

A demon had been responsible for the lives lost in Xandor, and we had yet to unmask who, but there wasn't a doubt in my mind now that these cases were related. As much as I wanted to bring that up, I knew I couldn't. But there was something else.

Staffan was trying and failing to get a grip on the conversation. "Why would the saints—"

"This would be a good time to bring up the recent encounter us demons in Darthou have had with the saints." It was my turn to interrupt Staffan, and I stood, adjusting my jacket, more than ready to take him on. I needed to show the rest of them that there was a stark difference between the two of us. I didn't want to be associated with him any more than he wanted to be associated with me.

"Not now, Kadriel," he warned as he pushed himself up from his chair. The hatred in his face showed that he was losing his grasp on the room. It was now or never, and I pushed on.

"There's a saint who has gone by many names, but until a few days ago, we knew him as his oldest name—Noliathan." I swallowed hard, pushing back the emotion that threatened to constrict my throat. "He's also responsible for the deaths of our late king and queen—my parents."

Whispers again. Surely, some had heard of Noliathan before. With a saint his age, I found it hard to believe that there weren't others aware of his existence.

Staffan looked at the clock again, but I couldn't let that sway me from what needed to be said.

"Normally, the saints work alone, right?" I looked at the countless faces that were turned to me; there had to be over two dozen. Some were more familiar than others, but I would strive to learn each one that I didn't personally know. "When two of my colleagues and I were on a mission to deal with Noliathan once and for all, we were ambushed. What started out as a handful of saints that should have been easily disposed of, turned into a battle that we were ill-prepared for. They were ready to fight."

"What do we do?"

"What do they want?"

The room was growing louder, and I almost missed the goblin king who slipped away from the room in the same direction as the serpent. The trolls were following suit, leaving us all behind.

My eyes locked on Staffan, and the gut reaction that something was amiss was stirring again. He was fuming, fists balling at his sides as we held each other's stares.

There were too many leaders and not enough guards. Staffan and I weren't the only ones without someone else in tow for protection. You hoped you never needed it, but were always prepared in case you did.

His gaze flicked to the clock again, and at that, I had to say something. "Who traveled here today without some sort of guard present?"

Staffan's face broke at my question, his expression showing a chip in his hardened exterior. The murmurs grew louder and the room began buzzing with countless voices at varying levels.

"Everyone leave, the islands have been compromised!" I ordered as I made a beeline for Staffan. The scuffling of feet and scooting of chairs caused a ruckus, and the room fell into chaos.

"You little shit!" Staffan spat at me. He pulled back his arm, but I dodged it and landed a blow to his chest where he kept his pocket mirror. It broke beneath my knuckles, ensuring that he wouldn't have the chance to merely disappear and get out of this one. There would be no hiding or running away from me now.

His rage only pushed me further, unforgiving as I finally set words aside and let my fists take over for once.

And it felt good.

The seam of my jacket split near my shoulder blade as my hands surged forward on him again and again, as if he were my own punching bag. I could see—better yet, I could *feel* him concentrating on healing himself, and it was slowing his response to fight.

Fucking amateur.

"You set this up!" I seethed as he missed me again. It almost wasn't fair, considering he was no match for me. Why had he been given so much control when he couldn't even fucking fight? It should be the other way around. I was maybe an eighth of his age and yet he was stumbling, missing hits and holding a poor frame. He should know better.

I landed a blow to the underside of his jaw, and he fell back and over his chair. I used my foot to strike him down by his lower back where his kidneys were. A gush of air left him as he groaned in agony.

"Kadriel, get out of here!" I recognized the voice of the troll I had met when we first arrived. It carried over the emptying room, and when it reached my ears, I turned in his direction only to find saints filing in through both entrances with weapons in hand.

They were headed straight for me, cutting down anyone in their way. The troll included.

Before I could react to the loss of life unfolding before me, I grabbed fistfuls of Staffan's shoulders and transported us back to Darthou and to the council chambers.

With the heel of my palm, I drove his face down into the ground. A crack sounded as his jaw hit the floor and his bellow echoed through the room. I shrugged out of my jacket, placing it on my chair, and undid the buttons at my wrists so I could roll my sleeves up. This was far from over.

Rafina would sense his pain soon, if she hadn't already. I would have to be ready for her to join in on the fun when she arrived. I was adamant to finally get some answers. If I had to test the bonds of their tethering to do so, then so be it.

A scream sounded, and I whipped around to locate it, but no one was there. I searched every nook and cranny my eyes could scour to find the woman's voice, but found nothing. Then a man's voice joined in. Begging. Wait, no. It was *pleading* for someone or something to stop.

Together, the voices sent a numbing chill up my spine. There was something familiar to their sounds, as if I knew them, and I feared for them and their safety. Bloodcurdling screams erupted from the woman, her strained cries making me think she had lost all hope.

A blow to the back of my neck sent me forward and to the ground. My head hung low as I caught myself on all fours, but

Staffan's hand wrapped around my neck, catching my breath as he picked me up and slammed me against the wall. My larynx was being crushed, and I fought to breathe. When I met his eyes, an image began forming, and someone came into view. A woman knelt down, holding her arm as if injured, and with a look of defeat. Hopelessness was evident in her features that reminded me of my sister. They were too much alike.

Mom.

"They will conform or I will end them. Just as I have ended you," an image of Staffan declared as he slaughtered her right before me. It was as if I was the one committing the act, and it made me want to vomit.

The image shifted to that of my father, on the ground and beaten to a pulp. I had never seen a demon so broken down, yet still alert even through his torment. He was then set on fire by a faceless man on my right. Screams erupted as the flames consumed him, tearing away his life.

It had been years since their deaths. The preconceived images that I had constructed in my memory were now being overrun by these new visions. This wasn't what I had been told had happened. These weren't the facts that my uncle, Aleena and I had been presented by the council when they informed us of my parents' deaths by a saint.

I couldn't breathe as the image began to shift once more, to another face that wouldn't quite form. My vision was fading, and fast. The fuzziness told me I didn't have long before I lost consciousness.

Instead of fighting Staffan's hold on me, I fumbled to retrieve my blade. With a click, I brought it up and rammed it through the soft spot beneath his chin. Staffan's mouth parted at the impact, the metal barely visible inside as blood began to seep out and around my hand. The shock gave me enough of a reprieve to catch a breath of air before my foot landed on his chest, sending him flying to the ground as he scrambled to remove my weapon. Blood spurted as he withdrew it, tossing it to the floor.

I heaved as I tried to speed my healing. A fury was settling in my blood at the images of my parents. All this time I had been led to believe that Noliathan was responsible for their deaths, because that was what I had been told. What Staffan *specifically* had told me. Us.

"You fucking liar!" I raged as I took off toward him, tackling his form to the ground with such force that my shoulder throbbed.

"You killed them! You fucking killed them!" I cried out, distraught that I would never be able to unsee their deaths. They played on repeat in my mind, terrorizing me. I would never be able to wash it away.

My eyes were watering with the onslaught of emotions cascading through me. I felt an urge to tear him apart, limb by limb, for what he had done. For the lives taken, and for leaving Aleena and me orphans. And for what? Why did he have to take them from us?

My fists began pummeling him, and each time he tried to raise his arms for cover, I swiped them away and kept at it. I could feel the break of his nose, a crack to his skull, and when that wasn't enough, I stood. Sending my foot down, I shattered a number of ribs, but it still wasn't enough. The garbled sounds emitting from his throat did nothing to slow me, and only drove me further.

Reclaiming my knife from the ground, I approached him again. A hum in my ears was so loud that it was swallowing up any other sound as I came to a stop at his side.

My parents hadn't deserved that. Aleena and I didn't

deserve to be left in a world without them. I wouldn't give him the opportunity to speak again. He would never get the chance to persuade, bargain, or plead. If he had any last words, I wouldn't hear them.

This ended now.

My throat strained as I let out a shriek that shut down my hearing. Everything became muted as I attacked him with the small blade, slicing the arteries on his neck and wrists and then moving to his chest. I lost count of the stabs, and when the blade broke off on his collarbone, I let my hands continue to beat him, long after he took his last breath.

Staffan's blood soaked me just as fast as it covered the stone floor that surrounded us. My mind went blank. I didn't think about the next move, only the urge to drive him into a pulp until he became one with the ground below.

Something wrapped around my upper arms, pulling me off of him, and I aggressively shoved it away. It was a back-and-forth of me breaking free only to be snatched up and pulled away again, dragged from the murderous man who was responsible for so much pain. I thrashed about, adamant to escape so I could continue. I hadn't had enough yet. I hadn't had my fill of revenge.

It wasn't until Violet came into view that I finally snapped out of it.

CHAPTER 24

Violet

I gasped for air, suddenly overcome with an anger so great it swept the substance from my lungs. Clutching my chest, I moved to the side of the bed, trying to figure out where this was coming from. I couldn't catch my breath, and I lost my balance getting up from the bed, stumbling.

Kade.

Something was wrong. Elias still had yet to retrieve me for training, and with my horrible sense of direction, that only left me with one other option for help.

Taking off in my bare feet, I ran out of our home and down to the next door. I tried the handle just in case, but it remained sealed, denying me entrance.

I panted, knowing full well that I couldn't use the mirror in the bathroom as it wasn't meant for travel or communication of any sort. I was stuck, unable to contact anyone or travel anywhere, unless it was by foot.

The debilitating agony swiped at my chest again. Kade was livid, hurting in a way I had never experienced before. There was no denying that, given our connection. Over our time together I had felt numerous emotions through him, but nothing of this magnitude.

What in the hell was happening at the Summit?

I would beat on Aleena's door until my fists bled if I had to. Right now I was fearing for Kade's life, and I wouldn't stop until I had someone's attention. Anyone. Secrets be damned.

I was sweating profusely, as if I'd run five miles. My legs shook, and I braced myself on my knees before repeating my assault on the door. If anyone else were to hear me, then so be it. I would rope them in to help me if I must.

I'd been successful in locating Kade once before. With the severity that I felt right now, surely I could do it again if I had to. I couldn't afford *not* to find him.

"Aleena!" I hollered, my voice a jagged shrill. My right hand beat the door as I called to her. If she wasn't here, I would beat on every door I found until I was able to find someone to help. I was struggling to stand, leaning on the doorframe as I pushed harder, pounded harder. My voice cracked as yelled her name repeatedly.

Just as I released an armful of weakened strength, the door flung open and I went flying forward. Aleena fumbled to catch me, sending us both to the ground in a heap of flailing limbs.

"What the fuck, Violet?" She pushed off the ground as she scurried over to help me up.

"It's Kade," I rasped, overwhelmed to the point I thought I might pass out. "Something's wrong, we have to find him!"

My throat closed in, as if I was being held by it. I clawed at it as if I could pull something off of me. I was losing air, failing to breathe in, and my eyesight was going awry. I couldn't focus on Aleena.

My eyes went wide with alarm. Kade was declining, and my heart pounded as I sensed his condition. The thought of his impending death made tears fill my eyes.

Fight, Kade! Fight!

"Let me grab Elias, hang on!" Aleena vanished from view and I hunched over onto the floor. My eyes ached and began to sting, straining as I fought to find some sort of sanity.

The fear of losing Kade was very real. The line between us splintered before me, and I had never felt so helpless. I was losing hope and the ability to see straight; it was agonizing and felt like it drew out forever, second by second, a torturous spiral of defeat and despair.

"I've been searching for Tamian but I can't find him." Elias's voice came closer. "Violet, what's wrong?"

The chokehold on my throat disappeared and I sucked in precious air. My lungs expanded over and over, trying to replenish what I had lost. A newfound strength was surging through me, a power that was taking over and making itself known.

"What the fuck?" Aleena muttered beneath her breath as I met their faces. I searched her eyes, witnessing shock, an expression I hadn't experienced with her before. "What's wrong with your eyes? I mean, are those tears?"

The moment our eyes met, my sight made itself known. Images and scenes began filtering through my mind. A death began to unfold of a man with greasy hair and a serious overbite. Something wrapped around his neck, and then I heard a snap. The light dimmed from his eyes before my sight moved on to another man.

Shit, shit, shit!

I closed my eyes, shaking my head in irritation. I had left without grabbing my coins. I hadn't even been actively trying to find anything when I looked at Aleena, much the same as when it happened with Kade.

I swiped at my eyes, becoming even more aware that black tears were staining my face. But we couldn't get into that now; we had to find Kade.

"Is he alright? Kadriel? Can you feel him?" Elias pushed past Aleena.

I nodded. "I think he's close. Can I have your pocket mirror?"

Elias stiffened, silent. As I met his eyes, images began unfolding in my mind and I blinked away, growing aggravated. "Dammit, Elias! We don't have time!"

Aleena reached into the pocket of her skintight leggings and retrieved hers, handing it to me. My thumb swiped over it, producing an image of Kade pummeling something. Better yet, someone.

The high-pitched sound emitting from him was a clear indicator of what was going on, even if I didn't understand why or how. I clasped my hand over my mouth, terrified not by the act that he was committing, but by what it meant.

"Is that the council chambers?" My voice was small as I let Elias see the image in my shaking hand. He was already pale, but I swore he turned white as a ghost. He popped out of view without a word or sound.

"Take me there, please." I held the mirror out to Aleena and she hesitated to reach for it. She knew something was awry with me, and it read all over her face. She didn't even try to hide it. Looked like we had some explaining to do before the coronation tomorrow after all.

If there was still going to be one.

"Please," I urged, desperate to get to Kade.

She nodded slightly, touching my shoulder and the glass surface, taking us to the council chambers that I had only been to on rare occasions. I wasn't even sure if you could walk here or if it was the same as Rafina's infirmary that could only be accessed by a mirror.

Elias was trying to pull Kade off of what looked to be a man, but he was no match for Kade. Kade fought him off, driving himself right back to the being on the floor that was beaten beyond recognition.

There was so much pain, so much built-up anger radiating off of Kade, that it was impairing. My heart ached for him, and I was unable to mentally process what he was going through even though I could feel it. There weren't enough words.

Aleena brushed past me and on toward the scene. Elias took one arm and Aleena the other, drawing Kade back and finally hauling him off. He thrashed back and forth, trying to fight off those attempting to detain him. The front of him was blood soaked, his shirt torn and a madness in his expression that shook me to my core.

Coming out of my frozen state, I took off and rounded the three of them as I made my way into his line of sight, trying to put a barrier between him and whoever the dead man was on the ground. I had a hard time believing that any demon could heal themselves and come back from that. Maybe it was all the images of death I had seen between the witch, Kade, and Elias, but the murder scene behind me didn't even faze me. I just wondered who was responsible for Kade's wrath.

"Kade," I said, urging him to look at me and not at the unknown man who he was fixated on. He ignored me, and I raised my voice, lowering to the point that one of my knees hovered above a streak of blood from Kade being dragged away. I grappled to take his face in my hands. "Kade!"

His eyes flicked to mine, and the disorder came to a standstill. Kade remained suspended between his sister and best friend, shuddering now that his violent movements had ceased. I could almost see the wheels turning inside his head, coming to terms with where he was and how we had come to be here. His chest moved rapidly as he began to come down from his exertion.

But there was so much hurt. So much suffering.

"Somebody get Zan," I ordered gently, careful not to break eye contact now that I had his full attention. "Now."

In tandem, Kade's arms were released cautiously and his arms sagged. I attempted to ignore the crimson that now stained the two behind him, and the mess I was kneeling into as I came down to his level.

Elias took the initiative and disappeared, leaving the rest of us behind.

"Kade?" Tears began spilling from my eyes as I took on his affliction. I had no idea what had transpired or what had brought us to this moment, but it was devastating. There was no denying it.

"What—" I hiccupped as I tried to get the words out. "What happened?"

He held my gaze for a moment, then surged forward, collapsing into a heap of hoarse sobs at my front. My arms wrapped around him as I held him close, wishing I could comfort him, but I had no idea how. His body quaked beneath me, jerking each time he inhaled.

We sat there for a while, merely existing in whatever pits of destructive sorrow we were in. It was all-consuming and I couldn't concentrate on anything but the constant flow of tears and the gut-wrenching sadness that rendered us useless.

It wasn't until his cries drew to a close and the room fell quiet that I lifted my head from his. Zan was now centered between the other two, carefully studying the scene behind me. Elias was staring at the both of us, arms crossed and waiting. Aleena's lips were pressed thin, eyes fixated on me. And it was one hell of a hefty glare.

There was so much explaining to do, but my troubles paled in comparison to whatever Kade was going through.

Releasing my hold on him, I nudged him to sit up and look at me. His eyes were almost hollow, face puffy, and stubble had formed around his jaw. It was like he had been the victim of a crime and not the one who committed it.

Kade moved his mouth as if he were going to talk, but not a sound came out. He shook his head, confused. Once again his lips moved, but there was nothing.

I swallowed hard when his eyes met mine again, my brows raising in alarm as he reached up for his throat. There were markings around it, as if someone had been strangling him. But I knew deep down that that wasn't the only cause of his lost voice.

Aleena was the first to break the silence. "Anybody care to share why Violet is crying black tears and there's a dead body in the council chambers?"

Kade's eyes widened, probably realizing for the first time that we weren't alone. His jaw dropped slightly, unease spreading rapidly. There was no talking around this without the truth.

Zan held up a hand to shush Aleena, but she only shoved it away. I stood, wiping my cheeks with a clean and unmarked part of my sleeve, the black tears a greater contrast than the red against my light purple sweater. I didn't think there would be any saving this top, and the amount of clothes that had been ruined by blood or tears was seriously annoying. And I wasn't even going to take into account the garments Kade had gone through, shredding them in attempts to get to my body.

"Aleena," I began, treading lightly, not knowing how she was going to take this news. We had been lying to her for weeks, months even. Literally ever since I had come to Darthou. I had an inkling that there was no way this could go well. If I'd been in her position and was just now finding out, I would probably be pissed too.

"What are you?" Her voice rose, anger brimming beneath her features as she stepped forward. Zan tried to hold her back, but she popped out of view and appeared inches away from my face. It should have startled me, but I stood my ground.

"Aleena, we'll explain everything," Zan pleaded, and before he could join us, I held up my hand for him to stop.

"Well somebody had better!" Aleena fumed.

Kade stood and met me at my side. I took his hand in mine, ignoring the texture of dried blood on our hands as they joined. He might have been silent, but it appeared he was coming back into himself again. His shoulders straightened as he focused on his sister. I turned my attention back to her too.

"I'm not all demon, and not by choice." I spoke very matter-of-factly, and as calmly as I could.

Aleena shook her head, her nose turning up as she raised her head slightly. "What the hell is that supposed to mean?"

"We aren't sure how it happened exactly, but I am also part fury and part banshee."

"Bullshit," Aleena spat. "They were exiled ages ago. They're probably dead. Do you think I'm an idiot?"

"Never," Elias spoke up, and her head whipped in his direction.

"And you knew?" She stepped toward him. "You all fucking knew? You hid this from me?"

Now Zan joined in. "It was in your best interest—"

"Fucking bullshit! You've been lying to me!"

If nobody else was going to say it, then I was. I hated the bitch anyway and I had no problems inserting her name into the conversation now that we had found ourselves here.

"Because Rafina is involved." I raised my voice to get her attention. Aleena's body stilled, but I could sense that the name had struck a chord in her. I had never seen the two of them together in any kind of entanglements, but I could only assume they were discreet if they were still involved. Since Rafina was tethered to Staffan, I didn't think he would take too kindly to that kind of affair.

"How?" She took a small step back, but she was still dangerously close to my bubble and I could feel heat radiating off of her like a furnace.

"We're still trying to figure that part out," Zan said. "We know you two have a history together, and we didn't want to put you in the middle of everything until we had some answers."

Elias dropped his heavy gaze from Aleena and turned his head away. This wasn't the first time I had witnessed this reaction when the topic of Aleena and Rafina was brought up. It was obvious that this was more than uncomfortable for him.

Kade brought his free hand up to his neck again, and while his energy felt depleted, he pushed on as he tried again to heal himself. I squeezed his hand, hoping he could draw on me for whatever he needed to right himself again. He closed his eyes in concentration, and I willed everything I had in me for him to be successful.

"Aleena," was the first word out of his mouth, and he

dropped his hand away from his throat. I wanted to be relieved, but I didn't know if there was anything he could say to help make all of the information we had held secret sound any better.

We had lied to her. Repeatedly.

The hurt was returning, taking me by storm. Before I could say something, Kade held up a hand to quiet me. I didn't want him spiraling like this, not again.

"Blame me if you must for not bringing you in earlier, but there's something you need to know."

I squeezed his hand, unsettled by what he might be leading up to.

"There's something all of you need to know." His chest expanded slowly a few times, before he continued, "I killed Staffan."

Collectively, we all turned to face the man on the floor who Kade had been pried from, the lifeless body that none of us had put a name to since arriving. Or at least, if anyone had, nobody spoke about it.

"That's not—"

"It is," Kade cut Elias off.

"I recognize the suit," Zan spoke up as he came around. He was careful not to step in any blood as he approached the body, kneeling slightly as he examined it closely.

"What? How?" Elias was just as confused as I was. "Was there any sign of Rafina?"

"No." Kade shook his head. "Never saw her once."

"And you wouldn't have." Zan stood. "If you take a look at his wrist, his tethering has been severed. And it's fresh too."

Silence consumed the room as Zan made his way back over to us. His eyes flicked to mine, and then back to Kade. "What exactly happened at the Summit today?"

Kade filled us in on the events of his short time spent away. From the importance of the place picked for the day, the lack of guards, and the leaders that conveniently began sneaking away before Kade had warned everyone it was a trap. From the sounds of it, Kade was lucky enough to have made it out of there just in time before saints had shown up and begun to take on whoever was left.

"Okay, but even if Staffan was a part of the setup, why kill him?" Aleena was furious. It read on her face and in her body posture. "He could have been useful. I could have got information out of him."

Now all eyes fell on Kade once more, and we waited for him to inform us as to why the acting leader of the council had been snuffed out. It was a violent end that should have been a disturbing sight to see, but I only wanted to know why. I'd never liked Staffan anyway, but to come down to this level, there had to be a major piece that we were missing.

"He…" Kade was turning sorrowful again, but there was something else stirring, mixing into it and muddling my senses. "He killed our mom and dad. I…I saw it."

"Wh—what do you mean you *saw* it?" Aleena's voice thickened with skepticism. "Noliathan killed our parents."

"You saw it?" My voice was so tiny in comparison to the others. I was shocked, but this news further explained his warring emotions. He had been led to believe one thing all this time, only to be so close to the demon who had killed his parents, and for years. Kade had sat by his side in this very room. Just days ago we'd thought it was Damian—er…Noliathan—and now this?

Confusion swept through us all.

"Just like…how I…" I searched Kade's eyes, and he offered a slight tip of head to acknowledge that I was on the right track.

My eyes widened at the realization. Was Kade really capable of the sight just as I was?

"You can draw on Kadriel's abilities. I suppose it makes sense that he might be able to do so in return." Zan stated what my mouth was failing to iterate.

"But I didn't think that tethering capability was possible between different creatures. It's only between demons," Elias said.

"Well, I think they are living proof that it's possible." Zan was studying us as he came back around.

Three sets of eyes fell on us as I looked up to Kade, but it was evident by Aleena's pinched face that she still hadn't come to terms with the information unfolding.

"I'm still fucking lost." She passed us as she moved over to the man who resembled nothing of Staffan. Even his slanted nose was nowhere to be seen. "Staffan's dead and isn't tethered anymore. Noliathan didn't kill our parents, he did. And Violet is some weird concoction of creatures that shouldn't be possible but is?"

I hated that we were only skimming the surface with Aleena. There was still so much to unpack, but I couldn't deny the fact that I was so relieved to bring her in. I was more than ready to start discussing these things with someone other than Sarah. She could only help so much, since she was human. Aleena, however, could provide new insight. Now that she was becoming aware, I had to believe it was for the better.

Swallowing, my gaze dropped before my mouth decided to start moving. "I hate to say it, but there's more."

CHAPTER 25

Violet

It took some time, but a game plan was formulated before we all went our separate ways.

Zan, Elias, and Aleena took it upon themselves to get rid of Staffan's body and clean up the messy end he had been met with. There was already a small search party underway to find Tamian, and they'd chosen a select few to carry out the task discreetly so they wouldn't raise any alarm. And within the next hour, they were planning to go to the islands where the Summit had been held in the hopes of finding survivors, collecting the dead, and perhaps fighting a battle if it came down to it.

I really, truly hoped it didn't come to that last bit.

Even though we had been met with the revelation that the murder of Kade and Aleena's parents—once thought to be the responsibility of a saint—had actually been committed by none other than Staffan, the news did little to calm our worries about whatever storm and agenda the saints had planned.

Kade and I returned home so he could shower and change. I took it upon myself to join him. Without words, I washed him, careful and unhurriedly, much like what Kade had done for me when I'd been coated with that black mess after my transition.

I wanted to ask him so much. Questions burned in my mind, as they so often did. Normally he would meet each one without much hesitation, and satiate my inquisitive mind, but it didn't feel like it was the right time. Kade wanted to be ready when he was retrieved to go to the islands. He wanted to see the aftermath himself and lead the others in, preparing them for what they might see, hear, or come in contact with.

There would be pushback, but I was adamant about joining him. I was tired of sitting on the sidelines unable to help in any way, shape, or form. I firmly believed that we were stronger together, if only I didn't have the coins on me.

Wrapped in my towel, I stepped out of the shower. The heat was swirling around in clouds of mist as I made my way over to the sink where I kept my coins. I had yet to tell Kade about the crack in the one.

He was beginning to look more like himself again. Gone was the stubble and hollow eyes, but there was a light missing. That charm of amusement, that spark that always lifted my spirits, was nowhere to be seen.

"It was personal." The words were out of my mouth before I could comprehend them.

"What?" Kade asked as he took the coins from my hand and placed them back on the counter.

"Staffan. If you saw him kill your parents, no wonder you

went off on him. It was personal. Just like when I killed Brett, I was blinded by rage.”

My throat had been raw and my voice had left me with nothing to speak with. I had been so lost in my own fury that nothing else around me mattered until he was gone. Until the threat of him was over. Kade had been met with the same aftereffects when he killed his parents’ murderer.

At least he had been able to finally heal himself, even if not right away.

“I wonder why you never experienced the sight before today.” I spoke aloud, forgetting to hush my thoughts. “I’m sorry, I’ll shut up.”

“No, I think you’re onto something.”

My brows lowered, curious as to what he meant by that.

“It’s only happened a few times, and I just brushed it off as a recurring memory rearing its head.”

“What?” I pushed on, wanting him to spill.

“On occasion, when I look at you…”

He paused, and I took his hands in mine as I pleaded for him to continue. “What is it, Kade?”

He blew out a steady breath as I waited patiently.

“Sometimes, I can see flashes of you killing Brett. But it’s quick, as if the memory just decided to stir and come to the surface. I never thought much of it before today. Until after I killed Staffan.” He swallowed, and I swore I could see the skin around his eyes hollowing again. “It wasn’t until I saw you in the council chambers that I put it together. The images of my parents were almost identical to what you’ve described. It was as if I were committing the act, even though I merely witnessed you killing Brett. I rewatched it countless times and at different angles, so I didn’t realize that I was the one doing it, so to speak.”

"And I've only taken one life. So of course that's all you would see. There isn't any special highlight reel of all of my kills like when I look into yours and Elias's eyes."

"Right," he confirmed.

"How were we to know? We're still navigating our relationship and figuring out what the hell I am and what I'm capable of." I then corrected myself, "What *we* are capable of."

Kade drew me in, wrapping his dampened arms around me. His towel hung low on his hips as I embraced him back. We stood in silence for a while, simply existing in the comfort provided by the presence of one another. These past few days had proved more than problematic, and it didn't show any signs of slowing. That very thought was daunting.

"We need to talk." I was the first to break away. And while I didn't want to be the one to do so, I needed to get the words out of my head before I lost my grip on them. I had no idea how much time we had before Kade was summoned away.

"About?"

Stepping back, I leaned up against the counter, crossing my arms in the hopes that my towel might stay up better. It had a tendency of slipping down the more that I moved.

"About leaving me here…alone. Kade…" I was getting frazzled, reflecting on the time I'd spent here in our home, knowing something was seriously wrong with Kade and unable to reach out. I had no means of communication whatsoever. "I know you don't trust me enough to let me have access to a mirror, but when I thought I might lose you today—"

My sentence broke off as my throat began to constrict. My eyes stung, and I clung to whatever strength I could find to push through it.

"Kade, I could hardly function. I was all out of sorts on a

level I had never even imagined possible. For all I knew, you were dying and I had no way to contact you or attempt to reach out to anyone else. Had Aleena not been home, I would have been so lost. Hell, I'm lost ninety percent of the time here in Darthou.

"But once I had Aleena's pocket mirror, I was able to find you. Without my coins, by the way. Which I accidentally left here. I don't ever want to be put in that position again. I was really, really scared."

Tears escaped down my cheeks and I untucked my towel so I could brush them away. It was pointless, though, as more began to fall.

Kade took me by the hand and led me out of the bathroom and into his watching quarters. I shivered now that we had left the heated room of our steamy shower and clutched my towel at my front as I followed him to a stop. He opened one of his desk drawers and pulled out a pocket mirror that was identical to the one he used. It was encased in black obsidian, just like my necklace. It was a bit more worn, showing it had withstood time and a few dents and bangs, but could still be useful.

"For now, in case of emergencies, you can have this. I know you haven't had much training with these, but if you have to take it with you, make sure the glass is facing away from your body. That way, if you want to travel, you can focus all of your energy on where you want to go and *then* touch the surface."

"So...if the glass were facing me in my pocket, I could merely think of a place and transport there?" I wanted to make sure I understood what he was saying.

"Right."

"But, if you have yours in your pocket all the time, how do you keep yourself from zapping in and out all over, all the time?"

Kade tried to smile, but his lips barely moved and it didn't reach his eyes. "That happens a lot when someone first gets their pocket. For now, I would advise you to keep it in a safe place here, and again, only use it for emergencies. We can work up to traveling with one."

I nodded in agreement. With the mess of a headspace I had between my two ears, I had no doubt that I would be popping in and out of places both here and back in the world I used to call home. While I appreciated that I hadn't been met with any pushback, this pocket mirror now felt a little more dangerous than what I had planned. But he was trusting me with this. And that alone meant so much.

I took it from his hold, letting the smooth back side sit in my hand as I examined it. Careful not to touch its reflective surface, I curled my fingers around its curved edges.

"Thank you, Kade."

Tapping came from the wall of mirrors, and we exchanged glances before I took off for the doorway so I could be out of view from Elias. Kade strode over and I could hear his best friend clear as day as he came through.

"Are you sure you want to go?"

"Yes, how many do we have?"

"We have members of the guard, and a few seekers are willing to help."

Instead of standing there to eavesdrop, I took the opportunity to get a head start on finding undergarments, darting for the bathroom so I could start to dress in my protections. I all but ripped my brush through my hair and chose to ignore the strands that I had painfully pulled from my head that were now stuck in the brush. Wanting my hair out of the way, I pulled it back into a tight and low bun. I had just finished putting myself together, feeling a small ounce of pride as I zipped up the back of it, before there was a knock at the door. All I was missing now was my boots, my coins, and the hardest thing to get—Kade's approval to accompany him.

I grabbed my two coins and swung the door open to find him already dressed. His eyes quickly filled with rejection as he surveyed my attire.

"No," he stated, and I sailed past him and to the closet once more.

"I'm going, Kade."

"The hell you are." He followed after. "You have the pocket mirror now in case of an emergency."

I pulled my boots on and fastened them before retrieving what few weapons I was allowed to carry on me. "Is Aleena going?"

"Well yeah, but—"

"I'm tired of sitting on the sidelines. I will remain close and keep my mouth shut."

"You're not ready." He took a step forward, worry and anger fusing together in one swift gut punch that almost knocked me over.

"Will I ever *be* ready? At least to your standards? You said it yourself that this might be no more than a rescue and recover mission."

"I said that it might be a rescue mission as I can't see the saints sticking around for long after their attack."

"Then what harm is it if I go?"

Faint tapping sounded again. I knew what Kade was thinking, so before he could try to escape without me, I grasped onto his forearm in the nick of time, piggybacking on his transport.

"What the hell are you doing?" His frustration lashed out.

But he wasn't the only one getting riled up. Was he really going to just up and leave me like that? I removed my hand and took a step away from him.

We were now in a room, surrounded by several demons all dressed in their protections. Their eyes were all fixed on me as they each hesitantly bowed.

Recognition hit me, having passed by this room from time to time when I met Elias here for training in one of the smaller areas. But there was a feature I had missed before, as I'd never actually been in this particular room.

There was a row of mirrors, each identical in size and a few feet taller and wider than me. They were unlike those used in watching quarters, that were all smaller and of numerous different sizes. The room was brightly lit, showing off the outside world and the frosted trees in the distance. There were markings on the concrete floors—scrapes, divots, and holes that showed signs of what I could only assume to be training sessions or sparring. There was no way they were from normal wear and tear.

What the hell was I doing, indeed. I was out of my fucking mind.

"She's not coming," Aleena's voice sounded, and I met her hardened stare. I hadn't had the pleasure of seeing her in her protections yet, and she was the epitome of lethality. Her hair was still dark and arranged in a style I could only describe as Viking warrior. Tight braids at the sides of her face led to wild and unruly hair at the back. She was wearing the same claw fingertips that she had worn at our tethering celebration, and blades on her thighs.

"She is, and you will remain by her side, as will I," Kade ordered, before tilting his head down toward my ear. "We are not going to cause a scene here. We will discuss this later."

Swallowing my shock was difficult. He wasn't trying to send me back, when seconds ago he had tried to leave me in the dust. I didn't doubt that he was partially worried I might try to come after him, now that I had a pocket mirror of my own, and figured this was the safest way to keep me under his thumb instead of letting me blindly transport myself to find him.

I had yet to decide if this was a victory or not. We were more than likely headed into a heated argument about this whenever we returned home. So be it.

"We will enter at the southeast side of the last island, where there is a structure that we will need to surround before we make entry. Enchantments prevent us from traveling or viewing the inside. I am only aware of one physical entrance and exit, so keep your heads on a swivel. The interior room will easily fit all of us, but should we be met with any force, it could get tight."

"Are we taking any prisoners?" a man asked, one who I had never seen before.

"The only one I want is Noliathan. Any other saint, end them."

The group surrounding us seemed pleased with Kade's order. There were nods of excitement at the mere mention of getting to end the lives of saints. Their collective disdain for their enemies was clearly evident.

Zan popped into view, now wearing normal day-to-day clothes, but he had definitely changed since I'd last seen him in the council chambers. His face was grim as he approached us, and he brought news that swept the room into a hush.

"Tamian has been found," he said, but I knew that wasn't all of it. There were a few quiet murmurs, but nothing I could make out.

"And?" Kade poked, growing impatient.

"He was found in the dungeons. Nearly drained of his blood and left for dead. Had we found him any later, he would be gone."

They had dungeons in Darthou? Why hadn't I heard of them before, and where were they?

The volume around us grew louder and someone stepped forward on my right—Lorenz, from the kitchen. It took me a second to recall that he had once been a seeker before he switched careers. He might have been much smaller in frame compared to most of the men surrounding him, but he still looked every bit the part of a soldier among those here today.

Lorenz opened his mouth to speak, but Kade cut him off. "I admire your willingness to volunteer, but you should go to him."

"Thank you, please let me know if I can be of any other assistance." Lorenz bowed and vanished from sight.

I knew that the two of them had been conversing in the kitchens, but I didn't know the extent of their relationship. Judging by Lorenz's desire to leave, they must be pretty close. Although the news that Zan had brought was unsettling, I was just grateful that Tamian had been found and wasn't dead. But it just made me wonder who had tried to kill him in the first place? Hopefully, depending on how fast he healed, we might know that answer soon.

"Thank you, Zan," Kade said to him as he left. Zan opened his mouth when he made eye contact with me, but I remained quiet, turning my attention away. I was sure he was on board with everyone else, wondering why the hell I was here to begin with.

Kade was now at the wall of mirrors, dragging his hand across the surfaces and bringing forth images of a sandy beach shrouded in darkness. Frame by frame, another world came to life. Well, I wasn't sure if I should call it a world or a realm or what. Whatever it was, it brought forth images of destruction and death.

I gulped as I took in the sights of what looked to be bodies scattered about. Dark spots stained the bright sands, and I took a step forward, examining the scene. It looked like it had been a bloodbath of a battle.

"Sure you still want to go?" Elias spoke over my shoulder. Although I couldn't find my voice, I removed the blade from my forearm and held it in my grasp as I nodded. "Aleena will be on your left, I on your right, and Kade will lead. Do *not* break away from our formation."

"I know." I gritted my teeth. It was the same formation we had used on our first visit to Xandor. I only hoped I wasn't so much of a distraction that it pulled away from the focus the ones surrounding me needed.

Kade nodded. "Wave one, north side."

A group of about five men and one woman made their way toward the mirrors and crossed through and into the sands. They had various weapons in their hands; some held shiny blades while others used tools, some that I recognized and some I didn't. Once they were in position, Kade swiped at the images and cleared our view for a new location.

"Waves two and three, go," Kade ordered, and two more droves of demons crossed through. The determination was palpable as they made their way in, their footsteps quieted as they hit the sand. They, too, disappeared as Kade made quick work of revealing the site that would take on the rest of us.

"The rest of you, follow us." Kade made his way toward the center, and his apprehension hit me like a brick as Elias and Aleena flanked. I offered a small nod to try and reassure him, but his lips only thinned. I knew he was upset with me, by both our connection and his demeanor, but this was my chance to get involved. I knew it wasn't in the way he was hoping for, but I wanted to be a part of this, and I wanted to be by his side.

My feet sank as they stepped onto the sandy shoreline. It was still here, save for the rolling waves that were closer than I thought they'd be. While I wanted to appreciate the night sky that reminded me of home, the sight before us was staggering.

Everyone surrounding me was on high alert, searching high and low for any sign of life. Blood soiled the sands, and the bodies scattered about made my stomach turn. Some were human-like, others resembled creatures I had come across at the underground club. Body parts were strewn about, and it was evident that no life was present in the bodies we passed with our soundless movements. My heart ached for the lives that had been lost around us. It pained me that they had met such a violent end.

It reminded me of the chaos that had befallen Xandor, and my stomach stirred vigorously with that recognition.

Kade came to a stop on our way toward some sort of building. It looked old and honestly, not safe to enter if you asked me. I was unsure if it would still be left standing if a giant storm were to blow through here.

He knelt down, observing a body that was dressed in some sort of armor. It was a body that looked human. Kade's blade-filled hand slammed down into the man's chest without so much as a word or warning. The man's body remained stiff and unmoving, but I could feel disgust rolling off of Kade as he withdrew his blade and stood.

I suspected, from that action, that the man before us must have been a saint. Perhaps Kade was merely making sure he was dead, or he just needed to take some frustration out, I couldn't be sure. But this side of Kade was one I would have to get used to if I were going to make a habit of sticking by him through trials such as this. For so long, I had wondered what I was missing, all the facets of who Kade was and what he did, and now I was seeing it firsthand. Kade didn't kill without reason.

I wasn't sure how to tell a guard from a seeker as they were all dressed in the same protections of head-to-toe black, but one on my far left knelt down and inspected some sort of creature with reptile-like skin. He picked up his arm and paused, before gently setting it back on the ground and rising again. He rejoined us as we began to close in on the stone building.

There was already so much death outside; I hated to think of what might await up ahead. My grip tightened on my blade, wishing it was bigger right now. To do any damage to someone, I would have to be in close proximity to them. I wanted to believe that we wouldn't run into any trouble here, but I hated the little voice in my head telling me that wouldn't be the case.

In my periphery, there was movement on both sides, and my head snapped back and forth. My heart sped up as I squinted, as if I could make the images of the ones approaching us any clearer in the dark. I looked to Elias and Aleena as we all came to a halt, but neither of them seemed fazed. A few seconds later, I realized it was only the first few "waves" as Kade had called them, coming back from scouting around the island. The leader of each triangular formation held up their hands, signaling something to Kade. He mimicked the same movements they did, and we began to move once more.

The first and second waves began to blend in with our group, and their two leaders came to join Kade. My stomach twisted as if a knot was forming, and my free hand settled over it. I took a deep breath, unsure of why I was coming down with this, and my face started to warm. It was like the onset of a stomach bug and fever, and the timing couldn't have been worse.

Until a low scream formed in my mind.

No, it can't be. Not now. This can't be happening. I have my coins!

Kade picked up on the stress that my ailments were causing, and he hung back while the formation adjusted to fill his void. He gestured for the others to continue, and the one to the right of him paused, as if he wasn't going to follow through with what he was instructed to do. I noticed how his gaze seemed to linger on Kade, and the unease I was experiencing increased.

Kade flinched as he approached, almost as if he was holding back something painful. I wondered if it was the ringing in his ears that was causing it, and I worried that my being here was hurting him and his effectiveness.

I was fucking stupid for coming along. I should be home and without my coins, allowing him to be free of their side effects. I was probably putting him in more danger, and it was all my fault.

My heart was racing, and not in a good way. I was panicking. The last thing I ever wanted was to put Kade in harm's way. Who was I to think that after being in Darthou for a few months, I was ready for something like this? Kade had every right to be mad at me.

"Something's not right," I whispered as Aleena and Elias held back as well. The other demons passed us, some casting glares my way and others paying me no mind whatsoever.

"What do you mean?" Kade asked, in all seriousness. His voice was impossibly low.

Demons were now filing through the crooked doorway and into a black abyss that awaited them. I had no idea what they would come to find, but I was nervous for the lot of them. Were all of the saints really gone? Did they really just come, kill, and leave? None of this felt right.

"I don't know. I…" My hands were shaking, to the point that the blade I held threatened to jump out and fall to the ground.

Kade pressed the back of his hand to my cheek, then to my forehead. "You're burning up," he stated.

"You have no business being here," Aleena seethed, and I tried to ignore her.

"Do you have your coins?"

I nodded at Elias. "Of course I do."

Well, usually that was the case. With the exception of Kade's situation today, I always had my coins tucked away somewhere on me when I left our home.

"Give them here." Elias held both of his swords in one hand, and held out the free hand for me.

I gave Kade a worried look as he pinched the bridge of his nose before reopening his eyes and agreeing. "Do it."

Pulling the coins out of a small pocket at my hip, I let them fall into Elias's hand with a few clinks. I did a double take, noting how three pieces fell instead of two. The one coin that had been cracked was now split in two. I stared at them in disbelief and fear.

Kade rubbed his temples, oblivious to what I was witnessing but relieved in their absence.

Elias shot me a concerned look, and all I could do was shake my head. I only hoped that he would hold off on saying anything. I couldn't deal with this right now; it wasn't the time or the place.

The scream from moments ago returned, but its volume was elevated. I whipped my head around in search of it but found nothing around us. It droned on, fading as if it were moving away, but I couldn't tell where it was coming from.

The three around me stared, but I only had eyes on Kade. "Did you hear that?"

"Hear what?" Kade asked.

"What is it?" Elias pushed.

One. Two. Three. Four more screams, and I bolted past them through the doorway of the building. Heading into what, I had no idea.

CHAPTER 26

Violet

A temporary state of darkness messed with my vision, but it was the sounds of utter mayhem that sent me surging forward.

"Violet!" Kade called, hot on my heels.

Grunts, hollering, and metal clashing made me think that a battle was just up ahead. A small flicker of light came into view, and I darted off to follow it. I rounded a corner and found a fight underway.

It was a clash of demon black and what I assumed to be saints in midnight blue. Some were stumbling over corpses on the ground while they fought. There were those duking it out with hands and others with weapons. My mind was spinning, as in my panicked plight I could no longer tell if the screams were confined to my mind or actually present.

A man came barreling toward me and I ducked, only to find Kade unleashing his sword from behind and ramming it into the man's abdomen. Elias was right behind and cut through the man's neck, decapitating him swiftly before moving on to another aggressor. It was a not-so-subtle reminder of what I had witnessed from one of his kills. The man and his detached head dropped to the floor. Only, I didn't hear either of them hitting the concrete, as the screams began to overtake me once more.

Aleena was off and cutting her way through the crowd, disappearing quickly as she was swallowed up by the lot of them. I surveyed the area as my grip tightened on the handle of my blade.

Death. I sensed it, practically felt it. Impending and stale death. It seared through me and heated my blood.

The desire to end life myself was surfacing and rearing its head. There were murderers in here, that much I knew. It was called for, like the times I had witnessed Kade, Elias, and Aleena killing those who deserved it. Similar to those individuals I had picked out in Kade's watching quarters. I knew there were those present who deserved to be punished, and I could taste sweet vengeance on my tongue.

"Violet!" Kade's voice was more like an echo in a cave as he rounded me, stepping in front of me and blocking my view.

I blinked, refocusing my attention on Kade, but I was struggling.

"Violet—"

"Look out!" A tall man approached with an intent to take out Kade, but my fist was flying before I even had time to process it. My blade sank into his eye socket and he screamed as he dropped his weapon. Kade finished him off, slicing through his clavicle before withdrawing and laying a fatal blow.

A hand came from behind and wrapped around my neck, slamming me against the ground and knocking the wind from my lungs. It was disorienting, and the room spun as someone fuzzy applied even more pressure, cutting off my air supply. My hands were now empty, and I clawed at him as I attempted to get some kind of relief. Kade had been just steps away; where was he now?

I could barely focus, but a demented grin formed as a man jeered, "Stupid girl."

The man was wearing black. In fact, recognition set in as my nails dug into his hands. It was the man who had been at Kade's side before entering. Perhaps he was the one who had spurred that uneasy feeling. I was now fighting for my life beneath him, and his strength was overpowering. Skin curled beneath my fingernails, but it didn't even seem to faze him.

As I met his eyes, an image of Tamian began to unfurl in my mind. I knew now that while Tamian might not be dead, his death had been the intent. The large guard, who had such a deep voice, hadn't begged for it to stop, nor had his body caved or responded to the strikes delivered. It was like he was frozen. He had taken each hit, each cut that the man before me provided, and it fueled my rage to new heights.

I should have been growing weaker, but there was a newfound energy that I tapped into. I clawed at his eyes, and his frustration grew. When he loosened his grip to try and swat me away, I inhaled sharply before kicking him off. I sat up to find Kade raising his arms, and down came his blade. Blood sprayed from my attacker's flesh, and the man cried out in pain as Kade continued to cut him down, cursing at the traitor as he did.

The clashing and fighting around me paled once more,

overcome by the sound of screams. It was maddening, and my hands covered my ears as if that would provide any comfort.

A blow landed on the back of my head, and I fell forward. I gasped as I tried to recover, rolling to the side before pushing myself back up again. Someone grabbed ahold of my hair as their other hand put me in a chokehold. I rammed my elbow into what I assumed was their stomach, and they bent over. I scuffled around to get my bearings.

What was the obsession with going after my neck?

Retrieving another blade from my ankle, I turned to face my new attacker. To my surprise, it was another demon. Just how many fucking traitors were there?

Aleena came out of nowhere, her metal fingertips digging into the man's neck and tearing out a chunk. Blood spattered her face, but it didn't even bother her. She left and the man dropped to his knees, and I took it upon myself to approach him.

His eyes searched mine frantically as he tried to hold his neck together.

"You chose the wrong side," I said, and I swung at him. His neck contorted into an unnatural shift, and I heard a crack before his lifeless body fell to the ground next to a large being who I could only describe as a troll or ogre of some sort. From what I could tell by the pallor of his skin, he had already been dead for some time.

"Violet, we have to get you out of here." Kade was pulling at my arm. Before I could refuse, a saint's pommel made an impact on his jaw and he stumbled back. Nabbing the sword that Kade had lost his grip on, I held its base with both hands, ready to take on his attacker myself.

The tall man took a menacing step in my direction, and without thinking, I retreated back a step of my own. Kade's sword was heavier than I had anticipated and I fought to keep it upright. How in the hell did he hold on to this thing? And Elias? He held two!

I was in way over my head.

"How's the hybrid life treating you?" The man's features morphed from that of a man in maybe his forties, into a face that I could never forget. A clean-cut hairline, brown eyes, and that crystal clear voice and youthful face.

My former boss, the saint in the flesh formerly known as Damian. "Noliathan."

Rage ignited low in my belly at the sight of him. But what my sight revealed as I met his eyes might cause me to burn the fucking place down.

"Oh, Violet, you can call me Nolan now."

Images of death began unfolding in my mind, deaths of both demons and creatures that had taken place in this very room. There was no mercy with the ending of each life. I shook my head, trying to bring myself back into the present. I couldn't afford to get lost in his past killings. I had to focus.

"Hybrid…" I sneered. His use of that word made me cringe. Just how much did he know? Apparently, enough to know that a demon wasn't all that I was.

A body came at us and I jumped out of the way, narrowly missing a hit. A demon struck the wall, but quickly stood and regained his bearings, zapping out of view and popping up again on the other side of us to face his opponent.

Damian drew back his arm, ready to take the demon by surprise with an attack, but before I could think it through, I was flying forward. I rushed into him, knocking him to the ground, and his weapon slid across the floor. I landed a punch to his face, but it wasn't enough, and he threw me off of him. My head hit the ground and there was pain, but my adrenaline kicked in and I stood once more, ready to face off with him.

"So tell me—" Damian was already standing, eyes fixated on me. "How come you haven't killed him yet?"

I blinked in confusion. "Killed who?"

The only life I had ended was Brett's, and that felt like ages ago now. There was no way Damian wasn't aware that Brett wasn't among the living anymore. Especially if, as we suspected, he was the one who had helped Brett move around undetected.

His eyes narrowed as his head cocked to the side.

Images began filing through my head again, and I bit back the bile of watching him murder all over again. I hated the replay, and it only made me despise him all the more.

"Kill who?" My voice rose as I took a step forward.

Kade came out of nowhere and was suddenly fighting face-to-face in a battle with Damian. I had no other choice but to back up against the wall to get out of their way. It was then that I realized how sparse the room was becoming.

It had been full when I first stepped foot in here, but now there had to be more bodies on the ground than there were standing. I would have a better chance counting the ones still alive than the lifeless mix of those fallen. There was so much destruction and lives lost that my head was spinning.

I searched for Aleena and Elias, but I didn't see either of them. My heart pounded, just as worried about each of them as I was Kade.

Screams overtook me once more, and I became furious. My forehead broke out in a sweat and my chest heaved as I tried to keep my feet steady, but I was struggling. I was reaching my boiling point, and I felt entirely useless.

I let out a shriek that tore from my throat. My eyes clenched shut as my vocal cords strained. The torture was worse than when I had killed Brett, as if this act alone would strip me of my voice and any future ability to speak. Then, as if the cords themselves snapped, I drew to a halt.

Out of breath, I choked on the air that I tried to take in. I could sense my black tears streaming down my face and wetting it. My throat burned as if I had swallowed fire, and when I reopened my eyes, it was like my worst nightmare coming true.

My brief moment of hysteria must have been enough of a distraction to allow Damian the chance to gain the upper hand.

"No!" I screeched.

Kade was on his knees ahead of me, a blade protruding from his stomach. The flickering of flames from a nearby light source caught the glint of blood that dripped from the pointed end. Damian withdrew it with a sharp pull, and I watched in horror as Kade's body fell forward and onto the ground, almost in slow motion. The pain registering on Kade's face as he went down resonated with me. My tethered arm burned in tandem along with my abdomen, and while I wanted to run to him, I felt compelled to go after the one responsible.

I rushed after Damian as he fled, pushing past Kade's pain that I was experiencing through our connection and using it to fuel me. I couldn't let him get away. I wouldn't. We couldn't let him escape.

Retrieving a random sword from the ground, I chased after him. I was temporarily blinded by the darkness of the hallway on my way out toward the beach, and then the ground beneath my feet turned sandy. Running on this terrain proved difficult, but I pushed harder. I had no other choice.

Damian turned, and I noted how his eyes had been seeping blood from their corners. I was closing the gap between us and felt the odds tipping in my favor.

I surged forward, barely latching onto his legs, and took us both to the ground. My whole body ached, but it didn't stop me from clambering up and onto him, fighting to keep him below me so I could get the upper hand. His armor was stiffer than my protections, his movements not as fluid, but restricted. I straddled his upper half, our arms flailing to ward each other off, and I screamed in frustration.

My fingers dug into his neck and a dark liquid began to pool at my touch. Damian struck my face before flinging me off of him with a spray of sand. He coughed and sputtered, his wounds attempting to close.

Returning the favor, I punched him right back before scrambling back on top of him, intent on ripping his throat out with my bare hands.

I squeezed with all of my might, his neck caving at my touch as he flailed, trying to pull my arms from him. I couldn't explain the strength that coursed through me, but I welcomed it. And just when I thought I didn't have any voice left whatsoever, a shrill sound erupted from my throat once more as I stared at him head-on.

Images began to filter through my mind, clips of death playing fast and unfolding before me. What was confusing, however, were images of some who didn't die. Like Brett, who was a frozen memory and nothing more. Even people I used to work with, and various other humans from my past life.

My fingers sank in until they disappeared about halfway into his flesh. The warmth that coated them was a reminder that I was capable of doling out his death, and I would take way too much pleasure in ripping the life from his body.

Countless lives, numerous creatures of all shapes and sizes, had met their ends by his hands. But it was images of two individuals who reminded me of Kade and Aleena that caught me off guard. Damian might not have committed the act himself, but he had sure as hell been involved. He'd been there, and he was witness to it.

Damian's eyes bulged, light slipping from them as his panic reached its peak. His fight was faltering. His hair turned gray and his eyes began to leak red from both corners once more. His life was draining away, and rapidly. He would never be able to toy with anyone else. Deceive or manipulate or betray. Death was his only future.

My fingers were ready to rip his windpipe from him. Victory was within arm's reach, until arms hauled me off and away from him.

I thrashed about, unaware of who was removing me from the scene. I didn't know if it was another traitor, saint, or what.

Elias and another demon were at Damian's side, rolling him onto his stomach and securing his hands behind his back with a thick strap that appeared to act like cuffs. Not only had Damian's facial features changed, but his body as well. He was now shorter and less muscled, a man I no longer recognized, as he didn't even fit in his chosen attire anymore. He was coughing up copious amounts of blood, but it wasn't enough.

I didn't want him to leave this island alive. Life was too good for him. He deserved to die!

Wiggling myself free from my captors, I plummeted forward onto the ground. I wasn't done with Damian. I wanted to fucking kill him!

I couldn't process what kind of state Kade was in right now. I wouldn't even be able to look at him until this piece of shit was wiped from existence.

Aleena popped into view before me, taking me by surprise. Before I could comprehend what I was doing, she caught my fist before I could punch her.

She mouthed words that looked like she was ordering me to stop, but I heard nothing. She looked so much like her mother, almost the spitting image of her. They shared the same shiny dark hair, and bone structure. They could have passed as sisters.

The same could be said for Kade and his father.

Aleena shook me by my shoulders, hard. It was enough to give me pause, and I began to examine the circle of demons now forming around us.

Some mouths were moving, others gaping, and there were those as still as statues. There were less than ten, a fraction of what we had in volunteers tonight. I only hoped that this wasn't all that was left of the army we had arrived here with.

"Violet, look at me!" Aleena shouted, and my attention slowly turned toward her. Her voice was fading in, but it was muted like I was underwater. And that was when my panic set in.

"Kade." I tried to speak, but it was the worst-sounding croak. My voice was almost nonexistent, and I didn't know if she could even understand me.

She released one of my shoulders, pointing behind me, and I whipped around.

Kade was staggering onto the beach, propped up by another demon, holding the site of impact from Damian's attack. Liquid ran down his protections and blotted the ground, but slowly. He was weak, but he was alive and moving. That was, until his knees gave out and he collapsed. The demon at his side helped to gently lower him to the ground.

I took off toward him. My hands cupped his face as soon as I was close enough, relieved that he wasn't still inside, lying in a pool of his own blood. I didn't know how fast he was able to heal a wound such as this, but I was grateful to have my sights set on him. Tears fell from my eyes as I wrapped my arms around him, willing every fiber of my being to heal him.

I tried to apologize as I pulled away, his pain clearly evident, but my voice was gone. I placed a hand to my throat, hoping I could dull the soreness there. I was pleased to find warmth beneath my touch, and once I could swallow without any ache, I pressed my hand to Kade's stomach. His eyes closed briefly, and together, we closed his wound.

I wanted to rejoice that Kade was alright, and that we had almost come out unscathed. But the lingering stares on the both of us squandered any hope of that.

"What is she?" I heard a murmur from behind me, and I searched Kade's eyes. Fear was creeping into every pore as it registered that the time for hiding had come to an end.

"Why are her tears black?" another whispered.

Kade took my hand and stood. There was a clear hole in his protections that showed no trace of injury, just drying blood.

"Is this all?" Kade spoke to someone on his right, and a burly man stepped forward. Something had slashed through his arm, tearing a chunk of his protections away, but the rest of him was unmarked.

"Seven severely wounded and sent back to Darthou. Zerin, Fao, Tanni, and Carron turned on us and claimed four in their attacks. You're looking at what's left."

Both mine and Kade's spirits plummeted. From what I could tell, we had about half of the demons we had arrived here with. The loss of life, within such a short time span, was devastating.

"Let's collect our dead and head back," Kade ordered, but the man spoke up again.

"Not until you explain this."

I couldn't bring myself to look at him as he pointed in my direction.

Kade scowled. "It's none of your—"

"What is she?" he called as he closed in on us, getting into Kade's face. "She's not a demon!"

"I am a demon!" I raised my voice and stepped between the two of them. I stood my ground as I brought my gaze to his. I wouldn't be talked about as if I wasn't here.

"Violet, don't," Kade warned, urging me to stop, but I pulled my arm away. Aleena was quick to join me at my side.

I hadn't wanted to expose myself, since we had been keeping it under wraps for so long, but I didn't see any other way around it. If we kept lying, the guard would have no reason to trust us and it would ruin Kade's reign. If we told the truth, there might be a glimmer of hope that we could earn their trust. Maybe not right away, but I chose to believe that this path was the better option.

Either that, or they would think I was an abomination and they might try to kill me right here and right now.

I didn't know if I would ever be fully accepted in Darthou, but it was a risk I was willing to take. There was no going back to the way things had been.

"We don't know how, and we don't know why, but my transition to demon wasn't exactly...traditional."

I glanced around, taking in each set of eyes that were fixated on me. I swallowed hard as I tried to pull the words out of my head with careful precision. I had always shied away from public speaking—presentations in school, or literally anything that would cause me to be the center of attention. But I thought I would gladly trade this group of scrutinizing demons who had just come out of battle for a classroom of peers right about now. I'd do book report, a science experiment…hell, even a math problem on the whiteboard that looked impossible to solve.

My heart pounded wildly as I pushed the past away and focused on the here and now. The chance to finally come clean and hopefully, control the narrative.

I stood tall, remembering what Aleena had told me about posture right before our tethering celebration, and took in as deep of a breath as my body would allow.

"I am part demon, part fury, and part banshee."

The silence that followed was almost more than I could bear. I didn't know if I should expect them to attack or argue. But I didn't expect complete stillness, making the ocean incredibly loud to my ears.

"But…you tethered to Kadriel, did you not?" The man beside Elias and Damian spoke up, and all heads turned in his direction, then back toward Kade and myself.

"I did. We are tethered." I gripped Kade's hand tighter, exchanging a look with him. He was just as worried as I was about spilling the information we had tried so hard to keep under wraps.

"Impossible," someone said from behind us.

"Furies and banshees were banished long ago," another chimed in.

"You can't tether to another creature." The man in front of us spoke again in disbelief. I could see he was having trouble coming to terms with it.

"Neither of us were even aware of her fury and banshee sides when we completed the tethering ritual. We soon found that out for ourselves later," Kade told them.

"Was it you who screamed?" Aleena questioned. I could feel my brows pinch in confusion.

"We could hear it from inside," Elias confirmed.

"You…you heard that?" I questioned, glancing around at numerous heads that were nodding in agreement.

"Stupid girl." Damian attempted to laugh through his broken voice. Perhaps I should call him Noliathan now, considering he looked nothing like my old boss. The marks on his neck had already healed most of the way.

"You should watch your tongue before I carve it from your mouth," Aleena fumed as she drew closer to him. I noted how a few of her bladed fingertips were missing, but that didn't stop her from slapping him, leaving a gash across his face.

Noliathan spat a mouth full of blood, a sinister grin playing out as if he weren't affected by the pain she'd induced. Although, it looked as if he could pass out at any moment.

"You were there." I crossed the short distance and approached him. His head wobbled back up to look at me. "You were there the day that Staffan killed Tarnon and Audra."

"What?" Kade was quickly by my side once more.

"Why?" I asked, rather heatedly. "What business does a saint have with a demon?"

"I don't know what you're talking about," Noliathan sneered. This time, I smacked him, and hard.

"Don't fucking lie to me. I saw you there." Images began flashing in my mind again as I stared into his eyes.

He was the first to break contact, but it was only to release a sadistic laugh that had me fisting my hands.

Kade raised his foot and landed a kick to his chest, sending him toppling over. "Take him to the dungeons. I want additional guards around his cell. The maximum that we can afford."

Elias and another vanished with Noliathan. I should have been relieved, but I didn't think I would be until his life finally came to an end. I knew that Kade had wanted to take him alive, but I didn't exactly understand why anymore. Why waste time in ending him? I refused to believe that anything good could come from it.

"Staffan killed the king and queen?" one of the women who'd accompanied us asked, her face stricken with shock.

Kade and I exchanged glances before turning to face the guards and seekers who remained. While I was glad they weren't coming after me with pitchforks, I was still uneasy with all of the attention, but I pushed forward anyway.

It was time for the truth to come out, and hope that it didn't come back to bite Kade and me in the ass.

Together, Kade and I recounted a watered-down version of what had happened so far. While he was earnest, graceful, and full of thought-out sentences, I was tripping over words and stumbling through knowledge that should have been easier to explain. I had lived through it all so far, so why was it so hard to finally bring it all to the light?

Probably because I feared for the worst. What if they wanted to banish me like the rest of the creatures in Xandor? Or worse, kill Kade and me for our lies and deception?

There was no holding back either. Kade led us all the way up to today and the Summit, even admitting to killing Staffan. The shock and murmurs from that revelation rolled through the small crowd like an avalanche, gaining speed and momentum as the atmosphere around us shifted.

They wanted more information. More details and facts about this crucial turn of events. My nerves were at an all-time high as Elias returned and stationed himself at my backside. It was like he, Aleena, and Kade were attempting to cage me in whatever protective stance they could.

The demons seemed split on the report about Staffan. There were those who appeared satisfied with the outcome, while others thought it an act of betrayal. After all, how on earth could Kade really *see* Staffan commit such an atrocious act?

"We have a problem." Zan appeared out of thin air, traipsing across the sands and making his way through the part in the small crowd. He looked utterly distraught and had splotches of red on his clothes.

"What is it?" Kade dropped my hand to meet him.

The amount of eyes on me instead of the newest arrival was unsettling, and I crossed my arms uncomfortably. Aleena must have taken notice, scooting closer to the point that our arms brushed against one another.

"Rafina is nowhere to be found. There is no one to tend to the wounded and we've already lost one of them."

My mind instantly went to Tamian.

Please, please *don't let it be him. There's already been so much loss today.*

"If Rafina severed her tethering with Staffan prior to the summit…" The voices around me quieted as I piped up, but there was still talk among them as they listened in. "Does she have any reason to stay?"

"She wouldn't have."

"No."

"What else are you lying about?"

Before I could shrink in fear at the rising ruckus, Kade cut in with a silencing order. "Enough!"

No one flinched or recoiled at his outburst. That one, single word brought about that troubling quiet once more.

"How do you wish to proceed, Kadriel?" His uncle tucked his hands behind his back as he awaited a response from the soon-to-be king. With Staffan out of the picture and Kade nearing the throne, it seemed as if the decision-making might be up to him in the meantime.

"Get in contact with other kingdoms to see if they can lend a hand. Tryadnee's healer should be our first attempt. Go."

Zan disappeared without a second to spare, and Kade pivoted to face Aleena. "Take Violet home."

CHAPTER 27

Violet

I should have been drained. Mentally, physically, and emotionally. Yet I was still trying to process the day's events, reliving it all scene by scene as I pried off my protections and hopped in the shower.

Aleena had returned me home as directed, where she ordered me to stay, like a puppy dog who had gotten into some serious trouble. I'd been too stunned to fight back, while also too scared to return to the island—to those who questioned all of the truths we were striving to tell.

From the fear of losing Kade, to Staffan's death, to the battle that had ensued on that island, it was a lot to take in. Disclosing almost everything that had transpired since my arrival in Darthou to the demons who had accompanied us had me shaking.

Then I was reminded of the blade protruding out of Kade's stomach.

I shuddered as I recalled the scene, hunching my shoulders as my breath caught. Damian—er, Noliathan, whatever the fuck I needed to call him—could have easily sliced through him. The man I had been willing to leave my old life for could have died today. Possibly twice.

Black tears began to fall in the shower, mixing with the water that fell from above and swirling down the drain. I was at war with myself for having gone in the first place, not knowing if I had caused more trouble in the long run. I had been so adamant to go, piggybacking on Kade's disappearance.

Should I apologize for coming along in the first place? Should I beg for forgiveness? Kade had every right to feel the anger and sorrow that I could feel vibrating off of him even though he was out of sight. I felt partially at fault for the shit show that had happened on the island. I never should have gone. I should have stayed here, in our apartment. Fucking alone and out of the way.

Turning the handle on the shower, I cranked it to hot. It temporarily scalded me, then my body fell into a numb state as I stood beneath it.

How bad had I messed everything up? Would the coronation still happen tomorrow? Staffan was dead, the Summit meeting an ambush, and two battles had taken place on that island that had taken countless lives. I didn't even want to know the body count. Sure, some of them probably deserved it, but I feared for the families of the ones who didn't.

When my eyes began to ache from the strain of crying and my stifled sobs came to a close, I finally turned off the shower. The bathroom was filled with a heavy mist as I stepped out to retrieve my towel. I wrapped it around me, focusing on taking deep breaths as I tried to muster up any courage I could find to exit the bathroom. The moment I opened the door, the stark difference in temperature sent an unwelcome chill through me.

I darted through the bedroom and into the closet, searching for comfortable clothes that I could warm up and curl up in. Finding a long black sweater and some pajama bottoms, I slipped them on and returned my towel to the bathroom.

A strip of light was illuminating the end of the hallway, and I tiptoed silently in its direction. I hadn't heard a peep from Kade since he'd ordered me away. As I approached, I realized that the door to Kade's watching quarters was closed and the light was coming from the bottom.

Placing the palm of my hand against the door, I paused. I assumed that since it was closed, he didn't want to be bothered. Had he left it open, I would have been granted access, and I could start on the slew of apologies I was arguing with myself over. But I didn't know if my apologies would even be enough. Still, I waited.

I waited at the door for a welcome that never came. My feet became cold on the bare floors, and a single tear escaped down my cheek. I didn't like being cut off like this. I would rather be fighting and begging for his forgiveness right now than met with this silence, this avoidance that cut me deep.

I was tired, exhausted even, and I felt as if I had no one to turn to. I was alone in a world that I had wanted to accept as my own, but I still didn't seem to fit anywhere. Without Kade by my side, I didn't know what to do or who to talk to.

Sarah was my only other choice, but she had a family of her own and I didn't want to burden her with anything more than what she was already dealing with. Aleena was pissed, and rightfully so. I wasn't that close to Elias or Zan, at least not enough to want to confide in them about anything.

Hopelessness consumed me, eating at me until I was raw.

I retrieved my blanket from its shelf in the closet and made my way over to the bed. I curled up beneath it, burying my head, and cried myself to sleep in the sleeves of my sweater.

"Violet?" I stirred slightly at the sound of my name, but only nuzzled my head deeper into the covers. My body was cozy, but my face was chilly and I sought warmth. But when the womanly voice spoke my name again, I popped out from beneath the blanket.

"Violet."

My eyes peered over the edge and settled on Aleena sitting on Kade's side of the bed. Dark hair was pulled over her shoulder, and she was wearing clothes that were a bit too big on her.

"Is everything okay?" I sat up, glancing around in search of Kade, but there was no sign of him. The bed was still made beneath her, and there was no indication that he had ever joined me.

Light was pouring in through the stained glass windows, and I rubbed at my eyes, unsure of how much time had passed since I'd been asleep. It was night when I had lain down, but I had no concept of time because of the lack of clocks around here.

It was seriously annoying.

"We need to start getting ready for the coronation."

I blinked at her, unsure if I had heard correctly. "Wait, the coronation? Is that still happening?"

She nodded, but I noted how her face fell as her eyelids lowered.

"But…after everything, we're still going through with it? What about Staffan? The council? The Summit, and me and—"

Aleena held up a hand to cut off my rambling. I pulled my sleeves over my hands and set them in my lap to wait, but I couldn't wait.

"For what it's worth…I'm sorry." My apology drew her focus back to me, but she remained silent and tight-lipped. "I'm sorry if I put you guys in jeopardy on that island. I'm sorry that we didn't bring you in and tell you the truth sooner. I'm sorry for everything that has been a fucking disaster ever since I got here." I choked on the last of my words as my emotions flared with anguish.

"I don't blame you, Violet." Aleena took a moment to herself before she began weighing something in her head. "And well, we're beginning to learn just how long ago things around here started going to shit. Now it's just uncovering who all is involved and taking action. There's a lot of things happening all at once."

I nodded in understanding. It had to be horrifying to believe for so long that a saint had been responsible for the deaths of her and Kade's parents, only to find out it was one of their own, a demon, who had carried it out. And it couldn't have been easy to accept that some of those they had been aligned with were traitors, turning on them in battle.

Kade had never promised me a picture-perfect world when I chose a life with him, and I had never expected it. Darthou wasn't without its own politics and problems; it seemed just as much of a mess as my old world, my old life.

"Have you seen Kade at all? Since the island?" My fingers twisted together, nervous about how she might respond. Would Aleena try to sugarcoat things, or would she be honest? I hated that Kade had shut me out and left me on my own last night. I wanted to clear the air, but apparently he had other plans. Ones that didn't involve me.

"He's been nonstop, all night. Taking charge and making plans. Calling in reinforcements for healing Tamian and the injured, searching for Rafina, communicating with the other kingdoms and creatures, decreasing the size of the coronation today for security purposes. I swear we're a few steps away from a lockdown."

And staying away from me.

"Kade had initially wanted Sarah to start getting you ready, but she was having problems getting ahold of Jacobi to watch the kids."

"Ah…so you're stuck with me again." I had an inkling that I would be doing a lot of apologizing. Apologizing to her, to Kade and Elias, maybe to just about everyone, that I had made their lives just a little more difficult. "Sorry about your luck."

"Look, I'm not going to pretend that I'm not upset about how and when I found out about"—she gestured to me—"you. But in hindsight, I do understand why. What I will say is that I'm looking forward to training you without any limitations. That is, if you still want me to."

"Yes," I stammered out without delay. "Yes, of course. I would really like that."

"Good." She grinned, meeting my eyes. Images of battle began to unfold. I blinked away quickly, trying to focus on something else.

"Now, how about you go wash your face and we'll head over to my place to get ready."

I paused, suddenly unsure. The last time I'd gotten ready at her home, we were headed for Torenca and I was dressed pretty provocatively. But then again, both Aleena and Rebecca had been responsible for my dress for the tethering celebration, and that dress was immaculate. Surely whatever coronation dress they'd designed would be appropriate for the occasion today.

I excused myself to the restroom and as I approached the counter, I took in my reflection. My hair was still damp from being swept up, my face was puffy, and smears of black showed the tears I had cried.

Scrubbing my face with my bare hands, I tried to rid myself of the marks on my cheeks. My skin reddened at the harshness of my touch, and I was angered that I couldn't even seem to cry like a normal human *or* demon.

And what was worse was Kade ignoring me. Instead of talking to me, he'd disappeared to start barking orders as if he were already king. He was obviously suffering, but by shutting me out he was hurting me in return.

I let my forehead rest against the edge of the sink on my forearms, and took deep and steady breaths. I had to get ahold of myself and calm the fuck down. In just a few short hours, I was going to be crowned queen, and I had to get a grip. I couldn't afford to spiral out of control, even though my raging thoughts threatened to do that.

Maybe I would be better off putting on a straightjacket and being thrown into a padded room.

"Violet? We should get going." Aleena's voice carried through the cracked door as she knocked. I shook out my hands before coming out and closing the door firmly behind me. I paused slightly as I cast my gaze down the hall. I didn't even know if Kade was in there, and if he was, would he even have time to answer if I knocked? I should feel him if he was, right?

Instead of taking a chance and finding out, I followed Aleena out. We made the short trip down the hall and into her place. She was quick to turn on some music and it began flowing through the air, the bass guitar leading into a melody that was quick to turn into something fast-paced and energetic. Little by little, her flavorful taste in music was turning me around and giving me hope to get out of my slump.

Conversation began to unfold quickly as she busied herself with her preparations for me. And instead of grilling me over the onslaught of information I had unloaded on the demons on that island, she came off as more inquisitive than offensive. Curiosity lit up her eyes as she hung on my every word. And for the first time, I didn't hold back my disdain for Rafina or Staffan in front of her. I bared it all.

One of the first things I wanted her to do after today—and Aleena was in agreement—was to go to Xandor as soon as the opportunity presented itself. The comfort and ease that I soon found in chatting with her was exactly what I had been missing last night. Someone to confide in, share my feelings and worries and plights. Now I could speak freely about anything and everything under the sun that was always hidden from view here. All I had ever wanted from Aleena in the first place was friendship, and this truly felt like the start of it. I wanted to get along with her and Elias more than anything, since they were so close to Kade. Elias, however, I might have to try to work a bit harder at.

Aleena was a pro when it came to getting dolled up, and to be honest, I quite liked being pampered. By her, anyway. She would work on me one minute, just to turn around and do something for herself but almost twice as fast. It was fascinating to watch her do her own hair. Her fingers twisted and turned in each direction, creating two braids in a halo around her head. She kept the rest loose, curling some of her strands.

"Are you going to have any special colors for your hair today?" She had a knack for picking vibrant colors, and I had yet to see her wear one that didn't work for her. But with her masterful skills with blinks and shifts, she could undoubtedly take on whatever hair and skin tone she desired.

"Actually, I think I'll be going all natural today. I might want to stand out most of the time, but today, I believe there's power in unity."

I considered her words. Today was kind of a monumental occasion. The first coronation in decades. Even though by her own admittance, the attendance would be considerably less than what had first been planned due to yesterday's events, I knew it would still draw quite a crowd.

But her use of the word "unity" sparked my curiosity, and it was pleading with me to finally question her about her relationship with Elias.

"Can I ask you something personal?"

"Of course." Her hands were working through my hair, creating a loose braid around the crown of my head.

"I know you said you didn't want to be tied down to a tethering, and I get that, I do. But what's going on with you and Elias?" I wished I could see her reaction, but she had turned me away from the mirror.

"I'm not sure I know what you mean."

"I don't mean to meddle, honestly." I tried to not sound too nosy, even though I definitely was. "I just want to know if I'm missing something. You both either seem scorching hot or freezing cold. Is there, or has there ever been, a middle ground between you two?"

Her hands stopped moving, and when the silence stretched on, I cautiously sat forward so I could face her. There was a sadness in her expression that caused me to stand. "I'm sorry, I didn't mean to pry. Forget I said anything."

Her throat worked to swallow and she batted her lashes before looking up and away. "A future with Elias is…it's too real. I know he would try to give me anything and everything if I accepted—"

"Wait, has he asked you to tether? Isn't that kind of a big deal?" My heart beat harder in my chest for her. So there was something serious between them!

Aleena nodded, her eyes becoming glassy. It was strange to see the all-powerful seeker before me being vulnerable in this way, but it was humanizing at the same time. Perhaps she just needed an outlet, someone to talk to as well.

"If I were to accept and go after a life with him, I would have to give up seeking. There's no way to have everything I want. I have to choose one or the other."

"Can you just be with him without tethering?" I still wasn't quite following, but I hadn't expected her to get so upset. I couldn't see Elias telling her to give up seeking, so what was I missing? "Do you love him?"

Aleena hushed, almost stunned by my inquiry. I held her gaze until death came into the picture. The scenes behind her eyes from the island threatened to ruin the moment, and I broke the connection by standing up and taking her hands in mine, looking at our hands instead.

"Aleena, do you love him?" I squeezed gently as I pressed her.

She didn't speak, and only nodded her agreement. That's when I chanced another look.

"Then if he loves you in return, which I'm willing to bet that he does, you two will figure it out. But you can't do that if you don't talk to each other."

"I don't even know what to say. I've pushed him away so many times." She hiccupped. "I'm not good with these feelings and stuff. What kind of human mind games are you pulling on me anyhow? You're making me soft." She offered a small laugh.

"Apparently, I'm a few things. But I don't have to be human to think like one," I joked. "I *was* one after all."

"That might be true, but…I could tell something was off about you the first time we met."

I rolled my eyes. "Please don't tell me that I smelled bad."

"Not that you smelled *bad*, just that you smelled *off*. I never really understood why, but now I know."

"That nose of yours is kind of creepy."

We both broke into small fits of laughter, and when it came to an end, I pulled her into a giant hug. I caught her by surprise, going off of her stiffened posture, and it took her a moment before she settled into it. Only then did I speak up. She deserved to know how much this conversation meant to me. "You have no idea how nice it is to talk to you now. To *really* talk to you."

When I pulled back, another tear cascaded down her cheek but she was quick to swipe the colorless substance away. Aleena cleared her throat. "Now, where were we?"

She shooed me back into the chair and curled my remaining hair into perfection. I noticed her retrieve something shiny from one of her drawers and she began looping whatever it was into the back of my hair. My fingers were playing with my necklace as I listened to the music and tried to relax. But it was of no use.

"Do you think I'll get the chance to talk to Kade before the coronation?" I thought of him and the night he had gifted me this necklace, flowers, and that yellow teddy bear from the carnival. Nerves were growing rapidly, and I couldn't stop fidgeting. I had to think about literally anything else.

"I will make sure of it."

I drew my index finger back and forth along the black obsidian bar, wanting nothing more than to just see his face. I didn't like being in the dark about what was going on, or being left out of whatever decisions were being made. Perhaps I would only be a distraction and nothing more. I knew Darthou was in a fragile state right now, but I hoped that the current situation wasn't any indicator of his future as a leader.

"I remember when he was making that." Aleena returned to my view and began assessing me. I assumed she was done with my hair and moving on to the finishing touches of my face.

"What? My necklace?"

"Mhmm…" She took a pin from a tiny box on her desk and picked a strand on the right side of my head. "He made it years ago. Cut and formed it himself."

I briefly recalled Brighton mentioning something about that when we'd first met. The thought of Kade going through the trouble of making something such as this, long before we ever met, was heartwarming. It was rare for me to not wear it, and now knowing this, I cherished it even more. "Will I be able to wear it today? I don't even know what my dress looks like."

"Definitely. Rebecca and I assumed you would want to."

I grinned as I teased her. "You two definitely understand your clientele, don't you?"

"Damn right. Sometimes better than they know themselves."

After Aleena finished with me and finally gave me permission to stand, I took in my reflection at her vanity. My hair fell in luscious waves that cascaded down my back, and the sides were scooped up by that braid. When she lifted a handheld mirror, I could see the back, and I almost gasped. Silver streams of something were threaded through my hairstyle, shimmering whenever my head moved. It made my hair almost appear red in color.

There was a blush to my cheeks and a neutral shade applied to my lips, making me appear more regal than the daring look she had chosen for me for our club visit. I swore my eyelashes were somehow longer too.

I couldn't stop complimenting it all, even as Aleena finished getting herself ready. From the looks of it, she was also choosing a color palette that was more subtle than severe, but her beauty was still bold.

"Backtracking to my necklace. Is there someone besides Kade who could make something for me? Well, something for him?" I leaned up against the wall as I watched her apply some lipstick, finishing herself off.

"Of course. What did you have in mind?"

"Would they be able to keep it a secret? I would like it to be a surprise, but it's not something that I need right away either."

Aleena tapped the tips of her fingers together, eager to get in on this. "Yes, but you have to tell me what it is or no deal."

Sighing playfully, I rolled my eyes. "Deal."

CHAPTER 28

Violet

Aleena dropped me off in the small room just outside the great hall. The same tiny space Kade and I had briefly occupied before greeting everyone who had showed up for our tethering celebration. My nerves were at an all-time high, fingers twisting until they ached from the strain and heart pumping viciously. I only hoped the next face I saw would be Kade's.

The dress that Aleena and Rebecca had created for me was nothing short of breathtaking. The gray fabric hugged every curve and swerve of my upper half and fit like a glove without it being too tight. The material glistened, much like whatever was weaved through my hairstyle. No one would have any troubles seeing my necklace, as it was nestled perfectly between my parted breasts.

The skirt pooled around my feet now that I was standing still, but there was a daring slit in the side that showed a good amount of leg if I took large steps, and thank goodness they had remembered my fondness for flats instead of heels.

But not even my reflection could sway my panic for long. I was going to be queen. One that the people of Darthou might not even accept. The truth was coming out, and I was sure with news like mine, it would spread alarmingly fast. Rafina's disappearance, Staffan's demise, and the attack yesterday were just adding to the complexity of the issues surrounding us.

What if we weren't met with welcoming faces, but with those who blamed me for everything that had gone wrong? What if they tried to withhold Kade's crown because of me and what I was?

An overwhelming sense of passion began spreading over my body, and it stalled all thoughts. A need to fuck and find release. The urge to come undone and cry in ecstasy. My knees wanted to buckle. The feeling was quick, heady, and all-consuming. It aimed to take over me whole.

"How lucky am I, to fuck a queen tonight?"

Kade's voice heated my cheeks, and as much as I wanted to turn around and jump him, I also wanted to give him a good piece of my mind. His distraction had almost worked.

"Are you even going to come to bed tonight?" I shot back, still hurt that he had sent me off without a single word yesterday. I couldn't explain why I was so angry all of a sudden, but it hurt that he was choosing to ignore his recent absence.

"I deserve that."

"You shut me out, Kade," I pressed, attempting not to waver.

This wasn't exactly the route I had planned to go once we were finally together again. But his sudden appearance, need to screw, and my terror of being crowned a queen that Darthou's inhabitants might not accept when they all learned the truth, was almost more than I could handle.

Kade moved gradually, coming into view from the shadowed corner of the room as he rounded me. I couldn't bring myself to look him in the eye, and kept mine cast down, fearful that if I looked up, I would cave. I might surrender to him if I looked at that face that I loved so much. The demon who I now couldn't imagine my life without. He had to know that what had happened last night wasn't fair to me. He was supposed to be my rock, the equivalent to a husband, and I'd needed him but he wasn't there. He had ordered me to be taken home, and he'd been silent ever since.

"Violet," he said softly, begging for my attention, but I remained still. When I didn't respond, he reached for my hands and pulled them apart before tilting my chin up. He forced me to look into his eyes. "I'm sorry."

While I had initially wanted to do all of the apologizing, it felt good to hear it come from him in return.

"I didn't know if you were mad at me for spilling everything. Ticked at me for tagging along in the first place. Getting in the way for Damian to—" My words faltered as I recalled Kade with a sword protruding from him. The image would forever be burned into my mind, and it gutted me, for lack of better terms. I shook the remnants of the memory away before it could become too much. "And now this? Doesn't it feel wrong to go on with the coronation?"

"Violet." He raised his voice slightly as he placed his hands on my arms and bent enough to come to my level. "The truth was going to come out eventually. There was no way we were going to be able to hold on to that forever. But I think you'll be surprised just how many are backing us."

"But I have no idea how to be a queen. I have no idea how to be a demon, or a fury or a freaking banshee. How am I supposed to stand up there with you as if everything is okay? I'm not ready for this!" My voice cracked as I spoke, and he stilled the shake in my hands.

"But you *are* ready. What you did yesterday? Yes, it was fucking crazy and wild to tag along, but you took down Noliathan. With your scream, you immobilized him. You then took control of the situation, and instead of trying to keep up our cover, you told your fellow people point-blank every goddamn thing that has transpired since you came here. Now *that* was brave."

"Or incredibly stupid."

He shook his head. "No, it wasn't. I think you earned more respect yesterday than I might have in my entire life so far. Embrace this, Violet. I think you are exactly what Darthou needs."

It was hard to believe the words coming out of his mouth. What did Darthou stand to gain from me rising to power with Kade? How would I ever be beneficial to this world that I still knew so little about? I wanted nothing more than to find my place here, but I didn't want to be in the spotlight for that to happen. The pressure of being some sort of royalty was now minutes away and I was petrified. None of it had felt real, until now.

"You're not mad at me?" I sought for clarification, as if that would be any help right now with a crowd gathering for us. I noticed lines of silver embedded into his gray shirt beneath his suit jacket. He exuded the flair of someone of great importance, fitting for someone about to be named king, and he was fucking hot as hell with his hair that he had attempted to tame and style.

Something shifted between us as I held his gaze. His chin dipped down as his sight traveled down and toward my lips, then my breasts. Lust was returning, and in full force. It began to heat my core as I imagined peeling him out of his jacket.

"Couldn't be further from it." He sought my mouth, but I held my hand up to halt him.

"Kade, we can't. Not here," I urged, even though my body wanted nothing more than to surrender to him right here and now. I would gladly trade this coronation to stay sequestered in this tiny room and grind out our problems in the best way we knew how. "My makeup."

"Is that a challenge?"

I swallowed, trying to suppress the need and excitement that was coursing through me.

He tilted my head to the side, pushing my hair over my shoulder as his lips found my neck. Gripping my ass, he pulled me in close. I longed to feel his fingers dig into my flesh instead of my skirt, but it didn't keep me from whimpering at his touch. The nearness that I desired, the communication I wished we'd had last night, was all coming to a head as Kade located the slit in my dress. His hand dove in and under my panties, straight for my center. I moaned into his ear as he made his way inside, reveling in this small touch even though I wanted so much more.

"Is there ever a time when you're not wet for me?" he mused, and I could sense his gratification.

"Not even when I'm asleep," I purred, breathless.

His fingers moved, twisting and turning while also giving a teasing amount of attention to my clit. It was slow, sensual and gentle, and took my mind off of everything except the demon who was right in front of me.

"I love you," he said, his face barely an inch away as he met my hooded gaze. My lips parted, taking in his exhales as if he was giving me air to breathe. My chest bloomed with the comfort of hearing those words. From the first time he had spoken them until now, he had never given me any reason to doubt them, or him.

"I love you," I gasped as he touched that spot inside that wanted to send me into a crumbling mess on the floor. Kade fought not to take my mouth with his. His lips hovered so near, grazing mine as if he were testing to see if I would allow him access. Each brush made me feel lightheaded, as if I were floating but he was keeping me grounded.

A series of raps on the door made me jump, but Kade was quick to lock me into place with his free hand while the other continued to work. My eyes were wide with alarm, afraid that someone might try to come in and witness our scene.

"Just need a minute," Kade gritted through his teeth, never breaking contact with me. He leaned in toward my ear, air whizzing past it as he lowered his voice. "It's up to you whether you come loudly or quietly."

His thumb rubbed circles against my clit, and I fought against the urge to bite my lip. My body was growing hotter by the second.

"I would decide quickly," he teased, amusement evident as he watched me climb. The worry that we might be caught worked together with his fast fingers to build me up for a release, and I struggled to keep my stance.

This time, someone beat the door, and by the sound of it, with their fists. "Kadriel!"

With Elias on the other side of the door, I began pulling Kade out of me by his forearm. Aggravated, he pulled out a handkerchief from inside his jacket and began wiping his fingers off as I sorted myself out, smoothing my dress down.

The desire between my legs had soiled my underwear. I half contemplated removing it altogether.

Kade swung open the door and was met with his equally well-dressed best friend. Elias's attention shot to me and I froze, before he turned back to Kade. I had the suspicion he knew what had been transpiring in here, though thankfully he didn't verbally confirm it.

"Everyone is waiting. Your family has already taken their places."

"Everyone?" Kade repeated, folding the cloth he had used to clean his fingers and returning it to its concealed spot.

Elias only nodded once, then vanished from our view.

"I guess we'll have to finish later." Kade returned and took me by the hand. "Are you ready?"

There was a very good chance that I was going to pass out. My legs weren't sturdy, and my heart was threatening to kill me. "No, not really."

The corner of his lips turned up as he looped my arm around his. I didn't know how he could remain so calm right now. I could sense he was trying to put me at ease, but I was too much of a mess to accept it. "Just keep your eyes on me. Once we're crowned, the rest should be smooth sailing."

"Crowned? Wait, we actually get a crown? Crowned? How come nobody said anything about that?"

Kade laughed, and the humor he was finding in my confusion did nothing for my nerves. "What can I say, I told you I was fucking a queen tonight."

My lips pressed thin, and I was stunned into a momentary silence before we exited the room. We began our descent down the corridor that would lead us to the main entrance of the great hall, and when the large doors came into view I stopped.

Kade's brows furrowed as he awaited a reason.

"This new king better fuck me real good tonight," I warned. I was scared beyond measure to turn the corner and pass through the crowd that awaited.

"That, I can certainly promise you." His wickedness returned, and it heated my blood once more as he kissed the back of my hand. For a fleeting moment I forgot about my sky-high worries and brewing troubles. That was, until Kade proceeded to lead me into the room that would change our status and our future.

There was that word again. *Change.*

I still had no idea what change Rafina had referred to. It couldn't be this, could it? A hybrid, as Noliathan had called me, rising to power? No way. How could anyone benefit from that?

Holding my breath, I rounded the corner, and a sea of fancily dressed demons turned in our direction. A scream began to erupt in the back of my mind and I tensed, tightening my grip on Kade. These screams really did have the worst timing.

CHAPTER 29

Violet

I knew one of my coins had bitten the dust, but what of the other one? Did Elias still have it? Surely if it had come into Kadriel's possession, he would have given me the remaining piece. But would it be of any help to me now?

Another scream chimed in, and I bit the tip of my tongue. If Kade was hearing it too, or if he sensed my distress, it didn't show as I stole a glance up at him. His head was held high as we moved down the aisle, passing by rows and clusters of faces that I couldn't bring myself to look at as they bowed. It was a gradual dip of a wave that followed us as we moved.

The weight of their stares was harsh, and I struggled to breathe as if I were in an ill-fitting corset restricting my rib cage.

As we crossed the halfway point, I began to settle my focus

on those at the front. Zan, Sarah, and their kids were on the right side where Kade would soon join them. On the left, I noticed that Aleena wasn't alone. Elias was by her side this time, hands clasped in front. He hadn't been up front for our tethering celebration, as he'd been working, but he was with Kade's family now, and Aleena in particular.

They looked perfect together; despite the stark difference between his platinum hair and her natural dark color, they complemented each other. Aleena's maroon dress might have been simple, sleek, and formed around her body, but it was the perfect match to the man beside her.

Whether Elias was at the front because of Kade, Aleena, or at both of their requests, I was just glad to see him up here and a part of the group, like he was.

Prior to today, we had never had a run-through, or talked about the proceedings, and I had no idea what awaited us. But then Zan stepped forward, as if preparing to address the crowd. He rounded the two thrones that had been in storage, now positioned front and center.

We came to a stop before him and waited. There was a genuine and warm smile on Zan's face, a pride that I had seen once before when he had completed our tethering ritual.

"Thank you for joining us today to mark this special occasion. It is with a heavy heart that we were unable to involve other creatures for today's festivities, and we hope to make it up to them once the time is right."

The acoustics here were amazing, and each word he spoke echoed through the hushed room. If only the screams in my head would shut the fuck up and let me listen without interruption, that would be great.

"Whether you were here when the late king and queen were crowned, or are joining us for the first time on this Blood

Moon, welcome. We are honored to have each and every one of you here for this historic moment."

My gut started to turn. Queasiness flooded through me at an alarming pace as another voice screeched near my ears. I flinched as the screams combined and built.

So many voices, so many cries and shrieks. They rapidly drowned out Zan and whatever speech he was delivering. I searched through what few crowd members I could see on my right, as if I might be able to pick up on where my plight was coming from, but there was nothing obvious. Black eyes, dotted with a few colored human ones.

Kade used his right hand to squeeze my arm, and I turned to face the front again. Zan and Aleena were now before us, crowns in hand, but I was in a daze. Almost like I was on the outside looking in. I couldn't even concentrate on the shining objects they held.

Shut up, shut up, shut up!

I was unsteady as my mind fogged over, and my vision turned blurry as Aleena lowered the crown onto my head. The weight of it threw off my balance but Kade only strengthened his one-armed hold on me.

Everything about my vision was cloudy. And while this was ten times worse, it reminded me of the night when Kade had first made his appearance. I had forgotten all about the injury that had made me feel like I was in a dream when we first met. And now, the blurry vision paired with the cacophony in my head was almost paralyzing. I thought I might literally pass out from the strain of it all.

"Murderer!"

As if some mystical force released me, the haze fell and the screams came to an abrupt halt that caused my ears to instantly start ringing. I stumbled as Kade and I broke apart, spinning around to see who had interrupted. The masses turned their heads to find the cause of the commotion, bodies moving and parting as they created a path for a figure almost three fourths of the way back.

Rafina stepped into view, and the people of Darthou gave her space. Had she been in the crowd this entire time, or had she just arrived? Her black attire covered every inch of her, a gloved dress that fell to the floor and came up her neck. Her hair was pulled back tight and high, making her look as severe as her distraught facial expression.

"Tell the people of Darthou how you murdered Staffan!" She forced her once calming tone into one that stretched into a shrill sound.

Audible gasps and murmurs began to filter through the room as it began to stir into turmoil. If there were those who hadn't known of his death before now, Rafina was certainly creating a spectacle to inform them of it. She took a few more steps forward, pointing to the ground as she raised her voice again.

"Tell them how you led several demons into battle yesterday, and of the lives that have been lost!"

My hands fisted at my sides. She was trying to get them to turn on us. Striking matches, ready to let the world burn. I had little doubt that someone of her standing might be able to do it, pull it off and play the victim even though I knew she was involved, even if I couldn't prove it.

"Tell them about the abomination of a tethered mate that you have chosen to have at your side!" Rafina sounded strained, as if her voice wouldn't hold out for much longer. "Who you have chosen for a queen!"

Kade took a step forward, but I swiftly pushed past him. I was unable to stay quiet any longer. Some men and women were moving out from the crowd and closing in. I had no idea if they were friend or foe at this point, as I was solely focused on Rafina. This was my first time in her presence without my coins, and if the screams erupting in my mind as I approached her were any indication, I was about to get an onslaught of information out of her. I just needed to get closer.

This was my chance; it might be now or never.

"How about you tell them that Staffan was working with a saint?" I bristled, not really knowing how loud my voice was. "How about you inform them that it was Staffan who murdered Tarnon and Audra? I find it incredibly hard to believe that you knew nothing about that!"

Rafina stilled, shock registering on her face, and I grinned as I closed in. I had her. Now if I could only get my fingers around her neck.

Kade was at my side in a nanosecond, no doubt using his pocket mirror to keep me within his reach. He let his voice fill the room as he joined me. "Tell them all about how you conveniently severed your tethering to Staffan just before he went to the Summit yesterday. The ambush that he was in on. The destruction he helped orchestrate, on our own kind no less."

She shook her head, her face showing no remorse and no sadness. It only maddened me all the more. Her expression morphed into something that I could only describe as pure evil.

"They'll never accept you," she snickered as she began to close the distance between us. "They'll never trust you once they know what you are." She was no longer the graceful, blond beauty. Instead, she was a venomous viper, spewing everything she thought she had in her arsenal to turn the tables in front of the people of Darthou who stood by and watched.

"It is you who we should no longer trust."

The crowd parted for the deep bass of a voice, and I couldn't hold back my surprise. It halted me in my pursuit.

Tamian moved forward, joining in with the familiar faces I was now recognizing from the fight yesterday on the island. The faces that I had told my truth to. Those who had listened and judged and asked many questions that I so desperately wanted to know the answers to but regretfully, didn't.

He was alive. By some miracle he had survived and was standing right here, Lorenz popping in by his side. Whatever healer had ended up helping mend him, I would have to give them my thanks.

"Staffan poisoned me, beat me, and left me for dead." The crowd stirred again at this revelation. Thank goodness somebody else was stepping up, someone who had no direct connection to Kade or myself, providing his firsthand account of his experience with the man who had taken charge of Darthou. "And he wasn't alone."

The crowd grew louder, combatting the screams in my mind. Stealing a look at Kade, I noted how Aleena, Elias, and Zan had all joined us on the floor amongst the kingdom's people. Sarah had stayed behind with the children, which was probably a safe idea.

I dragged my gaze to the guard who had entered into the picture, taking a stance between Rafina and us. By looking at him, you wouldn't guess that he had been so gravely injured yesterday.

Others came forward too, creating a barrier, a line separating us from Staffan's ex of a tethered mate. It appeared as if they might be trying to protect us, capture Rafina, or maybe even both.

I could only assume that the hunt for Rafina had been

ongoing since last night after the bloodbath at the island. Darthou's most valued and respected healer had been nowhere to be found. She had abandoned her people when they needed her.

"Fucking fools," Rafina hissed, and she vanished from sight. Multiple demons around us disappeared too, possibly trying to go after her. I only hoped that this time, they would be successful in retrieving her.

The chorus of screams lessened greatly, but a few still remained. I shook my head as I blinked repeatedly, almost coming out of a trance and taking in my surroundings.

Kade was already instructing demons to find and capture Rafina. Bodies were popping away at an alarming pace, some on Kade's orders and probably some who just wanted to get the hell out of here.

I wanted to tell him about the screams, that something wasn't right, and about the earlier fogginess that had clouded over everything in front of me as we were crowned, but I was being pulled away by my wrist. Aleena was ushering me away from the chaotic outburst and up toward Sarah as Zan and Elias disappeared into the throngs that were still awaiting instructions. The spikes on Kade's crown were barely visible when more demons arrived, dressed in protections.

It felt as if they were readying for another war. Was this really necessary if they were only going after one person?

Ajax and Brighton were clinging to their mother, fear etched on their sweet little faces. Sarah was trying to keep them calm as we approached, but her words barely rose above the pandemonium.

"Let's get you and the boys home." Aleena's voice was stern. Sarah was quick to grab onto the boys' hands, and once Aleena landed a hand on her shoulder, we were transported into their home. It was disorienting going from one extreme scene to another that was drastically quiet and undisturbed. Well, except for the poor boys who had no idea what was going on. Tears were rolling down their faces as Sarah led them to their rooms, leaving Aleena and I behind.

"I should head back." Aleena tried to take her leave, but before she could disappear, I grabbed onto her arm.

"Take me with you," I begged, but it came out as more of an order. One that had Aleena raising one perfectly shaped brow.

"No." With a firm grip, she removed my hand from her. "The safest place for you is here. And for the love of everything you hold dear, don't you *dare* open a door for anyone."

Her swift departure felt like a slap in the face—a reminder of probably the biggest mistake of my past being thrown at me by none other than Kade's sister. It made me drown in all of the bad decisions I'd made over the course of time, and made me question the time I spent with Aleena earlier, sharing secrets out in the open for once.

But now?

Sobs from the boys attempted to sway my attention, and while a small part of me wanted to go and attempt to help Sarah with them, I had a feeling that I might mess that up too.

Would I ever stop feeling like such a liability?

"Violet?"

The skirt of my dress swooshed as I whipped around to find Jacobi standing near the entrance. He wasn't wearing the attire I would have expected him to be in for the coronation, but casual sweats and a T-shirt. His face, however, harbored a gloomy expression that had me inching toward him.

"Are you okay?" I cupped my hands in front of me, treading carefully. "I know Sarah and Zan were trying to reach you earlier."

He swallowed before looking away, taking his time to answer me. Jacobi had never been one for much talk to begin with, but he seemed…off.

"Was any of it true?"

Halting my approach, I shook my head, not understanding. "Is any of what true, Jacobi?"

A single tear slipped from his right eye, rolling down his face in a rapid descent. "Never mind, it's too late."

Just as I was about to ask why, something sharp stuck me in the neck. The pain radiated out from the point of impact and spread through my entirety like ice filling every inch of my body, inside and out. My breathing labored as panic set in, my body not responding to my need to turn and find my attacker.

I was frozen. Unable to call out for help or tell Sarah of this intruder in her home. I couldn't alert them or tell them of the danger nearby. How would Sarah be able to protect Ajax and Brighton against this…whatever this was?

My eyes shut without my saying so, just as Jacobi stuck his hands in his pockets and his head dropped low. His afflictions were no longer visible.

What have you done?

"Thank you for your service, Jacobi. Your father would be proud."

My body remained set as if in stone. Cold, hard, and solid. The air coming and going couldn't be any more than one might suck through a straw.

While the paralyzing agent working through me was frightening enough, it was nothing compared to the terror I felt when I realized I was at Rafina's mercy.

ACKNOWLEDGEMENTS

If you've made it this far in Violet and Kade's story, from the bottom of my heart, thank you.

There's a reason I dive into the paranormal and supernatural elements so much, and that's because anything is literally possible. If I can take readers' minds off of whatever is plaguing them in their daily lives, then I consider that a major accomplishment.

I have to thank my husband (how much longer do we keep your name under wraps?) for pushing me to keep going. For telling me to keep editing, keep writing, and don't quit. If he wants to know what happens next, surely some other people do, right?

From being my supporter, formatter, cover designer, and ears that have no other option than to listen to my downward spirals, thank you. None of these books would be possible if it weren't for you. These stories would forever be sitting in my Google Docs. I love you!

Rebecca at Rebecca Joy Editing, thank you! You're another that has been with me since the beginning, and I sincerely appreciate all the work you put into editing. Because of you, I'd like to think that I am becoming a better writer—looking for overused words or phrases and saving me from odd line choices that would make zero sense to readers. You are the reason I praise editors and their hard work.

Special thanks to my sister-in-law for reading and supporting me long before I put my face out on social media. She is my sister in all things spicy and smutty.

Shout-out to the ladies at my day job. Thank you for ARC reading, catching typos, sharing your excitement with my books, and giving me a place to discuss what comes next.

Many people will drop off after reading the first book in the series if it's not their thing, and that's ok. That's something I've had to come to terms with. But for the readers that have stuck with me up to this point, thank you, thank you, thank you!

Please rate, review, or spread the word however you can. An author can only do so much, but your actions and word of mouth can help find more readers.

See you soon with the final installment of the Tethered to You series with… Unleashing Me.

ALSO BY KRYSTAL KAE

Tethered To You Series
Watching Me
Altering Me
Revealing Me

The Rose Duet
Chasing Petals

If you enjoyed this book, a quick rating or review on Goodreads, Amazon, or wherever you got your copy would mean the world to me. Your support helps others discover the book – thank you!

ABOUT THE AUTHOR

Krystal Kae lives in the corn-filled Midwest with her husband, children, and pets. Her love of reading and writing started back in high school, but it was over a decade later when she decided to put her overactive imagination to work again and began filling blank pages.

Fascinated by all things paranormal, fantasy, and romantic-you can find these topics the center of her writing universe.

When she's not working her full-time office job or buried in a story, she loves to create memories with loved ones, travel, and take long walks in cemeteries.

Get the latest updates at **KrystalKae.com** and follow
@krystalkaewrites

www.ingramcontent.com/pod-product-compliance
Lightning Source LLC
Chambersburg PA
CBHW020234010826
48973CB00006B/1504